Animal
Wrongs

Animal Wrongs

a novel

Stephen Spotte

THREE ROOMS PRESS
New York, NY

Animal Wrongs
BY Stephen Spotte

© 2021 by Stephen Spotte

ISBN 978-1-953103-09-3 (trade paperback original)
ISBN 978-1-953103-10-9 (Epub)
Library of Congress Control Number: 2021935385

TRP-091

Publication Date: October 19, 2021

BISAC category code
FIC014020 Fiction / Historical / Medieval
FIC034000 Fiction / Legal
FIC064000 Fiction / Absurdist

COVER ILLUSTRATION:
Daniel Fishel: www.o-fishel.com

BOOK DESIGN:
KG Design International: www.katgeorges.com

DISTRIBUTED BY:
Publishers Group West: www.pgw.com

Three Rooms Press
New York, NY
www.threeroomspress.com
info@threeroomspress.com

For Lucia

"History just burps, and we taste again
that raw-onion sandwich it swallowed centuries ago."

Julian Barnes, *A History of the World in 10½ Chapters*

Animal
Wrongs

PART I

Monsieur Rat
in the Dock

*"We often think someone is a man,
and he is only a ghost,
a dead man on vacation."*

—Hugo Ball—
Flight out of Time

MONDAY MAY 1ST, YEAR OF GRACE 1508—
CHASSENÉE AWAKES AT HIS COUNTRY ESTATE OUTSIDE THE
CITY OF AUTUN AND ANNOUNCES TO MADAME CHASSENÉE THAT
HE HAS BEEN NAMED DEFENSE ATTORNEY FOR SOME RATS

I, BARTHÉLEMY DE CHASSENÉE, BORN IN the year of our Lord 1480 at Issy-l'Evêque in Burgundy, attempted to roll from my back onto my stomach in sleep, but the intended angle of one hundred-eighty degrees stopped abruptly at ninety. The reason was simple physics, the momentum of my turning proving inadequate to overcome the elevation of my paunch. Beside me Madame Chassenée groaned and exhaled loudly. I opened my eyes uneasily, hoping the cloud of her foul breath that had coalesced overhead in the night had not drifted menacingly lower. Birdsong filtered through the closed windows while sunbeams plastered quivering scalene triangles against the ceiling. "Good morning, Madame," I said.

Her eyelids fluttered, and she succumbed suddenly to a coughing fit, spewing gobs of yellowish phlegm onto the coverlet. When the spasms at last subsided she said, "And to you, Monsieur." She wiped her nose and mouth on the sleeve of her dressing gown, descended laboriously from the bed, and disappeared into the hall where I heard her pissing a loud stream into the chamber pot. At the top of the stairs she shouted for our maid. "Échive! Where are you, stupid woman? Bring our tea at once, and then empty the pot!" Fitting, I thought, that our servant's name is derived from eschiver, meaning to evade or avoid. But then, who could blame her?

After Madame had settled back into bed I remarked that today was May 1st and suggested we open the windows and let fresh air and sunshine flush our stale room. It was, I pointed out, a beautiful morning. Perhaps we ought to be grateful for our good fortune and enjoy it.

Her face soured. "Not on your life. And risk a cold gust? What if an insect or a bird should enter? Perhaps the Black Death is peering at us through the glass as we speak, eager to ransack our bodies and send our souls winging toward Heaven. Well, mine at least. You would do well to study the Holy Writ and put aside your stupid law books. *First Corinthians*, chapter fifteen verse fifty-two: *for the trumpet shall sound, and the dead shall be raised incorruptible, and we shall be changed.*" She looked at me in a superior way, as if having said something profound. "Anyway, here comes Échive with the tea, which I intend to take exactly where I am."

Échive set the tray on the dressing table, poured two cups, and handed them to us. We sipped in silence, separately thinking murderous thoughts.

Madame Chassenée and I had adopted a mutual loathing almost from our wedding day, and as time passed the relationship abnegated into splenetic bickering and unremitting disgust. To my relief and her feigned disappointment, our rare and unenthusiastic copulations never had produced a child, adding further to what has evolved into a persistent malaise: now one could accuse the other with impunity of being a vessel of defective seed or ova. Our predicament will endure until one of us dies. Like the fairy tale, each dawn signals the start of a joust between two inept, opposing knights, neither able to unseat the other. We battle until bedtime when a truce is called that lasts only while we sleep. At sunrise the skirmish begins again.

"I have some news," I said.

"Tell me your news, and I'll do my best to stay awake. Before you start, I have a suggestion."

"By all means tell me your suggestion," I said venomously.

She looked at me as if conducting an inspection. "I suggest, Monsieur, that you wear a hat at all times when out and about, considering your head has become totally bald. Sunken as it is between your narrow shoulders it looks like an egg in an egg cup with the small end pointed up."

"And you, Madame, might as well put away your prosthesis and gum it. Having turned quite witchly, why not advertise as much?" I was referring to the dentures carved from cow bone that she placed on her bedside stand at night and had cost me one hundred sous to have made by a master carver. She always kept them nearby when they weren't in her mouth so upon hearing God's angel blow his horn on Judgment Day she would not waste time looking for them and delaying her ascent into Heaven. How quickly the toothsome wenches become toothless witches. But Madame has no excuse to complain about my appearance now, I who have been ungodly ugly from the moment of birth.

So, the day's joust had commenced as usual with jabs of the lance intended to draw blood. "But about my news," I said. "I've been summoned by the bishop of Autun to serve as attorney for the defense in an upcoming ecclesiastical tribunal. I accepted his offer and must pack at once. I'll be staying at the only decent inn, Le Coq et la Pie."

"Ah, yes, the one where the serving girls double as whores. And such a fitting name, The Cock and the Foot. What could be more appropriate? How long will you be away?" She said something else, but was just then inserting her dentures. The sound that emerged was moist and unintelligible.

I said in anticipation, "How long will I be away at Autun? Who knows? A few days, a few weeks, but if the proceedings drag on I'll come home intermittently. The court can summon me when events resume."

She repositioned the dentures more firmly. "I shall miss you, Monsieur. I feel for you as I do our bedbugs and the rats in the stables. Who are you defending?"

"Rats," I said. "A bunch of rats that ate last year's barley in the fields and municipal granary."

"I ask you a serious question, Monsieur, and you reply with sarcasm. So, I ask again: who are you defending, and will the client pay generously?"

"I'm defending a group of marauding rats. It's the truth, Madame. The client is the municipality of Autun. The pay is meager, but the trial should gain considerable publicity from which I expect to attract future high-paying clients."

"And you're hoping to get these rats exonerated? To what purpose? I detest rats. And what will my refined lady friends think of this? At the next social gathering I shall surely remind them of my rising status. 'Ladies, I shall say, my bald, stunted gnome of a husband—the renowned lawyer Barthélemy de Chassenée—has recently been elevated to loyal defender of the rodent tribes. He is now legendary among vermin, protector of the foul and whiskered who shit in your pantries, steal your bread, and converse in squeaks.'"

"You don't have any lady friends, refined or otherwise. You're a hag, Madame, a fishwife living far from the sea and eternally ungrateful for a life of ease you don't deserve."

"*Me?*" She sat up suddenly. "It's I who married beneath my station. You're a homely gnome no one else would have. I regrettably took pity on you and find myself trapped in a loveless, barren marriage. Ah, the pool of handsome noblemen in which I could have angled using my beauty and charm as bait. A life of gaiety, of parties, dancing, fine clothes, adoring friends." She looked at me with hatred. "And instead I have . . . you."

Mankind needs marvels, even unpleasant ones, to distract from the banality of our empty lives. Just an occasional small happening to inject a little spice would be adequate, but in my situation such a blessing seems improbable. You see, I awaken earlier than Madame Chassenée, typically even before daylight at the liturgical hour of lauds. The first thing I notice as the room brightens is her ruffled nightcap that rises to a crooked point at the center, like the bent beak of a defective chicken. From there my eyes are inevitably drawn downward to her nose, its extraordinary length and how it spreads like a mushroom toward the end, nostrils aimed slightly upward. Folk knowledge claims that a pregnant woman who lets a pig run between her legs while straddling rows in a field will deliver a child with the snout of a porker. How else to explain this example except through a careless act by Madame's mother?

Four stiff black hairs clustered at the tip of Madame's nose bend back and forth like wind-blown trees as she sleeps, dancing in synchrony with her polyphonic snoring. Their resemblance to hog bristles is striking. French girls are warned from an early age never to eat pork when eventually becoming pregnant for fear the child will be born with just such repulsive accoutrements on their snouts. I often wonder if Madame Chassenée's mother had never been told this or simply ignored the advice.

Were our bedroom scenes not so disquieting at this early hour of prime I might refold my eyelids and perhaps experience the more banal dreams of others instead of my hopeless fantasies. Well, in truth, at least somewhat less fantastic. I might, for instance, dream about Never-Never Land and its cornucopia of endless food and sex where the citizens go around naked and fornicate randomly at all the liturgical hours. They take tumbles in pastures, in haylofts, in the furrowed fields oblivious to the hoeing and singing of happy serfs. Baby animals frolic all around, and children (to my great delight) are never seen or heard. Willing, angelic women with jiggling breasts thrum golden harps under the azure sky. They smell of spring meadows and morning dew and sunshine. Unlike Eden, which appeared when the world began, Never-Never Land is anticipated to take form when the world ends. It represents Paradise regained, a place I'll doubtfully ever visit.

Tuesday May 2nd—Chassenée, François, and Alvin Depart the Manor for Autun, Arriving after Sunset and Checking into the Inn Called Le Coq et La Pie

A FEW DAYS AGO A COURIER arrived with a letter from the bishop of Autun, my former place of residence until Madame Chassenée and I joined the landed gentry in the countryside. The words were clear enough, if a little strange: the bishop had appointed me as lawyer in an upcoming ecclesiastical proceeding to defend some rats accused of destroying much of last year's barley crop, both in the local fields and at the municipal granary within the city walls. The proceeding will be conducted by the diocese and judged by a judicial vicar designated by the bishop. My adversary, if I chose to accept, would be the renowned prosecutor Humbert de Révigny. I had come up against Révigny twice before in more conventional civic trials and know him as a worthy opponent: brilliant, iconoclastic, erudite, and extraordinarily well prepared. I would need to be at the top of my game.

Business had been slow through the winter, and I wasn't looking forward to an uptick in the writing of wills, representing clients in boundary disputes, handling land sales and title searches, and becoming involved in similar mundane tasks that fill an attorney's hours. My experience until now had been relegated to secular law; here was a chance to participate in the canonical arena. The clients were certainly unusual, but then so was the opportunity. Plus, the impending tribunal provided a means of escaping Madame Chassenée for weeks or even months, a change no doubt beneficial to us both.

The remainder of the day was spent packing and leaving orders with the manager of my vineyards, orchards, fields, and pastures, who also oversees maintenance of the manor house, stables, and all other buildings on the property. Madame, as usual, would supervise the household staff through intimidation and disparagement.

To assist and provide an illusion of protection along the way I planned to take François and Alvin. I introduce this pair with trepidation. Both are cowardly, disloyal, and guaranteed to abandon me instantly in the face of danger. As to intelligence, neither is competent to fasten his own shoes. Hoping to bestow a semblance of responsibility (no doubt futile) I've pronounced them my footmen when traveling. Frankly, they serve no useful function in this context or around the manor and likely would die of hunger if locked inside a bakery. Even the rats I'm about to defend have the good sense not to starve in the granary.

The plan was to leave before sunrise, I riding the palfrey, the only decent riding horse in my stables. François and Alvin would follow behind seated double on a mule and leading a donkey loaded with baggage and other necessities. Assuming no delays we should reach the walls of Autun by evening. Along with my written acceptance of the case I had asked the courier to reserve a bed for me at the inn, a table in the tavern downstairs, and stalls and sustenance for my animals. François and Alvin would sleep in the stable and have their meals delivered by a serving girl.

Madame couldn't be bothered to see us off. In fact, she was still snoring loudly as I dressed and tiptoed from the bedroom feeling lucky not to have awakened her. It was barely light. Downstairs, Échive emerged yawning from the servants' quarters to serve me a breakfast of tea and yesterday's baguettes with butter and jam.

My footmen were waiting outside. François wears a fixed smirk at all times. He has stuffed the shoulders and upper arms of his tunic with rags, thinking I don't notice. In this way he hopes to lessen my whip's sting. He also knows I have yet to strike him across his smirk or anyplace else, no matter how tempted, and remains confident in believing I never shall. We both hope he's right, but on this morning I came close to breaking our unspoken contract. "Would His Lordship like the stirrups raised?" Another way of mocking me. François has purposely lowered the stirrups while saddling the horse so he could make fun of my height, or rather the lack of it. In truth, I'm barely taller than a carnival midget. He boosts me into the saddle, then jumps backward anticipating a deserved kick in the head, but with my short legs I miss by a wide margin. François' smirk never morphs into a laugh, although his eyes crinkled this time when he looked up at me.

Alvin, his backward teenage son and assistant, watches without interest, having no understanding of human interactions regardless of how outrageous. He spins clockwise in circles, head tilted and arms spread wide imitating a bird in flight. "Je suis un oiseau!" he shouts repeatedly to the stars now blinded by the rising sun, or maybe to butterflies or imaginary creatures only he can see. "Regar de moi voler! Regar de moi voler!"

Our modest cavalcade departed in the still air just before daybreak, riding across a land drenched in morning mist obscuring lurking demons and goblins. We rode carefully, eyes darting, expecting one of Satan's minions to leap into our path at any moment. The way forward followed a series of familiar livestock trails through pastures where cows and sheep were already grazing despite the early hour. They raised their heads in momentary interest, chewing dully, any of them potentially a demon in disguise.

Fear consumes our waking hours and most of our dreams. We fear the guarantee of Purgatory and the possibility of Hell afterward, but also the demons, goblins, imps, giants, dwarfs, ghosts, and elves that haunt our earthly existence. Griffins and other winged fiends patrol the skies; forest spirits, hobgoblins, and trolls populate the woods and fields; water-sprites the streams and rivers. A cockatrice or dragon could appear suddenly; miniature dragons and fierce salamanders might lurk in the low flames of the hearth fire. All around are witches, werewolves, and vampires masquerading as ordinary human beings. We distrust everyone and everything. The family cow could momentarily go mad, trample someone, and abruptly return to being just a cow as if nothing had happened. A neighbor or even someone of your own flesh was possibly a demon in disguise or infested by a demon. There was no telling, no way of knowing whether even cream rising to the surface in a bucket of milk wasn't actually a demon waiting to enter whoever drank it. And always in the background God and Satan monitored every move, judging dispassionately, knowing our fates from cradle to grave and leaving us to fumble and quake in ignorance and uncertainty. We distrust everything and everyone, and rightly so.

At last the sun rose, and we breathed easier. By mid-morning the paths had merged onto the road leading east, muddy now from spring rains. We rode until near the noon hour of sext, stopping in a small copse to sit a while in the shade and take a meal of bread and cold meat. After tea prepared by François over a small fire of sticks we mounted and continued the trek.

The house roofs of Autun, foreshortened by distance, rose obliquely behind the city walls across the rivière Arroux. They resembled a continuum of chines, indistinct and strange as if glimpsed through sleep-encrusted eyes. The sun at our backs indicated the time was past the mid-afternoon hour of nones. We would enter Autun a little past vespers, or just after sunset. I paid the merchants' toll at Porte d'Arroux, and in the rolling twilight we passed through the western gate.

Once inside the city proper we splashed through overflowing sewage, past stinking public latrines and the decaying carcasses of animals littering the streets and alleys. Pedestrians on late-afternoon errands tiptoed around puddles seeking drier ground, the women lifting the hems of their dresses, the men slogging ahead grimly. Dripping manure wagons rumbled past, the drivers yelling and whipping their oxen and mules, drenching passersby with feculent slop and oblivious to the shouts and curses hurled their way. The streets and alleys crawled with scavenging rodents and cockroaches. The air was stulted by the hoarse croaks of vultures, rooks, and carrion crows and the relentless barking of dogs.

We continued down rue de l'Arbalète to rue des Marbres Antoine, then turned right onto the narrow and curiously named rue de la Jambe de Bois. The inn was immediately before us. Blocking the way, however, was a dead mule. Mangy dogs fought among themselves tearing at the hide and ripping out chunks of muscle and viscera. I ordered François to dismount and drive them away. He grumbled but obeyed, taking my whip to the nearest ones, beating them until they yelped and fled. He remounted the mule, and we made a detour around the carcass. Night had fallen, and the innkeeper was lighting the oil lamp by the front door of the tavern. He saw us and gestured that we follow him to the stable in back.

The innkeeper raised his lamp inside the stables and showed two stalls reserved for me: one for the horse, the other for the mule and donkey. For a few sous charged to my account François and Alvin could take up living quarters in a nearby mini-stall rented for this purpose and filled with clean hay. They had brought their own cups, blankets, and spare clothes.

The innkeeper hung the lamp on a peg and watched while my footmen unpacked the donkey and separated their belongings from mine. They carried my valises inside the inn, and we followed the innkeeper up some narrow stairs to the second floor, where he again hung the lamp on a peg and waited. Under the pitched roof were four beds, two already occupied by pairs of dozing men. I would sleep in one of the two empty ones, sharing space with a man I had not yet seen. While unpacking I took note of my belongings in case of thievery and laid everything out on a shelf.

I said, "Does your establishment harbor bedbugs and fleas, monsieur?"

"No," he lied. "I run a clean inn. In spring and again in autumn my wife washes the sheets using strong soap. She scrubs them vigorously against the washboard and afterward dries them in the wind and sun. No vermin could survive the torture to which she puts her sheets. I assure you, monsieur, if you encounter vermin in your bed then you or your bedmate has brought them."

After I unpacked we all went downstairs to the tavern. I asked the innkeeper to show my men where to find water and hay for the animals and provide them a lamp to carry out their duties. I was tired and sore from the day's ride. I needed food and drink. I also needed a night's sleep and hoped my bedmate snored more softly than Madame Chassenée.

As the innkeeper was leaving I instructed him on feeding my men for the duration of our stay. He was to provide them breakfast near the hour of prime, including a bowl of small beer each, hot tea, barley bread, and cheese. At the end of the day at compline they were to receive a flagon of green Spanish wine along with barley bread, beans, and meat. If beans were not available, cabbage or onions were adequate substitutes. I emphasized just one bowl each of small beer in the morning and a single flagon of wine at night, stating that I refused to allow more. "François, the older one, will complain, promising to pay for extra beverages from his own pocket before we leave, but I assure you, monsieur, his pocket is empty."

The innkeeper said, "You are exceedingly generous, monsieur. Your footmen will not have a cause to complain."

"They will surely think of one," I said. "Now, I need sustenance for myself. Is my table ready?"

"Indeed, monsieur."

Wednesday May 3rd—Chassenée and Révigny Take Supper Together in the Tavern; Révigny Reveals His Otherness

⟨≈⟩

Le Coq et la Pie is Autun's only halfway reputable tavern. The merchant and noble classes are served their food and beverages in clean utensils of pewter and latten. The lower classes get by with tableware made of fired clay and wood. These are seldom washed between uses, and many a smithy or cattle driver has been given his porridge in an earthenware bowl ringed with thickening accretions of previous meals.

Suddenly, Révigny, my opponent in the impending tribunal, appeared in view. I had not seen him in several years, but he seemed to have changed little. He was thin, tall, stooped, and forward-leaning, nose arriving a step ahead of the toes. He was now bald except for a thin ring of hair around the lower part of his skull, giving him the tonsured appearance of a monk. He saw me and approached, grinning sardonically. He walked slower and more hesitantly than I remembered, as if suffering some obscure ambulatory debility.

"Barthélemy! How well you seem! May I join you?" He still had that penetrating look of someone who recognizes his superiority and makes certain everyone else does too, a useful trait for intimidating witnesses, opposing lawyers, and even susceptible judges.

"Of course, Humbert." I stood, and we shook hands. His felt oddly limp and weightless, as if not connected to an earthly being. I put aside this fleeting impression as ridiculous and asked Révigny how his career had progressed since we last met.

He sat down, dismissing my inquiry with a wave. "Oh, this way and that. Nothing startling to report. What are you drinking?"

I said I had arrived only moments before. He turned and beckoned the innkeeper, who pretended not to notice and continued engaging in conversation with another patron. He looked up eventually, nodded at Révigny, and casually sauntered over, wiping his hands on a filthy apron. "Monsieurs?"

Révigny said, "We shall have wine, innkeeper, but none of that green Spanish squirrel piss or anything French with which you've diluted it. We want your best French vintage, nothing less. My friend and I are lawyers and might be around for weeks or months staying at your shithole of an inn, so this is your chance to profit honestly. But if you don't respond *immediately* when we beckon, or if you cheat us or fail to honor our demands and instructions, I promise that we shall take you to court and end up owning this property. Then you and your ugly wife will be left begging in the streets without a sou. Am I clear?"

The words hit home. The innkeeper was clearly terrified and started to sweat. "Yes, monsieur," he managed to stammer. "I have a fine red Burgundy fit for a prince and will fetch you a flagon immediately. I know this vintage well. It so happened I was buying supplies in the countryside on the very day the grapes were being pressed, and I swear to you I heard a hoopoe's call."

Révigny said, "Then I hope you were very young because otherwise the wine is still green. Pray to whatever deity you worship for reassurance it rises to your praise and that the hoopoe you say you heard wasn't a rook. Otherwise, we guarantee your corpse will be embalmed in the stuff after you die of starvation and leprosy in some nameless alley."

The innkeeper brought the flagon, poured us each a cup with shaking hands, and left it on the table. I had momentarily diverted my eyes from Révigny and was looking absently around the room, now filled with patrons and hangers-on. They comprised the usual assortment of city merchants and tradesmen, traveling merchants, whores doubling as serving girls, a stray dog . . . A mime was going from table to table offering to perform for disinterested and drunken clientele. A ragged beggar huddled in a far corner hoping for table scraps was being beaten by the innkeeper's sturdy wife wielding a heavy stirring spoon.

When I looked back at Révigny my heart nearly stopped, then suddenly began thumping asynchronously until I thought it might explode out my of chest. Without thinking I leaped from the chair, knocking it backward and spilling the cup of wine at hand. My erratic behavior and the subsequent disturbance seemed to go unnoticed in the raucous atmosphere of the tavern. When I dared look at Révigny again a chill like the cold hand of a corpse wrapped its fingers around my spine, and my flesh crawled with the goose-pimpled sensation of being tormented by a ferocious winter wind.

The being before me wasn't the Révigny I knew but a demon, a nearly skeletal entity encased in a transparent, wonderfully elastic membrane that mimicked his movements, contracting when he retracted an appendage, stretching to accommodate its expansion as if in anticipation, always keeping a constant minimum distance of separation from the body part in motion. When he pointed at the innkeeper to refill our cups the material stretched to accommodate his finger completely to the end of the fingernail without touching it. He wore this device like an outer skin, a plasma of some kind unknown to modern science. Filling the space separating this material from himself swirled a fulvous smoke that intermittently hid or revealed the features of the being inside. It tracked his movements after a slight delay, as water takes a fleeting instant to refill the vacancy left by a swimmer's hand pushing it aside. The being itself was bright green, as were his clothes.

To be specific, everything about him was green except the smoke enveloping him, and his eyes, which had no pupils but were similar to the depthless eyes of some fishes from the abyss. In their resting state, his were iridescent green. They glowed with the phosphorescence of summer fireflies only more intensely. As the days passed and I spent more time in his presence I noticed how they brightened and changed color depending on his moods, the intensity correlating with Révigny's level of excitement: anger, boredom, disinterest, and so forth. When he was stimulated the phosphorescent green morphed sequentially into amber then to bright, sulfurous yellow. As his mood heightened further his eyes turned orange, sometimes exploding instantaneously into the blinding red of fiery coals. They appeared to have a physiological life separate from the rest of him because at all times they pulsed, slowly if he was calm but quickening as his moods heightened. This activity, however, was asynchronous with his breathing, the phenomena being driven by separate internal engines.

That first encounter astonished me. "Great God!" I managed to gasp, unsure whether to stay or depart the scene screaming and never return to Autun. "What the hell! Is that you, Humbert?"

"Aha! Two statements and a question, the first statement false, the second requiring explanation. First, God is not great; second, I'm indeed from Hell, but the nuances and ramifications of this will clarify in the coming days. As to your question, the answer is yes, it's the same old Humbert. Well, not quite my old self. Death has a way of changing people. No doubt you've been told how Hell is populated with liars, and some of that tendency toward prevarication seems to have rubbed off on me. Then again, I'm a lawyer. Must be the company I kept while kicking around up here on Earth, your esteemed lordship included."

At this little joke he grinned like a death's head. "Meanwhile, don't alarm the other patrons, who still count themselves among the living, if in name only. Pick up the chair, sit down, and let's calmly sip this wine, which actually isn't too bad. Maybe we'll allow the innkeeper to retain his business. Anyway, what could be more boring than owning an inn?"

I did as instructed, but my hands were quaking, and I felt slightly ill. In looking around I failed to notice anyone watching us. Just then a serving girl set down two bowls and a platter of coarse barley bread, the look of which did nothing to help my queasy stomach. In the bowls some chopped vegetables and a few lumps of greasy meat floated in a barely warm broth. She then walked away, apparently not having seen anything unusual, like possibly a bony green demon and a bald paunchy gnome sitting down to supper.

From across the table Révigny gave off a faint acrid odor I couldn't identify immediately. Not a foul rutting smell that supposedly trails Satan, nor an odor of putrefaction, either of which, I suppose, might emanate from a demon, but something inorganic and yet combustible. Suddenly, it became clear, or perhaps the correct word is opaque. I'd noticed that Révigny's whole body was immersed in a fulvous cloud, and when he or any of his body parts turned suddenly the cloud was set in motion and various parts of himself disappeared momentarily until he stopped moving. Then the cloud ceased swirling and settled around him. The smoke inside that strange, fluid cocoon emitted a faint odor of sulfur. I had been smelling burning brimstone! A little must escape occasionally, meaning that wonderful transparent membrane was permeable to some extent. I wondered if only I could detect the odor and learned later this was indeed the case.

"I see your dreams, Barthélemy, the ones in which you appear handsome and horny, obviously not yourself. Speaking of which, do you think women might find me more attractive in horns?" He leaned forward to show me the top of his head, which bore two stubby protuberances. They must have been there all along. How could they not? I wouldn't have noticed had Révigny not bent over to my eye level. He's very tall, at least two meters, or about Madame Chassenée's height. They both tower over me, meaning that in most circumstances the tops of their heads are well out of my view.

"Your head looks like a polled calf's," I said. I was gaining confidence. The wine was helping, or perhaps Révigny was trying not to seem excessively weird and threatening. The wit and mannerisms of this strange being had already convinced me it really was Révigny, or at least a convincing facsimile, and that I should relax and simply accept him as my old friend and adversary. It was merely a matter of adjusting to his new appearance, or so I kept telling myself.

"How about now?" Instantaneously, his head sprouted two enormous curled ram's horns.

"Good God, Révigny, don't do that!" I glanced quickly around the room, which had become quiet, but everyone was looking at me, not at him. It must be true, I thought. They see him as an ordinary human being. I looked at Révigny again, and his head had returned to normal, if a pea-green head bearing two nascent horns could be called that.

"Better tone it down, my friend. People are staring at you. To them I'm a harmless old man, merely your farouche dinner companion." He gave a little chuckle that resounded from inside his cocoon like a badly cast church bell. "Isn't it marvelous, Barthélemy? Only you can see me in this guise. To other poor souls I appear perfectly human, maybe even pitiable, a lonely geriatric shuffling toward the grave. Little do they know that among them walks a Devil's advocate, Satan's personal servant and number one admirer!"

"Why me?" I said morosely, picking up the flagon and refilling our cups. "Why choose to appear to *me*? Have I ever done you any wrongs?"

"Of course not. You've always treated me civilly and with respect. But don't consider this as punishment. Think of it as a chance for enlightenment, to experience the mysterious 'Other' firsthand instead of imbibing drivel spouted by bishops and curates. Believe me when I say they're clueless. What a tremendous opportunity I'm offering you!"

Being barely taller than a midget has many drawbacks. For example, while sitting in a chair your feet never touch the floor. The undersides of your knees are squeezed against the leading edge of the seat, cutting off circulation to the lower legs and eventually turning the feet numb. Scooting forward doesn't help because then you can't lean back without becoming nearly prone. "I must stand a minute," I said, and slid out of my chair.

"I understand," Révigny said. "Your feet have become numb."

Irritated, I muttered, "Do you know everything about me?"

"Pretty much, but setting aside unimportant details, consider this. There are two planes of wisdom. The lower is recognizing we're each other's delusion. The higher is embracing this condition. Think of our situation as a little experiment during which we shall test and monitor your progress toward wisdom's higher plane. After, of course, you've accepted the lower one. The upcoming tribunal should determine that." Révigny settled back and stared at me, eyes idling alternately between green and amber, a state, I was to learn, indicating thoughtfulness.

"Incidentally," he said, "we shall be sharing a bed for the duration of the tribunal." He quickly held up a hand, palm forward. "But don't worry. I don't snore."

THURSDAY MAY 4TH—CHASSENÉE WALKS TO THE CATHEDRAL TO MEET THE BISHOP

I AWOKE AT THE LITURGICAL HOUR of prime to see hints of the encroaching day through the one grimy window. Révigny was absent, and the bed looked as if only I had slept in it. I remembered being drunk and the innkeeper and Révigny helping me up the narrow stairs the night before. Around me the other patrons were still sleeping. I crept down the stairs to the privy outside, then went into the tavern. Révigny was sitting in the same chair as before.

"Good morning, Barthélemy! How did you sleep? In case you didn't notice, I don't sleep these days. There's far too much mischief going on in the middle of the night, and I hate to miss it. So, you basically have 'our' bed to yourself. Stretch out as much as you like."

"Thank you," I said, pouring myself some tea.

"Off to meet the bishop this morning?"

"That's right. Are you coming along?"

"No, I've done that already. Today I'll just, well, do nothing except bask in eternity."

After a breakfast of tea, small beer, and bread and cheese I set off walking through the streets and avenues to the Cathédrale for my meeting, taking note of the urban life I had abandoned for the quieter countryside.

City noise can be deafening. Carts rumble past, ungreased axles screeching, wheels grinding against the stones, the drivers shouting and cursing at their animals. Tradesmen call to one another over the din. Children shriek, pigs grunt, roosters crow, mules bray, and horses neigh. Two men-at-arms riding thick war mounts clanked past. Small boys ran beside them, wide-eyed at the dented pauldrons in their armor, the remnants of contests or even battles. Pilgrims led by a priest stood patiently in the muck waiting for them to pass. The streets teemed with peddlers, beggars, peasants from the countryside seeking work, unemployed soldiers and sailors, and whores hoping to snare a merchant on his way to a business meeting. Maids leaned out open windows gaily crying *gardez l'eau!* as a warning to pedestrians below before emptying chamber pots into the streets.

Wagons and two-wheeled carts are common in the towns and countryside throughout France, but coaches, because of the extravagant cost, are rare except in Paris. In Autun only the wealthy fishmonger Jean Philipot owns one. I see it stopped near the corner in front of the dressmaker's shop. Its occupants, Madame Philipot and her daughter whose age, so I'm told, is eleven years or thereabouts, have just stepped out. They move daintily, careful not to soil their dresses and shoes. Both hold frilly parasols above their heads despite the fair weather, gossamer devices that could doubtfully repel even mist. Madame pauses to say something to her postilion, who has stepped down to open the coach door, probably ordering him to wait or run an errand. Carpenters are at work adding a room onto the back of the Philipot house on the next street, ostensibly for a permanent servant of some sort. Rumor has it (via Madame Chassenée) that Monsieur Philipot has hired a coachman who soon will arrive from Paris to replace the postilion, thereby giving his coach—and his wife—even more status. According to Madame Chassenée, source of all gossip masquerading as knowledge, the new room surely will be for him.

Most of the populace travels on foot. This includes friars, monks, and other members of the lower clergy, and the peasants. A professor, clerk, or someone else educated but still of poor means might own a mule, donkey, or bony horse. The bourgeois and wealthy merchant class, the nobility, and the higher clergy ride fine horses. A select few of them, as I've mentioned, might even own coaches with iron-rimmed wheels, although in terms of comfort a horse with a stable gait is more sensible considering the rutted, pot-holed thoroughfares. Jouncing over cobbled streets in a wheeled contraption even at walking speed is sufficient to upset the stomach and loosen the teeth, unless the passengers are seasoned mariners adept at clenching their jaws and gripping tightly attached objects to keep their balance.

Since selling the house in Autun and becoming landed gentry, Madame Chassenée has pestered me to buy a coach and pair of trained horses to pull it, and, of course, engage a full-time coachman from Paris as permanent driver. For obvious reasons I've resisted her entreaties. Foremost is the initial expense, which is outrageous. Then you must factor in future repairs. Some part of a coach is always breaking, usually a wheel or axle. Meanwhile, there would be two more horses to feed, not to mention a coachman growing fat on my bread and drinking the wine from my vineyards, living in my house, and drawing a salary for mostly sitting around. How many days each week must Madame be driven the several leagues to Autun for clothes and victuals and then stay overnight with relatives? Not many, I assure you. Finally, Madame Chassenée's only reason for wanting such an extravagance—and which she never admits—is to enhance her social status, which in my opinion is inadequate to offset the negative aspects.

The day was turning hot, and I had a hangover. It would be interesting to learn later how Révigny felt. Do demons suffer from too much drink? If not, then Hell might be the better option after all, especially if avoiding spending eternity in the company of Madame Chassenée could be negotiated with Satan. Maybe Révigny would agree to serve as my intermediary. The idea was curiously amusing: I the client, Révigny my lawyer, as judge the Devil himself. The previous evening was almost too strange to contemplate, although my feelings of initial shock and fear had largely passed. I had always liked and admired Révigny and saw no reason to change this opinion simply because he was presently dead and existing in the form of a green demon. Admittedly, this reasoning made less sense once I was sober.

Just before midmorning I arrived at Cathédrale Saint-Lazare d'Autune at Place du Terreau, built to honor the Old Testament Lazarus. The devout believe his remains are entombed somewhere under the stone floors. How he got from the Holy Land to France and why he came to Autun have never been sensibly explained. This is simply another "fact" propagated by the ecclesiastics, its truth buoyed by unquestioned faith. The importance of the Cathédrale is evident from the condition of the streets in the immediate surroundings, which are surfaced with cobbles allowing them to drain instead of turning to mud in foul weather. Bishops are inclined to keep their shoes and the hems of their fine robes clean and dry.

On entering I passed under the tympanum of the Last Judgment displaying the Kingdom of Heaven and signed by Gislebertus, its sculptor. The right section shows the demons of Hell. One of the demons and a heavenly angel are weighing souls on a balance, each contesting to tip the scales in his favor. Neither, I noticed, resembled Révigny. Strange that with all the demons running about a sculptor of Gislebertus' prowess might never have been shown a suitable specimen to copy. On Judgment Day the souls from Heaven and those residing in Purgatory and Hell will be released to gather for the final judgment. The lesson ought to be that both sides cheat, but every good Catholic knows that an angel's heavier thumb tips the result in the Lord's favor.

I continued through the narthex and was met just inside the nave by a priest who politely asked my business. I stated my name and said I had an appointment with the bishop. He bowed and led me through the open choir to the apse at the far end. If Lazarus was indeed lying beneath the floor, I had stepped on his remains while traversing the choir.

I followed the swaying robe around the altar. Tucked in a corner behind it was a door, which I presumed must lead to one of the chapels. However, the door opened instead into an airy windowless room, its lower reaches lit by banks of candles, the upper part hidden in blackness. The bishop sat in an ordinary chair at an ordinary table on a platform raised a half-storey above the floor. It appeared to be his everyday workspace because he was obviously busy at a task. The priest turned and disappeared without a sound, closing the door behind him.

This was my first audience with a bishop. Hat in hand I stood before this literally elevated holy person. I felt the cool draft on my bald scalp and watched it torment the guttering candles. The pen continued scratching as I shifted nervously from foot to foot until at last the great man set it to rest beside the inkwell and peered down at me over his spectacles. Both His Holiness on his high perch and the bells now ringing the hour of terce high in the belfry were closer to Heaven than I. The reverberation through the thick stone of the walls and floor was making my flesh tingle, although not from any spiritual awakening. Maybe this was the point, a reminder that humble aspirants to Paradise are relegated to queuing up at ground level until beckoned.

"You are the lawyer Barthélemy de Chassenée?

"Yes, Your Holiness."

"And you took a law degree at the Université de Paris in the year of grace 1502 and have been a lawyer working here at Autun since the year of grace 1506?"

"Yes, Your Holiness."

"And you agree to serve as lawyer for the defense in the upcoming proceeding in which you will represent the rats accused of eating our barley?"

"Yes, Your Holiness."

"Very well. Prosecuting the tribunal will be the esteemed Humbert de Révigny, who also took his law degree at the Université de Paris, although his predates yours by some eighteen years. The proceeding will be held outdoors at the Théâtre Romain. Do you know it?"

"Yes, Your Holiness. As a boy I attended the Ecole Préparatoire to the south of that place and west of the cimetière." I didn't mention that I had been teased and bullied mercilessly there and often beaten by the bigger boys, who included nearly everyone enrolled. My tiny stature and peculiar facial features have continued to be a source of ridicule throughout my life. What I also knew but kept to myself is that the Théâtre Romain once held twenty thousand Gauls who gathered periodically to witness the mayhem and slaughter that in ancient times passed for Roman culture. The impending circus in which Révigny would prosecute some rats and I would defend them could only be the modern equivalent, if less bloody.

"I should mention one more thing," said the bishop. "Call it a dilemma of sorts, but one you need to know about before formally accepting this case. Not long ago, in the year of grace 1487 to be exact, His Excellency the vicaire-général of this very city of Autun addressed a similar issue, that of a plague of grasshoppers ravaging the fields. He noted that the insects might not obey his precept because of *instigante Satana*, or 'Satan's influence' in the vernacular.

In doing so he drew a clear line between living creatures and the Devil, who might lead them astray just as he does humans. The dilemma was and remain this: if the accused were under Satan's influence, how could they possibly be granted a defense attorney? What Christian would agree to defend demons? In addition, how could the community, with the Church's blessing, set aside a piece of land for these and future demons to occupy if negotiations came to demand it? If the accused were indeed infested by malevolent spirits, this raised more potential problems than if they were just grasshoppers—or in the case before us, rats."

I bowed and said, "I understand the dilemma and its ramifications, Your Holiness, and nonetheless accept responsibility for defending the rats."

"Very well. I admire your courage and pray God shows sympathy to your situation and protects you. The proceeding will be conducted by a judicial vicar of my recent appointment. Because this is to be an ecclesiastical tribunal his verdict is final; there can be no appeal. Each day that court is in session the proceeding will commence at midmorning, or terce, the liturgical third hour." He then raised his right hand and ended the interview: "Go with God, my son."

After meeting with the bishop I returned to the inn, stopping at the stable to check on François and Alvin. François reported they were being fed. Alvin looked at me curiously, as if seeing me for the first time. He and I bore a strange resemblance: unusually short, enormous belly, head scrunched between narrow shoulders giving the look of not having a neck, a chin so recessed as to offer bare solace for a beard, and at age fourteen he was already prematurely bald. For some reason his appearance annoyed me. I ordered him to fork more hay for my animals and muck their stalls. I then admonished François for not having kept the water buckets filled and threatened a beating if the task wasn't accomplished at once.

That evening Révigny and I again assumed our chairs at the table I'd reserved for the duration of my stay and ordered a flagon of wine. After a serving girl had poured us each a cup and left I looked at Révigny sitting across from me, pulsating inside his cocoon. "How did your meeting go with His Holiness?"

"About as expected. Surely you know."

"That's true, but from your own mouth?"

"He told me about the dilemma brought up by His Excellency the vicaire-général of Autun in the year of grace 1487. I was seven years old at that time and naturally don't remember, but you no doubt do. I'm referring to the business about a local grasshopper plague and the possibility of *instigante Satana*. He asked if I'd still defend the rats after hearing this, and I said yes."

"I recall that case, and it's been discussed at great length in Hell."

"With what conclusions?"

"None at all."

I said, "On a more interesting subject, I never did know what happened to you. How you met your end, I mean. I have vivid memories of our court days together representing opposing sides, then you went off to Paris to prosecute a case of common greed. Rumors of your death later circulated, but no details. What happened?"

He raised the cup to his lips where the skin of the cocoon became instantaneously thinner, allowing him to sip from its rim. "I died," he said simply, then added, "except actual confirmation of the event was never transmitted afterward. In other words, for reasons known only to Satan the news of my death never got out except as rumor. I suspect he wanted it that way so I could come back and walk among the living without controversy. In many situations it's more convenient if your demoniacal qualities remain unrecognized."

"That I can understand," I said, "but tell me the details anyway." Our bread and soup arrived just then, and we paused to eat.

After one bite Révigny wrinkled his green nose and pushed his plate away. "Terrible food. I think I'll pass on tonight's swill. Reprising my story, it began with a secular trial. I'd been summoned to Paris by the civil authorities to prosecute the bishop's cousin, a Parisian merchant accused of extortion. This defendant, keep in mind, was a blood relative of the bishop of Paris, one of the most powerful men in France. The whole affair had become scandalous, and the great man was in fear of seeing his reputation tarnished, such as it was. I'd learned through private channels how the defense attorneys had bribed the presiding judge, setting the stage for me to lose but collect a sizeable fee and afterward exit gracefully without fanfare, but that isn't how things turned out.

"Through various manipulations orchestrated by Satan and unknown to me, I won the case. On the day of this unexpected victory, feeling elated and self-congratulatory and intending to find a jolly tavern in which to celebrate, I departed the Grande Chambre du Palais de Justice and stepped into a quiet alley dominated by shadows. There a band of truncheon-wielding thugs waylaid me. Before I could yell for help they stuffed a rag in my mouth and beat and kicked me unconscious. Was it ordinary robbery? No, my purse had not been taken. The attack was clearly personal. Its occurrence immediately following the verdict could scarcely have been coincidental. So, I lay there bleeding onto the cobbles, my soul uncertain whether to stay or depart." Révigny took a moment to cross one bony leg over the other and gaze thoughtfully across the room.

"Then what?" I said.

His gaze returned to me. "Some good Samaritans came along. They carried me, unconscious and half dead, to a nearby doctor who began immediate treatment, but I was too far gone. My brain had cleared a little when the bishop himself stopped by two days later to administer last rites. It was strange that he came in person. Guilt? Probably.

"Although barely able to summon breath, I called him a fat pederast and said to stick his worthless babble and fake piety up his ass. Screw your Sacrament of Penance, I told him, I don't feel shame about anything I've done; I have nothing whatever to repent. But you, on the other hand, have lots. I figure you sent those thugs after me. You're nothing but a coward, a hypocrite, and an overfed capon.

"Well, the bishop completely lost his mind. He became apoplectic and told me I was the one going straight to Hell, and then he stomped out. That prognostication wasn't completely accurate. I didn't go straight to Hell, much as I would have liked. I went instead to Purgatory like everyone else, expecting to spend a few millenniums picking lint out of my navel when not joining the choir of shrieks, but lucky for me Satan had been watching the whole episode, including the trial. He laughed so hard, he later told me, that he actually cried tears of boiling brine, a revelation even to him. I no sooner got to Purgatory than he reduced my sentence to a puny six months, which was unheard of, and after I'd served it he ordered a pair of dark angels to deliver me nonstop to Hell where I've been warming my heels ever since, except for occasional trips topside to participate in tribunals and trials Satan considers amusing or a threat to his hubris. Image is everything, even down . . . there." Révigny pointed dramatically at the nether region lying far beneath the floor.

"You see, Barthélemy, Satan and I had earlier made a contract. It was what I wanted because at the moment of death I was guaranteed a light sentence in Purgatory and afterward a straight shot to Hell with no chance at Heaven. Satan promised a good life in fiery eternity, although his prevarication is famous. Still, I believed him, and he kept his word. No torment, he told me, none of the legendary fire that burns hot but never consumes. As a bonus he would occasionally send me back among the living to carry out his mandate, which is to make existence miserable for Christians by using the canonical and secular courts as theaters in which to perform. The idea of watching me work amused him. As a lawyer I knew my options, and they weren't appealing: suffering untold years in Purgatory followed by an eternity of damnation with the great unwashed of humanity. So I accepted his offer. Heaven had never been an option anyway." At this last admission he tipped back his head and laughed, a sound like the merging echoes of stones bouncing off the walls of a bottomless well.

"Aha! There it is," Révigny said. "Why would God make the world this way if not for the striking contrasts?" He shook his head slowly in seeming disbelief, sending the ever-present cloud of smoking brimstone to oscillating out of synchrony.

I was shocked. For a moment I hesitated, unsure how to respond, before blurting out, "What you're saying is blasphemy!"

Révigny was examining one of his shoes and seemed not to be paying attention.

"Did you hear me?'

"Of course. So, what can the keepers of all that's good and holy do, send me to Hell? Odd how one shoe became scuffed in the mugging and stayed this way through all the chaos of Purgatory and the Netherworld. What we have here, Barthélemy, is a metaphysical mystery, something strangely disturbing is scratching its hairy back against reality's doorpost. Oh well, it's only a shoe." He looked at me and smiled his oddly sad grimace, displaying green teeth behind green lips. Then he playfully stuck out his tongue. It emerged extraordinarily long and thin, like a green serpent. The end was sharply forked, each tine terminating in a tiny serpent's head with a pair of fiery red eyes. He flashed his own eyes red, and the tongue waggled around as if searching, seemingly of its own initiative.

FRIDAY MAY 5TH—COURT CONVENES THE FIRST DAY
OF THE TRIBUNAL; THE JUDICIAL VICAR EXPLAINS
WHY AN ECCLESIASTICAL PROCEEDING IS NECESSARY
AND EMPHASIZES THE COST INCURRED

⬥

COURT CONVENED AS SCHEDULED AT THE Théâtre Romain, the large amphitheater mentioned previously and built in Roman times on the city's north side. A makeshift courtroom had been set up on the stand, or large stone stage, at the far northern end. Its furnishings comprised a long table with three chairs on one side facing the gallery to the south. A dock in the form of a stockade perhaps four meters square had been erected between the main table and stone bleachers directly in front of the judicial vicar at a distance of four meters. It contained a single chair and a nearby table, the one bearing no connection with the other. The chair was for the witness; the table held a caged rat, representamen for the accused. Offset to one side of the main table but between it and the dock, a table and chair had been reserved for the clerk of the court whose duty it is to record events of a legal proceeding as they occur and afterward enter them into the official record.

Several hundred onlookers had already gathered in the gallery at the Théâtre's southern end, which forms a semi-circle facing the court and its paraphernalia. Most occupied the ring of stone bleachers rising in twelve levels up the embankment facing the dock and the stand behind it; other onlookers sprawled in the grass between the bottom row and the stand. Many had brought food and drink, anticipating a day of leisure and entertainment. Because the area is a common, sheep and goats grazed placidly on the level floor of the amphitheater and among the carefully placed banks of stone bleachers.

The event was taking the appearance of a spontaneous festival. On officially sanctioned festival days Autun's town square typically features a religious procession through the main thoroughfares to the Cathédrale led by the clergy, its ranking members dressed in fine robes and bearing crosses and banners. Temporary booths line the streets selling food, drink, and religious and apotropaic trinkets. These last, of course, would be missing from the tribunal about to begin, although we could still look forward to the hangerson: thieves, roving vendors, pickpockets, whores, mimes, acrobats, beggars, and sometimes even a podicinist (breaker of wind) to entertain the crowd, a mix of locals and visitors from the countryside. In the way that vultures quickly locate a carcass, a mime and a juggler had already appeared, plus several musicians and some vendors selling food and drink. With minor variations this scene would define the gallery of spectators in the weeks to come.

The day was pleasantly warm and sunny. The liturgical hour of terce had just been signaled by the distant bells of Cathédrale Saint-Lazare. After the clerk stood and announced opening of the court the judicial vicar, resplendent in a white robe, rose from his chair behind the main table and addressed the gallery. "The accused—that is, the resident rats of the city of Autun and surrounding countryside—are charged with the crime of having destroyed barley crops in the fields during the previous growing season and devouring most of the winter's harvest stored at the municipal granary for benefit of our community. If the issue recurs this winter the peasants will have insufficient supplies to see them through. Without their barley bread and porridge it's possible some will starve.

"Last month the bishop ordered me to convene an ecclesiastical tribunal to assure saving this year's crop by taking preventive measures. Specifically, the objective will be to eliminate the rats before seedheads form on barley stalks in the fields, permitting a full harvest to be gathered and that portion designated for the granary rendered safe from despoliation. It means, quite simply, getting rid of the rats before midsummer; that is, no later than the middle of the growing season.

"This will entail tangible expenses to the community. The equivalent benefits are more nebulous. First and foremost, elimination of a specific danger or annoyance to society, in the case before us the voluntary exodus or consequent punishment of the rats determined to devour food allotted by Divine intent exclusively for the only beings created in God's image. The defendants sowed no barley, nor should they be entitled to reap any.

"Court proceedings, whether ecclesiastical or civil, are not without costs, which in this case will be borne by the community through tolls and taxes paid to the municipality of Autun. It means, good citizens, that you will pay them indirectly. Among these will be fees of the procurators—that is, the lawyers—and any additional advocates representing the complainants or defendants, along with those of expert witnesses for either side whose testimony might be solicited. The bailiff doesn't volunteer his services, nor does the geôlier charged with incarceration and care of the accused until sentence is pronounced and carried out. And, I should add, nor do their assistants, servants, and guards. All these men must receive their usual fees. I have nothing more to say about the matter." With these last words his gavel struck the sounding block, officially ending further discussion.

It was barely past sext, time for the noonday meal for those having it, and already the day's session was over. The spectators seemed nonplussed. A man had appeared leading a donkey, his cart burdened with a cask of wine for sale by the cup. Another vendor arrived with loaves and pastries. The music had started, children were fighting and shrieking, and drunks were already staggering about, both men and women pausing to piss openly on the ancient bleachers.

With the afternoon free I went to the stables and found François and Alvin napping in the hay, having not bothered to return their breakfast dishes to the tavern scullery. I prodded them awake, pointing out that the stalls needed mucking and the water buckets filled. Because the day was pleasant I ordered them to take all three animals outside, crosstie them, and brush their coats. These instructions having been discharged, I went to the inn and took a nap.

Révigny and I met in the tavern around the liturgical hour of vespers. After a cup or two and some moments of relaxation I mentioned that I had some questions about his metamorphosis and present life as a demon.

"Ask away," he said. "My life is open to your enquiries."

"You claim not to sleep, and I've never seen you sleeping, at least in a conventional sense, and you appear to be unaffected by alcohol; that is, you don't get drunk or have hangovers."

"We demons don't require sleep. Why? I don't know. On the other topic, little is known about the alimentation of angels, good and bad. Demons and angels belong to the same tribe, the former simply being naughty doers of evil. The ecclesiastics at least got that distinction correct. Without sounding too professorial, eating is the chewing and swallowing of food. Alimentation encompasses the fate of food or liquid through four stages: first, mastication and swallowing, or 'eating' and 'drinking'; second, passage into the stomach; third, digestion in the stomach and intestines followed by absorption of the dissolved nutrients and liquid into the body; fourth, the excretion of unnecessary components." Révigny put both elbows on the table, bringing his horrid face close to mine and giving off a whiff of sulfur. His eyes had turned bright yellow, and he was obviously enjoying the discussion.

"Let's break apart the sequence and consider each stage separately," he said, as if presenting a lecture from a university podium. "All angels both good and bad can accomplish the first two, but the third and fourth exceed their capabilities. In place of digestion, absorption, and finally excretion of the remainder, food and drink dissipate into the loosely constructed matter serving as an angel's earthly facsimile. Whether living humans or angelic beings we're all constructed of compacted molecules. The particles comprising those of us in the latter state are simply assembled more loosely; that is, with more empty spaces among their component parts. This also explains how some of my brimstone smoke leaks out.

"A demon, the subject of this discussion, can eat and drink with humans, animals, or other demons, although it gains no corporeal benefit from doing so. Then, of course, it needs none. Obviously, neither can it suffer the ill effects, say, of poisons and hangovers. And the remainder of a meal? Nothing is left, just as nothing was used and incorporated, so naturally angels both light and dark neither urinate nor defecate. Let's be practical: have you ever seen an angel of either sort with an asshole?"

"I confess that I've never looked," I said.

"Well," Révigny said, "put that aside a moment because the deeper question is whether Jesus had one. Learned ecclesiastics assure us that in Christ's body the alimentary sequence was complete, but because He was Glorified He required neither nutrients nor water. The food and drink He ingested and swallowed were incorporated into His body instantaneously with nothing remaining. Seems illogical to me, but if true the man was a paragon to the conservation of matter." Having finished his oration he leaned back and folded his arms, eyes dimming slowly to amber.

I said I thought we ought to have another cup of the middling vintage, and Révigny immediately agreed. After all, he reminded me, the weekend was upon us. Ahead was only an absurd trial of some rats, irrelevant exempla of Eden's countless delinquents.

MONDAY MAY 8TH—THE JUDICIAL VICAR EXPLAINS
THE DIFFERENCE BETWEEN ECCLESIASTICAL AND CIVIL COURT
PROCEEDINGS, OUTLINES THE STEPS TO BE FOLLOWED,
AND INTRODUCES MEMBERS OF THE COURT

AFTER THE CATHÉDRALE'S DISTANT BELLS FINISHED announcing the hour of terce the judicial vicar stood and addressed the court. "In trials involving pests it isn't possible to put each accused individual in the dock. Instead, we prosecute them as a group, presuming if one is guilty so are they all. Keep in mind that such proceedings pit mankind against indolent nature, those who labor for their sustenance versus those who would leave the hard work to us and steal what we have earned.

"If convicted their punishment must be anathema rather than death, for two reasons. The first? Because there are too many to charge individually. Locating, arresting, and interrogating every rodent or grasshopper in the surrounding fields, each fly in a pesky swarm, is impractical, not to mention disgusting. Imagine if we were to see the court overrun by thousands of rats. Therefore, we put a representamen on display in the dock—Monsieur Rat over there—and assess the innocence or guilt of his comrades *in absentia*. I emphasize that the objective of canon law is prevention of future harm, not punishment for past harms, and this standard applies to mankind and animals alike."

I jumped to my feet. "Pardon the interruption, Your Grace, but may I speak?"

"Yes, monsieur."

"Your Grace, this objective seems contradictory. The rats here at Autun are charged with a past crime, that of eating last year's barley crop, not a crime that might or might not occur in the future. The canonical court, however, claims such an assumption to be false based on the general agreement among ecclesiastics that insensate large beasts, and also small ones like grasshoppers and rats, typically referred to as 'bestioles,' lack agency, making them immune from conventional punishments. Then why any punishment at all? From what I've heard so far this tribunal is being held solely for the purpose of deterrence, to prevent the same crime from happening at a later time by the identical creatures. If true, no matter how fiercely our citizens hate these particular rats for what they did to last year's barley crop the past is irrelevant insofar as the court should be concerned. In other words, Monsieur Rat, his relatives, and their associates aren't here to be punished for eating last year's barley. As you've said yourself they're to be prosecuted instead for eating a *future* barley crop, a crime that might not even occur. Am I right? And if it doesn't happen, how will we know it's because these rats have been properly chastised and warned of dire consequences or the actual preventive mechanism is no reason at all but merely coincidence?"

"We aren't here to question longstanding tradition, Monsieur Chassenée," said the judicial vicar. "Now please sit down so I may continue. The second reason is the Church's ban on its clergy from participating in tribunals in which the penalty could involve the shedding of blood or sperm, the latter being of no consequence in this case. If found guilty and subsequently executed, blood then would be on the Church's hands. I know of only one possible exception, and that is when Saint Bernard de Clairvaux while preaching in the church at Foigny cursed a swarm of flies disrupting his sermon. He cursed them with the words *Excommunico eas!* In the vernacular it means, 'Excommunicate them!' I say this is a 'possible exception' because he might have meant to kill them. If true, flies are bestioles, some forms of which do not always bleed, or at least not so we can specifically distinguish blood from other juices when their bodies are squashed.

"If held under aegis of the Church a proceeding such as this can hand down only canonical punishments. However, if the verdict excludes the possibility of capital punishment an ecclesiastical judge may assume civil jurisdiction if secular authorities agree, but this is the only exception and irrelevant here. I remind the court that the situation in human trials is similar: a heretic tried in ecclesiastical court is never explicitly condemned to die; rather, the case is assigned to a civil court for formal sentencing and seeing the sentence carried through.

"So, how is it decided whether the accused must appear before a clerical or secular court? The determination isn't so complex as it seems. In the case of animals, local communities have control over activities of their livestock. When a domestic animal or recognizable group of such animals commits a direct crime against a human being, when a certain pig, say, or herd of pigs recognizable as distinct individuals, kills and eats a child the accused perpetrator or perpetrators may be arrested and incarcerated. Formal charges are brought, and the crime is then tried in civil court under secular law.

"When rats, mice, grasshoppers, and other wild creatures living independently and *not* under human control commit a crime they are brought before an ecclesiastical court such as this one and prosecuted under canon law. In such instances many individuals—often uncountable, not just one or a few—have acted in concert to perpetrate the crime. After all, who could honestly testify, 'It was this very grasshopper I hold between my fingers that I caught in the act of eating my wheat, not the one over there.'" At this the gallery had its first of what would be many laughs.

"The Church then intervenes with supernatural functions, ordering the pests to stop their carnage and crimes against mankind and God and depart from the fields, granaries, vineyards, or orchards as the case may be. What you are about to witness will be such a proceeding, and I shall preside and decide guilt or innocence and what punishment, if any, is appropriate."

The Judicial vicar then described what to expect in the coming tribunal, emphasizing again that it would not be a trial in the commonly understood sense of how that term is applied in secular law when the accused is charged with a past crime; rather, it will be, he emphasized, an *ecclesiastical proceeding* or *canonical tribunal*. Events will follow established procedures sequentially, first one, then the next, and so forth in their proper order. These steps and the rules governing them are the foundation of the Church's canonical legal system.

An ecclesiastical proceeding is initiated, His Grace explained, when the Church receives a complaint of a crime from the community. The aggrieved party submits a requeste des habitans (request for redress). If the accusation is merited the bishop dispatches one or more investigators to assess the damages and determine whether the situation warrants prosecution and should be assigned to a canonical or civil court. If the former, public processions and prayers are ordered in the hope of staying God's anger prior to initiating a formal proceeding. Why? Because the people— that is, the complainants—had obviously sinned, making them responsible for the events about which they were now complaining. Still, the people are God's children despite being afflicted with sin; consequently, the Church is obliged to act on their behalf.

If processions and prayers fail—in other words, if the rats ignore holy admonishments and directives and persist in their despicable habits—the bishop, having duly discharged his obligations as God's representative on Earth, appoints a cleric trained in canon law—a judicial vicar—to oversee matters from this point forward. In rare and unusually important circumstances the bishop might assume the task himself. The next legal steps are the plaidoyer des habitans (the plaintiffs' plea) followed by the defense's plea on behalf of the clients, or plaidoyer pour les rats in the impending case here. Steps four and five are replication of the plaintiffs' plea (réplique des habitans) and the rejoinder of the defendants (réplique du defendeur).

The judicial vicar's first act is to appoint two lawyers who can be either clerical or secular (the Church has no preference), one to prosecute the defendants on behalf of the plaintiffs and Church, the other to represent the defendants. In the sixth step the procurator for the plaintiffs—who also represents the ecclesiastical court and is thus the bishop's procurator—presents his conclusions. The last step is when the judicial vicar delivers the sentence (sentence du juge d'eglise). Throughout, those present will hear the case presented and argued in French; that is, the vernacular, or vulgar, except for the sentence, which is always read in Latin. Why?

Although God is fluent in every language whether vulgar, barbarian, or formal and understands the demotic idioms of each, it's clear to all that He prefers Latin. Therefore, if Latin must be used in court the word or phrase must be followed immediately by a vernacular translation. As presiding judge the judicial vicar is expected to remain impartial throughout, reserving judgment and sentencing until after both sides have been heard fairly.

The tribunal starts when the court summons the leaders of those causing the offenses demanding they appear and report to the procurator designated to defend them. If they fail in this duty the court issues an edict ordering them to vacate their present places of residence within a predetermined time on threat of specified punishment. The edict might include inducements, like offering a parcel of vacant land to which the accused can migrate and dwell in safety. If the edict is ignored the accused are declared *contemnors* (those who show contempt), setting canonical proceedings in motion; that is, the steps listed above. All this the judicial vicar explained to the court and spectators, which the latter largely ignored, their attention siphoned away by the many diversions.

He then introduced his judicial associate and the two procurators, and we stood in turn as our names were announced. "Sitting at a separate table off to the side of us is the clerk of the court whose duty it is to record the events as they occur. I, of course, am the judicial vicar and the judge of this proceeding. At the main table here on the stand and seated in the chair to my right is Monsieur Humbert de Révigny, lawyer for the complainants, who will prosecute on their behalf and the Church's. On my left is Monsieur Barthélemy de Chassenée, lawyer for the defendants, meaning the rats."

The rest of the day wasn't memorable, the judicial vicar droning on citing relevant precedents. The afternoon became overcast, and by nones a light rain had started to fall. Unwilling to get his white robe wet (or perhaps afraid he might melt), His Grace dismissed the court, and the two score or so spectators who remained drifted slowly away. His final words to us members of the court were to bring our mounts the next day.

Anticipating this change in the weather, I had ridden to court with François and Alvin following on the mule. Their orders were to wait until the day's proceeding ended and accompany me back to the inn. I found them near the entrance to the Théâtre Romain. My horse was tethered to a tree, the mule untethered and grazing nearby. François was talking to a peasant girl. She was giggling about something he said. Alvin, meanwhile, was making his bird motions, turning in circles with arms outstretched. Neither was watching my animals. I shouted, and François immediately broke off his conversation and ran to get the horse.

Alvin paid no attention until I approached him from behind. He turned with a startled gaze on hearing my footsteps, but made no other movement. I shouted in his face, "Obtenez la mule!" In response he looked at me curiously as if trying to discern my species. His expression suggested a decision might be imminent: rabbit or squirrel, which could I be? "La mule," I said, this time in a normal voice, and pointed to it. Finally, recognition and a response. Alvin spread his stubby arms and directed his tubby torso to "fly" more or less straight toward the animal and gather its reins.

That night at the tavern Révigny was quieter than usual, as if he had something on his mind. He kept tapping his foot on the floor, and the echo was making me feel cross and uneasy. "Can't you do something about the echo?" I said.

"Sorry, it's the cocoon. And the anti-echoic chamber hasn't yet been invented. We still have a few centuries to wait for that."

"Will you be around to greet it?" I said. I had no idea what he was talking about and meant the question as a joke, but Révigny didn't smile.

"Consider this," he said. "I might not have been long *in* the world, but I've spent part of eternity *of* it. And to think that I was once a normal man. Or was I? Today feels like I've been around forever."

"You claim to be immortal?"

"Your words, Barthélemy, but they do have an enticing ring."

I once watched a butterfly struggle out of its cocoon then rest on the remnant as its wings dried and straightened. It was a lovely creature, but how would the being before me look if suddenly free of its cocoon? I shuddered to imagine.

Now Révigny did offer a sad grin. "Nice of you to think of me as a beautiful butterfly, Barthélemy."

TUESDAY MAY 9TH—COURT CONVENES ONLY BRIEFLY;
THE GALLERY EXPRESSES DISAPPROVAL; OFFICIALS DEPART FOR
THE MUNICIPAL GRANARY TO INSPECT DAMAGE TO THE BARLEY
STORED OVER THE PREVIOUS WINTER; THE COURT GETS DRUNK

⚜

WE RECONVENED AT THE USUAL TIME, then adjourned almost immediately. The judicial vicar insisted that we court officers inspect the granary and personally assess the reputed damage to barley stored over the winter. By late spring the stores would have been largely depleted anyway and not replenished until the autumn harvest when landowners from outlying farms and villages bring their allotments of grain to be measured, recorded, and deposited. By law, every landowner must contribute a share of his crop to sustain indigent citizens of the département de Saône-et-Loire through winter, spring, and during especially destitute times even into summer. The gallery complained loudly at the inconvenience of our abrupt departure, having anticipated a day's entertainment.

I remembered the granary from my childhood, an austere stone building on open land bounded by Chemin de la Croix Verte where it extends parallel with the Promenade des Marores before this thoroughfare bends north. Boulevard Mazagran forms a boundary toward the west and Boulevard Laureau another to the south. The area is roughly the shape of a right triangle. The granary, which occupies the southern and wider portion of the plot, has been a fixture of Autun for two centuries or longer.

The building is constructed of gray field stones now plastered with colorful lichens. It has the shape of a rectangle standing vertically and rises to a height of two storeys. The rough-cut stones are not fitted tightly, making it necessary to plug the larger openings with smaller ones. Each summer the bishop orders all cracks large and small caulked to minimize the leaking of grain, although spaces inevitably remain.

Near the top of the structure on one side is a shuttered opening through which baskets of barley are emptied. Above it a sturdy cantilever of oak protrudes, and from its end dangles a pulley. On either side are two ladders set close enough that a man standing on one can touch the shoulder of his companion on the other. Together they climb the ladders in synchrony and once at the top muscle full baskets raised by men on the ground to the mouth of the opening and tip the contents inside.

The interior wall is the exterior's mirror image. When grain is removed two men standing atop the pile inside fill a basket using shovels and raise it by pulley to the opening. Two men on the outside ladders pull the basket toward them, attach it to a hook on the exterior device, and from that cantilever it is lowered to the ground. During dry weather the shutters are opened to allow a change of air, which helps prevent mildew.

Wearing the robes of our profession we rode to the granary as a group, parting throngs of bony dogs and tattered pigeons approaching for handouts, often bumping shoulders in the effort to avoid piles of manure and garbage, some more than a meter high. Beggars accosted us requesting alms. Their reward was to be knocked down if failing to step aside. The judicial vicar looked at them with distaste, muttering on one occasion that an ordinance should be issued to keep such vermin outside the city walls, especially the cripples and lepers whose infirmities made them an eyesore.

A man is judged by the clothes he wears and the horse he rides. To honor the legal profession and reinforce personal standing as a prominent land-owning citizen of Saône-et-Loire, I dress well and ride my palfrey when called to meetings in the city. This provides exercise for us both and allows me to display my status in the community. My mount is young and vigorous with a smooth gait, and he possesses the stamina to go several kilometers at an ambling pace before needing food, water, and rest.

An hour or so before sext we stopped at an inn and took refreshment. It was mid-afternoon when we reached the granary, all of us slightly drunk. The judicial vicar suggested a rest in the shade of the building prior to inspecting it and while doing so offered additional refreshment from his private cellars. The day had turned hot, and no one objected. His Grace's servant passed among us handing out cups of white Burgundy from vines with roots deep in the limestone ridge of Saint Aubin in the Côte de Beaune region. It was a magnificent wine, crisp with a slight citrus flavor. Révigny was thrilled and transmitted his pleasure in glowing language to our host, at one point stating that, no disrespect to our own deity, but this vintage must have passed from mythical hands on Mount Olympus directly into His Grace's.

Rats were everywhere, oblivious to the bright light. They scurried between our feet, often stopping to look up at us inquisitively. They seemed completely unafraid, certainly having no premonition of what the court planned for them, nor did they offer indication that I was their potential savior. "Such disgusting creatures," the judicial vicar said. "I hope the coming proceeding produces the desired results. Think of the poor people who draw grain from here. Surely each basketful is equal parts barley and rat turds." He requested that a basket be raised from inside and lowered to us on the outside. Subsequent examination proved his prediction correct.

By the time the inspection was finished the sun was tipping toward the western horizon, and we were tipping every which way. Unknown to us François had found a battered cup in the street and was stealing wine from His Grace's barrel. He was as drunk as the rest of us. I ordered him to bend down and interlace his fingers, providing me a step to mount my horse. It was a maneuver he had performed a hundred times, but in this instance his fingers came apart when I set my foot, and we both tumbled into the mud. Upon regaining my feet I reached for the whip and began scourging him and shouting curses, which startled the palfrey. He began high-stepping and turning in circles with François still holding the reins in one hand and raising the other arm over his head to protect himself from my blows, none of which found the mark. At one point the horse nearly trampled me, and I barely got out of its path, slipping and falling again. The rest of our party watched with mild curiosity, eventually turning and gaining their own mounts, although not without difficulty. Only Révigny made it into his saddle gracefully.

Alvin, who was even drunker than François, turned in erratic circles while loudly announcing to the sky his prowess of flight. *Regar de moi voler!* he shouted repeatedly. *Regar de moi voler!* As we watched he slipped and fell several times, looking more like a misshapen gargoyle following each tumble into the mud. As our group rode away he and François were still trying to mount the mule, which resisted their clumsy efforts by sidestepping and swinging its hindquarters out of reach. They eventually got astride and made it to the inn some two hours later, hooting their arrival. After stabling the mule, both fell asleep underneath it in the dirt and manure.

THE JUDICIAL VICAR HESITATED A MOMENT until the bells stopped ringing and the clerk formally reconvened court before rising to speak. "The people afflicted and inconvenienced by these ravenous rodents were interviewed prior to the start of this tribunal. Mitigation measures were implemented promptly, but to no avail. Witnesses agreed unanimously that during the previous year rats had indeed caused considerable destruction both to their crops in the field and at the granary. In an effort to stem the hairy hordes, keepers of the granary tried the usual methods of rodent control.

"As a first step, feeding scraps to the many resident cats was forbidden in the hope of piquing their interest in ratting. When this proved ineffective more immediate methods were implemented, namely poisons known to be lethal against the rodent tribes. I have before me the two recipes deployed. The first: mix aconite and arsenic in pig fat, and into this beat wheaten flour and eggs. Stir to the consistency of bread dough then bake in an oven. Cut into strips and nail to boards placed where rodents are known to inhabit. The second: take hellebore root, grind together with wheaten flour, add honey, pig fat, and cheese. Stir these ingredients together into a paste and set out in spoon-sized dollops where rodents frequent.

"Neither recipe proved effective. The rat hordes continued to increase, the grain stores diminishing concomitantly. Court officials inspected the granary yesterday and we deem it infested well beyond acceptable limits. The findings of clerical inspectors sent into the surrounding villages prior to this proceeding came to the same conclusions about infestations in the fields. Based on mitigation attempts and the observations of experts and nonexperts alike the court concludes that steps must be taken to remedy the problem. God's help has been requested through our prayers, and a procession here at Autun dedicated exclusively to expulsion of the rats has been held, obviously without result. I ask everyone—noblemen, merchants, and peasants—to immediately increase tithes, give more alms, and attend extra Masses praying for heavenly intervention in this trying time, never forgetting that human sin has precipitated the plague." His Grace glared pointedly at the gallery, where those gathered stopped talking and laughing and avoided his eyes.

"Based on the evidence, I hereby declare the plaintiffs' petition valid. Ordinarily, the next step in these tribunals is summoning the defendants themselves—meaning the rats—to appear in open court. Not all of them, of course, but a few of their representative leaders would be required to show themselves and accept any consequences on behalf of their families and comrades. However, I'm electing to issue an edict instead, insisting they vacate the fields and granary. If they disobey this command I shall proceed directly to anathematization. Does either procurator for the prosecution object?"

Révigny immediately said, "I don't object, Your Grace."

My strategy had been in place from the start. In cases like this the defense attorney is almost certain to lose anyway. Therefore, a common first phase is to establish various legal roadblocks in the hope of slowing the proceeding toward its inevitable denouement. In a legal context, attempt to avoid or blunt all arguments against my clients by using dilatory motions. With luck, some unforeseen event or factor might eventually reverse the tide. I had counted among my tactics a prolonged argument aimed at postponing a summons. This was no longer possible.

Delays of any sort have limits, including the risk of angering the presiding judge when he eventually loses patience. In the absence of a summons I was left no choice except to focus on the edict, which I hoped would be only the first of three. When the rats failed to honor it—as they inevitably would—the law allowed me to request up to two more. If the last of these is dismissed as not valid or irrelevant the only hope of vindicating my clients would default to other options, and these are few. In truth, none came to mind at the moment.

Has such a strategy ever worked? I was left no choice, and the moment had arrived. I rose from my chair. "May I speak, Your Grace?"

"Of course, monsieur."

"I request a delay of one week to better prepare my case on behalf of the defendants."

"Can you offer a specific reason?"

"Three, Your Grace. First, you are passing over a summons and proceeding directly to an edict, which will force a change of plans by the defense. Second, the message received at my estate in late April was terse and uninformative, mentioning only that I would be defending some rampaging rats. No details were provided. For example, I hadn't known that His Grace actually began the tribunal unofficially before appointing Monsieur Révigny and myself as procurators. Neither of us knew about those early attempts to rid the granary of rats by making the resident cats hungrier, then deploying poisons, nor had we been told beforehand that around the same time clerics had been dispatched into the countryside to solicit the opinions of citizens about their rat troubles. Finally, this is the first I've heard about a procession. My comments aren't meant as personal criticisms of His Grace, whose integrity and fairness are above reproach, but learning of these events so late has placed me at a disadvantage."

His Grace looked from me to Révigny. "Do you feel the same, Monsieur Révigny? Could you also make good use of an extra week of preparation?"

"Yes, Your Grace, very much so."

"Then a reprieve of one week is granted. Monsieur Clerk?"

The clerk stood and said, "Court will next convene at the usual hour on Wednesday the 17th of May. Court is dismissed."

I didn't see Révigny until vespers, when he appeared and joined me at our table in the tavern. I also hadn't seen him at breakfast when he failed to appear or the previous evening when I skipped supper and went straight to bed in a drunken stupor. He sat and beckoned the innkeeper, who jumped at once, cringing and wiping his hands as usual on his dirty apron. "The new wine," Révigny said.

A flagon soon appeared. Révigny raised his cup as in a toast. "Wait until you taste this. It's straight from the judicial vicar's cellars. I stopped by to pay my respects after court recessed. During our conversation I remarked how much you and I had admired his white Burgundy from Saint Aubin yesterday. His Grace was so pleased by the compliment he presented me with a gift of an entire cask, which he said would be delivered this very afternoon. That was after we'd had a cup or so in his private quarters to test its quality. A full cask just might see the two of us until the end of the tribunal. If not, I'm not above groveling at His Grace's feet for a replacement. No more rodent piss for us, my boy. From now on, only the best." I duplicated his gesture and raised my cup in gratitude.

Révigny pushed back his chair a bit and made himself comfortable. "In Hell we drink only the finest wines from Burgundy and Bordeaux, the reds aged in oaken casks at least two generations. And the fatted calf Yahweh abhorred when sacrificed to pagan gods? Delicious! We feast on it daily. Yes, only the finest."

"I thought demons can't digest and excrete."

"They can't, but we can surely taste. You seem troubled, monsieur. What's bothering you?"

"I'm feeling slightly guilty for the abuse I occasionally heap on François and Alvin, but mostly Alvin. François understands events happening around him and deserves whatever mistreatment I can muster because he purposely tests my patience. Alvin, however, is a pitiful simpleton who doesn't comprehend anything, making his shortcomings excusable, and which in turn makes my failure to acknowledge them a shortcoming of my own."

Révigny leaned forward and lifted his cup to his lips. "Ah, still muddling over that matter of paternity, are you?" His eyes changed from green to amber, and he flashed his death's head grimace. "I've been anticipating this. Remember when I mentioned that I don't sleep after dark because of all the mischief about? Well, Satan and I were at your festivities that night of François' wedding when Madame was conveniently far away from your estate and here in Autun. We were disguised as two peasants and correct in our thinking that because all peasants look alike to their lords there was little chance of your noticing a couple of strangers."

I said, "Seriously, Humbert? You were there?"

"Indeed I was, in the company of our dark lord and master, who incidentally truly despises masquerading as anyone other than a nobleman or knight. It took quite a lot of compliments from me and assurances that he still looked handsome even in rags before he could stop complaining and enjoy himself. Please don't mention this if you ever have the pleasure of meeting him."

"Uh, certainly. But why were you there? I'm just an average member of the gentry, nobody special."

"Oh, but you are Barthélemy! You have no idea how special. We were there to scout you as a potential member of Hell's inner circle." He waved his hand in dismissal. "But not to worry, I mean a *future* member of course. There's never any point in hustling anyone into Hades prematurely considering the length of eternity and such. No hurry at all. Relax. I'll pour us another cup of His Grace's excellent wine."

He refilled our cups and sat back, eyes now flashing bright yellow. "Suppose you tell me the story from your perspective?"

And so I did.

I told him how with every birthday of Alvin's I wondered again about his paternity. I noticed that he ceased to grow as a young boy. I saw his girth expand and noticed how his hair (always thin) had mostly disappeared even before puberty. Like my own hands and feet, his remained tiny, terminating in stubby fingers and toes, nor did his arms and legs grow to normal length. Unlike my mine, however, his brain failed to develop. He was now an adolescent with the mental capacity of a six-year-old, or thereabouts. He was an eternal child close to assuming the unlikely and false appearance of manhood.

I explained how François had a way of communicating with him, an unspoken language the nuances of which I never learned. It consisted of a system of subtle prompts and signals, culminating in Alvin's rote response. I said that I doubted even François was aware of how it worked. It might be innate, similar to the gift some have of training dogs and horses.

Tempting Alvin into any kind of useful activity requires making it a game. To pitch hay, for example, François calls Alvin's name and after getting his attention sticks the pitchfork into the pile and slings the impaled hay toward its destination. Alvin then stops turning in circles and, after watching François perform this motion a couple of times, runs to him and tries to take the pitchfork. François resists momentarily, as if not wanting to give it up. Once in possession of the tool Alvin enthusiastically forks hay until François interrupts and tempts him with another game, perhaps filling the water buckets, or distracts him with an apple or some such treat.

But could it be true? On the day François married my swineherd, a scrawny, toothless woman with one fixed eye that wouldn't turn, I opened two casks of green Spanish wine destined to be blended with some of my own vintage and sold at the Autun market in the public square. I thought my serfs might see this donation as a generous gesture. By the time of the evening marriage ceremony everyone working on my estate, including most of the household staff, was stinking drunk, and among the drunkest were the bride and groom. Madame, having anticipated such a scene, had gone to Autun to stay with relatives, refusing to participate or even closet herself safely inside the manor house.

Naturally, I joined the festivities, attended by a manservant carrying a flagon of my own palatable wine. Near nightfall I announced to my debauched peasants that I intended to invoke my lord's right of *jus primae noctis*, in the vernacular, droit du seigneur (the lord's right of the first night) and that François would have to wait his turn starting the next night.

Amid cheers and huzzahs my appropriated bride and I staggered through the front door of the manor house and up the stairs to my bed, where I ravished her then fell soundly asleep. When I awoke the next morning she was lying there watching me with a disconcerting smile, one eye staring at me and the other at the ceiling, hoping she was now my bride and not François'. I quickly ended any such idea, immediately banishing her back to the pigsties with orders to commence mixing the day's swill. Nine months later, almost to the day, she gave birth to Alvin.

"Very accurately told, Barthélemy. Satan and I watched the whole performance and know the outcome. Congratulations, Papa! Perhaps your backward offspring will someday become a bishop and make us proud. I can see him now in his little white robe and golden slippers, holding a miniature standard of the cross and shouting, *Je suis un oiseau! Regar de moi voler!*"

WEDNESDAY MAY 17TH—CHASSENÉE ASKS THAT NEW WITNESSES BE INTERVIEWED ABOUT THE RAT SITUATION AND THAT THEY BE SUMMONED TO TESTIFY BEFORE THE COURT INSTEAD OF DEPOSED IN THE COUNTRYSIDE; HE REQUESTS A TWO-WEEK DELAY

No sooner had court reconvened than I asked permission to speak. The judicial vicar nodded.

"I've just completed a week of intense planning, working day and night until my eyeballs feel like they were rolled in sand. The time was well spent, although one crucial obstruction remains, a dilemma of sorts, and until seeing it resolved I can't properly represent Monsieur Rat and his colleagues."

"What is troubling you, monsieur?" the judicial vicar said.

"I feel almost too embarrassed to raise it considering how patient and thoughtful His Grace has been already."

The judicial vicar sighed and leaned back in his chair. "Bring it up anyway, Monsieur Chassenée."

I bowed and said, "Thank you, Your Grace. My problem is this. I believe the court is moving too quickly, skipping ahead of the evidence toward a conclusion unlikely to benefit my clients. In describing the depositions taken in April by two clerical investigators Your Grace referred to the respondents as 'the people,' a universal term lacking adequate definition. Who exactly are 'the people' and what specifically were their testimonies, not collectively but individually? Do we know their names, sexes, and addresses? How many persons were interviewed, and are their statements representative of the département's residents? Is there a written record, or must we assume on faith that such testimonies actually occurred? In the absence of records, including the questions asked and exact replies of the respondents, what guarantee do my clients have that the information is unbiased and accurate? This worry could be allayed if the defense is given permission to interview them."

Révigny said, "I'm willing to accept His Grace's blanket statement as free of bias and untainted by inaccuracy. He is, after all, a man of God sworn to uphold the truth, whether in an ecclesiastical or secular context. So were his clerical investigators. Such men do not lie."

"Thank you for the vote of confidence, Monsieur Prosecutor," said his Grace, "although Monsieur Chassenée for the defense makes a valid point. Why indeed should he take my word alone? His duty is to defend his clients. Monsieur, there is admittedly no written record of witness depositions. The court's investigators spoke to several aggrieved parties, some in their dwellings, others while laboring in the fields. I regretfully declined to ask how many persons were interviewed and whether they represent a fair sampling of the département's inhabitants. The investigators' conclusion of unanimous agreement was based on these conversations. However, it's unofficial, as you say, having been transmitted to me orally in chambers and from my lips to the court. What do you suggest?"

"Your Grace is extraordinarily generous," I said, and bowed to him. "But in the interest of fairness the record ought to be made official before any conclusions are reached. Furthermore, consider that it will serve as a guide in perpetuity. Legal scholars will study this tribunal—its progress and conclusions—centuries from now; a good showing is essential. Your Grace's name will be stamped in history." At this His Grace struck a thoughtful pose with quill partly raised, as if sitting for a portrait while about to sign an important document. "I ask that twelve witnesses be summoned and instructed to testify openly before the court, and that their comments be entered into the official record. Anything less is a disservice to my clients. As defendants they have the right, through me, to confront their accusers and hear any charges against them firsthand."

"I don't object, Your Grace," Révigny said.

"Then so be it," the judicial vicar said. "Twelve persons chosen randomly by clerical investigators will appear in court approximately two weeks from today prepared to testify about damage suffered personally at the jaws and paws of rats." The clerk of the court rose and handed him a piece of paper. He examined it quickly and looked up. "According to the clerk's calendar the appointed date is Tuesday the 30rd of May, one day short of two weeks. This ought to suffice. Court is adjourned until then."

I went to the inn and ordered François and Alvin back to the manor with my used laundry and gave François a note with the date he and Alvin were to be back, which was a week and a day. They were to pack the donkey with my belongings, as usual, and ride double on the mule. Separately, I included a list of items they were to bring on the return trip, including a couple of volumes from my library. Their orders were to leave at the liturgical hour of prime the following morning after breakfast. François was to hand Madame Chassenée the note and list of items personally on arriving home and not simply give it to a maid or anyone else on the household staff. In it I asked Madame to see that my bumbling footmen maintained the schedule and didn't tarry, that there was much work to be done here at Autun. I also included a few lines describing how the tribunal was shaping up, not that Madame would be the least bit interested. I then told the innkeeper of this impending absence and warned him about falsely charging me room and board for my men, mule, and donkey when none would be requiring such resources in their absence, and to see that my horse was cared for. Now I could only hope François didn't become distracted along the way, get lost, or lose the instructions.

Gathering everything together, organizing François and Alvin, and inculcating them with their orders, straightforward tasks though they were, took the rest of the day. I got to the tavern shortly past vespers to find Révigny seated in his usual chair and viciously kicking at a cripple begging a piece of bread from underneath the table. The innkeeper's wife, a large beast of a woman, appeared from the scullery, grabbed the man by the remnants of what once had been a tunic, and hustled him out the door still with his hand outstretched in the hope a few crumbs might fall into it.

Révigny looked up and saw me. "Ah, Barthélemy, you caught me in the act of carrying out Christ's instructions to love our fellow man. I noticed you were late and ordered bread to stay the imaginary hunger. Seeing your footmen off with the dirty laundry, I hear."

"Yes, and a list of instructions, which I trust Madame will see is fulfilled, assuming François and Alvin don't take a wrong path or Madame decides not to leave her bed on the day of their arrival and my orders are given to a swineherd instead. Here you sit beating the less fortunate and carrying out God's work while I contemplate

Hell's environment here on Earth and thank Him I've escaped it another few weeks. I refer, of course, to my own manor and loving wife. However, it does raise a subject I've been hoping we could discuss, namely, what's Hell really like? Nothing compares to a firsthand description from one of its most erudite and discerning citizens. Oh, and I presume you know for certain that the man just evicted really was a common beggar. You've surely heard the admonition about not treating a stranger unkindly because he might be Christ in disguise. Now, I must remember to remind the innkeeper again each morning to feed and water the horse while my footmen are absent."

"You flatter me, Monsieur Chassenée, not that your words fall on undeserving ears. And yes, the one who accosted me was only a stinking beggar made crippled, I suspect, by an 'accident' he would vigorously deny was self-inflicted." He gave out one of his hollow-sounding chuckles. "Incidentally, I applaud your baiting His Grace into giving you a two-week reprieve. Very clever and, as you say, a good excuse not to return home.

"But to address your question, in a word, Hell is shambolic, but only slightly moreso than the situation here on top of the ground. Think of being continuously inside the maelstrom of a fierce battle, one in which you know in advance there won't be any survivors. Look around at all the fools currently alive and consider that in Hell all the fools who ever died are current residents, and their numbers grow daily. Soon Satan will be petitioning God for room to expand, although I have to say he's making impressive inroads right here in France. Maybe France will be Hell's next outpost and Autun its capital. I would need hundreds of assistants just to keep pace. Hades, if I haven't mentioned before, is overrun with lawyers. There wouldn't be a shortage of eager and rapacious volunteers.

"Up here I eavesdrop on conversations in which people imagine and describe monstrous forms of life all around, a sort of self-made Hell on Earth: a sow with a man's face, a monk with the tail of a snake and countenance of a dog, a fish with a lion's head who cries like a human baby. The Dominican Giacomo Affinati insists these creatures are various incarnations of sin placed among humans by God as life-lessons. My guess would be they are harbingers of war, famine, or pestilence, or maybe demonstrable consequences of heresy: disrespect God and you'll end up a grasshopper with wiggly antennae sticking out of a skull shiny as a monk's. In any case, they transform creatures created in God's image into animals.

"But then, I have no particular expertise in such matters. I don't read many religious tracts these days, except when called back among the living to prosecute someone or some*thing*. Hell's library of Christian literature is woefully incomplete, as you might expect. As to tomes on devil worship, we have complete sets of everything ever set to parchment and paper, etched in clay, chiseled in stone, and painted on cave walls. If you need anything pertaining to this genre jot down the title after the trial. I'll deliver it to you in facsimile the next time I'm sent here."

"Then what's the point of subjecting a soul to torture if there's no lesson to learn, no possible penitence, no realization of remorse?"

"The point is the pain itself, Barthélemy, the agony of perpetual torture. Body and soul are separated at death. As we've discussed, even in Purgatory and Hell the body, although absent, has transferred its exquisite sensitivity to physical pain and attendant mental anguish to the soul. Regret? Contrition? Remorse? Hope of redemption? Use any term you like, but it's too late. The time, as you imply, has come and gone. Such opportunities are available only in life; they vanish the instant death knocks at the door. But all this talk of death and theology makes me thirsty, if only figuratively." He turned and raised his arm. "Innkeeper!"

Tuesday May 30th—Court Reconvenes after Chassenée's Requested Two-Week Delay; A Witness Testifies to Personal Suffering Caused by Rat Infestations (At Least We Think So)

❧

Court reconvened on schedule. I expected to see people waiting to testify queued behind the main table, huddling in the chilly rain under the temporary waxed-canvas awning, but there seemed to be only one witness. A smaller awning had been erected to cover the dock, where the witness testifying and Monsieur Rat could remain dry. The judicial vicar had ordered more permanent fixtures built over the main table on the stand and the other used by the clerk of the court, although construction had not yet begun. In the meantime servants would be posted behind members of the court holding umbrellas above our heads. Our main concern was keeping the documents dry. The gallery proved to be a fair-weather crowd, and the inclement weather had reduced the day's attendance considerably.

The clerk called for order, after which the judicial vicar rose to speak. "Nearly two weeks ago, on Wednesday the 17th of May, this court ordered two clerical investigators to venture into the various communities within the département de Saône-et-Loire closest to Autun, pick twelve representative citizens at random, and issue summonses requiring their appearance before us today, Tuesday the 30th of May. Of those twelve, just one has obeyed the court's order. To find replacements would delay the proceeding. Consequently, we must be content hearing testimony from she who has honored the call and agreed to perform her civic duty. This good citizen is Madame Cloutier. Will Madame please enter the dock?" An older woman limped into the dock and stood beside the chair. She was barefoot, eyes clouded by cataracts, and wearing a coif on her head. The clerk of the court quickly swore her in.

My interrogation technique includes putting witnesses in a comfortable state of mind before questioning, hoping they might be more inclined to be open and truthful. I had not anticipated the sly ways of country peasants and how this one was about to make me look foolish. "Good morning, Madame Cloutier," I said with a smile. "Thank you for coming to court and swearing before God to tell the truth."

"If you say so, monsieur. Has anyone ever told you that you're short?"

I ignored the insult, no doubt spoken out of ignorance. "The surname Cloutier has its origin in the trade of making nails." I said. The intention was to put her at ease by opening with a subject she knew best, her family. "Does your husband have a forge or smithy where he produces these useful items?"

"If you mean Roul, he doesn't make much of anything, useful or otherwise. I don't think I've ever seen someone as short and fat as you. Or as ugly either."

"I see. Do you know why you've been summoned to court, madame?"

"I assume it's about Roul. I've never been to Autun until now and can't say I like it much. The priests who handed me the paper and told me to come here said it was about five leagues north of where we live near Le Creusot, but it seemed much farther in the farm cart with Roul complaining the whole way about the stress it was taking on the mule. Aren't mules supposed to pull carts? That's another of his, well, you surely know because here we are."

"Excuse me, madame? I don't understand. We surely know what?"

"That Roul buggers our farm animals, and not only the mule. Right now he's somewhere out in the gallery hiding among the rest of the riff-raff. Ask him yourself. I never imagined seeing so many wastrels and derelicts in one place. What a sideshow, and you're part of it! Why aren't they tending their fields? It's planting season."

I looked at the gallery and saw everyone eyeing everyone else, trying to pick Roul out in the crowd. There was considerable murmuring and laughter. "Are you certain of this, madame?" I said.

"Of course. I even asked our village priest if buggery is a crime, not mentioning my husband, and he said yes. Is it true, monsieur?"

"Definitely, madame, and a very serious one. Bestiality expressed as buggery is a sin as well as a crime. It's mentioned often in the Old Testament. Chapter twenty-two verse nineteen of *Exodus* reads, *Whosoever lieth with a beast shall surely be put to death.* This applies to both men and women. And *Leviticus*, chapter twenty verses fifteen and sixteen, also tell us that not only humans but the offending animals involved in this unholy behavior must be put to death as well. In modern France the act is so repugnant that when referring to it lawyers say, *cujus ipsa nominatio crimen*, or in the vernacular 'to say the very name is a crime.' An exaggeration, of course."

Madame Cloutier became agitated. "Put to death? Our priest didn't mention that."

"Madame," I said, "we must return to the reason for your appearance here today. It has to do with rats."

"Rats, monsieur? To my knowledge Roul never buggered a rat. I would have heard the squeaking. No, monsieur. I'd surely know if my husband ever switched his amorous allegiance to the rodent tribe. That thought is truly disgusting."

I said, "Madame, the subject of the summons is whether it's your opinion that the rats on your land have been eating more grain than in previous years."

"The what, monsieur?"

"The summons given you by the priests ordering your appearance in court. The paper."

"Oh, that. Well, Roul and I never learned to read. Even if I could my eyes are too blind these days to see the letters. We really didn't understand why you asked us here. The priests who gave us the paper weren't too helpful. All I know is that tonight we'll be sleeping in the farm cart somewhere between here and home. I hope it isn't still raining. Oh, and if you're going to put Roul in jail at least let him take the mule and me home because we can't find the way on our own. You can come out to fetch Roul and take him to jail another time. May I leave now?"

I said, "Please answer the question, madame."

"Which question?"

"In your opinion, were there more rats last year than in previous years?"

"What a stupid thing to ask. How would I know? Even if I could see I wouldn't waste time going around counting rats. I can't even count. Now may I leave? I've got to find Roul. I expect he's in that crowd cooing in the ear of somebody's horse or mule. And you, monsieur, should think about joining a circus."

"Certainly, madame, and thank you for coming."

The few moments with Madame Cloutier in the dock, although entertaining, proved unhelpful. She had the gallery in stitches, and even the judicial vicar couldn't help showing a hint of a smile despite trying to hide it by putting a hand discreetly over his mouth. Révigny displayed (at least to me) his usual inscrutable rictus. Only the clerk remained implacable, busily scribbling his transcript of Madame Cloutier's unorthodox testimony.

The day's proceeding ended just as the bells intoned the onset of nones, the ninth hour. His Grace paused a moment to listen in reverence until they finished, then allotted the clerk a week to prepare Madame Cloutier's testimony in preliminary written form along with a summary and conclusion and deliver copies to him at his office in the Cathédrale and to Révigny and me at the inn. That would be Tuesday the 6th of June. We three were to independently provide our written comments of acceptance or rebuttal for the clerk to pick up after another week, or Tuesday the 13th of June.

The clerk, who had been looking at his own calendar, interrupted to note that because Easter Sunday had fallen on April 23rd, Ascension Day would be Friday the 2nd of June. No work could be done then or Sunday of that weekend. Sunday was never a day of work, but now an extra day would be lost. He recommended pushing his June 6th deadline forward to Friday the 9th. His Grace, Révigny, and I would then have until Friday the 16th to prepare our written comments.

The four of us would meet at the judicial vicar's office in the Cathédrale at terce on Tuesday the 20th to negotiate any last details, His Grace being final arbiter of any disputes. The clerk and His Grace would then get together Friday the 23nd to prepare the final draft. The clerk would read the finished report aloud in court the morning of Monday the 26th and afterward submit it into the record of the tribunal.

No one objected. The judicial vicar approved the schedule and made it official by dropping his gavel on the sounding block. This was all very tedious, although necessary to be certain the required days of rest and worship would be observed. We had huddled in a standing group in front of the judicial bishop, who remained seated, discussing the details in normal voices among ourselves. The gallery, unable to hear us, fidgeted and expressed displeasure with boos and hisses at being excluded.

MONDAY JUNE 26TH—THE TRANSCRIPT OF THE WITNESS IS READ ALOUD AND ENTERED INTO THE RECORD; THE JUDICIAL VICAR RULES IN FAVOR OF THE PLAINTIFFS AND ANNOUNCES INTENT TO ISSUE AN EDICT ORDERING ALL RATS TO VACATE THEIR DOMICILES; CHASSENÉE COMPLAINS THAT THE WITNESS TESTIMONY IS INADEQUATE TO FAVOR EITHER SIDE

❧

BY THE TIME COURT RECONVENED I was well rested and becoming bored by inactivity. I was also prepared for the various possibilities that might be put into play.

The clerk stood and read his report summarizing Madame Cloutier's testimony, which was officially accepted and entered into the record. The judicial vicar then proclaimed that her evidence as presented was adequate to support the plaintiffs' claim of damages. He announced the next step in the proceeding, which was to issue an edict commanding the rat hordes to leave the fields and municipal granary, adding for benefit of the spectators and the record that the witness list had not included any granary workers because members of the court had inspected that facility personally and found extensive rat damage to the barley stored there.

This was one of the possibilities I had anticipated. I jumped to my feet and objected. "Pardon me, Your Grace, but of twelve witnesses receiving the summons eleven didn't appear or send proxies to represent their views. Eight of these might as well be phantoms. The record shows that three others excused from appearing complained of rat damage before being given wine by the interrogating clerics, who were taking their midday meal among the rows. On that day and under the wine's influence all three peasants confessed ruefully to shorting their landowner several measures of grain. Your clerics, using 'confidence of the confessional' as justification, excused them from appearing in court while nonetheless entering their statements as legal depositions. Even assuming such chicanery were condoned by the Church, how can the discrepancies in grain measures be attributed to anything except human thievery? I demand those records be struck, leaving only Madame Cloutier's unreliable testimony, which is neither here nor there. After separating the chaff from the grain it seems your decision is based on the testimony of one witness, nearly blind, who by her own account does not know how to count and can't confirm if the rat tribes inhabiting her fields had gained or lost membership. Under such circumstances a judgment favoring the complainants is hardly justified."

"Maybe you're right, monsieur, but it was you who suggested we interview peasants directly, and I'm not inclined to repeat the exercise or even summon eleven others to replace those eight who ignored the court's order to appear or were questionably excused. We're rapidly approaching peak growing season; this isn't the time to dawdle. Anyway, issuing an edict to the rat hordes won't bring the tribunal to a close. You have ample time to make your arguments."

"Speaking of which, Your Grace, may I present a formal argument against this proceeding?"

"Yes, Monsieur Chassenée, of course," He said, elbow propped on the table, chin resting in his hand. It was clearly a posture indicating ennui.

I turned to face the gallery and the dock, the latter empty except for Monsieur Rat in his cage. He seemed as bored as His Grace. "Your Grace and other members of the court," I said.

At that moment the judicial vicar pounded his gavel. "Court is adjourned until tomorrow."

The tavern was just filling up when Révigny and I arrived and took our customary seats. Two goats had wandered through the open door, and one was nibbling at the rags of the crippled beggar sitting on the floor in his accustomed corner and who seemed to be a regular inhabitant. The goat was becoming aggressive, and the beggar was trying to push it away. The innkeeper's wife emerged suddenly from the scullery and drove all three from the premises by beating them mercilessly with her heavy wooden spoon.

Révigny turned from the mayhem toward me and said, "Maybe we should kill these goats, subject their entrails to extispicy, and learn in advance how our tribunal turns out. The problem, of course, is finding someone to interpret the patterns of innards displayed randomly on a pagan altar. Good divination skills are so rare in these modern times, and praying for wisdom never yields the expected result."

Révigny shook his head in faux sadness. Then he turned and raised an arm. "Innkeeper! The wine!" Again facing me, he said, "Our learned ecclesiastics try to convince us that the sum of mankind's sins flows directly from a single headwater, namely the Fall from Grace of Adam and Eve. God's punishment was brutal and swift, and ever since that moment men have labored in the fields with calloused hands and bent backs, and women have suffered the pangs of childbirth, all because a serpent tempted Eve in the Garden of Eden. An interesting event. Let's reprise it.

"Two things puzzle me about the many illustrations depicting the serpent tempting Eve, the first being that the serpent has no legs in any of them. It's depicted as an ordinary snake. Why should that be strange, you ask? Snakes don't have legs. Right, but consider that God didn't condemn the serpent to forever crawl on its belly and eat dust *until* He learned of the tempting of Eve and her response; in other words, until *after* Adam and Eve were tempted and bit into the fruit of the forbidden Tree of Knowledge. So, I ask again, where are the snake's legs in all the illustrations we've ever been shown, some even with the serpent's head resting placidly on Eve's lap? It surely had legs while sweet-talking her. Strange, don't you agree? I conclude that the original 'serpent' resembled a skinny lizard that ran—or maybe waddled—on four appendages.

"Second, Adam and Eve were punished for eating fruit from the Tree of Knowledge, not for having sex, which is puzzling considering that God had already given all knowledge to Adam. Then he and Eve ate the forbidden fruit and suddenly were conscious. They alone became *aware* to the extent of being *self-aware*, making them unique among Earth's inhabitants. Sex had nothing to do with anything, at least explicitly. Adam and Eve sinned the instant they acquired knowledge, the accumulation of which requires consciousness. However, sex is far easier for the clergy to regulate than consciousness, eh? So, God's representatives on Earth simply deemed sex in its protean manifestations as evil *de facto*. Blaming sex as the reason for the Fall has been a cover-up all along."

Révigny then gave me a sly look. "You realize that in these modern times mankind is ultimately punished for his ignorance. In *Genesis*, chapter two verses nineteen and twenty, God placed all living and nonliving things before Adam, who named them. But what the Bible omits is that Adam did even more than this: *he told them what they were and delineated their places in the world.* Having completed his task Adam possessed all knowledge, the only other all-encompassing source being God Himself.

"Then Adam and Eve sinned and were no longer perfect. Adam's knowledge attenuated slowly over time as it passed through his descendants, then through theirs, and no one ever again could garner all knowledge and hold it in one hand. With each generation mankind lost a little more. So here we are!" Révigny leaned back suddenly in mock surprise and widened his eyes to the size of saucers.

"Just a few centuries ago scholars concluded that since the Creation we humans had misplaced our last flicker of enlightenment and become hopelessly stupid. What was left except turning to history for solace and attempting to unearth those few remaining crumbs of wisdom? In the 12th century of our Lord Europe experienced a mini-renaissance when writings of the ancient Greeks and Romans were once again 'discovered.' Plato, Socrates, Aristotle, Galen, Lucretius, Cicero—all had lived before Christ, placing them in humanity's lineage nearer Adam than anyone then alive. Logically, their erudition and percipience must be proportionately greater than anyone since, the disparity widening with each generation. At least a little of mankind's original intelligence might be recouped by reading their works."

The wine had arrived, and I was, as usual, much taken with Révigny's stimulating conversation. The fate of the serpent's legs had never occurred to me, nor apparently to anyone else. And in response to his assessment of mankind's collective ignorance, what could I say? I looked across the table. My dinner companion sat relaxed in his chair, eyes pulsing amber, a disconcerting grin pasted where a human mouth should be.

TUESDAY JUNE 27TH—CHASSENÉE ARGUES THAT ANIMALS
CAN'T BE ACCUSED AND PROSECUTED EITHER IN ECCLESIASTICAL
OR CIVIL COURTS; HE EMPHASIZES THEIR DIVINE RIGHT TO EAT
ANY HERB THEY CHOOSE; RÉVIGNY REBUTS BOTH ARGUMENTS;
CHASSENÉE HAS AN EROTIC DREAM AND FAINTS

COURT RECONVENED AT TERCE, AND WHEN the bells stopped
ringing I turned to my right, faced the judicial vicar, and said, "May
I proceed with my argument, Your Grace?"

"You may," he said, seeming more alert and energetic this
morning than the previous afternoon.

I stood and began speaking to the court, turning occasionally
toward the spectators, some of them actually listening. "As lawyer
for the defense I demand immediate exoneration of my clients and
the release of Monsieur Rat, their representamen, freeing him to
enjoy the rest of his life in the company of friends and family.

"I have two undeniable and irrefutable statements to make. First,
no court, ecclesiastical or secular, can claim jurisdiction over animals. No court, in other words, can legally accuse, prosecute, judge,
or sentence an animal, regardless of its level in the earthly hierarchy. The need to abnegate and abjure such pursuits, being
inventions of mankind, is undeniable. The places and rights of animals in the world have been secured by Divine intent. Earthly laws,
in contrast, represent an artificial system created by mankind that
reflects all his failings and frailties.

"I agree with Saint Thomas Aquinas, who writes of the futility
and doubtful legality of cursing animals, believing that 'brute
beasts' of any sort—including worms, insects, rats, and other lower
forms known commonly as bestioles—are incapable of committing
crimes against mankind because they lack reason." I then took my
chair awaiting Révigny's rebuttal.

Révigny stood, a sheaf of notes in hand, and asked to speak. When granted permission, he said, "Conversely, Aquinas sees value in persecuting rampaging rats and grasshoppers when they initiate famines causing people to die. When facing such threats, *not* to curse the culprits allows the possibility of homicide, a far worse crime.

"And please, let's keep Earth's lower life-forms in proper perspective. They were clearly stowaways aboard the Ark, making their presence illegal. Can you really picture Noah inviting pairs of every kind insect, rodent, serpent, and spider aboard? Some authorities even doubt whether such creatures are animals, suggesting they might be Satan's creations devised for mankind's discomfort and sanctioned by God to test us. God Himself worked hard for six days fashioning the world and everything in it. He would hardly expend His own efforts laboriously molding such monstrosities out of clay. These tasks take time. Consider just the millions of tiny legs, for example, each fashioned carefully to species specifications. Thus, the presence of bestioles we know as lice, bedbugs, and fleas that suck our blood and make us miserable, the rodents and grasshoppers that relentlessly attack our crops.

"As to pronouncing anathemas, numerous examples of humans cursing and intervening against nature can be cited from the Holy Writ and elsewhere. The original incident occurred when God cursed the serpent for tempting Eve in the Garden of Eden, and today the snake crawls on its belly in everlasting shame." Here he paused and looked at me, eyes pulsing an excited orange. "This is described in *Genesis*, chapter three verse fourteen: *Because thou hast done this thou art cursed above all cattle, and above every beast of the field; upon thy belly shalt thou go, and dust shalt thou eat all the days of thy life.* In *Second Samuel*, chapter one verse twenty-one, David cursed the mountain Gilboa and deprived it of moisture, having learned that King Saul and his sons died on its slopes after battling the Philistines. As the Israelites retreated, King Saul, unwilling to be captured by 'the uncircumcised ones', fell on his sword and died.

"Job, in his eponymous book, chapter three verse three, cursed both his conception and the day he was born, saying: *Let the day perish wherein I was born, and the night in which it was said, There is a man child conceived.* In *Mark*, chapter eleven verses twelve to fourteen, Jesus cursed a barren fig tree, not for its lack of fruit but because its abundant leaves gave a false appearance of fecundity. The tree lied, suggesting awareness and the capacity to deceive, thus eliciting Christ's curse and a death sentence. And Saint Bernard de Clairvaux famously cursed the flies disrupting his sermon in the church at Foigny, to which His Grace alluded earlier." Révigny paused to consult his notes. "Yes, His Grace's words were spoken in this court on Monday the 8th of May. If such anathemas can be justified—and Scripture and the solemn words of saints are evidence they happened—then man holds unquestioned dominion over all of nature and may use this authority as he pleases."

Révigny sat, and I stood immediately. "I remind my distinguished adversary that no statement taken verbatim from the Holy Writ may be challenged in any court, ecclesiastical or civil. Any direct rebuttal is precluded."

"So noted, monsieur," the judicial vicar said.

"So noted," Révigny repeated, as tradition requires.

"Can mankind justify punishing God's other creations?" I said. "Wouldn't doing so oppose God? And would not praying be the proper way of dealing with the problem, that and penance, giving alms, and increasing tithes to the Church? Could a bishop in modern France excommunicate the savages who have not yet been taught Christ's teachings? Not likely, and the same holds true for animals. Until animals learn to recognize which words and deeds formalized in Catholic doctrine and therefore in God's eyes constitute sins and afterward confess and offer penance they remain forever beyond the Church's reach. Curse and anathematize them all you want. Even exorcize them. It won't change anything.

"In *Coutumes de Beauvaisis*, French jurist Philippe de Beaumanoir objected to cursing animals based on the legal meaning of 'intent.' Aquinas grounded his own objection in reason. It's Aquinas' view that animals—by definition not human and thus insensate and irrational—exist apart from guilt, which in turn sets them apart from punishment. Curses and anathemas presume agency on the part of the accused; in other words, knowledge of culpability, recognition of why they're being punished, and the capacity to experience remorse and change their ways accordingly. When hurled at animals anathemas fall not on deaf ears, but ears that can't comprehend."

Révigny stood again in rebuttal. "As the judicial vicar explained at the beginning of this tribunal, an ecclesiastical court proceeding is not an actual trial; rather, it involves cursing the accused instead of trying him. It is, therefore, a tribunal. Also, the pronouncing of a curse is done by a cleric, God's representative, and in the name of God." He looked at me. "So, Monsieur Chassenée, His Grace and I aren't here to exterminate or punish these creatures you lament so loyally. Even were the Church to exorcise them they wouldn't die, but rather the demonic tendencies in their nature would be driven out, the result being that pests and humans could exist amicably side by side sharing God's bounty. They would spare the fruits of man's labor and instead eat coarse vegetation and other unwanted greens of the meadows and woods. They might even assist man by 'weeding' his gardens and fields. We expect them to modify their existence to our convenience. After all, they're unquestionably lower than humans in the earthly hierarchy. Is this too unreasonable to ask?"

Implying I didn't know the difference between ecclesiastical and civil proceedings was insulting, but I felt the sting only momentarily. The appropriate response was none. I let the slight lie fallow to wither unnoticed and instead drove directly to the point. "If the Church resorts to exorcism, then yes, it's indeed too much to ask.

What you're requesting of my clients in that case is extinction, not merely to depart the fields and forests but disappear altogether. One documented case of this sort the exorcism included the words *wherever you go, be cursed so that you may decrease from day to day, till nothing is left of you except what is needed for the use of humans. . . .* Do they support God's original instructions at creation to go forth and multiply? No, they say the opposite, and merely because some of His creatures have shown the temerity to inconvenience mankind. I posit that exorcism of my clients would be an act directly counter to the Lord's wishes and intent.

"Certain important philosophical issues are attendant to the exorcism of animals, one being their ontological status as conjurable objects. This places them in the same category as humans, but also plants, demons, items of food, and all else of proven substantive existence. Everything tangible is confined within the same system of forces. Therefore, the ultimate origin of a particular demon must be determined prior to exorcism. This necessitates conjuring the four elements air, water, fire, and earth and asking their cooperation: air and water not to retain the demon, fire (except hellfire) to reject it, and earth to consume and preferably direct it down to Hell. Exorcism is complex, dangerous, and not to be undertaken lightly, and I promise I shall fight until the end to spare my helpless clients its tortures and uncertainty." I sat down and mopped my brow, having just delivered one of my finer rebuttals. However, I wasn't finished.

Almost immediately I stood and reminded the court that at the beginning of my argument I said I had two points to make, the first being that animals are immune from the accusation and prosecution of crimes in both canonical and civil courts. I repeated that my subsequent argument defending this statement had been convincing and irrefutable.

I said, "I shall now present my second argument, that animals have a Divine right to eat any plants they choose. Why? Please follow the logic. Plants and animals existed in the world before mankind, who came late to the scene. No living entity has been created since; everything was already here. Animals were munching the vegetation when Adam, soon followed by Eve, arrived fully formed in the Garden of Eden."

I gazed into the distance, eyes focused above and beyond the spectators as if seeking heavenly guidance. Abruptly, I turned my back to them and again addressed the court. "Their sudden appearance and preordained place at the apex of the earthly hierarchy must have been a terrible shock to any animals happening to glance up from their endless banquet. To say this differently and certainly more simply, animals and the plants on which they dined were here first." Those spectators paying attention responded with a mixed chorus of laughter and boos.

I ignored the interruption and continued. "Consequently, every animal ever molded from clay by the hands of God and placed on Earth—whether creeping, crawling, swimming, flying, or walking—has the right to eat any and every plant it chooses by Divine right. This is indisputable and beyond discussion. I need only refer to *Genesis*, chapter one verse thirty, and I quote: *And to every beast of the earth, and to every fowl of the air, and to everything that creepeth upon the earth, wherein there is life, I have given every green herb for meat: and it was so.* God spoke these very words. What could be clearer? Note that the Scripture says *every green herb for meat.* God didn't specify one kind of plant or another. There wasn't any need because He included them all, every single one. Without exception. Both cultivated and wild. To Him there wasn't a distinction." I spoke these clipped sentences distinctly and slowly, emphasizing each word.

I paused for effect and again turned and looked at the spectators, trying to discern if anything had changed, but the scene was the same. Children still shrieked and chased one another through the stone bleachers. Sheep and goats, unperturbed, grazed and bleated. Picnics proceeded unabated, and the occasional drunk staggered to his feet and vomited or pissed a loud stream. However, here and there I discerned intelligent eyes looking into mine.

I raised my right hand. "If the damage caused by animals becomes excessive, don't blame them, blame yourselves because the reason is transparent as a cloudless day. God has punished you for your sins by weaponizing the animals He placed among us. Let's be specific: the rats have eaten your barley because you are unrepentant sinners, all of you, each and every one." I made eye contact with two individuals in the gallery who seemed calm and relatively sober and pointed a finger at the first, saying, "Do you doubt me?" Then I pointed at the next, "Do you?" I directed the same finger upward, jabbing it at the sky.

"To you doubters, ask yourselves why the bishop ordered prayers and led a procession through the streets of Autun prior to opening this tribunal. Try to remember his sole purpose, which was recruiting God to our side, hoping He might look down benevolently on the predicament of our aggrieved citizens and treat us favorably by making the rats disappear. While you continue sinning and blaspheming, don't try transferring the burden onto the rats; rather, keep it strapped across your own shoulders where it belongs.

"Mankind's memory is short and that of sinners especially so. Who recalls that procession led by the bishop, his intense effort to erase the evil destruction of Satan's minions to our fields and granary? Who recalls the prayer and repentance, the community's first remedial attempt at a solution? A tribunal like this one is the fallback position. The bishop, you will remember, directed all curates in the diocese to order their parishioners, regardless of age, sex, and degree of infirmity to follow them in procession as they bore the standard of the cross and splashed holy water throughout the fields and around their boundaries. The citizens were to chant litanies and exhorted to burn votive candles, to plead with God on their knees in the name of the Virgin and all saints to remove this tribulation and ease their trials. Pray to Jesus Christ our Lord and

Savior and the blessed saints Peter and Paul, they were told, and hope this hairy, whiskery plague departs and never again returns to damage the fruits of our labor, and if it does then pray in addition that it suffers an eternity from Heaven's curse."

With this I sat down feeling the silence descend gently, quietly, covering and muting the crowd like a soft blanket of autumn leaves.

Révigny rose. "My rebuttal to Monsieur Chassenée's argument is so direct and logical it needs no flowery language or falsely pious theatrics to illuminate the truth and in the end enlighten and convince. Man, of course, was created last, as my learned colleague states, but this was neither an accident nor the result of poor planning. God had to be certain everything mankind would ever need to survive and prosper was in place and functioning.

"He no doubt started with just a few animals and plants as a test of nature's balance, then added more of each until declaring the world in equilibrium and filled to capacity with life. Adam and Eve and their descendants were now free to pick from this bounty. And when the lands and seas had been prepared to His liking God placed man at the top of His earthly hierarchy, just below the angels in Heaven, which are just below Him. We know this because the Scriptures describe the process eloquently and in considerable detail.

"All nature has been created for the purpose of mankind's exploitation. Thus, beasts and bestioles that eat his food and cause him to go hungry behave contrary to God's will. Animals are inferior to man and therefore must obey his laws. One animal's relative position in the earthly hierarchy—whether higher or lower than another—doesn't matter because human justice flows evenly through them, top to bottom, from noble stag to lowly weevil.

"In verse twenty-eight of the very first chapter of *Genesis*, God tells Adam and Eve: *Be fruitful, and multiply, and replenish the earth, and subdue it; and have dominion over the fish of the sea, and over the fowl of the air, and over every living thing that moveth upon the earth.* My learned adversary states correctly that in verse thirty God gave the animals the green herbs and seeds as their meat, but in the verse before, verse twenty-nine, He says to Adam and Eve: *Behold, I have given you every herb bearing seed, which is upon the face of all the earth, and every tree, in which is the fruit of a tree yielding seed; to you it shall be for meat.* Mankind is clearly mentioned before the animals, indicating he stands above them in the hierarchy of life. As such, beasts or bestioles that eat his food and cause him hunger are acting contrary to Divine will, not in keeping with it, as argued by Monsieur Chassenée."

Révigny sat, and my turn came again. I rose from my chair and said, "The contradiction in ecclesiastical courts lies in the belief that man and animal are equal before the law because they bear certain similarities, but animals nonetheless are prosecuted based on their inferiority to man. Subsequent prosecution, judgment, and punishment of bestioles are thus administered in canonical courts by God acting through his human agents in the form of clerics.

"Other contradictions arise when denouncing creatures put on Earth by God without considering them in different contexts. I refer both to the unofficial and often blasphemous curses we hurl at them in the heat of the moment for inconveniencing us versus formal ecclesiastical curses, or anathemas. What might this contradiction be? I offer two possibilities. First, the creatures we curse in either capacity might be acting secretly as God's agents placed purposely in mankind's path to punish us for our sins. In such cases harming or killing them could be interpreted by the Almighty as sacrilege, man's puny attempt to upset the balanced world He has so carefully constructed. Second, occasional animals might be agents of Satan, acting under his evil direction against mankind and attempting to thwart God's wishes. In either instance the creatures to which we refer are mostly bestioles whose actions occur outside the purview of the civil courts and that consequently have no control over their fates. They are natural denizens of forest and field, not pasture, stable, or sty, and the notion of jailing swarms of grasshoppers or packs of rats, as His Grace has already explained, is impractical, assuming we could even coerce them into such confinement. Secular authorities defer to their ecclesiastic brethren to prosecute them metaphorically *in absentia*, as His Grace also explained previously."

The words were now rolling out of my mouth, too quickly to organize the thoughts propelling them. "It's common knowledge that God works in mysterious ways. The honored prosecutor evidently believes that because all animals were created for the use of man we can arbitrarily discard those he finds disgusting, unpleasant, not of use, or in competition with us for Earth's resources. God's intention surely was more complex. He is, after all, omnipotent and able to predict the future. If these creatures weren't in mankind's best interest, if not now at least tomorrow or the day after, He would not have put them here, except perhaps to test us. I therefore petition the court to assess and rule on what God's deeper motives were for placing creeping things among us that eat our crops, bite us and suck our blood, and by their very ugliness make us uneasy."

I felt light-headed. Révigny and His Grace moved in and out of focus. I could feel a vacuous smile similar to Alvin's start to spread across my face accompanied by a heightening sense of excitement: a tingling in the intestines, a tightening of the anal sphincter, sweat starting to glisten on my forehead. I sometimes experienced these and other odd sensations at the onset of an exceptionally vivid daydream ordinarily accompanied by a fierce headache. I then slip into a trance as if my entire being is shifting to a state of semiconsciousness, from which point events move at terrible speed. Helpless, I step inside the whirlwind. It sucks me upward, accelerating to dizzying speed. Just when I'm about to faint I emerge abruptly into stillness. The agonizing, nearly unbearable forces dissipate. Mind and body separate, and I'm suddenly suspended in a vacuum, floating and weightless, mind and senses at a higher elevation than the body just abandoned. I watch it drifting far below, arms and legs spread, eyes open but evidently sightless. It seems small, pitiful, insubstantial.

In this divided state I remain to some extent conscious. I speak sentences that seem memorized, although I've never thought, heard, or read them before. Hearing myself speak them, I'm as startled as any listener. The words reverberate inside my skull as they emerge through my mouth; all else is silence. Outside this invisible capsule nothing moves; there's no sound or light. Any other humans—if there are others—remain for the moment hidden, although I can sense their presence.

I heard myself say, "I've been thinking of returning Monsieur Rat to the granary and releasing him where he was captured so he can tell his friends and relatives about the excellent treatment received while in our company." The words sounded false and hollowed out, trailed by reverberations as if spoken inside a bell or from the depth of a barrel.

"I understand how some are outraged by the gentle care Monsieur Rat has received in captivity, dining on the king's white bread while citizens suffering in the countryside are relegated to eating moldy vegetables and stale barley bread dipped in cold porridge. But being a rat he has little choice except behaving as one. He is gluttonous, promiscuous, and unholy by nature. He lives outside the rules and teachings of both God and man. Imagine a world of plentiful food and rampant sex where life is unrestricted by morality. Picture our captive rodent in Autun's granary, the site of his capture, wallowing on a mattress of barley. Without even looking he can close his paw on a plump grain or turn onto his stomach to plunge his snout into an endless feast.

"Lady rats, as our resident expert will soon explain, come into their time frequently, when they eagerly mate with whichever male is handiest. Ah, to Monsieur Rat the granary is indeed a land of plenty: food for the taking day and night, voluptuous lady rats draped in glossy fur licking his ears with their pink tongues and tickling his belly with their delicate whiskers. They expect nothing but sex in return for such attention. Think of it! No guilt, no expectation of helping rear the young, no backbreaking labor to consume the hours, no frowning deity threatening a fiery afterlife, not even contemptuous in-laws or disrespectful offspring. In fact, does Monsieur Rat even recognize his children? Doubtful, my friends, highly doubtful. Among this throng of eager females clamoring to be his paramours might be his own daughters or granddaughters. Incest isn't frowned on in rat societies. On the other hand, let's not be quick to throw stones and cast aspersions until having assessed the facts. None of us would be here today had Adam and Eve's children not abased themselves in consensual fornication. Yes, *incest*, and we their descendants are still paying for their sins.

"But look at them, these ardent, receptive ladies lining up to receive Monsieur Rat's services. A virtual harem! He pretends indifference and absently masticates another grain. His ladies wait impatiently with itching vulvas while he demurs and teases those closest with feathery touches and soothing rat-talk, rat-poetry. Life is a game, after all, for rats and humans alike. He yawns. 'Soon,' he tells them. 'Soon.'"

A rodent dream-orgy seems about to begin, but I'm distracted by mingled odors of enticing perfume and delectable food. Out of nowhere the banquet appears, as is usual in these dreams, along with the familiar woman whose face I've never seen before. We're in a pasture with cows. She beckons, and I join her. We sit in the grass to eat. There's the usual flagon of wine (an aged red Burgundy this time) and two crystal glasses along with the succulent fruit and freshly baked bread, but the main dish is a standing rib roast directly from the oven, half of it already carved into steaming slices, their rims charred and dusted with spices, the centers seeping blood. Surrounding them on the platter are onions, carrots, and quartered potatoes cooked with the roast and served au jus. For dessert a strawberry sorbet, its source of ice a midsummer miracle.

The woman and I are kissing across the banquet, pausing to suck one another's fingers, lips, tongues. What comes next . . .

"Monsieur Chassenée! Monsieur, are you ill? Can you speak?" It's the bailiff. He's on his knees mopping my forehead with a wet cloth. I hate the end of these dreams, the long swim upward into consciousness, the loss upon surfacing of my handsome face and Grecian stature, my vanishing self-esteem and fading vision of the heroic selfhood. But I most regret losing a unique charisma never experienced in my waking hours that draws women to me like moths to the candle. And in sympathy with those moths who fall tragically to earth with singed wings from the candle's flame, so I plummet from dreamland's firmament to reality's hard and bitter ground.

I struggled to sit up. I'd fallen and landed on my back, the only place I could possibly end up. With a stomach that protrudes like an oversized melon, even were I to fall face down my body would inevitably roll into its present position like an obedient skiff seeking equilibrium. The bailiff helped me to stand. I felt wobbly, slightly nauseous. Everything was fuzzy, as if my eyeballs had been waxed. My head, bereft of any cushioning that hair might have offered, throbbed as if struck with a blunt instrument, evidently a gift of the stand's paving stones. Only the bailiff had spoken; the gallery was quiet as a church.

The judicial vicar cleared his throat. "That was quite the disquisition, monsieur. Yours was a magnificent rebuttal culminating in a dramatic act that the greatest Parisian actors might envy. However, I'm denying your petition that this court assess and then rule on God's motives for devising the forms of life He's placed among us. I would never be so presumptuous as to question His decisions and motives." His Grace's gavel struck the sounding block. "Court is dismissed until tomorrow." I looked at Révigny. He grinned, eyes pulsing red with excitement. Looking into them only made my headache worse.

Wednesday June 28th—Chassenée Continues His Argument that Animals Can't Be Cursed; Révigny Rebuts

꧁꧂

I FELT ALMOST NORMAL BY THE next morning when court reconvened, although a little weak. The dreams always had this aftereffect accompanied by a sense of peace as if the mind had been emptied out and refreshed.

The judicial vicar asked how I was feeling. "Much better, thank you. Your Grace is kind to enquire. If the court pleases I request permission to continue my argument against the anathema of animals."

"You may proceed," His Grace said.

I stood. "How many of my rats have been baptized I couldn't say. Nor can I state the number of Catholics among them, lapsed or faithful. I do know, however, that only a baptized member of the Church can be excommunicated, and if some of my clients fall into this category then by anathematizing them the court would be damning them to everlasting Hell. The very definition of 'excommunication' is *extra quam nulla est salvation*, in the vernacular, 'from which there is no salvation' and can only be enacted against baptized members of the Church. If this is indeed true and Your Grace agrees that it applies to animals as well as humans then the gesture isn't without consequences. The result might set a legal precedent causing inconvenience and confusion within the Church at large, even necessitating a papal bull.

"A curse might raise questions perhaps never asked before. For example, will those rats already Catholics be allowed to remain so following excommunication, the same as humans? And will they consequently be denied all sacraments except the Sacrament of Penance? These are important issues, Your Grace, and their disposition could have far-reaching influence, affecting how the Church conducts its business for centuries to come.

"As the court knows from yesterday's presentation, I claim a fallacy in this practice of curses and anathemas against animals, and certainly any notion of exorcising them. The Spanish theologian Martín de Arles y Androsilla questions whether clerics can properly adjure wolves, snakes, and other creatures considered noxious or enemies of man, concluding in the affirmative and citing a bit of writing by William de Auvergne, which turns out not to exist. He also cites Saint Thomas Aquinas. However, Aquinas actually says the opposite and brings us once again to the matter of exorcism. While admitting that exorcising demons *inside* animals is legitimate, Aquinas says nothing about animals themselves being demonic, a conclusion with which I agree. Demonic animals are entirely fictional entities.

"Nonetheless, our renowned theologian Arles y Androsilla takes the jump directly by unilaterally declaring serpents to be theriomorphic demons. Soon afterward all other animals we fear, loathe, or merely find inconvenient were tossed into this category. In other words, he made exorcism of the animals themselves legal, not just any demons that might inhabit them.

"To Aquinas, cursing God's creatures is blasphemous. Although demons can indeed inhabit animals, in such situations they're the ones who ought to be cursed, not their animal hosts. I therefore anticipate a serious issue with throwing curses and anathemas around haphazardly. They could easily hit and injure an unintended recipient. How do you know, for example, that the rats you curse aren't innocent, their detestable deeds not the work of demons inside them operating their jaws, moving their legs, and activating their squeak boxes? My point is, be careful what you curse. Identify and confirm its origin before taking action.

"My next statement regards a fallacy that seems unnecessary even to mention, but evidently some individuals and entities—the latter including the Church itself—have forgotten that to be excommunicated requires being human. It has no meaning otherwise. Why?

Because animals do not have souls. Therefore, the very notion of their excommunication is ridiculous based on two facts. First, to become a member of the Church requires baptism, for which animals are ineligible, meaning that only Church members can be excommunicated. Entities lacking souls have nothing to salvage after death, making anathema an empty exercise. Second, is there evidence that monitories are actually effective against bestioles, and rats in particular?"

Révigny stood and said, "The erudite musings of my colleague are fascinating, but best left to theologians and other deep thinkers. We lawyers are faced with practical matters, and Monsieur Chassenée has just posed an interesting one. He asks whether cursing bestioles is known to be efficacious, especially against rats. I can answer with certainty that indeed it is." He looked at the paper in his hand. "I shall quote the words of Malleolus, which to those unfamiliar with Latin means 'Little Hammer,' a loving nickname bestowed on one of our greatest inquisitors.

"The great Malleolus reported the following event. Here are his words: *At one time a portion of the French coast was infested by rats. These rodents were assigned to ecclesiastical authority, and a sensational proceeding followed its progress. When pronouncing sentence the bishop in charge of the dispute and his accompanying clergy went to the summit of a promontory where they waved crosses and enjoined the rats to go away. The rats ran from all sides and swimming bravely crossed the stretch of sea separating the coast from a small deserted island, where they remained confined.* Isn't this conclusive proof that deploying anathema against rats can be effective? It has quelled my own doubts, slight though they were, as it should everyone's. We sense in this report God's ineffable touch." Révigny sighed and looked heavenward, letting the gesture elide dramatically into reverie. He shook his head, audaciously pretending to break the spell before continuing.

"Another example involving bestioles occurred in the year of grace 890 when Pope Stephen drove away a plague of grasshoppers by sprinkling the fields with holy water. There are many reports of similar instances for those having the conscience and diligence to seek them.

"The law naturally relies on precedent to reinforce its validity, although precedent need not be grounded in tangible evidence. Miracles and legends also suffice. To bolster my case for the effectiveness of anathemas I remind the court how the bishop of Lausanne rid Lac Léman of eels, which had become so numerous as to interfere with bathing and boating. Earlier, he had cleansed the lake of lampreys that were preying on the large fishes, in particular the salmonids, a favored type eaten on fast-days.

"And, I argue, think of the cost savings to the Church and community. Nothing was required except an ecclesiastical curse, and poof! The problem disappeared. Another exemplum was the case of Egbert, Archbishop de Trier, who cursed the swallows that disturbed his homilies by shitting on his head while he stood before the alter, warning that henceforth any of them entering the sanctuary of the church faced instantaneous death. Although I could cite more, these exempla are sufficient proof to make all doubters tremble."

"Nonetheless," I said, rising again from my chair, "I urge caution when casting anathemas, and I shall give you an example of why. 'Benefit of Clergy' is a law in modern France allowing Church officials to escape prosecution under secular rules. Obvious advantages have been built into the system for those who qualify, particularly when it comes to the sodomy of choirboys and acolytes. In laymen's language a man of the cloth may be tried only by his peers; that is, other clergymen. And this holds for all crimes, whether mild or despicable. Consequently, who could say with certainty that the symbolic defendant on full view in the dock before us—Monsieur Rat, no less—isn't a member of the clergy disguised as a rodent? The burden falls on the prosecution to prove otherwise before guilt beyond credible doubt can be effected."

I faced the gallery and said, "So far, Monsieur Révigny has avoided this major impediment in his weak prosecution of my clients, but you, the common people, know better. Take a close look at Monsieur Rat. Don't be fooled by his beady eyes and twitching whiskers. Educated clerics tell you that animals on trial are irrational and insensate, but are you convinced, you who lived on the land and survive on what it allots? The creatures competing with you daily are hostile, clever adversaries, often able to exert supernatural powers. Think hard, Monsieur Révigny: if you occupied the judicial vicar's office and wore his robe, would you risk casting a curse down on the head of a possible bishop dressed in a rat's clothing? Except for the shoes, of course."

The judicial vicar was quick to admonish me. "Monsieur Chassenée, I have given you ample leeway in defending your clients, but this is stepping over the line and very close to heresy. Watch yourself."

"Yes, Your Grace, but I haven't demeaned the Heavenly Father merely by bringing up a legal item of pertinence to the case before us. In doing so I mentioned only the clergy, who last I looked are human, not especially heavenly. If you like, I can prove my point by citing a specific case of fraud perpetrated by field mice disguised as heretical priests."

The judicial vicar scowled and waggled a finger at me. "Another such comment, monsieur, and I shall charge you with contempt of my court!"

I bowed. "Yes, Your Grace. I beg the court's apology."

The gallery had immensely enjoyed my soliloquy on the law, the possibility of demonic shape-shifting empowering their peasant superstitions, and the impish exchange with His Grace. Even Révigny's mouth had relaxed into something of a grimace that in certain circumstances might pass as a smile. I felt something rub against my leg and looked down to see a small pig sniffing my boots. I sent it squealing with a kick to the ribs, causing my audience to howl gleefully.

Soon afterward the judicial vicar adjourned the proceeding, announcing we would not convene again until Wednesday the

5th of July. He then asked officers of the court to stay until the bailiff's men had cleared the Théâtre Romain of spectators. When at last we were alone His Grace explained the impending delay.

He would definitely issue an edict ordering rats infesting the granary and fields to depart. My arguments had not swayed him, although he agreed not to mention anathema or the threat of it, at least right away. To give the edict added weight he preferred to issue it via the bishop's imprimatur, but first needed his permission, and the bishop was presently out of town. The earliest they could arrange to meet was Monday the 3rd of July. Meanwhile, he dared not print hundreds of notices beforehand in case the bishop declined his request or approved it with changes. The edict would be issued in either case, whether through his office or the bishop's remained to be determined. When court reconvened on the 5th his clerk would read the edict aloud to all present; immediately thereafter the postings and public readings would commence.

Later at the tavern Révigny was elated, grinning maliciously and ready to crow about something, no doubt at my expense. "Nice try. I mean your failed dilatory tactic of asking His Grace to assess God's decisions and the motives behind them." He looked at the ceiling as if mentally adding numbers. "Such a task would require at least the convening of a Lateran Council, consuming months or even years, time enough to let your rascally, whiskered clients abscond into the fields and woods."

WEDNESDAY JULY 5TH—THE BISHOP ISSUES
AN EDICT ORDERING RAT TRIBES INFESTING THE
MUNICIPAL GRANARY OF AUTUN AND NEARBY FIELDS OF THE
DÉPARTEMENT DE SAÔNE-ET-LOIRE TO DEPART WITHIN SIX DAYS;
COPIES ARE POSTED IN THE FIELDS, INSIDE AND OUTSIDE THE
GRANARY, AND ON CHURCHES AND PUBLIC BUILDINGS

RÉVIGNY HAD BEEN CONSPICUOUSLY QUIET. AT this juncture I
expected a comment from him, at least a mild protest about some
element of my recent ranting. Instead, it was the judicial vicar who
spoke to the court and spectators, and his opening words were
addressed directly at me.

"I choose to ignore your little joust with heresy near day's end
the 27th of June, Monsieur Chassenée, and not issue a sanction,
but only to keep the Lord's business moving forward. I have bowed
in part to your arguments against anathematizing animals and
did not mention the threat of a curse specifically in the edict
about to be read publicly, but I warn you against igniting my anger.
Is that understood?"

"Yes, Your Grace."

"Very well. My investigations reveal that an edict or summons
written clearly in large letters and placed against a rock is adequate
to rid a field or manmade structure of its mice. These vermin, as
everyone knows, are the cousins of rats, making them all relatives
within the composite kingdom of rodents. Consequently, a method
effective at expelling mice ought to suffice against rats. I spoke with
the bishop, and he agrees to use the authority of his office to implement an edict that will end our rat troubles, God willing." He looked
askance at the clerk sitting at his separate table and nodded.
"Monsieur Clerk, please read the edict."

The clerk stood and read. *I, bishop of Autun, conjure the rats reading
this notice, or hearing it read aloud, to do us no harm and to prevent other*

*members of their race from doing so. I give you six days from its posting to
depart your present habitations and never return. If after such time I find
you still here, as God is my witness I shall cut you into seven pieces.*

The bishop had affixed his name and office to the document,
and several dozen copyists were already working diligently making
hundreds of reproductions to be propped against a large rock in
every infested field where a rat could easily see and read it. Other
copies were destined to be posted on public buildings (including
churches), and on all four sides of the municipal granary's walls,
inside and out. In addition, at each of these locations the notice was
to be read aloud at the liturgical hours of prime and vespers. Those
assigned reading duty and found remiss by such deficiencies as tar-
diness, drunkenness, or failure to appear would be subjected to
public flogging followed by three days in the stocks.

I argued that most rats were unlikely to notice or acknowledge a
blanket edict and asked that a copy be addressed and delivered to
my clients individually. I acknowledged their lack of fixed addresses
and apologized for the inconvenience, reminding the court that
notifying the intended recipients of an edict is the court's responsibility, not that of the lawyer for the defense. At this, Révigny barked
out his strange, hollow laugh, which undoubtedly seemed odd just
to me. His Grace said nothing, but dismissed me with a sour look
and an absent wave of his hand. At the least, I persisted, Monsieur
Rat might be released back into the granary where he was captured
in time to relate tales of the gracious hospitality shown him while in
captivity and urge his comrades, along with his wife and extended
family, that if they departed immediately God and the bishop might
extend mercy and not curse them. This sensible recommendation
was met with open derision by the spectators.

So, we waited. When such an edict is effective the community
offers prayers of gratitude. When it isn't the tribunal continues *in
contumaciam*; that is, in contempt of the court's directive.

Thursday July 13th—The Rats Fail to Appear; Chassenée Is Ordered by the Judicial Vicar to Explain

A WEEK PASSED. To NO ONE's surprise not a single rat was observed departing from any of the posted locations. When court reconvened Thursday the 13th of July His Grace insisted I explain and justify the disrespectful, obstinate, and embarrassing behavior of my clients, adding that he now considered them contumacious by not honoring the terms of the edict, contumacy being a legal designation in modern French law. I replied that I could think of several reasons, all justifiable.

"My clients failed to appear simply because attempting to contact them en masse goes against their nature, their way of life granted at the time of Creation by God. Although rats are sociable to a degree, each looks after its own interests and needs. The court might have gained positive results by delivering the edict to every adult rat, assuming that minors (including infants) who have not yet learned to read, and geriatrics whose eyes are clouded by cataracts, would be alerted by their parents or caregivers. Rats, may God forgive them, aren't generally monogamous, and mothers and fathers seldom inhabit a common dwelling." I paused for effect, crossing myself then looking down and shaking my head sadly at such blatant and despicable immorality.

"Think of the public square on market days when crowds gather from all over to buy and sell their wares and produce, some to peddle onions, others to purchase them, but each acting as an independent agent. Rats are no different in this respect. In addition, rats sometimes move from place to place, and many were probably in transit and doubtfully aware of the edict. Finally, even those literate enough to read the notice were likely too nervous to obey. An order handed down by an ecclesiastical court is intimidating even to humans, and no less so to a timorous rat, especially one in its infancy or coming into adolescence. Add to this an inborn fear of departing familiar surroundings for new lands perhaps teeming with predators, cats in particular, which lurk in every village and field. The very mention of cats strikes terror in their hearts." I mentioned that a person fearing for his safety may legally refuse a court order. I reminded everyone that under French law this privilege likewise extends to animals.

"We know," I continued, "that among men, power and wisdom are commonly associated with age. We need only look to the Scriptures and their stories of ancient Hebrew kings and prophets. Moses was old and tired when he led the Israelites to within sight of Canaan. Rat kings—those to whom all lesser rats genuflect and are subservient—are likely infirm with age, maybe crippled or even blind or deaf. They would have difficulty migrating and indeed might still be trying to depart their domiciles, striving with what remains of their failing vigor to obey His Grace's summons."

"What you claim as possible might be true, all or in part," His Grace said. "Conversely, it could be nonsense, dilatory blathering. Either way we labor on God's time, not that of some rats, whether kings or commoners. In fact, the time we spend sitting here isn't even ours because time belongs to God alone. If time is to be wasted it's entirely His choice. My inclination is not to be presumptuous and usurp a decision that's rightfully God's.

"One thing, however, is certain. If defendants involved in either a canonical or civil action ignore an official edict—in other words, are contumacious—they are automatically declared guilty of all charges and lose the case by default." The gavel struck with a resounding whack. "The rats are hereby declared guilty."

MONDAY JULY 17TH—THE OFFICIAL RAT-CATCHER OF AUTUN
EXAMINES MONSIEUR RAT DISPLAYED IN A CAGE IN THE DOCK;
CHASSENÉE BUILDS HIS CASE FOR THE LIMITATIONS AND FRAILTY
OF RATS; RÉVIGNY INTERROGATES THE RAT-CATCHER ABOUT
RAT REPRODUCTIVE RATES AND EMPHASIZES THE
URGENCY OF EVICTING THE RATS FROM THE GRANARY

⟨✦⟩

THE FIRST EDICT HAD BEEN ONLY the opening act of our little theater production. A second would surely follow, and a third was permitted under ecclesiastical and secular laws. I needed to move quickly and gain the upper hand.

We had not been in session since Thursday the 13th of July. Court had been canceled the day after because our presiding judicial bishop had another engagement. Then the weekend came. We finally reconvened. The clerk had barely declared court officially in session when I asked and was granted permission to speak.

"Members of the court, I introduce to you Monsieur Marcel Caron and call him to the witness chair. Despite his surname he isn't a cartwright, but the official rat-catcher of Autun. Monsieur Caron has made the study of rats his life's mission. No one within the entire département de Saône-et-Loire can match his knowledge of their wily machinations." Caron emerged from the lower gallery bleachers and took the witness chair inside the dock. After he was seated I said, "Monsieur, I ask you to examine the caged rat displayed in the dock since the beginning of this tribunal and describe to us what you see."

"I see a rat, monsieur." The gallery erupted in laughter, as did His Grace and Révigny. Only the clerk of the court failed to acknowledge the humor.

After the disturbance died down, I pressed on. "But what sort of rat? A sickly rat or a healthy one, and in either case explain to us how you, an expert on all manner and kinds of rats, can tell the difference."

"Certainly, monsieur." He got up from the chair and began at once to examine the rat closely. The rat approached that side of its cage and appeared unafraid, maybe even a little friendly and curious. For a moment the two were nose to nose, almost on familiar terms, a pair of beady black eyes staring into two large brown ones, man and bestiole trying to traverse the impossible chasm. Caron walked slowly around the cage, still watching its inmate intently. The rat turned too, tracking his movement. After several minutes Caron returned to the chair while the rat seemed to lose interest and shifted its gaze elsewhere.

"Well?"

"This rat is of the male sex," he said. "He's in superior condition. I would estimate his age at three or four years, quite old for a rat, especially a city rat forced to subsist on garbage in the streets, offal from the abattoirs, animal and human excrement, and tannery waste. Unless, of course, its home has been the granary. This rat is probably not just a father or grandfather many times, but also a great-grandfather and even a great-great-grandfather. Rats are prolific, as you know, monsieur."

"What else can you tell us?"

"His physical condition is superb, as I said. He's so fat I can barely see his feet, and his coat is thick and glossy. He's had an easy life so far."

Révigny rose to his feet. "An easy life, monsieur? He's led a life enjoyed only by the nobility, first eating barley in fields laboriously tilled, planted, and tended by these poor plaintiffs, many presently observing the proceeding from the gallery, and later wallowing in the municipal granary where he was captured while gorging on the bounty of their labor. For many weeks he's loafed in that cage and dined on the king's bread made of fine wheaten flour, not the coarse barley substitute relegated to my poor clients and at which Monsieur Rat would doubtlessly turn up his hairy nez. To anyone, rat or human, white bread constitutes a royal feast. Indeed, life has been easy for Monsieur Rat, but my duty as prosecutor requires me to transform it into one of misery at the earliest opportunity."

At these words the gallery shouted its derision. Among the many angry voices, three stood out. One yelled, "The rat eats the king's bread while we get cold porridge!" Another shouted, "Kill the cursed rat and be done with it!" And the third said, "Shut up, grande gueule!" Loudmouth, indeed! Révigny whirled away from the spectators, his robe billowing and his own distinctly green nez in the air as someone who has just suffered a penetrating insult from a gathering of equals and not the frustrated outbursts of stinking, illiterate peasants. He glared back at his detractors, then at me, eyes flashing red in anger, and sat down. I looked at the judicial vicar, who seemed oblivious to the ruckus and was focused instead on an interrogatory on the table before him. These documents are useful tools containing leading questions crafted to channel a suspect's responses toward a judge's biases. How it might be useful in an ecclesiastical proceeding involving some rats I could only wonder. Maybe His Grace was bored and studying in advance of an upcoming tribunal more important than this one.

The earlier slight seemingly forgotten, Révigny left his chair and approached the dock. "Monsieur Caron," he said in a kindly, condescending voice, "I beg your patience. What I'm about to ask you as the court's authority on all matters of rathood is a bit indelicate and likely even embarrassing to the more refined of our spectators. I shall therefore come directly to the point. It deals with, that is, with rat love-making." The gallery screamed its delight. Révigny, without taking his eyes from Caron, raised a hand for silence. "Tell us, monsieur, what you know."

"Yes, monsieur. I shall relate to you some facts about reproduction within the secretive rat kingdom, speaking of such matters as politely and discretely as possible."

"Thank you, monsieur. You are surely a gentleman."

Caron nodded at the compliment, either ignoring or not perceiving its sarcasm, and cleared his throat. "I shall start with the position. Put simply, despite being rodents, rats do it doggy-style." Again, the spectators responded with hoots and laughter.

Révigny took a step back feigning shock, looking first at the spectators and then at us. He shook his head and repeated Caron's words, "Faire l'amour en levrette."

Caron waited for the uproar to subside, then continued. "Rats become capable of producing offspring at about three months of age. If able to avoid the heavy boot of mankind, the sharp claws of cats and owls, and the piercing teeth of foxes and stoats, a rat lives perhaps two or three years, turning senile toward the end. Females suckle their young in the manner of horses, cows, dogs, and even humans. Their blood is therefore warm, unlike the chilly blood of frogs and serpents.

"A mother rat nurses her young for only several days before weaning them. She has from seven to fourteen pups in a litter and can produce seven to fifteen litters in a year, coming into her time within twelve hours of giving birth and then mating with any and all adult males available. Suffice to say, rats are very promiscuous. I mention this solely for factual reasons; any moral ramifications I leave to the ecclesiastics as being outside my expertise. It isn't my place to judge rat customs. I remain neutral and open-minded, as does any naturalist seeking only truth."

"Very commendable, monsieur," said Révigny, his eyes brightening from pale amber to intense, pulsating yellow.

"Thank you, Monsieur Révigny. But to continue. Assuming none of the pups is killed or dies of disease or other causes, a mother rat raises hundreds of young in a year. However, if we also consider the reproduction of her offspring, which are maturing, mating, and giving birth to pups of their own while she herself continues to remain sexually active, we're talking about thousands of rats being born in one year, starting with a single pair. The more food available the better will be their condition and the more rapidly they multiply. The population then expands to the maximum limit of its resources, which inside a granary is boundless."

Révigny leaned an elbow on the table holding the cage. He gazed down at Monsieur Rat a moment, then turned and looked at the court benevolently. "Exactly my point, monsieur! Leaving the rats for even a few minutes to carry on their unholy fornication, gestation, and parturition is too long. In no time we would be knee-deep in them."

"That's correct, monsieur, and your colleague Monsieur Chassenée would surely drown. The depth of rats across the landscape of France would extend well above his head." The crowd loved it.

Révigny paused for the din to subside before looking directly at the judicial vicar. "There isn't time to lose! The rats must be expelled with all possible speed, deploying every resource the court can muster. The complainants and I demand it!" At this the gallery cheered with throaty gusto. Révigny spun to face it, robe swirling after him. Like a conquering Caesar he raised both arms and nodded his head up and down, urging on the motley throng, momentarily a hero to these fickle, feckless peasants who had come only to be entertained.

After Révigny finished bowing to the spectators and once again had taken his chair the judicial vicar looked at me. "I see you fidgeting, monsieur, as if you have an important statement to make, perhaps in rebuttal to Monsieur Révigny's? If so, please speak it."

"Thank you, Your Grace, but my point is more aptly directed to you." I didn't mention that my feet had gone numb from sitting and dangling my legs over the edge of the chair. I was fidgeting because of the need to stand, and now given the chance was afraid of toppling over.

"You may speak."

"Again, I thank His Grace. I presume His Grace will soon issue a second edict and it will be the same one as before. Is this correct?"

"Not exactly, monsieur. You are correct that another edict will be issued, but wrong about its content. The wording of the new version has been changed because the court will now order the rats to vacate their present habitations and move to a piece of land recently acquired by the diocese. They will again have six days to migrate."

This was not entirely unexpected. The ploy isn't uncommon in ecclesiastical tribunals during prosecution of vermin. Nonetheless, I feigned surprise and confusion, angling for another delay. "Your Grace, where is this parcel of land set aside for my clients? I had no knowledge of it until now. I reserve the right to evaluate its suitability as a future rat habitation. For all my clients and I know the place is desolate, bereft of food, water, hiding places, and other life-sustaining resources, and maybe infested with cats, foxes, stoats, and other mortal enemies of the rodent tribes."

Révigny stood to nullify my protest. "Your Grace, I see no reason for Monsieur Chassenée's complaint. After all, who is better qualified to assess the needs of unthinking animals than the clergy, God's representatives here on Earth? I add that some learned scholars consider all vermin—insects and rodents alike—not to be animals at all but stowaways aboard the Ark, uninvited by Noah. This makes them irrelevant and unnecessary life-forms of Satanic creation. As I mentioned previously, you think that God, who labored tirelessly for six days would have wasted his energy molding such monstrous nuisances from clay? Any creation takes time."

"Only God can create new forms of life," I said. "This is well established and not debatable. And since when are vermin not animals? Every solid object is either animal, vegetable, or mineral. What else could rodents and insects be except part of the animal class? Do vegetables and rocks swim, run, creep, wriggle, or fly on wings? Hardly! And with no disrespect to the court, Your Grace, I disagree with Monsieur Révigny about the actual matter before us. Clearly, animals themselves are the best experts in matters of their own needs. Despite being dumb and insensate, God has endowed them with the will and means to survive and propagate in a competitive world. Who evaluated this newly acquired land, and what criteria were used to declare it suitable?"

The judicial vicar said, "Another cleric and myself inspected it, along with the landowner. Following some negotiation this pious man donated the parcel to the diocese in exchange for an indulgence. He is now guaranteed a shorter stay in Purgatory after his death."

I asked if the land was presently in cultivation.

"No," said the judicial vicar. "Not to my knowledge."

"And why is that? Could the reason be that its surface is bleak, barren, and inhospitable to vegetable life?"

Révigny interjected and said, "Monsieur, these are rats we're discussing, not connoisseurs. Rats, as everyone knows, dine happily on the foulest garbage, ingesting items that would make a starving man vomit. I see no reason to question the suitability of land selected by so renowned a presence as His Grace."

The judicial vicar nodded his appreciation at Révigny, obviously pleased by the compliment, then turned toward me. "What do you propose, monsieur?"

"I ask the court to postpone issuing its edict, allowing the defense time to evaluate the land for its suitability as a rat habitation. In addition, I request that Autun's official rat-catcher, Monsieur Marcel Caron, be appointed to the defense as advocate along with Monsieur Rat as official representative of his tribe. It will be our joint task to make the assessment and recommendation I shall subsequently read before the court and then submit as a document for the record."

"I have no objection, in principle," Révigny said. "However, not being lawyers Messieurs Caron and Rat are not qualified under French law to be advocates."

"Then designate them consulting experts for the defense without legal standing," I said. "Surely, they qualify in this regard. Monsieur Caron has studied rats most of his life and knows their needs and inclinations intimately. As to Monsieur Rat, who can possibly know more about what it's like being a rat than an actual rat?"

The judicial vicar said, "How long a delay are you requesting, Monsieur Chassenée?"

"How far is this land from Autun, Your Grace?"

"I estimate three leagues, more or less."

I did a rapid conversion in my head. "That is approximately seventeen kilometers, do you agree?"

"I suppose so," said the judicial vicar.

"And you, Monsieur Révigny?"

"That sounds right."

"Then I shall need three weeks," I said. I spoke the words with conviction, hoping to avoid a compromise.

"So it is," the judicial vicar said. "Three weeks from today the court will reconvene to hear your report. Meanwhile, you may add Monsieur Caron's expenses to your roster of fees. Monsieur Rat, currently incarcerated, will have his expenses extended for the duration of the tribunal." He looked at the clerk of the court just then examining his calendar. "Monsieur?"

"I shall also need the services of a recording clerk, Your Grace," I said.

"So granted." He was still looking at the clerk of the court. "Monsieur Clerk?"

"Three weeks from today is Monday the 7th of August," the clerk said.

"So be it," said His Grace, dropping the gavel. "Court is adjourned until then."

Monday August 7th—Chassenée Reads a Synopsis of His Report to the Court, Deeming the Land Selected Unsuitable

I STOOD, PAGES IN HAND, AND addressed the court. "Your Grace and other members of the tribunal, hear the words of this report. Three weeks preceding today, Monday the 17th of July, I requested and was granted permission to inspect the land selected by His Grace and a colleague for purposes of assessing its suitability as a permanent home for the département's rat tribes. For assistance in this task I engaged Monsieur Marcel Caron, official rat-catcher of Autun, and Monsieur Rat, both having maintained a permanent presence at court through the proceeding to date. I also attended the inspection personally with my two footmen. In addition, I retained with permission of the court the services of a clerk certified by the office of the bishop to officially record our observations as we made them. Expenses for this excursion are itemized in the appendix.

"We departed east from Autun through the gate of Saint-André on horses and mules a little before the liturgical hour of terce on Wednesday the 19th of July, eventually finding inferior lodging and sustenance for the night at an inn within a kilometer of the property's western boundary.

"Inspection took place the following day, Thursday the 20th of July, when we examined the parcel thoroughly on foot and from the backs of animals, starting at prime and continuing until just past vespers. We paused at sext in the paltry shade of a spindly tree and took an inferior meal of stale barley bread and moldy cheese packed by the filthy hands of the innkeeper's wife. This impoverished fare, I regret to say, was partaken with a green Spanish wine of the lowliest vintage rendered nearly undrinkable by the sun's heat. The day was still and hot as only the fields of Saône-et-Loire can be during midsummer. My party and I suffered greatly, and even Monsieur

Rat panted and came close to death from heatstroke. I still feel the effects of sunburn, as you can see from my peeling scalp, despite having worn a broad-brimmed hat. We again spent the night at the same inn, departing near terce the following morning, Friday the 21st of July, arriving back at Autun near the liturgical hour of nones.

"To reinforce the record the court has designated Messiers Caron and Rat its experts on rodents including their diets, fears, and habits. Monsieur Caron's comments and my own were recorded *in situ*, meaning in place, that day by the clerk who accompanied us; Monsieur Rat kept his own counsel while making his opinions known through actions. The clerk's notes, combined with some of my own observations remembered later, became the basis of this report, a summary of which reads as follows.

> The rats of Autun and surrounding countryside and villages have become habituated to a diet of grain, but no grain of any kind exists at the said parcel recently acquired by the diocese of Autun. The vegetation there consists of sparse weeds and shrubs and a few stunted trees but no grassy tassels nor anything resembling grain, wild or cultivated, that a rat might find nourishing. In Monsieur Caron's expert opinion a sudden shift in diet from nutritious grains to less agreeable weeds and fibrous forbs would surely cause the rats to suffer extended bouts of diarrhea, and those with weak stomachs could become permanently infirm and even die. Without an abundance of starchy foods, most of the new arrivals will eventually succumb to malnutrition. The tragedy will be magnified when hundreds of orphaned rats are left to fend for themselves. Who will teach them the necessary skills required to forage properly, avoid predation, and eventually rear their own young based on millenniums of rat traditions and lessons on rat morality passed down from loving, attentive parents and grandparents? Rats do not possess a written language, each generation depending on the oral instructions and guidance of its elders.

The site itself consists entirely of open ground, mainly clay that in hot, dry weather becomes hard as stone and after extended rain is transformed into a quagmire. When in the latter condition an ox would have trouble slogging across it, much less a rat with short, stubby legs and weak muscles. Rats are notably cryptic in their habits, needing places in which to sequester when predators are about, to shelter from heat and cold, to store food, and to rear their young. This place is unsuitable for any burrowing creature. Locating a reliable source of water will be problematic. The available supplies we found are limited to a few vernal puddles that will undoubtedly vanish during dry spells. Of permanent streams or ponds we found none. Rats can survive on polluted water, but all creatures die in the complete absence of water. French rats differ from their cousins inhabiting the deserts of Babylon, which have adapted over thousands of years to desiccated landscapes.

At six locations we released Monsieur Rat from his cage to ascertain his opinion. All rats value freedom. They want only to be rats: to live, love, and die as rats at the bosoms of their families, perhaps with an attending rat-priest summoned to pronounce last rites. A caged rat presumably hates mandatory confinement as much as an incarcerated man. However, in every instance Monsieur Rat, after a moment of sniffing about in his new surroundings, returned voluntarily to the cage, clear indication that this parcel is no rat paradise.

"With these words I submit this summary along with my entire report to the clerk of the court for inclusion in his record of the tribunal. Thank you."

Révigny stood. "May I question Monsieur Chassenée, Your Grace?" On receiving the nod Révigny said, "Monsieur, you say this land offers no suitable food for rats, is this correct?"

"Yes," I said.

"And when Monsieur Rat was released to inspect the property at six different locations and voluntarily returned to his cage this behavior indicated to you a negative opinion of what he had smelled, heard, and seen. However, was an incentive provided for him?"

"I don't understand your question, monsieur."

"Was there not a scrap of white bread made of fine wheaten flour waiting in his cage?"

"I suppose there was," I said.

"Aha! So Monsieur Rat was offered a reward for returning to his confinement instead of running away, and for this reason we see him still before us in the dock. Of course, that might not be Monsieur Rat at all. Perhaps he indeed escaped and now thrives in that so-called desert. Or he might lie buried beneath its inhospitable soil in an unmarked grave, his soul—if he has one—hovering nearby awaiting the clarion trumpeters to announce a new dawn of Rodent Judgment Day. To most of us one rat resembles another. I call Monsieur Caron to the witness chair."

When Caron was seated and reminded he was still under oath, Révigny said, "Monsieur Caron, is this caged rat the original one or another?"

"It's the same one, monsieur."

"Do you swear to it?"

"Certainly."

Révigny turned his back on Caron and faced the court. Suddenly, he whirled around, pointed his finger at Caron, and shouted, "*And did you offer the king's bread to this rat as an inducement to return to its cage while you were inspecting the parcel of land we are now discussing?*"

The viciousness by which he uttered this statement startled everyone to silence. From the corner of my eye I saw His Grace sit upright, as if in assurance he was paying attention. Caron squirmed in his chair and wiped his forehead with the back of his hand. "I did, but he would have returned anyway. Rats know when there's no food around."

"So you say, monsieur," said Révigny in a quiet, calm voice, "although at the least you don't deny he was bribed."

"If you call it that, monsieur."

"I do," Révigny said caustically. "And I want it so entered into the record of this proceeding." Révigny then finished his interrogation with a haughty, "You are dismissed, monsieur."

The judicial vicar announced he would read my report in its entirety and render his decision of whether to accept or reject its conclusions. If the latter he would issue the second edict as originally intended. Court was dismissed just before sext and scheduled to reconvene in two days, Wednesday the 9th of August.

We had just sat down at our table in the tavern and signaled the innkeeper to bring a flagon of His Grace's excellent white Burgundy. Révigny's eyes started flashing bright yellow in apparent anticipation. "Is this who you really are?" I said.

Révigny glanced up at the innkeeper as he set down the flagon and cups and watched his hands as he poured. Then he looked at me. "This is how you perceive me. Perception and reality aren't necessarily the same. For example, are you as you now appear, or are you actually an Olympian god who plays your role in that theater of dreams? Is one real and the other a facsimile? If so, which is which? Or is neither the 'real' you?"

Révigny no sooner finished his question than he became subsumed in a violent coughing fit. "God-*damn* this brimstone! Can't a demon get a breath of fresh air?"

"What happens when I'm not around?" I said. "The rest of the world doesn't see what I see."

"Good point," he said between hacks. "I fake it, basically. You see me as things really are; they see me as they expect me to be. A vast difference, wouldn't you agree? Incidentally, you've expressed curiosity about what you call my 'cocoon,' an appropriately descriptive term. It's my own invention, and I'm rather proud of it. I was trying to come up with a way of keeping a thick fog of brimstone smoke around myself and remembered a childhood event. I was in a stable when a lamb was born and reprised the sight of it squirming inside the birth sac, finally breaking through and taking a first gulp of air. What a marvelous device! It was an opaque purplish-blue, and all I could detect was the movement inside. I couldn't see into it, and obviously the lamb couldn't see out. That wouldn't do in my situation, so I simply made mine transparent. True, there's some leakage of smoke over time, but when the supply becomes too depleted I merely zip down to Hell and replenish it."

"Why the brimstone smoke at all?" I said. "Why not just rush around green and naked like a normal demon, so to speak?"

"Because I require a constant cloud of burning sulfur to inhale. I confess I've become addicted to the stuff, like some citizens of Cathay can't live without their opium pipes. Even Satan is addicted. I've tried quitting, but the withdrawal is excruciating. Anyway, once I get back to Hell there isn't any choice but to start breathing it again. Burning brimstone dominates the atmosphere. This cocoon lets me travel anywhere on Earth and carry along a personal supply. Back in Hell I shed it like a greatcoat and don't wear it again until the next trip up here.

"You can identify newcomers to Hell by their endless hacking until they get used to the fumes. For example, if there's a plague or a major war in progress topside and new immigrants are flooding through the gate by the thousands the coughing can actually drown out the screams of souls already in residence. Not to be outdone the demons then get pissed and ramp up the flames and various tortures until the shrieks attain maximum pitch. Raises hell with your concentration."

Another fit of coughing convulsed his thin frame. I rolled a sheet of paper into a narrow tube, poked it through the faux amniotic sac enveloping him, and shoved the end between his teeth. He flinched and looked startled, but quickly caught on, sucking on it and inhaling deep breaths of what to me was the foul, moldering air of the tavern but to him must have seemed like pristine vapor rising from a snow-covered meadow.

"God, that's wonderful, Barthélemy. How can I ever repay you?"

"By losing the case," I said, only half sarcastically.

He spit out the end of the tube and waved a limp hand in dismissal. The hole I'd punched in his protective sac annealed instantly without a scar. He said, "You disappoint me, Barthélemy. As you know very well nobody wins or loses one of these farces. The outcome, if not officially preordained, might as well be. A human on trial will likely be convicted in an ecclesiastical setting, except in cases involving compurgation when the odds are reversed and the accused usually goes free. Otherwise, the condemned is nearly always sentenced to die. Ecclesiastics, remember, are forbidden to deal with blood, and after conviction the matter is turned over to a civil judge who handles the sentencing and gruesome details of execution. Then Satan and I 'win' and you and the defendant 'lose.' If he's acquitted and you and your client 'win,' what's the difference when the ultimate outcome is still inevitable?

"In Hell we take the long view. The poor bastard you save survives another year or maybe a few years, not even the blink of an eye when measured against eternity. Sure, innocent people can be accused of crimes they didn't commit, but such situations are rare. The fact that someone is on trial is a good bet he's guilty or stupid. Either way, after all the shouting is done Satan hangs another soul from his belt. If an animal is on trial and sentenced to burn, who cares? So what if a pig ends its life as smoked ham or charcoal?" He grinned greenly, and the red glow of his eyes grew brighter. "Incidentally, mentioning that tale of the orphaned puppies was a nice touch, although it obviously didn't touch His Grace's heart. I presume you were talking about Jean Racine's play *Les Plaideurs* in which he parodied animal trials. That's the one in which a dog is tried for stealing a chicken and sentenced to the gallows. The defense attorney appeals for clemency, arguing that the dog will leave behind a litter of orphaned puppies. He brings the litter to court. The judge, himself a father, collapses in tears and pardons the dog."

I remembered saying something about it during my recent dream, but didn't recall any details. "That's the play," I said. "It was staged a few years back in Paris, and His Grace probably never heard of it. As you say, he seemed unmoved. At least to the best of my recollection."

Révigny, now bored with this subject, moved along to another topic. "The good angels report to God, the evil ones to Satan, himself once a grosse affaire in Heaven's angelic hierarchy. His name then was Lucifer. Mankind walks the narrow line between their kingdoms. God and Satan each grab an arm and leg of every newborn, one on either side, and tug endlessly throughout his life trying to pull him into one camp or the other, competing to capture his soul for eternity. Scarcely a wonder that living humans stray intermittently back and forth across that line, yanked alternately between the forces of good and evil. As Newton's third law will someday state, 'For every action there is an equal and opposite reaction.'"

"Excuse me," I said, "but who is this Newton?"

"Never mind, a little musing just slipping out. I sometimes have difficulty remembering the future and worry about encroaching senility. Please ignore it. If I may continue, the Church's function is to surround each member securely inside a circle of enlightenment, protecting its flock starting with its own magic ritual of baptism and continuing through our lives with strategic applications of holy water, prayers, conjurations, and application of astrology in its war against Satan's malevolent and powerful sorcery. The Church's job is made particularly strenuous by Satan's singular advantage of mankind being born into sin as a result of the fall of Adam and Eve from grace. Incidentally, I commend you on your vast knowledge of the Holy Writ."

"And I commend you likewise. If you weren't such a sinful demon you might make a decent bishop."

"Please stop with the compliments, Monsieur Chassenée. Satan wouldn't be pleased. Innkeeper! Another flagon!"

Wednesday August 9th—The Judicial Vicar Takes
Chassenée's Report about the Chosen Land's Deficiencies
Under Advisement and Considers It Within the Context
of Révigny's Accusation of Skulduggery by the Defense;
He Announces His Ruling

❧

When court reconvened the judicial vicar, as promised, announced his ruling on whether the land acquired on
behalf of the rats of the département de Saône-et-Loire was a
suitable habitation.

The court was scarcely seated and opened officially by the clerk
when His Grace spoke from his chair. "I've made a decision," he
said. "Having duly considering Monsieur Chassenée's detailed
report dismissing the suitability of the land chosen by me as a rat
habitation, and after factoring in Monsieur Révigny's accusation of
skulduggery by the defense for putatively bribing the rat serving as
expert for the defense, I rule that the land is indeed a suitable habitation, if not for mankind, certainly for rodents. A second edict
ordering them to vacate their current domiciles will be implemented
forthwith." He motioned to the clerk of the court. "Monsieur Clerk,
please read the edict."

The clerk rose, coughed once, and began.

> Hear this and take notice, all present and those not, of this
> edict issued by order of His Holiness the esteemed bishop of
> the diocese of Autun. The defendants, having been accused
> and adequately prosecuted by the plaintiffs, and the accused in
> turn adequately defended against said plaintiffs, and following
> due legal consideration, the court hereby promulgates the fol-
> lowing judgment: that the cohorts, relatives, and acquaintances
> of Monsieur Rat, so displayed in the dock, vacate the municipal
> granary and all cultivated fields near Autun within the départe-
> ment de Saône-et-Loire and move within six days from

tomorrow's date to the designated area chosen for them where crops are not grown and they can do no further harm to mankind by continuing to live from the fruits of his labor. This notice will be posted on the four walls of the municipal granary inside and outside, on all public buildings and churches within the vicinity of the city of Autun and adjacent areas of Saône-et-Loire, and infested fields where rats have sorely damaged the grain. It will also be read aloud at several locations within the walls of Autun, including the public markets and inside and outside the granary, at the liturgical hours of prime and vespers for six consecutive days starting tomorrow, August 10th. If said rats belonging to the accused rodent hordes refuse to honor the edict and still remain after the allotted six days they shall suffer the public disgrace, subsequent emotional anguish, and everlasting humiliation and ignominy of excommunication from God's Church.

With that, the gavel fell.

The ruling wasn't unanticipated, and my next move was already planned. I had lost the argument against evicting the rats from their current domiciles, but the length of time allotted in the eviction notice was still in play.

I said, "The defense requests a delay to consider and address this new situation."

"How much time do you need, Monsieur Chassenée?'

"I request that his grace withhold posting the notice for three weeks. My clients number in the thousands and are scattered throughout the département de Saône-et-Loire. I need to consult their leaders, then perform calculations to obtain a realistic time required for all of them to migrate. I anticipate endless meetings and negotiations. It won't be simple."

"I've given them six days. That's not sufficient?"

"Not nearly, if Your Grace means to be fair."

"Monsieur Révigny?"

"I don't object, Your Grace. Anything in the interest of fairness."

"So it is," said His Grace. He looked at the clerk. "Monsieur, please check your calendar."

"Three weeks from today is Wednesday the 30th of August. However, the Day of Assumption when Mary, Holy Mother of Christ entered Heaven, falls on Tuesday the 15th. From then through that weekend will be taken up with celebration and prayers. I suggest a postponement until Monday the 4th of September."

"Very well," His Grace said. "Midpoint of the growing season has passed, and with this postponement the late harvest is looming. It's God's will and can't be helped. Court is dismissed."

MONDAY SEPTEMBER 4TH—CHASSENÉE REITERATES
THAT SIX DAYS FOR ALL RATS TO VACATE THEIR DOMICILES
IS MUCH TOO SHORT, NOTING THE ESTIMATED TRAVELING SPEED
OF RATS; HE ADVOCATES CONFINING ALL PET AND
OWNERLESS CATS DURING THE MIGRATION PERIOD;
RÉVIGNY REBUTS, ARGUING THAT IF PET AND UNOWNED CATS
ARE CONFINED TOO LONG BOTH RATS AND THEIR MOUSE
RELATIVES WILL MULTIPLY OUT OF CONTROL

❧

COURT RECONVENED AS SCHEDULED, AND THE judicial vicar said, "Monsieur Chassenée, you have the floor. Please proceed."

I called Marcel Caron to the witness chair. When he was seated I said, "Monsieur Caron, have you ever measured the speed at which an adult rat moves and how far it travels during its normal forays?"

"Yes, monsieur. I have noted that a rat seldom goes more than fifty meters from its domicile and back while foraging at night, if confident no cats, owls, foxes, or stoats are in the vicinity."

"And how long is the typical foraging period?" I said

Caron furrowed his brow and stared into the distance as if pondering a complex philosophical question. "I would say about twelve hours."

I said, "And we know that adult humans, when walking just shy of briskly, move at about two kilometers per hour, covering some forty-eight kilometers in twenty-four hours. This assumes the ground is smooth, level, and devoid of impediments. It also assumes that the traveler walks at a constant speed and never stops for rest and sustenance. Does such an estimate sound correct?"

Caron stirred uncomfortably. "If you say so, monsieur. I'm a catcher of rats, not an engineer."

I ignored his qualified response and continued. "A foraging rat does not always travel forward in a straight line, but rather stops, turns, hesitates, and sometimes even reverses course during its nocturnal explorations to sniff out food and prospective mates, isn't this so?"

"Yes, monsieur, it happens often with the rats I have observed."

"Right. Prior to today we discussed this matter privately, so I knew before this present testimony what your estimate would be for the distance traveled by a foraging rat over twelve hours. In the interim I've put quill to paper and done some calculating. Consider a situation in which a rat has a specific destination and purpose and travels only forward in a straight line." I turned and gathered some pages from my side of the table and shuffled them into order. "The number I've derived is conservative because the rats you watched did not have a specific destination and thus wandered around leisurely. Had they been on a mission they no doubt would have traveled farther. Unfortunately, we have no information about mission-driven rats moving at a sustained pace.

"A kilometer for those unfamiliar with the term comprises a thousand meters. So, by doubling your original low estimate of fifty meters traveled in twelve hours we derive one hundred meters in twenty-four hours, or one-tenth of a kilometer. Therefore, a rat scurrying along as best it can would require ten days to travel a full kilometer. That is, ten consecutive days and nights of unimpeded walking over favorable ground without stops or detours. In comparison, a human walking at a moderate pace under the same conditions covers four hundred-eighty kilometers in ten days, nearly one hundred leagues! Can you imagine? I looked directly at every member of the court and then at the gallery, my arms spread and a wearing a startled, wide-eyed expression as if I myself were in disbelief. Révigny registered his disdain by looking at me with calm green eyes and yawning ostentatiously.

I paused in my exposition and looked at the gallery. The people were talking and laughing. No one was paying attention. Nonetheless, I continued for the benefit of the court, my primary audience. "His Grace estimates that the parcel of land where these rats are ordered to migrate is three leagues from Autun, or seventeen kilometers. We may assume that certain other rat-infested locations within the département de Saône-et-Loire will be closer, others more distant. However, taking the distance from the proposed emigration site at Autun as an example, our rats traveling nonstop will need one hundred-seventy days to reach their new home, approximately five and a half months! These numbers, of course, are merely the products of conjectural arithmetic. No rat or human could sustain such paces even for a single twenty-four period without halting for food, water, and rest, thus greatly extending the actual travel time. Still, my example stresses the obvious fact that rats suffer extreme disadvantages because of their short legs and for this deficiency alone ought to be given every consideration. I trust the court will agree.

"Therefore, here is what I propose. Pregnant rats should be allowed to stay where they are until any young presently in the embryonic or fetal stages have been born and nursed to weaning. According to Monsieur Caron, our authority who presented some of this information previously, gestation lasts three weeks. Rat pups open their eyes two weeks after birth. At three weeks they are weaned and able to take solid food, preferably soft cheeses such as Brie and spermyse. The average number of pups in a litter is seven. A mother rat can travel without ill effects on the day her pups are weaned. Assuming a rat is impregnated today, the longest time necessary to wait is six weeks hence.

"This, however, is only part of the story." By now I was well into my appeal, pacing back and forth in front of the big table, casting occasional glances at the court and spectators.

"Then you must factor in travel time from the farthest outlying areas of Saône-et-Loire, keeping in mind that rats are most active and inclined to travel at night, as are cats, their mortal enemies. Rats dash from cover to cover, seldom moving in a straight line. They also must stop often for water and sustenance, to give birth and nurse the unweaned young, to mourn and bury their dead, for observance of liturgical holidays, and to allow for abrupt and unpredictable changes in weather. Naturally, traveling on Sundays, God's day of rest, is prohibited. Being unfamiliar with the new countryside means more time devoted to foraging than would be necessary in familiar surroundings. I request that the allotted migration be extended from six days to five months.

"In addition, I asked the court to order all cat owners to keep their pets indoors until the inquiry is finished and the last rat has safely moved to the aforementioned land. During this time unowned cats will be rounded up under supervision of the bailiff and confined in a secure place from which they can't escape."

There were howls of protest from the gallery, prompting Révigny to rise and speak. "Preventing cats from preying on rats is one thing, but what about mice?" he said. "They eat the grain too, certainly less of it than the rats, although still sufficient to make an impact. A cat sees them both as rodents. Confining cats to protect rats also protects the mice. If all cats are confined during the entire duration requested by the defense, populations of both the mice and rats will explode, leaving no grain at all for my plaintiffs."

I was running out of room to maneuver, then suddenly remembered Aesop's fable about belling the cat. I rose quickly and was granted permission to speak. "If the court please, Monsieur

Révigny's mention of mice reminds me of an ancient Greek fable recounted by Eustache Deschamps in his ballades, each poem containing a moral lesson. Among them is one titled 'Les souris et les chats' and recounts a tale about a group of mice being preyed on relentlessly by a particularly ferocious cat. The mice hold a council at which it's suggested that one of their number volunteer to tie a bell around the cat's neck. A bell would announce the cat's arrival, giving the mice time to escape and hide. The idea was brilliant. The only obstacle remaining was, *Qui pendra la sonnette au chat?* Indeed, who will bell the cat? Not a single volunteer stepped forward, the lesson being that plans that are too risky yield no result, regardless of how good they seem."

I looked directly at His Grace, then at Révigny. "However, if all the free-ranging cats were captured and belled under supervision of the bailiff think of how many rats could be saved!"

Révigny then rose. "Who will cast thousands of these tiny bells, and who will pay for the casting and raw material? From where will the manpower come to bell thousands of cats? And how long must the process continue as more cats are born and turn into adult ratters? I see this belling of cats as excessively costly, endless, and obviously impractical."

Révigny sat down, and His Grace turned my way. He looked at me thoughtfully and said, "Your entire presentation today has been quite a creative endeavor, Monsieur Chassenée, although I don't see anything you've proposed actually going anywhere." He then turned to his right and looked at Révigny, and they both chuckled. "I shall take all comments under deliberation and announce my decision on the next court date, which will be this Friday the 8th of September." He then dismissed the court.

FRIDAY SEPTEMBER 8TH—THE JUDICIAL VICAR ACCEPTS
CHASSENÉE'S ARGUMENT THAT SIX DAYS IS INADEQUATE FOR ALL
RATS TO MIGRATE TO THE NEW LAND, BUT CONSIDERS FIVE
MONTHS UNREASONABLE; HE PROPOSES A COMPROMISE;
CHASSENÉE ACCEPTS GRUDGINGLY, BUT REQUESTS CERTAIN
CONDITIONS TO ASSURE HIS CLIENTS CAN MIGRATE SAFELY

❧

AS SOON AS COURT RECONVENED THE judicial vicar said, "At the
last meeting of the court, which was this past Monday the 4th of
September, Monsieur Chassenée argued that six days are too few
for the rat hordes of Saône-et-Loire to shift themselves and their
belongings to the new land allotted them. After due consideration,
I agree. The revised edict will remain in place with this change: *six
days* will be replaced by *four weeks from the day of announcement, plus
an additional fourteen days for any rats that are pregnant.* After this time
all rats still remaining in their original domiciles may be eradicated
by any means available, including the murder of pregnant mothers
and their young still in the nest. This last, of course, will not be part
of the edict but simply passed through the populace by spoken
word. The day of announcement is obviously today."

"May I speak, Your Grace?"

"Certainly, Monsieur Chassenée, but let's not make things too
complicated. Winter will soon be here."

"I thank Your Grace for considering my request and modifying
the second edict. Regretfully, the revision remains woefully inadequate and with onset of frigid weather many rats will perish,
including the innocent suckling, naked and blind and clinging to
its mother's teat. Still, we might take certain steps to limit the
carnage. I proposed that every cat, owned or ownerless, be
ordered to post a bond with the clerk of the court, swearing under
oath not to harass or molest the rats in any way during the allotted
migration period."

This suggestion was met with loud hisses and boos and a cascade of rotten vegetables hurled in the court's direction. The riot was quickly quelled by the bailiff's assistants armed with truncheons. When the sounds of sharp cracks against skulls and the groans and screams of pain had abated, a discussion ensued among members of the court about how the cats could procure sufficient funds to post bonds. Under ordinary circumstances a cat isn't gainfully employed and thus has no source of income.

His Grace mentioned that cat owners should post bonds on behalf of their pets, to which I agreed. Révigny objected, claiming that many of his clients were indigent peasants living hand to mouth on coarse barley bread and the occasional sliver of gristly meat. How were they to afford this added household expense? I watched as his eyes changed from green to just the orangy side of rage, indicating he believed his own words, but only half-heartedly.

Ancillary issues arose. A few spectators shouted from the gallery that they didn't know exactly how many cats they owned; others acknowledged that cats venturing around their dwellings seemed to be ownerless, showing up occasionally to forage for scraps before disappearing. After hearing the spectators argue and complain until well into nones the court decided that classifying any particular cat as owned or ownerless wasn't straightforward after all.

Not surprisingly, no individual or group stepped forward with an offer to absorb the cost of posting bonds for cats. I suggested the court do so for citizens without adequate financial means, and failing that the Church should bear the burden directly because this was, after all, an ecclesiastical proceeding.

The judicial vicar immediately objected to both, noting the absence of any legal precedent in which a clerical court had posted bond on behalf of cats. He then insisted that the Church did not presently own cats, nor had it ever owned them throughout its history and thus couldn't possibly guarantee any cat's bond, whether owned or ownerless, even if the definitions of such categories could be determined with certainty, which apparently was impossible. He added that saving souls was a full-time task and consumed all the Church's resources. His Grace noted further that excessive fornication among members of the feline race explained why Autun and the surrounding countryside were overrun by cats. In their case God's mandate to go forth and multiply had become just an excuse for unrepentant feline lust.

Révigny asked if my request for bonds included unweaned kittens too young to hunt, and I replied that it did not. "Well," he said pompously, "how very generous of you, monsieur. I see that you can be reasonable after all. But in any case how are we to determine the total number of cats inhabiting Saône-et-Loire, then partition this number into how many are fed by mankind versus those living off the land?" He then suggested that the entire idea be scrapped in favor of letting nature play out. Surely, he insisted, enough rats would be left alive to sustain the tribes. "Let it be tit for tat, or as the saying goes, *á bon chat, bon rat.* In other words, as cats become better ratters, the rats figure out ways to escape from them. In the end enough will survive to preserve the race."

I retorted that such a laissez faire policy was unacceptable to my clients, especially parents, which effectively included them all. In any case, rats would always be the prey and cats the predators no matter how the balance of power shifted. Furthermore, any difficulty calculating how many cats residing in the département de Saône-et-Loire depended on humans for food versus how many were self-sufficient wasn't the defense's problem, but the prosecution's. I said, "I admit to not knowing each of my clients personally, no less their histories. I haven't been present during their moments of grief, disappointment, elation, or triumph, although I dare to guess they share a common wish not to be eaten."

With this remark I subtly shifted the conversation and laid a foundation for pursuing safety concerns, stating that short of controlling the cats the rats must be provided with guards day and night along the numerous paths from their present fields and other domains to the new one. I justified it as a good-faith guarantee against predation. Once again I insisted that every cat regardless of ownership status be ordered to post a bond, now adding that it should be accompanied by a notarized affidavit promising not to harass or molest the rats in any way until two days after the date the edict expires so as to prevent endangering any stragglers.

I reprised the hardship dilemma, arguing that all guards assuring the safety of my clients were to be put under the bailiff's command and posted at regular intervals between the rats' present places of occupancy and the new location. My motion, I emphasized, was being made under the precept of equal justice for all. In legal terms there was nothing special or unusual about it. Rats are merely justiciables, or litigants, under modern French law, no different in this respect from humans. Both are subject to the same classifications as everyone and everything—clerical or laity, minor or adult—whether or not capable of a personal legal defense. I noted, for example, that such a demand would not be out of place if issued to protect underage children on their way to a trial or ecclesiastical tribunal, and His Grace agreed.

I also argued that because my clients lived at many different locations a single edict likely would be inadequate to notify each. His Grace agreed with this too, but reminded me that his edict would be read aloud at all locations where official complaints of rat damage and infestations had been reported, and in his opinion this was sufficient to discharge the court's duty.

I stated how my clients were respectable rodents who wished only to please the court, but that long-distance travel is difficult for animals with such short legs, and especially so for those who are burdened by unweaned young, are pregnant, crippled or otherwise infirm, or are too immature to travel. There was also the difficulty of acquiring sustenance during the journey.

I said, "Your Grace, I wish to raise a point regarding your threat—rather, yours and the bishop's—of excommunication if my clients ignore the second edict as they did the first. There's no need to read the entire content of that document before the court. Just the last sentence suffices. It states: *If said rats belonging to the accused rodent hordes refuse to honor the edict. . . they shall suffer the public disgrace, subsequent emotional anguish, and everlasting humiliation and ignominy of excommunication from God's Church.* I argue that because my rattish clients are bestioles and therefore dumb brutes they lack any capacity to reason. Furthermore, all beasts and bestioles lack souls. Everyone knows and accepts this fact. At death there's nothing left to save.

"How can a soulless creature be excommunicated from a church to which it can't possible enjoy membership? These aren't new arguments, as Your Grace well knows, although certainly pertinent. Saint Thomas Aquinas held that unreasoning creatures are immune to either anathemas or blessings *secundem se*—in the vernacular, 'by definition'—being unable to understand and interpret them. Instead, only human beings can be the recipients. Curses and blessings are thus aimed at animals indirectly, except in their relation to man; in other words, whether affected favorably or unfavorably we humans are the actual targets. When God cursed the ground He did so because of mankind's crucial dependence on the soil for subsistence. Job cursed the day he was born and also his mother's womb because as Eve's daughter she had infected him with sin, inside and out, then cast him from her womb into the world to suffer the consequences."

Révigny stood and without asking permission to speak said, "This issue can be seen differently by considering animals to be Satan's agents. Then cursing them is proper because the curse is hurled directly at the Devil, not at them. Remember that when irrational animals turn against mankind it can only be at Satan's instigation. Dumb brutes and bestioles certainly can't plot such devious actions on their own. Add to this the fact that some animal forms are inherently evil, arising from the egg or the womb with no purpose other than to harm us: serpents, mosquitoes, fleas, dragons, scorpions, the Leviathan . . . I could name many more."

I signaled His Grace and regained the floor. "Not being a cleric and poorly versed in canon law I'm confused about the definitions of anathema and excommunication. Are they synonyms? If not, how do they differ, or is the second a subcategory of the first? If so, wouldn't anathematization be the damning of a maleficent animal; that is, a type of 'animal excommunication'? Clarifying these points is critical to my defense."

The judicial vicar showed sudden interest, either because of the scholarly nature of my questions or from seeing an opportunity to display his erudition. "How so, monsieur?"

"Pardon, Your Grace?"

"How are the specific definitions critical to your case?"

"As I understand canon law animals can be anathematized but not excommunicated because their status as dumb brutes makes this last impossible, besides which they don't have souls. And humans who have not been baptized are immune from excommunication too. I argued this point in court on Wednesday the 28th of June, which Your Grace no doubt remembers. I ended that inquiry by asking if monitories of any sort have proven efficacious in cases involving bestioles, and rats specifically. Monsieur Révigny then presented an example of rats being expelled from an area of coastal France by ecclesiastics who waved crosses at them. Whether these offenders had been anathematized or excommunicated beforehand wasn't mentioned, either in Monsieur Révigny's rebuttal or the original report in his possession, which he graciously allowed me to read."

"Could you come to the point, Monsieur Chassenée?"

"Of course, Your Grace. If animals can't be excommunicated under canon law then your edict holds no authority concerning my clients and must be considered null and void. That is my point." I was halfway seated, then remembered something and stood again. "Oh, I almost forgot. If a third edict must be issued in which the word 'anathematized' is substituted for 'excommunicated,' what specifically will 'anathematized' mean, how does its canonical weight compare with 'excommunicated,' and how will its definition be implemented in actual measure? Stated differently, if my clients disobey an 'anathema,' what specifically will be their punishment?"

The judicial vicar leaned back in his chair and looked at me. "That's quite an order you've just requested of me. In short, the answers you seek have never emerged from the shadows of canonical theory. As its name implies, 'excommunication' is expulsion from the community of God's church. Such is the opinion of Gaspard Bailly de Savoy, as set forth in his *Traité des monitories, avec un plaidoyer contre les insects* (*Treatise of Monitories, with a Plea Against Insects*), isn't this true?

"As an ecclesiastical jurist trained in canonical theory I consider excommunication a consequence and thus a subcategory of anathema in being limited to those of the human race who have been baptized and accepted Jesus Christ as their Lord and Savior. Thus, anathema is folded within excommunication, the principal category, or the reverse of how you present the situation in your question.

"Animals of any kind and human nonbelievers are excluded by definition. Excommunicating them is impossible, as you state. No beast or bestiole could ever be 'excommunicated' according to the exact definition of this term. The souls of unbaptized humans at death enter limbo, where they remain for eternity. Animals don't possess souls, only flesh, and they merely die. However, it's been argued by some clerics of high standing that Scripture is fuzzy on these distinctions. Certain passages in the Holy Writ hint that corruption after the Fall infected every living thing without exception, and all forms of life remain hopeful of atonement for the sins of their forebears and redemption for themselves."

I said, "This seems unreasonable, Your Grace, and certainly incompatible with the position taken by Saint Thomas Aquinas. How could dumb, insensate beasts ever hold any hope of atonement and redemption if they can't reason or think?"

Révigny rose from his chair. "I believe I can predict where this is leading, Your Grace. Monsieur Chassenée is about to propose that your use of the term 'excommunicate' invalidates your second edict." He looked at me, eyes modulating between green and amber, indicating a low level of interest. "Am I correct, monsieur?"

"You are indeed," I said.

"In that case, I shall disappoint you, Monsieur Chassenée," said His Grace. "The terms 'excommunicate' and 'anathema' are deployed interchangeably in canonical writings and speech. These are often confused with 'malediction,' which is simply a curse not necessarily associated with religious overtones. Technically, an entity can be anathematized without being excommunicated, but this is a small matter. As I mentioned just a moment ago, any distinction—assuming there is one—has not been officially recognized. Therefore, whether the one is officially a subcategory of the other is irrelevant by being unknown. For our purposes each term is representative of its complement, making them synonyms for deployment in practical matters like the wording of edicts. The edict will stand as written. If ignored, a third will not be forthcoming."

"Thank you for the clarification, Your Grace," I said, and sat down. There was nothing more I could do.

His Grace said, "Monsieur Clerk, please check your calendar and choose a date closest to the end of the edict when the court can convene again to assess the result."

There was a brief pause before the clerk stood and said, "Assuming the time allotted to the defendants starts today, it ends Friday the 20th of October."

"Excellent," said His Grace. "Monsieur Clerk, you have assured me that sufficient notices have been prepared and distributed to various staging areas in Autun and the surrounding villages. Please order them posted at once and send the criers to read the edict publicly at the preordained times." With this statement it was obvious that any arguments I made today were destined beforehand to be ignored, although it had been my legal right to make them and the court's obligation to enter them into the record. The proceeding had effectively ended. "And Monsieur Clerk, one more item. Please alert Autun's rat-catcher, Monsieur Marcel Caron, to prepare to do his part. On Monday the 23rd of October, rain or shine, he is to dispatch his minions to every site where notices of the edict have been posted to check for evidence of any rats still inhabiting those places and report back to you within a week and a day. I shall expect his findings summarized by you and on my desk a week later. What will that date be?"

The clerk studied his calendar. The week and a day you request encompasses Allhallowtide, which begins Monday the 30th with All Saints' Day Eve and continues through the celebration of All Souls' Day on Thursday the 2nd of November. Then come Friday and the weekend."

"I'd forgotten. Please go on," said His Grace.

The clerk cleared his throat. "I suggest that Monsieur Caron deliver his findings to me no later than Monday the 6th of November. I can hand my report to you on or before Friday the 10th, if Your Grace finds this suitable."

His Grace said, "That's fine. We have no reason to meet until early the following week when my decision will be announced. Court will reconvene at terce on Monday the 13th of November." His gavel struck the sounding block.

Révigny and I returned to the inn, where I told François and Alvin we would be leaving for home early the next morning after breakfast. Everything of theirs was to be packed and the animals readied to depart by terce. They could fetch my luggage while I was having breakfast. I then arranged with the innkeeper to pay the bill and expect our return on Sunday the 12th of November. With nothing better to do, Révigny and I retired to the tavern and afterward, in my case, a good night's sleep. I would need to be well rested to confront Madame Chassenée.

Monday November 13th—Court Reconvenes for the Last Time

BY THE TIME COURT RECONVENED I knew one thing, and would bet on Révigny knowing it too. The case had taken a turn I'd seen before. A trial is a play, a stage setting, and the court officials, plaintiffs, and defendants are actors. As events meander unpredictably toward a dénouement certain individuals emerge as heroes, others as villains. In this instance the gallery had become sympathetic to Monsieur Rat and turned against Révigny. It seemed paradoxical that a rat could be admired when his tribe comprises some of God's most despised creations. However, it isn't uncommon for a charismatic thief to gain the sympathy of the spectators, none of whom condones theft.

When court last recessed more than nine weeks previously I noticed many in the gallery stopping by the dock to bid Monsieur Rat adieu and say they looked forward to seeing him in November. Some cooed at him lovingly, complimenting him on his handsome appearance, and children stuck their tiny fingers through the bars and stroked his fur, which he tolerated gracefully as might a tame cat or rabbit. Anyone expressing these good feelings would happily have taken Monsieur Rat home as a pet.

Put simply, the spectators had grown fond of the rat tribe's representamen—or, with his new popularity, call him envoy—while still hating his race. From inside his cage Monsieur Rat exuded a certain nonchalance, or charme cavaliere. Had he spoken French we might even have called it savoir faire. Not surprisingly, the gallery rained boos accompanied by rotten vegetables on Révigny when he had once proposed torture to wring a confession from Monsieur Rat about his evil deeds, perhaps putting him to the rack, then adding in jest that doing so would require a very small rack. This comment might have been amusing at the start of the proceeding, but not later after Monsieur Rat had become a daily fixture at court. No, at this moment the very idea of harming Monsieur Rat was abhorrent. And he obviously had not been forgotten during the ensuing weeks. If anything, his admirers had increased in number, and the bailiff's men were forced to shoo them away from the dock so court could commence on schedule.

When pests are anathematized and the process works as planned, various explanations arise other than God's intervention. For example, any plague of grasshoppers must end eventually when everything edible has been devoured, and instead of its demise being the result of a causal event it was more likely just a sequential one (i.e. *post hoc, ergo propter hoc*). And if the plague fails to end when predicted the blame can always be placed on the sins of the villagers, their inadequate tithes, or a combination. However, considering that anathematizing animals seldom works the Church's fallback position is to increase tithes in an attempt to gain God's mercy.

Monsieur Caron's report showed no detectable movement of rats from any posted locations in the département de Saône-et-Loire to the newly acquired land. If anything they were even more numerous and bold. His Grace promptly anathematized them all and naturally demanded more tithes from everyone, reminding us again that the ultimate cause of the rat plague had been the people's sins.

He also reminded us that during the plague of grasshoppers in 1487 several specimens of the offending insects had been brought to court and publicly executed as a symbolic gesture of what would happen to their compatriots if they ignored clerical directives to abandon the sites of their crimes. As if the prospect of immediate demise wasn't sufficiently threatening, the judicial vicar judging that trial had proposed the additional horror of sprinkling of holy water over the infested areas. That, our judicial vicar announced, would be his own fallback position, although first he had something else in mind.

He summoned Marcel Caron, Autun's official rat-catcher. "Monsieur Caron, I call you to the dock to perform the task we discussed earlier."

Monsieur Caron emerged from the crowd and strode to the dock, shifting the cage holding Monsieur Rat to expose an open space on the table.

His Grace stood and raised his right arm toward the dock. "The rats have ignored my second edict just as they did the first. Therefore, Monsieur Rat, as their representamen it's you who must pay the price. As I vowed when issuing the first edict, 'as God is my witness I shall cut you into seven pieces,' and that time has come." Caron reached into the cage, extracted the rat, and pinned it to the table. He then produced a knife and cut off its nose, followed by its head and then five more pieces before being submerged under an avalanche of enraged spectators.

"I think it's time we left," Révigny said. We four members of the court grabbed our documents, lifted our robes, and sprinted for the entrance of the Théâtre Romain where our mounts awaited. From there we retreated with all speed. Monsieur Caron's fate is too gory and awful to recount, although I can report that the office of rat catcher of Autun is presently vacant and accepting applications.

PART II

Madame Truye
in the Dock

*"Pigs suffer, it is true, and their
pain purifies and ennobles them."*

—Roberto Bolaño—
By Night in Chile

MONDAY MAY 5TH, YEAR OF GRACE 1511—
MADAME AND MONSIEUR CHASSENÉE LEAVE THEIR MANOR FOR
AUTUN, MADAME TO VISIT RELATIVES, MONSIEUR TO VISIT THE
LIVESTOCK MARKET; THE DONKEY RECEIVES A SURPRISE;
CHASSENÉE IS SUMMONED BY THE BISHOP TO DEFEND A PIG

⤫

I HAD FINALLY CAPITULATED TO MADAME Chassenée's constant nagging about wanting a coach and ordered one from Paris, along with two trained horses to pull it and a professional coachman named Aufrey, now a permanent resident of our household. He had arrived with Madame's beasts and contraption two years previously in April, driving it laboriously through the spring rain and mud, a distance of about sixty-six leagues over roads so rutted and potholed that the front axle and two of the wheels broke during the trip, requiring delays for repairs and forcing Aufrey to hole up in vermin-infested inns.

These events were harbingers of what I had feared all along, that coaches are not only slow, inconvenient, and uncomfortable devices but unduly fragile, their design and construction incommensurate with the demands placed on them. Put simply, modern French roads are barely passable for saddle horses and farm wagons, relegating coaches to expensive toys for the wealthy. And until a clever engineer improves on the present arrangement of the habitable cabin portion in its current position—slung from chains attached to curved standards at the four corners and suspended above the chassis—every bump and depression threatens to loosen teeth and jar limbs from their sockets. Someday an invention will come along that absorbs the shock of the jolts. Until then I refuse to ride in this one.

I had instructed the Parisian agent to engage a coachman also skilled in coach mechanics so he might keep the machine in proper repair, and fortunately Aufrey has met this requirement. For the trip to our estate he packed the coach with all the spare parts he could cram inside and even strapped two extra iron-rimmed wheels to the outside of the chassis where space permitted: one against the back, the other underneath.

Aufrey is well organized, and when he reaches Autun and drops Madame with her relatives to visit and shop he then makes the rounds of the various trades where he leaves the rig with the black-smith, wheelwright, or leatherworker as the specific repair requires and the horses with the farrier if they need to be shod. He then waits in a tavern until summoned by a tradesman's apprentice after the work is completed. He finishes his beer and pays the tab, settles with the tradesman and gets receipts for the work, and appears at the appointed time to collect Madame and her parcels for the trip home. If she remains in town overnight to attend a party or other social gathering, Aufrey stays at an inn.

Aufrey has become my most trusted and valued employee, and I ignored Madame's early complaints that he was rumored to be sleeping with the maids. I told her that if she valued her present lifestyle with a coach and coachman it would be wise not to inter-fere. Aufrey, I reminded her, is a model worker. Others in town and in manors throughout the countryside would gladly hire him if he became unhappy and left us. The advice seems to have been received, and although she continues to berate the rest of the household staff she has nothing but smiles and compliments for Aufrey.

We had just lurched and slogged through Autun's west gate, where I paid the merchant's toll and prepared to leave Madame with the coach at the home of her relatives. I had a minor errand to

STEPHEN SPOTTE

discharge at the livestock market and brought along the donkey for this purpose, although it carried no burden. Alvin was holding its tether as it trailed behind the mule on which he and François rode double. A chilly rain had fallen nearly the whole way, and all except Madame were soaked and shivering. I gave Aufrey instructions to deposit Madame at her desired destinations when she was ready, take care of his errands, and drop Madame at the home of her relatives when her shopping was finished. He was then to meet François, Alvin, and me at the livestock market with the empty carriage. Today was pig day, and the place would be jammed with pigs of all ages, swineherds attempting to control them, and many a local owner and itinerant porcatier buying and selling. I wasn't in need of pigs, but rather a peculiar service likely to be found where pigs in large numbers are bought and sold.

Then I saw the man I was seeking, oddly dressed and obviously not a resident of Saône-et-Loire, but someplace on the other side of the Pyrenees. He was the castraire, a feared and respected semi-vagabond who performs his task, says little, then moves on. It was his services I needed. These castraires live in groups of relatives like gypsies, meaning nowhere in particular, often setting up temporary camps on the outskirts of towns. Although pigs are his major source of work, he castrates other domestic animals too. He's a marvel of dexterity with his fleams, his needles and thread. Few experienced surgeons can match his skills.

He castrates male piglets to dampen later adolescent aggression and so that they gain weight more quickly. Sows are castrated to prevent their breeding. To castrate females requires the greater skill. A sow is felled and its legs tied together to keep it prone. The castraire then makes a slit the length of a forefinger through the thick skin in the side of the lower abdomen, reaches in and digs around until finding a pocelhièira, one of two reproductive pouches the size of a newborn baby's hand and filled with tiny grapelike objects. He pulls it out, ties it off at the base with a length of thread to prevent bleeding, slices away the pouch with its contents, and stuffs the remainder back inside the abdomen. Then he fishes for the second pouch. Having removed both, with a threaded needle already prepared he takes a half-dozen stitches and closes the cut. The entire procedure lasts just a few minutes, then the sow's legs are untied and she stumbles to her feet. This skill is usually kept in the family, passed down from a father to his sons and grandsons.

The itinerant castraire is often summoned to treat boys— naughty, stubborn, or bad-tempered boys who disobey or become disruptive by crying constantly and perhaps erupting in frequent tantrums. "Testicular hernias" are blamed for these conditions, and castration of young boys from one to seven years exerts the same calming effect it does on male piglets. I needed his services for my donkey, which was becoming difficult to handle. It was Alvin's duty to lead him while riding behind François on the mule, but lately the presence of a horse or donkey in heat was making him bad-tempered and even dangerous.

A crowd had gathered around the castraire to watch him perform, applauding at the end of every procedure when a pig stood following surgery and disappeared into its herd. François, Alvin, and I sat astride our mounts and watched too, I unaware how my own life would soon become entwined with the lives of pigs. The man had finished his work for the day, and the crowd was dispersing when I approached him and requested a moment of his time.

"Certainly, monsieur," he said in his strange accent. He put away the last of his instruments and looked up at me, squinting into the light rain. "What is it you want?"

"I want my donkey castrated, but he's in no mood to be handled."

The castraire moved closer, inducing the little beast to snap at his hand and stamp a forehoof. "He's a feisty one, isn't he?" The man signaled to two young associates nearby. "My sons," he said. They enveloped the donkey's legs in their arms, muscled him to the ground, and quickly bound his feet. Their father went to work with his tools and within minutes the job was finished and the scrotum sutured. The castraire stood and held out his hand. "Five sous, monsieur. Your donkey will gradually become calmer and more docile. I paid the man just as Aufrey pulled up at the edge of the market driving the empty coach. Darkness was descending when we arrived at the home of Madame's relatives. I told Madame it was too late to return to the manor. There might be highwaymen lurking, and anyway the rutted road was too treacherous for night travel. She was to spend the night where she was; the rest of us would go to Le Coq et la Pie on the Street of the Wooden Leg to pass the night and return for her around terce the following morning.

The innkeeper settled my footmen into an empty stall in the stable behind the inn and ordered their supper and a flagon of green Spanish wine delivered to them by a serving maid from the tavern. The three horses, mule, and donkey were stabled and the coach secured for the night. Aufrey and I had just sat down at a table in the tavern and ordered wine when the bishop's courier appeared. "Monsieur Chassenée, at last I've found you. His Holiness requests your decision on this matter. He's waiting and would like it immediately." He handed me a scroll closed with wax embossed by the bishop's seal. The document I unrolled was brief, a request that I represent a sow charged with homicide in an upcoming ecclesiastical tribunal here at Autun. The trial would be held outdoors at the Théâtre Romain, prosecuted by Humbert de Révigny, and judged by the same judicial vicar who had previously overseen the tribunal of the rats in the year of grace 1508. I read the request again to be certain I understood its details. Something about it was unusual.

Animals considered to be vermin and under God's control alone are traditionally tried in ecclesiastical, or canonical, courts following accusatory legal procedures. A single individual isn't on trial, but rather all regional members of the species, as in the case of the rats. Animals brought to civil courts are under mankind's control, inevitably domesticated species, and tried under inquisitorial procedures. This sow, obviously a domestic animal, nonetheless would be held accountable by a canonical judge, not a civil jurist presiding in a secular court. The matter required explanation, preferably from the bishop himself. Preparing my case for the defense would depend on the system of rules applied.

Each court has pros and cons. Depending on how events played out the animal was likely doomed either way. All a defense lawyer can do is prolong the process and hope for a miracle. My opinion always has been that a domestic animal ought to be considered similar to a lay person from the law's perspective. However, its legal advocate is always free to argue for his client belonging to a clerical order (*ordinem clericatus*) with the caveat that the defendant present adequate proof. At any rate I was bored with my usual legal work, and this would be an interesting change. I told the courier I accepted the case and signed the document.

TUESDAY MAY 6TH—MADAME AND AUFREY RETURN
TO THE MANOR; CHASSENÉE, FRANÇOIS, AND ALVIN REMAIN
IN TOWN; CHASSENÉE VISITS THE BISHOP TO CLEAR UP QUESTIONS;
RÉVIGNY ARRIVES AT THE INN; THE PLOT TURNS MURKY

❧

DURING BREAKFAST WITH AUFREY I INSTRUCTED him to pick up Madame in her coach and take her home. He was to explain to her that the rest of us would be staying in Autun because I had been summoned by the bishop to defend a new client in a homicide trial here. He was to omit mention that the client was a pig, in part to avoid hearing Madame's laughter and sarcasm aimed at me.

I had brought along only one change of clothes, not having anticipated being held over for a trial. The innkeeper's wife could keep one set clean while I wore the other, but I needed spares of everything, plus additional court attire. Before releasing Aufrey to drive Madame back to the estate I instructed him to return in two weeks in the coach if she wanted to come or alone if she declined. I gave him a list of necessities, plus some books from my library. I advised him to arrive prepared to stay three days or so, that I had a task for him here in town. If he came alone he could saddle and ride one of the coach horses. As things later worked out, Madame decided to stay behind.

After Aufrey departed I tracked down the innkeeper and notified him that I, my footmen, horse, mule, and donkey would be staying an indeterminate period and that arrangements were to be the same as in the year of grace 1508. He was to provide François and Alvin two meals daily, a dry stall with clean hay in which to sleep, and stalls for the animals along with water and hay to sustain them. My footmen would see to their care.

I added that my coachman would appear occasionally, with or without the coach but with at least one horse, and additional accommodations would be needed at such times. Aufrey would require a bed, although not a place at my table. He could entertain himself at day's end when Révigny and I needed to discuss business privately.

The innkeeper was again to provide François and Alvin breakfast near the hour of prime, which included a bowl of small beer each, hot tea, barley bread, and cheese. At compline, or earlier if that was more convenient, they were to receive a flagon of green Spanish wine along with barley bread, beans, and meat. If beans were unavailable cabbage or onions were adequate substitutes. My men always traveled with their own cups, bowls, and cutlery. I emphasized just one bowl each of small beer in the morning and a single flagon of wine at night, stating that I refused to pay for more. I reminded him that François would complain and promise to buy extra beverages with his own money, except that he has no money nor any hope of obtaining it.

As before I reserved a table for myself in the tavern at which to take breakfast and supper and a bed on the second floor of the inn.

The innkeeper nodded agreement and assured me he remembered these details from three years ago and would diligently see to each. I also told him that Révigny should be arriving soon and asked for him to be assigned as my bedmate. This way I could have the whole bed to myself, knowing that demons are insomniacs. Naturally, I omitted mention of this last. Révigny would no doubt still resemble a harmless old man, tall and bent, and reveal his demonic incarnation to me alone.

It was a beautiful spring day filled with birdsong and sunshine, and I was feeling happy and confident knowing a lengthy reprieve from Madame was ahead. In this auspicious state of mind I could push aside even the unpleasant aspects of Autun: its stink, mud, lepers and beggars, animal carcasses decaying in the streets, and sing-song warnings of *gardez l'eau!* by maids emptying chamber pots out second-storey windows. When I went to check on my footmen I found François mucking the stalls entirely on his own initiative, a minor miracle, and Alvin was happily turning in circles with outspread arms, announcing his ornithological proclivities to an uncaring world. Everything seemed right, and I could now concentrate on business.

I decided to take advantage of the fine weather and walk to the Cathédrale Saint-Lazare d'Autune at Place du Terreau and petition the bishop's gardes du corps for a quick audience. Several matters needed clarification. The structure of the impending trial was shaping up as a peculiar hybrid of the ecclesiastical and secular, and a better notion of its exact conformation would be helpful for planning my strategy. I also needed documentation of the crime and its timeline, a copy of the witness list and notice of witness availability, and any other information pertinent to the case.

I arrived at the Cathédrale near the hour of terce only to wait another hour before being summoned into the dungeonlike room with a simple elevated table where His Holiness oversaw the Church's business. Hat in hand I approached, bowed, and announced myself.

"Barthélemy de Chassenée in your service, Your Holiness. Thank you for meeting with me on short notice."

"Welcome, Monsieur Chassenée. Back for another go, eh?" He seemed unchanged, peering at me as before over his spectacles and fiddling with his quill as if agitated by the interruption. But at least his greeting contained a fragment of humor.

"Yes, Your Holiness, but I have two questions."

"Ask them."

"Foremost, I'm confused by which rules this proceeding will follow. It seems outwardly based on canon law, yet the defendant is a domestic animal, which by tradition would be tried in a secular court. Knowing the rules beforehand would be helpful in preparing my defense."

"I understand your concern and confusion, monsieur. The laws we enforce were not delivered to us mortals chiseled on stone tablets. Those were the Ten Commandments. French civil laws as written and interpreted by men are flexible, canon laws less so, although not entirely inflexible. As you know, ecclesiastical tribunals are often overseen by competent lay jurists, and a civil trial judged by a judicial vicar is uncommon but hardly rare. For reasons that need not concern you I wish to keep my finger on the pulse of this proceeding. The easiest way of doing so is having a clergyman preside, thus retaining the issue within ecclesiastical jurisdiction and applying elements of civil law as necessary to meet the standards by which decisions and the evidence that determine them coincide to guarantee fairness. Term it a 'trial' as you would in a civil court setting, alternatively a 'tribunal' befitting a canonical proceeding. Either is suitable, or not, because in carrying out the mission it will contain elements of both.

"The truth is, I want the matter handled by a clergyman, not a lay judge, and this is best accomplished by giving it the Church's imprimatur but bending toward the secular as exigencies demand. Numerous precedents exist for such overlap. I've cleared the matter with appropriate secular judicial authorities representing the Crown, and they approve going forward as I've just outlined. In summary, think of the impending event as driven by a blend of canon and civil laws acting in the interest of justice. The judicial vicar I've put in charge is the man who presided at the rat tribunal. He will decide which rules to apply as events move along. He has been informed of the situation, as now you have. I shall meet with Monsieur Révigny later today.

"To anticipate your other question, copies of all applicable documents will be delivered to you and Monsieur Révigny at Le Coq et le Pie on rue de la Jambe de Bois before the hour of vespers. The trial will commence each day at terce, as announced by the Cathédrale bells, with weekends and religious holidays as days of prayer and rest." He stretched out his right arm. "Go with God, my son."

I heard the pen already scratching as I turned to leave, and walked back into the sunlight no less puzzled than on arrival.

Near vespers, as I was settling into my chair in the tavern, Révigny lurched through the door looking no different than when I'd seen him during this same month three years previously. He moved awkwardly, like the tired, harmless old man he supposedly was. This is how the world sees him, not suspecting that his outward appearance is a disguise meant to deceive. I alone knew that Révigny is actually a demon, once a brutal lawyer who died years ago, went to Hell, and returns to Earth periodically to litigate in both canonical and civil courts. That he actually works on Satan's behalf is a secret only I know. Révigny had been my prosecutorial adversary in the renowned trial here in Autun in the year of grace 1508 when I defended a bunch of rats accused of eating the citizens' barley.

He looked around the room, and limped over on spotting me. "Barthélemy! We meet again and on such a propitious occasion! You've been well, I hope." He pulled out the chair opposite and sat down, transformed instantaneously into the familiar tall, skinny green demon with a head like a fleshless skull and eyes that pulsed in different colors depending on his mood. He smiled his evil rictus, displaying a green mouth with teeth to match. Already his eyes were pulsing amber and turning a brighter yellow with growing excitement. "I've just come from my meeting with the bishop and hearing his little pep talk, the same drivel he gave you, I presume."

I stood to shake his hand, my short stature demanding it, while he remained seated, which put us on the same level. His handshake still felt like the golem's: limp, damp, and ethereal. "I'm fine, Humbert, and yourself?"

"Oh, you know . . ." He let that statement trail off and waved absently in dismissal. The plume of fulvous smoke still engulfed his head and neck, obscuring these parts of his anatomy at times. It seemed to have a life of its own, but its movement actually depended on Révigny's own, following along as the physics of drag and turbulence dictated.

"Your cocoon still seems in fine shape, and also your cloud of burning brimstone," I said.

He stretched his arms and legs to demonstrate the cocoon's remarkable flexibility. It had no earthly complement. Satisfied with my wide-eyed approval he once again relaxed. "Yes, as I mentioned before I take the damn thing off while relaxing in Hell and only put it back on for these visits topside. I need it to hold in the brimstone smoke, which is still addictive as ever. Never leave home without it." He laughed, a sound a hoarse troll might emit from the bottom of a very deep barrel. "And how is the lovely Madame Chassenée, vicious as ever?"

"You have no idea, Humbert. Our mutual hatred reached its zenith a while back. From pining to conceive she began living in fear of it, or as she phrased it, 'of having a defective child' with all my faults, which she never tires of enumerating. Truly, when Madame suffers, everybody suffers."

Révigny leaned back and feigned a thoughtful gaze into the far distance, the real distance being a few meters to a soot-stained wall

of the tavern. "Let's forget the past for a moment and think ahead."
He held out his arm and passed his hand slowly back and forth in
front of his face, palm outward, as if conjuring a vision. "I can see
the future," he intoned solemnly. Then he dropped his arm and
grinned. "Well, the near future, at any rate."

"Do tell," said I. "And what might the near future look like?"

"Ah," Révigny said, "I have your attention. The near future will
arrive as a child of chaos borne on the wings of scandal." He gazed
at the ceiling as if seeking suitably descriptive words. "Think of it as
the deformed spawn born of the unwieldy conjoining of ecclesiastical and secular law, a monstrous cockatrice of discordant parts
embodying a tragedy encompassing four of Autun's prominent citizens plus a fifth whose identity and destiny were to have remained
unspoken." He looked at me and jabbed a skinny green index finger
into the air above his head. "I further predict you will hear the news
before any other outsider, even Madame Chassenée, Saône-et-
Loire's deepest, most reliable reservoir of cruel and incendiary
gossip. In fact, some of the sordid details won't leak for months. No
one will know the true breadth of skulduggery in which you and I
are destined to immerse ourselves. Our only requirement is to feign
ignorance and watch the drama unfold, all the while keeping our
mouths shut."

"That soliloquy was quite a performance itself, Humbert."

He grinned and chuckled, eyes flashing bright yellow. "And I'm
only beginning. May I continue?"

I nodded and reached to refill our cups. "I see you've already
sweet-talked our judicial vicar into parting with another cask of his
fine white Burgundy. Good work, my friend." We raised our cups in
a mutual toast. "Now, please continue."

Révigny leaned forward, elbows on the table and his terrible face
practically touching mine. "We must keep our voices down, you
understand. Nothing, absolutely not a syllable, must advance beyond
this table. Agreed?"

"Of course," I said.

"Good. You know Jean Philipot, the wealthy fishmonger of Autun and his wife, she of the expensive clothes and gilded coach."

"Naturally. I represented him last year on purchase of a pig farm east of the city. He's expanding his business from fish to include pork. Soon he will add poultry."

"Do you recall his daughter? She's now fourteen years old, or thereabouts, and well developed. A child hidden in the body of a young woman is a dangerous creature best avoided by mature men of good social standing. They bring nothing but trouble, and assuredly such was the situation with this one." Révigny's voice now dropped to a raspy whisper. "As I mentioned three years ago during the tribunal of the rats, we demons rarely sleep, intrigued as we are by the mischief happening after dark. It seems Monsieur Philipot's daughter became hysterical on having her first menses, no one having explained beforehand that such an event is both normal and inevitable. Upon awaking one morning atop bloody sheets she went temporarily insane, shrieking, running around tearing at her hair and nightgown, and generally acting deranged. She couldn't be consoled. Finally, her mother and a maid got her dressed and, not knowing where else to go, took her to the Cathédrale where the bishop was informed of their distress and agreed to an immediate audience. After all, the Philipot family is one of the biggest contributors to the Church in all Saône-et-Loire.

"The bishop was naturally sympathetic, saying he understood the situation completely and offered to counsel the girl, assuring the mother that any discussions would retain the privacy and privilege of the confessional. He explained that female hysteria was likely at the root of the issue. He had seen it many times in young women, recognized the symptoms, and knew a tried and true palliative, which is to stimulate the clitoris manually. The girl will naturally scream and hyperventilate as if undergoing a minor exorcism, but after achieving relief becomes placid and compliant for days or weeks until another treatment is required. Madame Philipot was naturally relieved by this diagnosis. In the great man's calm and holy presence her daughter finally stopped weeping and gained some control of her emotions. It was agreed that she would meet with the bishop in the privacy of his chambers on Sundays at the liturgical hour of compline, during which time she would reveal to him her fears and troubles, and His Holiness would offer counsel and guidance, and, of course, the physical stimulation needed to temporarily alleviate her emotional burden.

"Demons, as is commonly known, can move at lightning speed, so fast as to be undetected by mortals. And we can change shape and size in a flash, becoming literally a fly on the wall. So it was that I began spying on these sessions, detecting at once the hypocrisy of the bishop's prayers. He's sly, that one, and before long he had his unsuspecting ingénue nude and horizontal on his couch, holy fingers arousing previously unimagined passions. Soon they were riotously en flagrant délit, her screams of pleasure echoing off the cold stone walls. What did she expect of him? To abandon the priesthood and all his accumulated power and prestige for a horny teenage girl who believed she was in love? And with a bishop, no less. Who knows, but neither could he stop abusing her. That the flesh is weak isn't a cliché.

"If God's servants around them masquerading as low-level priests—and I mean those pale creatures who creep through the dank corridors on silent sandals—were aware of anything immoral they kept it among themselves. More likely, the bishop made a practice of performing these rites on troubled young women, and the disturbance they heard was merely the expulsion of another demon. Who knows the reasons for their silence? You can't decipher the motives of true believers. Anyhow, news didn't escape the Cathédrale grounds, and the bishop's private chambers remained sanctified, in word if not in deed.

"Then the inevitable happened. A miniscule seed injected into Mademoiselle Philipot's belly took root and a fruit began to grow.

One month passed, then two. At three months the degree of ripening was impossible to hide. Sobbing mournfully, Mademoiselle Philipot confessed to her mother the truth about the nature of those confessions to the bishop, how the guidance had been passed and received while confessor and seeker lay with Mademoiselle's legs spread, eagerly receiving the turgid, holy member of God's earthly representative."

My feet had turned numb, and I scrunched back in my chair. I could only say, "How extraordinary."

"But the story doesn't end there," Révigny said, "and what we shall be dealing with at trial is the aftershock."

"Meaning what?" I said, my mind still dazed by the information revealed just now. What more could there be?

"More pointedly, who knows what? We may presume that the bishop and the three members of the Philipot family know about the sordid affair. If any of the household staff has been included such knowledge is irrelevant for our purposes. The important question is how much—if anything—the bishop has told his judicial vicar, which we can probably educe as the trial proceeds through its various stages. In addition, we can be sure that no one suspects the depth of our knowledge."

"I said, "You mentioned the narrative is still playing out. What did you mean?"

"The trial, of course. What I've revealed occurred several months ago. Mischief called, and while skulking around in various guises I heard every conversation between Monsieur Philipot and the bishop and also those exclusively within the Philipot's family, including several from which Mademoiselle was excluded. Obviously, decisions were being made that would affect her, but over which she would have no control. There were lots of words thrown around, not a few heated and tearful. Monsieur and Madame Philipot were terribly concerned about their family's reputation and how the scandal might be glossed over, or at least minimized. The bishop had risked his own reputation and future in the Church, and this bothered him greatly. Although unlikely, he could be charged in a court of his peers of breaking his vow of celibacy, in addition to deflowering a virgin. At worst, he could be banished from the Church. Fortunately, he has a compatriot in Paris, a bishop who survived the embarrassment of a similar event years previously when he was a mere priest, his passion having been for a young boy. At any rate, he had been 'cured' of this addiction and managed to climb the ranks despite the blemish on his record. He meets clandestinely with Autun's bishop, helping devise a strategy they hope preserves his rank and limits punishment to exile in some bleak département in the north.

"Mademoiselle's child, a son, was born in the midst of this strife, by which time she no longer resided in Autun but had been moved out of sight to the main house at the pig farm. Two women from that household staff attended her and the baby, and Madame visited occasionally. No doubt her coachman knows but has been sworn to silence. Monsieur and Madame Philipot's plan was eventually to adopt the child, claiming it to be an orphaned nephew of Monsieur's whose parents had drowned in a shipwreck on some distant coast. If necessary, they agreed to wait until he reached an age of two years so the tale would seem believable; in other words, they would be spared explaining how a tiny baby survived a shipwreck. More than half the children born in France die in their first year, and the Philipots and the bishop continued praying together fervently asking God to gather this one into his arms soon, as befitting a poor little bastard."

"And the daughter?" I said. "What were their plans for her?"

"Ah, the daughter." Révigny made an effort to look resolute. "With the bishop's clandestine assistance arrangements were made for her to enter a convent at a remote location in Bordeaux and spend the rest of her life atoning for her sin by praying and mopping the cloister floors. No more lacy parasols and silk slippers."

Révigny leaned back in his chair and crossed his arms. His eyes were flashing red, a guarantee that more was coming, much more.

I refilled our cups and scooted to the edge of my chair once again and let my legs dangle freely, now that the feeling in my feet had returned. "And how does all this affect us?"

"Cogently, my friend. One day while Mademoiselle's baby was sleeping in its bassinette at the pig farm a sow belonging to Monsieur Philipot's newly acquired herd came along and ate it. This is the same sow I shall be prosecuting for homicide and you will defend."

MONDAY MAY 12TH—MADAME CHASSENÉE'S COACH DESCRIBED; THE PROCEEDING FORMALLY OPENS; MEMBERS OF THE COURT ARE INTRODUCED; THE JUDICIAL VICAR OUTLINES THE COMING LEGAL PROCEEDING; RÉVIGNY SUMMARIZES FRENCH PIG TRIALS TO DATE

❦

I MENTIONED EARLIER HOW I WELCOMED the tribunal (or trial) about to begin, in part because it relieved me of spending time with my wife, but I had forgotten the influence of her coach now that it was part of our lives. She was no longer confined to the estate but free to travel as she wished. Madame became as attached to this rattling composite of iron and wood as some women are inseparable from a lapdog, horse, or lover. Her life now revolved around planning trips to visit friends and neighbors throughout the countryside and her relatives at Autun. What had been the occasional familial visit to town became monthly excursions and stays extending several days. It seems there was nothing more rewarding than being seen sitting like royalty looking out at the unfortunate bourgeoisie hoofing through the slop while she rode airily above it. A major highlight was passing Madame Philipot coming from the opposite direction in her own machine of conveyance and having the pleasure of seeing who could tip her nose higher while looking askance as if unaware of the other. Although I would be staying at the inn for the duration of the proceeding, it would not be unusual to encounter Madame while going about my daily business.

Considering how our lives have been altered by this contraption, a description of its arrival at the estate and its stunning effect on Madame are worth recounting. It came mud-spattered and filled with spare parts, but Aufrey went to work with cloths and buckets of water, aided by François and Alvin. Within hours the machine was restored to pristine condition and the horses that pulled it were washed and curried. Even their harnesses and traces had been cleaned, dried, and oiled. The spare wheels and other parts were stored in an alcove off a stall now modified into a weatherproof garage.

The craftsmanship was astonishing. The upholstery smelled of new leather and citron mingled with a faint scent of exotic woods from tropical Africa. Madame's given name had been inlaid in ivory on the dark mahogany panel facing the seat and also embroidered on the pillows and lap rugs. Every detail was thoughtful and elegant.

Madame, who had denied herself the experience of seeing the coach arrive, fearing, I suppose, disappointment, now descended the stairs of the manor house to the circular driveway trailed by the housekeeping staff. After fixing eyes on the object of her dreams she clasped her hands as if in prayer and started to weep, a new and extraordinary experience for us all, no doubt herself included. Aufrey, dressed in a clean coachman's outfit, doffed his hat, bowed, and opened the door.

Madame stepped inside and immediately swooned on seeing her name, stunned by the olfactory stimuli that must have stirred the quartet of black hairs on the end of her nose to vibrating like tuning forks. She let out a groan and toppled over onto the seat, unseeing eyes fixed on the ceiling. Aufrey and I rushed to her aid. Her eyes had rolled into her head, revealing only white sclera, and her mouth was foaming. She began to moan, softly at first, then with increasing intensity. Then as quickly as she had fallen over she sat up and flashed a toothless smile broader than any I had ever seen on her face, a happy, almost angelic smile. It was short-lived, of course, like any tenuous link of Madame's disposition with the realm of angels, although her infatuation with her new possession has never wavered.

A week had gone by since Révigny and I checked into the inn and received copies of the pre-trial documents sent over by the bishop. They contained nothing novel or out of order. Révigny's spying had revealed the bishop in a new light, and we vowed to stay alert to any unusual wrinkles that could affect the outcome as matters moved forward. Did the bishop have a plan? If events followed the usual course the sow would be tried and executed with only local fanfare, offering relief and closure to the Philipot family, a result no different than if the matter had been deferred by protocol to civil court. The bishop's insistence on retaining control under a canonical umbrella was puzzling. Were we in the middle of a conspiracy? If so, was the judicial vicar a co-conspirator of the bishop's or as ignorant of his personal situation as we supposedly were?

Révigny had been correct that night during one of our conversations in the tavern. It was during the year of grace 1508. The rat tribunal was then in progress, and he dismissed the notion that he and I were competitors. The outcome of such proceedings, he claimed, is preordained, and we and the rest of the court are just actors in a play. Every drama requires adversaries, and in being more staged than real neither side either wins or loses. The important element was to stage a good performance by vigorously arguing our respective sides in windy, erudite performances for the gallery's entertainment. After all, we were being paid decently and enjoying ourselves. Révigny had received a temporary reprieve from Hell and I from Madame, Hell's earthly equivalent. What else mattered?

Just as the Cathédrale bells stopped ringing the liturgical hour of terce the clerk of the court stood and officially opened the proceeding. He announced that the trial would be judged by His Grace, who rose grandly attired in a white robe. The defendant was the sow in the dock accused of homicide, having murdered a child of three months of age, or thereabouts, and eaten parts of his body sufficient to cause death. The child was thought to have been a foundling, no persons claiming to be the parents having come forward. At the time of the incident—near the liturgical hour of sext on the 10th of April, year of grace 1511—he had been under care of the household staff at a pig farm east of Autun owned by Monsieur Jean Philipot. The child had been lying in his bassinette on the lawn when the sow came along and attacked him while the caretaker's eyes were averted, showing him no mercy. The perpetrator then was seen running away and later identified, arrested, and restrained by field workers who rushed to the scene after hearing the caretaker's cries.

As in the trial of the rats three years before, a long table had been set up on the stand in the open-air arena known as the Théâtre Romain and facing the spectators occupying ancient stone bleachers stepping up a berm. The clerk's desk and chair were set off to the right of the stand. A few meters in front, between the stand and bleachers, stood the dock, modified into a sty sufficient to hold several adult pigs, although at present containing only the one large sow on trial. Beside it a witness chair faced the stand.

By protocol the judicial vicar introduced the clerk of the court, who had just spoken, and explained that the clerk's duties included keeping the calendar, recording minutes of the proceeding, and assembling the minutes into later reports for entry into the official court record. After introducing Révigny sitting beside him to his right and me to his left he began reading to the gallery from a prepared speech outlining in general terms how the trial would be conducted, a tedious but not uncommon prelude.

"Trials and the implementation of laws provide a social framework of egalitarianism. They offer a standardized mechanism that binds a community, sustaining social equilibrium by elevating order over chaos. When preceded by adequate publicity and conducted openly and fairly animal trials give citizens a chance to express diverse opinions articulated on a common moral stage.

"Any trial's purpose is to adjudicate a dispute between biased opponents, an impossible task in the absence of a narrative; that is, a story having a beginning, middle, and end. Storytelling is ingrained in our humanity and serves as the bridge linking us with other humans and the world at large. A trial represents a ritualized contest between two narratives for the purpose of deciding which is more compelling. In acting out the narrative, lawyers for plaintiff and defendant present different sides of the same story on behalf of their clients. Each side bolsters its viewpoint through witness testimonies, documents, and other forms of evidence, the objective being to assemble a story that sounds convincing while attacking and disparaging the other side's version as false. In the end the blindfolded and unbiased Lady Justice, personified as a civil or ecclesiastical judge, weighs the relative merits of the two sides and educes a fair verdict based on which way he sees the scales tip.

"Domestic animals and humans tried for homicide proceed through the legal system in a sequence of stages: arrest, formal accusation, and imprisonment. A judge and two lawyers are appointed, one for the prosecution, the other for the defense. The defendant appears in court where the respective lawyers present evidence of guilt and innocence and plead their cases. Because animals can't—or won't—answer questions directly, or at least respond intelligibly, we strap them on the rack to test their innocence, the exception being if the accused was actually caught in the act of committing the crime, as attested by witnesses. In such situations guilt has automatically been demonstrated.

"The rules for humans are the same. Why? Although blessed with the capacity of speech, humans often lie. Animals, being dumb and irrational are incapable of telling lies. When asked to confess, an animal on the rack squeals, brays, howls, or emits the sound of guilt assigned to its kind at creation. Animals are always truthful under torture, and the cries squeezed from them can be interpreted confidently as confessions, the logic being that a truly innocent animal or human declares as much and offers evidence before torture, hoping to avoid it. If unable to speak French the accused's lawyer offers testimony on his client's behalf. The process of obtaining confessions of guilt from animals is both reasonable and foolproof.

"Having obtained a confession a guilty verdict by the judge follows, and the accused typically is sentenced to death. At a final hearing the defendant stands before the court to hear the verdict read aloud in Latin. The mode of execution depends on the crime. Animals declared guilty of homicide are usually hanged or burned but occasionally buried alive. For lesser crimes the accused animal theoretically can be released under supervision of its owner, scourged, incarcerated, or banished from the community with the proviso that guilt had not been confessed under torture. I personally fail to see how this last contingency is possible in the case of an animal, considering the noises they make represent *de facto* confessions.

"There can be no higher appeal of decisions handed down by ecclesiastical courts. A verdict from a secular court may be appealed directly to the king by submitting a Letter of Remission and accompanying Pardon Tale through proper channels. The latter is the suppliant's written narrative presenting mitigating circumstances of the case and reasons for deserving acquittal. To my knowledge an animal has never petitioned the king as a suppliant for the obvious reason that they can't speak French and thus communicate their thoughts to a clerk. I am now ready to hear arguments."

Most of this monologue went unnoticed. Many of the spectators were already inebriated, having arrived early with food and drink to better enjoy the spectacle. A fistfight between peasants erupted in front of the stand just as His Grace finished speaking, and the bailiff's men moved immediately to break it up with truncheons. The trial had only started, but vendors were already moving through the crowd selling wine, beer, and religious trinkets. Musicians, clowns, jugglers, and mimes had also sniffed out a nascent festival and appeared with the speed of blowflies to a newly dead corpse. Shrieking children ran everywhere. Beggars, pigs, and dogs moved through the crowd at knee level begging and scavenging for scraps, receiving indiscriminate kicks and curses for their efforts. Only the sheep and goats grazing among the stones and bleachers stayed calm, lifting their heads now and then to look around with vacuous indifference.

Révigny asked and received permission to speak. He rose from his chair slowly, importantly, straightening his robe and clearing his throat. He grasped a fold of his robe in each hand and let his elbows hang. In this ostentatious posture he began to talk sonorously. "Before anything else, let's put to rest the matter of precedent about holding animals accountable for crimes against humans. Such trials in the Christian era date at least from the year of grace 824 when moles were excommunicated and ordered to leave the Valley of Aosta, Italy. Domestic beasts of many kinds have been charged and convicted successfully for killing Christians: horses, mules, donkeys, bulls, oxen, goats, dogs . . . the list goes on.

"And pigs, of course. In fact, mainly pigs, who are unique in murdering humans for the purpose of eating them. The others kill out of fear or anger against mankind generally, but of the domestic beasts none except the porcine race has an inherent, insatiable yearning for the taste human flesh, particularly the tender meat and sweet blood of children. This simply can't be denied in the face of evidence gathered over centuries in France alone. I shall cite some examples for doubters.

"A brief historical overview of these events is both interesting and necessary to lay proper groundwork for prosecuting the sow presently in the dock. Therefore, I intend to present details of several pig trials held in France of which history has left a record. Many, perhaps most, have involved the murder of humans by pigs, although other crimes have been charged and the defendants convicted. For instance, the year of grace 1394 saw a sow hanged at Mortaign for eating a consecrated wafer and thus committing sacrilege.

"My homicidal examples will be pigs exclusively, not bulls, dogs, and other domesticated creatures known on occasion to turn rogue and attack mankind. I shall not delve deeply into these cases but simply mention several as proof of precedent, a porky smorgasbord, so to speak, with a tiny taste of each." He looked at the spectators and smiled despite no one having noticed his joke. "Berriat-Saint-Prix, the eminent jurist, assembled and reviewed proceedings from several trials of homicidal pigs from the 12th and 13th centuries, occasionally providing information on their sentencing and the costs incurred when such information was available in the record. I recommend that scholars consult his works directly." This was an obvious dig at the illiterate rabble gathered around.

Révigny paused to look down at his notes spread on the table. "In the year of grace 1266 a pig was executed for killing a child at Fontenay-aux-Roses outside Paris, and two years later in 1268 an adolescent pig was arrested by justice officers at the monastery of Sainte-Geneviève, Paris, after having eaten a child. The culprit was burned. Unfortunately, no details of this case survive, just a record of its occurrence. And in the year of grace 1386 the judge of Falaise condemned a sow for tearing away the arm and face of a child who subsequently died of his wounds. This trial was peculiar in several ways, and I shall say more about it later. On the 18th of April, year of Grace 1499, the foster parents of a young boy named Gilon of about five and a half years, or thereabouts, were fined eighteen francs and imprisoned until the fine had been paid to the bailiff of the abbey of Josaphat, commune of Sèves near Chartres. Their crime was not taking proper care of the lad, who had been killed by a wandering pig. The pig was hanged.

"In rare cases some of the accused are declared innocent and released into custody of their owners. A trial held in the year of grace 1457 is unusual for such an outcome. Six piglets were shown leniency by the court of Savigny based on their young age. A sow attended by her litter had been caught en flagrant délit while killing and intending to eat Jehan Martin, a boy thought to be about five years. All were imprisoned, tried for murder in front of the seigneurial justice of Savigny, and found guilty. The piglets were released on bond into custody of their owner. However, resenting the social stigma of the murder and trial and fearing the piglets might commit crimes on their own, he relinquished them to the court a month or so later. The sow was sentenced to death and hanged upside-down from a gallows. Her offspring were pardoned despite having been covered in human blood at the time of capture, in part because the mother had set a bad example of parenting, and they were declared too young to make independent decisions. Helping seal the sow's fate was her demeanor. Throughout the trial she squealed and grunted incessantly in the dock, causing considerable distraction to the judge, bailiff, and lawyers.

"Another example of leniency took place after a homicide on the 5th of September, year of grace 1379. As two herds of pigs were foraging together near the town of Saint-Marchel-le-Jeussey, three old sows suddenly stopped rooting and as if on a demonic signal attacked and trampled the swineherd's son to death. His father had left him in charge, and he had been teasing some of the pigs. The sows were promptly arrested by citizens who rushed to the scene. They were incarcerated immediately and held under guard for trial. The matter seemed straightforward, except for witnesses describing how the rest of the swine milled around the crime scene squealing, bumping one another, and behaving aggressively. In the end all remaining individuals of both herds were arrested as accomplices to homicide.

"At the trial the lawyer for the defense stated that executing the three sows known to be guilty should be sufficient deterrence for the rest against further attacks on humans. Philip the Bold, Duke of Burgundy, serving as civil judge and who earlier had condemned all the pigs to death, was convinced by this argument. In addition, Friar Humbert de Poutiers, owner of both herds and worried about being left pigless, appealed to Philip requesting clemency for all except the three murderers. The duke honored his petition and declared the other pigs exonerated. He made the decision official in a letter de grace pour en faire raison et justice en la manière qu'il appartient (a letter of grace to make justice right and fair as it should be), ordering execution of just the three convicted sows. Without the duke's reprieve all would have been executed. Use of the rack with the three condemned pigs was unnecessary because their crime had been witnessed by human observers; confession would have been superfluous. The three sows subsequently went to the gallows; the other pigs were released with a stern warning. Thus, pardons in animal crimes are rare but do occur, to which these two cases attest.

"Costs to the taxpayers of trying and executing pigs can be considerable, no different from those involving humans. Following trial and prior to execution, prisoners, whether human or pig, are paraded through the streets in carts or sometimes dragged with ropes. Renting a cart, driver, and draft animal adds another cost to the community. I've personally examined two receipts dated the 9th of January, year of grace 1386, the first submitted to Guiot de Montfort, notary at Falaise, by the executioner and totaling ten sous and ten deniers in payment for dragging, then hanging, according to local civil laws a sow of about three years, or thereabouts, who had eaten the face of the son of Jonnet le Maux while he lay in his cradle and was about three months of age. The child died of his wounds. This second receipt was submitted by the executioner to Regnaud Rigault, Vicomte de Falaise. The executioner had been summoned from Paris, a considerable distance of fifty-five leagues. No mention is made of his travel expenses. In an appended note the executioner declares his satisfaction with the said sums and in good faith now takes leave of the king and viscount. I shall say more about this peculiar trial at a later time.

"In the year of grace 1393 an executioner named Niquando traveled more than seven leagues from Bescançon, for which he was paid a salary of sixty sous for the hanging of a pig and seven more for travel expenses. In still another case an executioner having been summoned by the bailiff and royal procureur rode nearly ten leagues from Paris to Mantes to hang a pig at a total cost of fifty-four sous.

"Guilty pigs are usually hanged from fourches located on the outskirts of towns and villages and visible to passers-by. If a community doesn't have one the victim is dragged or carted to the closest properly equipped bailliage. In the year of grace 1317 a pig convicted of murdering a child at Bouffémont near Paris was dragged nearly seven leagues to Noisy-le-Grand and there hanged from its fourches. Carpenters were hired if the fourches needed repair or reinforcing prior to the execution. I know of a case at Pontailler where the task required five carpenters working steadily for two days. About their salary there is no record.

"Rental of a cart to transport the condemned animal and a beast of burden to pull it these days typically costs six sous. For ropes to bind and drag an adult pig add two sous, a suitable hanging rope ten deniers, and new gloves for the executioner perhaps two deniers. The gloves have special meaning. After a guilty verdict the hangman, or bourreau, known jokingly as maître des hautes oeuvres (master of high works) is notified and asked to appear. In addition to his fee and travel expenses he requires new gloves to complete the metaphor of carrying out justice with clean hands while incurring no personal guilt for his actions.

"Add to these expenses the prisoner's board while incarcerated. In the year of grace 1408 Toustain Pincheon, geôlier of the royal prisons of Pont de Larche, when submitting an invoice for having attended his prisoners, listed a number of men and one pig, the latter incarcerated from the 21st of June to the 17th of July. All received equally the 'king's bread' at daily cost to the Crown of nineteen sous and six deniers.

"This," said Révigny, "concludes my argument for validation of the upcoming prosecution." He turned and bowed to His Grace and me.

"And it also concludes the court's business for today," said His Grace. "An excellent summary, Monsieur Révigny. Court will convene again tomorrow at terce." He picked up the gavel and struck the sounding box.

I had just entered the tavern after checking on François and Alvin to find Révigny already sitting at our table. Before taking my chair I signaled the innkeeper to bring our cups and a flagon of wine. "How did you accumulate that information?" I said. "Your erudition in this arcane area of legal history is remarkable."

Révigny had been scanning the room. He turned suddenly to face me. There was again that slight delay in the brimstone smoke's movement inside the upper part of the cocoon as if deciding whether to refill the space left by his head's abrupt turn or stay where it was and defy the physics of drag and turbulence.

"Don't be too impressed, my friend. We have it all logged into Hell's library. The only bottleneck occurs in the drudgery of finding, retrieving, and organizing it. As you know, many learned persons spend eternity howling in Hell's fires, some of them educated clergy condemned for lying, thievery, gambling, sodomy, greed, pride, and other sins both venial and mortal. They make excellent clerks, these fallen priests and even bishops, cardinals, and popes. Being offered the light duty of gathering and organizing information despite aiding Satan grants a temporary reprieve from the eternal flames that burn hot but never consume. They volunteer with alacrity to the point of acknowledging their envy and deceit by slandering one another in competing to be chosen. It's a joy to see these hypocritical men of God reduced to their immoral, obsequious selves.

"One of Hell's advantages is that good help isn't hard to find. Such educated persons arrive daily, weeping and hand-wringing and loudly lamenting fate, and so it will continue until some enlightened being discovers and implements a cure for stupidity. That could only be God, of course, but He evidently prefers humanity in its present twisted state.

"Hell also houses some quite famous personages, Barthélemy. I'm sure you'd find discussions with many of them fascinating. Genghis Khan . . ."

"I never pictured Genghis Khan in Hell," I said, "but where else would he be?"

"You interrupted me. I started to say that Genghis Khan and all other evil pagans are automatically excluded. Damnation ought to be ashamed because their presence would enliven the atmosphere. But just in the last century we gained a true celebrity who had broken dramatically from the Christian ranks. That would be Vlad the Impaler, noted for driving sharpened stakes into the rectums of his victims, then standing the stakes upright and watching the impaled struggle in anguish. The pain is much greater than being burned, which is over quickly once the fat combusts, or nailed to a cross. According to one tale Vlad ordered two monks impaled, and when their donkey brayed pitifully at seeing its masters so treated the donkey was impaled too.

"No, we have a restricted clientele down in Hell. Our citizens comprise fallen Christians and atheists who rejected Christianity." He spread his arms as if metaphorically encompassing limbo, extending them to twice their normal length in the manner of an octopus and setting them to undulating seductively. In this pose he sang in falsetto a nonsensical tune about something somewhere over the rainbow. The melody rose a full octave from the first to the second syllable of the opening word. What came after was a string of notes so primitive in rhythm and inflection it might have been the mating call of an unknown bird God created and then rejected from the avian tribe for lacking talent. Révigny is a very strange being even for a demon.

Tuesday May 13th—Révigny Presents
the Reasons for Animal Trials; Chassenée Rebuts

⌬

COURT RECONVENED AT THE APPOINTED HOUR. Again, Révigny asked and was granted permission to speak. He rose, notes in hand. "Animal trials serve any number of functions. I shall briefly review the three most important in no particular order and end with several of lesser relevance. First, these trials reinforce mankind's control over the lower animals and restore balance within God's hierarchy. A pig who murders a Christian challenges man's exalted station at the apex of all earthly life. Homicide is simultaneously a sin and a crime whether committed by animal or human, although only humans may be excused for homicide under certain conditions. Legally sanctioned execution is one example, war another, and so are self-defense and avenging the adultery of a wife or daughter by murdering her and the lover. Guilt is not even an issue if the woman and her paramour are caught en flagrant délit.

"The jurist Jean Papon lists thirteen such extenuating circumstances, under none of which an animal qualifies for exemption. The framework of the Universe has been ordained by God. The hierarchy of His devising and divination is not for us to question or attempt to change. The puny laws we write and enforce are backed by biblical mandates. Revolt against them, whether by humans or their domestic animals, disturbs the equilibrium of the Christian world and in all instances must be suppressed.

"Animal trials also serve the function of deterrence, which takes two forms: avoidance of recidivism by former criminals released back into society, and prevention of similar crimes by future perpetrators. A pig known to have committed homicide becomes a serial murderer if it kills again after release. In the public at large deterrence is effective only if potential criminals take heed and as a direct result refrain from carrying out future crimes. However, deterrence plays no role in the case of an incarcerated pig or human convicted of homicide and sentenced to die. In such situations the possibility of recidivism ends at the moment of death. Whether humans or animals are deterred by public executions of the proven guilty remains speculative.

"We can list revenge—specifically retribution—as a third function of these trials. In legal terms this is *lex talionis,* or the law of retaliation, in the vernacular an eye for an eye. A spectacular example involved the sow executed at Falaise in the year of grace 1386, alluded to earlier in my overview of pig trials in France. This event was clearly an act of *lex talionis.* How so? Because while still alive the sow was mutilated in the foreleg and head, then her snout was cut off as she squealed and replaced with a mask of a human face. She was then dressed in men's clothing—jacket, breeches, haut-de-chausses, and gloves on her front hoofs—before being dragged into the public square and hanged upside-down. The peculiar wounds inflicted prior to execution were the same as those she had inflicted on her victim. Her body was evidently maimed and dressed to *re*-present the male child she had killed. Are we to think this was a vicarious exorcism meant to erase memory of the event by *re*-enactment? Who can say after the passing of time, but its memorable nature suggests the opposite, now forever fixed in the annals of judicial history.

"Other, more obscure functions come to mind, such as the maintenance of social order, which includes not only human societies but those of domestic animals over which humans exert control. Still another is the putative erasure of painful memories, especially in homicide cases. A sense that justice has been carried out helps heal the community.

"To summarize, animal trials and subsequent punishments are necessary, not specifically for retribution against individual animals but to restore justice. We see this in the wording of verdicts handed down, such as 'we wish to proceed as justice and reason desire and demand.' Homicide by an animal is an unnatural act and disrupts the hierarchy of the Universe; that is, contrasted with humans killing other humans, which has been an integral part of our heritage since Cain and Able. They help dampen the general fear of lawlessness felt by peasantry and nobility alike. God's order must be sustained at whatever cost, and human laws are simply the trickle-down extension of those ordained by God." Révigny took his chair looking pleased with himself.

I mentioned to His Grace that I wished to comment.

He nodded. "Proceed, monsieur."

I rose to speak for the first time, tugging down my robe so it draped a little straighter over the sharp curve of my belly. Révigny's talking points were common knowledge in civil and canonical legal circles, and I could rebut them without having prepared an argument beforehand.

"Many great thinkers have sought to untangle the logic behind executing pigs who eat children. Perhaps punishment is merely ceremonial, meant to reinforce the yawning power disparity dividing vulnerable citizens from the invincibility of Church and Crown. If so, its delivery in a public forum exposes the consequences of crime to as many people as possible, young and old, inducing awe and terror in the observers and heightening the asymmetry of power between citizens and the law, whether ecclesiastical or civil. In a more abstract sense a crime, being an anomalous act, indeed upsets the social order; perhaps public displays of punishment serve to 'reconstitute' and heal the community.

"Executions aren't the only public spectacles. There are noncapital punishments as well, although their efficacy in punishing pigs seems doubtful. Milder forms meant to cause embarrassment and humiliation in civilized societies like France include posting public notices of fines, amende honorable sèche (publicly begging forgiveness from the offended party), and putting law-breakers in stocks in public squares or making them wear straw hats and sit backward astride donkeys while paraded through the community. Harsher, nonlethal penalties we enlightened cultures advocate include imprisonment, branding, scourging, mutilation, temporary or permanent banishment, and life sentences pulling oars in the king's galleys.

"From Monsieur Révigny's list I suspect that deterrence seems most satisfactory to the majority. Does it work? Only if the convicted pig and its compatriots understand that a crime has been committed, which is doubtful. Has anyone ever confronted a pig, posed a question to it, and waited in expectation of an answer? Only a dimwit. Has a pig ever knelt in public and offered amende honorable sèche to a family whose child it has just eaten? Not to my knowledge. We might fine pigs for lesser crimes, except they have no money. Could a pig be embarrassed into changing its ways if we posted a public notice describing its unlawful behavior? Unlikely. If pigs are indeed moral creatures we should also expect them to attend Mass with the rest of us and afterward confess their sins. 'Father, I have sinned,' a pig might whisper in the confessional. 'I've wallowed in my own shit and fornicated in public.' The priest listening from the other side of the curtain says calmly, 'God forgives you, young porker. Say ten hail Marys and don't do it again.'" The gallery, itself a restless composite animal, chuckled and hissed.

"If deterrence is the principal objective of punishment, where's the evidence that it reduces the incidence of the crime it was intended to deter? No one in modern times can say with assurance that it does, and I doubt that great thinkers of the future will know either. The passing of centuries is an ineffective tool for unwinding true dilemmas. And if punishment as deterrence actually works does its efficacy depend on making the intensity proportionate with severity of the crime? If so, we're assuming that harsh penalties are greater deterrents than moderate ones, although if this were the case then death sentences for capital murder would have extinguished homicide from both animal and human cultures millenniums ago, and yet it remains, rampant as ever.

"What lesson can we take away? Among learned men of our modern age the consensus to parents seems to be, don't leave your babies and young children untended so they fall prey to wandering pigs. And to farmers, keep control of your livestock so they can't injure and kill people. However, I see a third possibility, which I again direct at parents: don't eat children because you see what happens to pigs when they do this. They go to the gallows!" The spectators exploded in laughter.

"But here's the problem: if punishment is truly didactic, how does the public execution of a pig instill visceral fear of punishment and subsequent deterrence of the crime leading to it by other pigs? At exactly whom is the lesson directed? Or, say, when a human prisoner escapes and an effigy is punished in his place? Or when a human prisoner dies before his sentence can be carried out and the corpse is punished anyway? In the year of grace 897 Pope Stephen VI had the corpse of Pope Formosus, a predecessor by then eight months dead, set on a throne and tried for perjury. Who or what is deterred from committing future crimes other than bunches of straw and decaying bodies, both dressed in old clothes?

"As Monsieur Révigny states, animal trials portray the accused as 'human' in a representative context; that is, a surrogate for mankind, a higher elevation than any animal deserves in God's earthly hierarchy. What he omits is that such trials simultaneously keep the accused sufficiently 'animalistic' to be prosecuted, convicted, and executed for crimes against mankind, notably homicide. Because animal trials are identical to those in which humans are prosecuted they demonstrate man's parallel inhumanity to animals and fellow humans. But God's hierarchy is confirmed in the Holy Writ. Biblical auctoritates are unassailable, so I'm blocked from offering anything further in this regard.

"I argue that deterrence, Monsieur Révigny's proposed second function and the effectiveness of which he leaves open, can work only if other members of the species pay attention and absorb the lesson. It likewise projects to any humans thinking of committing a similar crime. Stated differently, if this is how we treat pigs, don't think your own future trial will be any different if you and Madame Truye on trial in the dock were to switch places. In the case of animals deterrence tacitly presumes the accused understands French and agrees in a general sense with Christian moral and cultural values. We make the additional assumption that an animal accused of a crime is capable of ethical and rational decisions or it wouldn't be there. And all these necessary precursors further presume that the animal on trial, a pig in this case, is Catholic. In truth, we know only that pigs are 'catholic' in the dietary sense, accepting any morsel of food regardless of its origin.

"The courts make use of both retributive and consequentialist justification for their verdicts and sentencing. The former is backward-looking. The latter looks ahead and means to reduce future transgressions; in other words, to deter. Consequentialist justification has three benefits. First, incapacitation through physical restraint, by which I mean imprisonment; second, specific deterrence directed at the criminal to prevent recidivism, for example, parole with restrictions; and third, general deterrence directed toward the populace for prevention of similar crimes. If punishment culminates in execution then retributive justification has collapsed into incapacitation alone, any possibility of recidivism and deterrence having been eliminated. How so? Logically, the dead can't commit future crimes. Animal trials usually end in execution, never incapacitation or specific deterrence. As I shall argue, whether deterrence alters the behavior of either animals or humans is unproven, as Monsieur Révigny has just verified in his opening statement.

"When executing a pig the purpose clearly is punishment for crimes already committed against mankind or there would be no accusation and no trial. Any trial is predicated on a historical event; in other words, the accused is on trial for something that has already happened. If the verdict is meant to deter, this presumes a direct species-specific effect, in this instance that hanging the offending pig will serve as a lesson to other pigs against devouring children. But where's the evidence of efficacy?

"*Isaiah*, chapter eleven verse six tells us, *And the wolf also shall dwell with the lamb, and the leopard shall lie down with the kid. . . .* But has anyone ever witnessed scenes like these? Remember, much of the Holy Writ reveals itself in fables and parables. Wishes and hopes are inadequate substitutes for actual evidence that punishing a criminal prevents future crimes by others. In truth, such proof has not been forthcoming, meaning it does not presently exist. And if the court's main objective is punishment of the accused for upsetting God's earthly hierarchy then deterrence is questionably effective at best. Is this a notable deficiency in the system? Probably not, although neither is it a confirmed verity. Not surprisingly, citizens of modern France seem more concerned with punishing past behavior than preventing future recurrences, and fear of lawlessness is of more immediate concern.

"So, Monsieur Révigny, if a principal objective of the law is to teach the pigs of Saône-et-Loire that death is the penalty for eating our children, how will news reach them and so become a lasting deterrent? I don't see any pigs sitting attentively in the gallery absorbing this lesson and looking suitably contrite, although dozens regularly wander among us disrupting the proceeding with their squealing and snuffling. I count four hefty porkers presently blocking passage between the gallery and dock, but they seem uninterested in my admonishments, intent instead on scavenging food dropped by gawkers and vendors. Is it possible they don't understand French? Perhaps the tribunal should be conducted bilingually. By chance, does my learned adversary speak with a porked tongue? If failing to address Madame Truye and her colleagues in swine vernacular we might try Pig Latin." At this the spectators clapped and cheered.

I waited for the disturbance to dissipate, then continued. "Rehabilitation isn't even a consideration, as it isn't with humans.

Incarceration and torture serve only to punish, not alter future behavior, and execution is the ultimate expression of both, surely in this life, the only one any animal or human has yet experienced. In secular trials of animals the accused is nearly always executed. Nor is deodand especially useful, being limited in this case to Madame Truye's market value as pork on the hoof.

"Monsieur Révigny's suggestion that trying and convicting an animal has a healing and soporific effect on the community, I might dissent. Gratian, the Italian canonist and author of *Decretum Gratiani*, in the vernacular *Gratian's Decree*, agrees with Monsieur Révigny. He too believes such trials are necessary so people can forget the traumatizing act that brings them about. I have doubts. A sensational trial followed by public execution of the condemned tends to promote memories, not amnesia. Certainly, the sight of the mutilated sow dressed as a man and hanged upside-down at Falaise was fixed permanently in the memories of all who witnessed that event.

"Try to answer this question: why do we maim pigs and dress them as humans to then execute them for being inhumane? For that matter, why do we dress human corpses before interring them? And if we dress a sow, why not in women's clothes? Is a sow not female? Perhaps women's attire of suitable size couldn't be found in time. Finding men's clothes of appropriate fit undoubtedly would be easier considering the many overfed clerics waddling among us who regularly donate their everyday wear to charity when becoming too porky." Again, cheers and laughter from the gallery.

In the tavern Révigny said, "I liked your 'porked tongue' reference. A little play on words." He stuck out his forked tongue, the ends tipped with miniature serpent heads that peered around with ruby eyes and their own flicking tongues, looking for something to bite. I scooted back in my chair, hoping to be out of range, but Révigny's tongue lengthened frighteningly, coming almost within reach of my face.

"Stop!" I said, and the tongue retracted.

Révigny refilled our cups and continued as if nothing had happened. "As I've always maintained, we four—prosecutor, advocate, judge, and accused—are actors in a play. The true judge and composite of our critics is the gallery. That's who assesses whether the show we provide is sufficiently entertaining and whether the ending meets expectations. Despite pious claims to the contrary our duty isn't to God, Church, and Crown, not even to the law. Our daily duty is performing to the highest standards. We're participants in a life-and-death drama and must faithfully portray our roles. Once delivered to the hanging site the execution becomes the spectacle. After all, *lex talionis*. Don't misunderstand me. A few spectators might actually care. Relatives and friends, perhaps. But the rest come to be entertained, and we must never bore them. To be boring is the worst sin of all for us lawyers. Nothing invigorates the body and stimulates the emotions like a rowdy trial followed by a satisfying execution." Révigny sighed contentedly. He clasped his hands behind his head and smiled at the ceiling.

"Life is a series of linked narratives and shifting scenes, often featuring shifty characters, mostly ourselves. As individuals we're either actors or spectators, the watched or the watching. A play comprises a story with a hero and villain. Bit players fill the empty spaces, create distractions, or serve as moral props. There's often a virgin on the verge of devirginization by the villain. Only the hero can save her hymen, that tiny, meaningless sliver of tissue for which men in their infinite stupidity risk honor, lives, and kingdoms. Will the hero arrive in time to allay penetration by the evil doer? It's all about who's first in the queue, eh? The brave, the strong, the lucky . . . we identify with them according to our hidden perversions. *We are them.*

"Nothing matters in the end except the play and the fact that it happened. Remember these words: *totus mundus agit histrionem,* in the vernacular 'all the world's a stage.' They will someday be posted above the entrance of a famous playhouse in London. Few today in modern France could imagine the English being so advanced. At present they're barely more civilized than the druids dancing on those windswept moors. The Irish, of course, are trapped in an even more primitive state, only lately having mastered the capacity to wobble about on their hindlegs."

Révigny's guffaws culminated in a coughing fit that doubled him over until he disappeared under the table. The coughs finally stopped and his head reappeared. "God-*damn* this brimstone. It's vile and acrid and possibly fatal. Good thing I'm dead. Maybe I'll only last through eternity and succumb afterward."

WEDNESDAY MAY 14TH—RÉVIGNY ARGUES FOR MOVING THE PROCEEDING TO CIVIL COURT; THE JUDICIAL VICAR AND CHASSENÉE DISSENT; CHASSENÉE TOSSES OUT A RED HERRING

RÉVIGNY ASKED AND WAS GRANTED A chance to speak. "In ecclesiastical trials the presiding officer of the court is a judicial vicar or his appointee, either a layman or another cleric trained in canon law and qualified for service as God's representative on Earth in legal matters. In civil trials the presiding court official is a member of the judicial laity. In my opinion, Your Grace, Madame Truye's case belongs in civil court, not here. Pigs are domestic animals, by definition under ownership and control of mankind. Rats, grasshoppers, and other vermin and pests aren't owned by anyone except God and by tradition are tried in ecclesiastical jurisdictions."

The judicial vicar took immediate umbrage. "That's highly presumptuous, monsieur. Are you questioning my authority as a cleric and by extension the Church's? Let's be sure I understand your argument. Because the sow in the dock whom you and Monsieur Chassenée call Madame Truye—which incidentally seems a tautology—is charged with homicide, and because pigs are domestic animals her case is properly a civil matter, unlike situations involving vermin and pests and other bestioles, which fall entirely under God's jurisdiction and can only be anathematized in canonical proceedings, not given death sentences directly by a cleric because we're banned from spilling blood. And sperm, I might add. Is this is your viewpoint?"

"That's correct, Your Grace," said Révigny. "Madame Truye is a domestic pig who until her arrest and incarceration wandered unsupervised among humans on a pig farm outside the city of Autun. She was, and still is, the property of Monsieur Philipot and therefore firmly within the category of chattel, not vermin."

His Grace was becoming agitated. "Because you continue to lobby undeterred for moving the court, I shall demonstrate with finality that your argument is baseless." He gathered some documents and arranged them into order. "On Monday the 12th of May, during your summary of pig trials held in France to date you mentioned *in this court* a certain case adjudicated in the year of grace 1499." He looked at the clerk of the court, who said, "That is correct, Your Grace."

The judicial vicar continued. "I have before me the very text of the decree read aloud to the condemned by the bailiff, the abbey of Josaphat, commune of Sèves. Note that the sentence issued involved a collaboration of ecclesiastical and secular jurists. I shall now read it in the vernacular. The original, of course, is in Latin.

> Given the criminal trial made before us at the request of the public prosecutor, abbot, and convent of Josaphat near Chartres, about the death of a child named Gilon, about a year and a half ago, who was killed at age three months by a sow, and, having regard to the instruction of the religious prosecutor of this jurisdiction, has been seen and brought to a close, and with regard to the said pig and for the reasons resulting from the trial we have condemned her to be hanged at the end of the hearing, within the scope of the jurisdiction of the plaintiffs, given under the seal of our bailiwick, the 18th of April, year of grace 1499.

"To refresh the court's memory, including its lawyers assigned to this case, ecclesiastical cases are typically initiated after a specific animal or person accused of a crime formally declares innocence, at which point publicizing the plea becomes the court's principal objective. Local citizens are expected to already know the facts, so investigation and assembling them isn't a court's principal objective, whether civil or canonical. Settlement of disputes through mediation in canonical courts to achieve a spiritual judgment is a reason for initiation of many others. In both situations trial and punishment is not the main purpose of the Church becoming involved in civil crimes.

"So you, Monsieur Révigny, experienced in civil court trials, are apparently concerned that an ecclesiastical court might merely anathematize this sow, a sentence you would consider too light for the crime of homicide. Is this correct?"

Révigny bowed. "We don't deal with anathemas in civil court, as His Grace knows. I think you need to be closer to Heaven than we secular lawyers can manage standing here on level ground with our shoes in mud and pig shit." On hearing this the spectators broke into raucous hoots and laughter.

I quickly gained my feet. It was in my best interest (or rather, my client's) for the case to be tried in canonical court, especially if I could successfully make use of purgation, a line of attack I was keeping secret for the moment. Persons accused of theft, murder, and other capital crimes of a secular nature often fared better in ecclesiastical courts. This was especially so when the accused requested and was granted purgation. In general, clerical judges were more concerned about community harmony than punishment, and leniency (an apology or fine) was a common alternative to harsher sentences. Even when the defendant was declared guilty, consequences ordinarily were lighter compared with civil courts, often no more than public penance.

"I object to Monsieur Révigny's petition to shift the proceeding to a secular setting," I said. "My client and I are perfectly content to be judged by His Grace, known to all as a fair-minded jurist. No one contests that Madame Truye committed homicide. However, her intent was neither malicious nor premeditated, and she should be declared innocent in the same manner as a minor or insane adult, neither of whom would be charged with murder based on lacking *mens rea*, or consciousness of guilt in the vernacular. Madame Truye's mental status, at best, is that of a very young child, or perhaps a backward older child. She has no control or understanding of her thoughts and emotions."

I then threw out a red herring in case either His Grace or Révigny began to suspect my strategy. I feigned indignation, drawing attention to my emotional self and away from my words. I pounded the table and said, "Furthermore, I object to my client being displayed in public during court days. This is highly irregular in trials of domestic animals. The accused is usually jailed out of sight, its prosecution and defense argued by the lawyers. I can only conclude my client is denied this tradition to emphasize her status as an unreasoning brute. Subjecting her to public ridicule and embarrassment can only foster negative bias and act against her possible exoneration. I therefore request that the court apologize to Madame Truye, beg her forgiveness, and return her immediately to the peace and obscurity of her jail cell."

"That isn't going to happen, Monsieur Chassenée," the judicial vicar said. "She's a pig. Please drop the matter and continue with your defense. However, I approve of your willingness to stick with an ecclesiastical tribunal. Therefore, I agree to bend a little and consider certain aspects of canonical philosophy to come into play in the interest of fairness to your client." The judicial vicar smiled slyly, a subtle signal his compromise came with a caveat about to be revealed.

I bowed and said, "Yes, Your Grace," having now been alerted that at least one aspect of the narrative was about to become clear. None of the subtlety had been lost on Révigny, which I deduced instantly when he glanced at me, eyes emitting red pulses. I could only wait. Court was adjourned until the next day.

That evening in the tavern Révigny said, "You realize what His Grace has in store, don't you?"

"Meaning what?"

"The hinted *quid pro quo* in your favor, his willingness to, as he put it, 'bend a little.' He plans to raise the issue of *jejunium sextae* thinking you won't be expecting it. But you and I both expect it. What could be more obvious? Therefore, I intend to raise it myself to keep him off balance. First mention must obviously come from either the prosecution or the putatively unbiased judge; for you to make the point would damage your own case."

"Won't you be damaging yours?"

"Not so much. The matter will arise anyway, and anything that prolongs the tribunal lengthens my stay up here among the mostly living. I'm enjoying myself too much to go back to Hell right now. Anyway, the transportation still isn't what it should be, and the prospect always makes me nervous."

"I don't understand," I said.

"Where do you think the phrase 'bats out of Hell' originated? From peasant shepherds who occasionally witnessed Satan's dark angels bearing dignitaries like me crash-land in their fields on moonlit nights. Bats aren't very aerodynamic when straight-line speed is required. All that flapping and zig-zagging results in unbalanced flight, and eventually we fall to the ground in a heap. Let me tell you, the so-called 'dark angels' are dumber than fence posts. From my standpoint, being dead has certain advantages. For example, I can't be killed, but it does raise hell with my cocoon. I have to lie around waiting for any puncture wounds to anneal then calculate the direction and remaining distance to the target site. If it's a long way I need another lift, which can be troublesome if the angels have dusted themselves off and departed. Besides being stupid they're hopelessly inept at solving problems on their own. In my unfortunate experience getting from here to there is often a big pain in the ass."

"I thought demons could zip from place to place faster than the eye can follow."

"That's true for short distances. For long distances we need to hitch rides like everyone else. Don't read me wrong. I love it down there, but I also appreciate the occasional holiday. Hell is a fascinating place, Barthélemy, provided you know the rules. This means, quite simply, getting in Satan's good graces and becoming one of his sidekicks. For those select few, life—or death, if you prefer—is good, especially if you can devise and suggest new tortures for the lesser inmates. I'm proud of one I offered recently and that Satan enjoyed immensely. I proposed the creation of a large shitfield contained within a pond. This shitfield existed in a suspended phase-change midway between liquid and solid. In other words, it was, as the tired saying goes, that perfect consistency: too thick to drink and too thin to plow. When some howling souls nearby were offered a brief respite from the flames they readily accepted a change in venue, only to be thrown into the pond and made to bob for apples!

"Among the perks for those of erudition are weekly séminaires during which Satan mounts a stage and lectures to his audience. Naturally, the rabble and uneducated are excluded and confined to their fires, and because they account for the majority by far of Hell's population there are always plenty of empty chairs for the few remaining. Mankind might be the only creature to whom God granted the capacity to reason, although just a handful takes advantage of His gift. Most of Hell's denizens are there because of their own stupidity."

"What does he lecture about?"

"Many different things. Satan is a very learned being, occasionally able to receive glimpses of the future. He sometimes passes along titillating tidbits. One day or night—in Hell there's no distinction—Satan explained how pigs locate truffles. In case you've ever wondered why only mature sows are selected to sniff for them around the bases of oak trees it's because truffles release a specific chemical also found in boars' testicles. On locating a truffle, even one deep underground, the sow assumes what in animal husbandry is describe as the 'standing posture'; that is, standing still and rigid waiting to be mounted and receive the boar's weight on her hindquarters. The chemical's composition is complex, well beyond the knowledge of any contemporary alchemist. In fact, the discovery wasn't made until the year of grace 1982, nearly five centuries from now."

"Do you believe this?"

"Of course! As a corollary, when young women were provided a sniff of the pure compound and shown an image of a young man their equivalent 'stance response' was activated, metaphorically speaking, and they ranked him higher on a scale of attractiveness than women not given a sniff. This is because human males, like boars, produce the substance in their balls, but also in their sweat and saliva. Satan intends to purify the stuff and use it as a lure to recruit female witches. Excuse the platitude, but when he told us about this everyone attending that week's DÉMON discours laughed like hell.

"In the distant future there will be speeches called TED discours in which a recognized expert in a particular field of knowledge—science, religion, philosophy, economics, and so forth—standing on a platform delivers a speech transmitted around the world through the ether. People will see it and listen using personal illuminated receivers. Even the rabble will possess these devices, which they operate by pressing buttons like trained monkeys. Their reward for this mindless activity is a perpetual stream of lies and slogans often interrupted by atonal sounds the unsophisticated confuse with music. Satan, disguised as a recognized expert in some field or other, intends to participate in these events to recruit future empty-headed souls, which by that time will number in the billions. He foresees occasions requiring him to stand in public and bullshit the masses, in some cases helping to prop up leaders whose credulity exceeds even theirs. Sophistry will rule. Science and technology will be highly advanced, but people will remain as gullible, passive, and superstitious as they are today. Entrepreneurs will become fabulously wealthy selling snake oil to the unenlightened as cures for their many ailments, real and imagined. The people will be blinded by demagoguery and value physical beauty above all else. We know this from history: technology always outpaces the acquisition and application of wisdom and rational thought. Maybe I'll strive to be emperor of all the world." His head was suddenly transformed into that of an obese older man with an orange face, white teeth, a pile of combed-over preternatural blonde hair, dead reptilian eyes, and a pouty downturned mouth like that of a dissatisfied trout.

THURSDAY MAY 15TH—JEJUNIUM SEXTAE; NOS INTER ALIOS; POSSIBILITY OF TORTURE

RÉVIGNY, HAVING BEEN GIVEN PERMISSION TO speak at the court's reconvening, rose from his chair, straightened his robe, and looked out at the spectators. "Were Madame Truye not a surrogate for a person we would not be here debating her fate. Any murder of a human—a being formed in God's image—is a sin whether committed by man or beast. In this instance secular court would be a perfectly appropriate forum were the sole accusation the murder of a child, except for an important caveat.

"However, the matter I'm about to broach can be distilled to a question of legal interpretation. Nonetheless, it merits discussion by the court. The sow prominently and deservedly displayed didn't merely dispatch with supreme indifference a child of God. She did so and afterward disgraced the Church—and God indirectly—by devouring his flesh on a Friday in violation of *jejunium sextae,* or 'fast Friday' in the vernacular, a sacred mandate and Church tradition. And in the animal kingdom pigs aren't alone in these violations. A werewolf captured in Franche-Comté was found guilty of eating one of his victims on a Friday in violation of *jejunium sextae.* It was inexcusable.

"Consequently, a valid argument can be made that canonical court is the appropriate venue despite my misgivings. The crime was extraordinarily vicious. Keep in mind that Madame Truye was seen fleeing the scene but not actually committing homicide. There aren't any firsthand witnesses, just one of the caretakers who reported seeing a pig running away. This indirect evidence makes Madame Truye eligible for torture to extract a confession of her foul deed. I trust this serious declaration of the plaintiffs—the child's guardians, Monsieur and Madame Philipot—will be taken under advisement by the court, assuming a voluntary confession is not forthcoming."

"Duly accepted," said the judicial vicar.

I stood and asked for clarification in the matter of torture. I finished with an apology to the judicial vicar for this interruption, making a slight bow to him and pretending to look shamefully at my boots. Révigny gave his robe a righteous tug, glared my way, and took his chair with faux authority, as if he controlled the proceeding.

I continued after Révigny was settled. "I understand Monsieur Révigny's point, Your Grace, but it seems inconsistent. Torture to gain a confession assumes the individual subjected to it is sentient, self-aware, and capable of having intentions. Yet, we refer to animals, including Madame Truye, as 'dumb beasts' and deny them emotion and reason. Madame Truye has been called cruel and ferocious, but how is a dumb beast to make a distinction between a human baby and a newborn squirrel fallen to the ground from its nest? If encountered while foraging, both are food so far as a pig is concerned. How can Madame Truye be tried and convicted based on a mental capacity and knowledge of intent—the *mens rea* in legal terms—she has never been credited with possessing?

"It's a matter of law that animals can't be criminalized for what they do naturally, not if the situation involves exigencies in the struggle for survival. When a cat kills a mouse for its food, that isn't murder. It's when an animal kills out of malice or passion that murder is deduced. But how is a foraging pig supposed to distinguish a small child from any other source of food?"

"You will receive clarification, monsieur," said His Grace. "Your cat and mouse example is relevant to nature, but irrelevant here because the cat did not commit homicide. If it had we would put it on trial. And it's not unreasonable to expect even dumb brutes to distinguish examples of mankind from squirrels and act in accordance with their inferior place in God's earthly hierarchy. Homicide is a civil crime, but also a sin against God as acknowledged by the Church and our secular and canon laws. On this there can be no disagreement. These are the rules we live by.

"I remind you that neither civil nor ecclesiastical courts partition the murder of humans into categories. Legally, there isn't a distinction between murder with intent and murder without it; therefore, homicide involontaire and homicide volontaire are treated the same. Nonetheless, an accessory violation associated with a principal crime like homicide can't be dismissed without due consideration."

The judicial vicar had effectively refuted my attempt to attribute Madame Truye's behavior to mere nonselective foraging. I saw where we were headed and felt certain Révigny would grasp this loose end and attach it somehow to his prosecutorial strategy. I blocked such an opening with a wedge of flattery before it could expand beyond my control. I said, "Your Grace realizes that violating *jejunium sextae* is only a venial sin, not a mortal one, and scarcely worthy of your precious time."

The judicial vicar pursed his lips and looked thoughtful. "It's true that my time is valuable. Lord knows, I'm pushed and pulled this way and that. Thank you for mentioning it in this public forum, monsieur. But back to your point, a person committing a venial sin has essentially two ways of achieving forgiveness, namely confession and penance. Both are recommended. Expiation can be achieved in four ways. The most effective is going on a pilgrimage to a holy site and asking forgiveness from the clerics tending it. The sinner can also confess to his local priest and donate alms. The benefit of attending Mass is obvious. For any of these fasting is a nice finishing touch. I presume nothing would change if the sinner is a pig, but without precedent we may only speculate."

Révigny rose suddenly. "May I speak, Your Grace?'

"Of course, monsieur."

"I remind the court about the legal juxtaposition of principal and accessory crimes in canon law. A case like this is now before us. It's well documented that placement of the boundary separating canonical and secular crime has been much disputed. *Nos inter alios,* a decretal of Pope Alexander III and in the vernacular 'among others, we,' does not provide guidance on the matter. Pope Innocent IV and canonists who follow the *Glossa Ordinaria* say no, the Church can't convict and punish secular crimes, and, by extension, assign an accessory. This means that an accessory ought to follow the principal through trial and conviction. Under such a scenario an accessory can come only after the more serious principal has been adjudicated.

"In many ways this makes sense. Were *nos inter alios* to become the law of the land there would not be any secular courts, and the Crown would lack all power in criminal matters. The clergy would then rule the legal system, the demarcation between secular and canon law having dissolved, and all crimes committed by the laity would be tried exclusively in ecclesiastical venues. Opponents of *nos inter alios* are right to protest its universalist claims."

There was momentary silence followed by some coughs and murmuring in the gallery. It was doubtful any of the spectators had understood the relevance of what just happened. "What do you suggest, Monsieur?" said His Grace.

Révigny said, "I believe we need His Grace's position on this matter prior to introducing accessory crimes, and ask him to consider if perhaps the trial should continue under civil authority." He sat and turned toward me, eyes flashing red. It had been a remarkably pointed peroration, not the rambling, disjointed speeches we lawyers usually make.

"I need to consult the bishop," said His Grace. "Court is adjourned until tomorrow."

Later at the tavern Révigny said, "I applaud your deployment of *mens rea* in your client's defense. Even more, I admire your timing when sucking up to the judge, anticipating his next move, catching him unaware and thus weakening the surprise he intended, which was to introduce *jejunium sextae* himself. Excellent work. Yes indeed, proclaiming a desire to remain in canonical court will certainly place you in His Grace's good graces to the point he should approve your future petition for purgation. Madame Truye will subsequently stand a chance of acquittal, however slight." He waggled a green index in my face and grinned. "Depending, of course, on how you overcome the minor dilemma of using pigs as compurgators and convince His Grace it makes sense."

I was scarcely surprised to hear this, knowing Révigny's intelligence, guile, and capacity to read minds. "How did you anticipate I was planning to introduce purgation as an accessory?"

"Elementary logic, dear boy. From your side of the aisle, what other option is there? For one thing, you lobbied hard to keep the proceeding in clerical court. We both know that *jejunium sextae* is just a distraction, like pounding the table yesterday and demanding our sow not be displayed publicly. Purgation, if you can pull it off, is a brilliant strategy, but it won't matter in the end. Your client will be hanged anyway. The public will demand it. What really matters is the entertainment value of the trial, which grows daily. I'm sure Satan is having a grand time viewing it from somewhere in the gallery.

"As to our more clandestine matter, His Grace's urgent need to consult the bishop has two interpretations. On one hand we might take it as tentative evidence of having been kept in the dark by the bishop about his dalliance with the Philipot daughter and its unsavory outcome. Maybe His Grace suspects your strategy and rushed off to alert the bishop. An accused pig requesting purgation would set a legal precedent, bringing our little court proceeding enormous publicity through its associated 'public fame' mandate of alerting all dissenting citizens of Saône-et-Loire to come forward and testify. Notices would have to be posted widely, and soon everyone—including the king—would learn that for the first time in French history a pig has requested purgation. The bishop surely would see this notoriety as detrimental to his fragile situation, stimulating an inclination to duck for cover and quickly shift the proceeding to secular court despite relinquishing control. And he could do this still without explaining his motive to the judicial vicar.

"On the other hand assume both His Grace and the bishop are still ignorant of your strategy, which I suspect is the real situation. The only accessory in the record so far has been the mention of *jejunium sextae*. It's highly doubtful His Grace and the bishop have even considered the possibility of another. Therefore, think of it in terms you already have as a red herring cast unintentionally before the court to distract from what's to come when purgation appears suddenly out of nowhere. This alternative theory will be confirmed if the proceeding continues in its present ecclesiastical setting, you then petition for purgation, and His Grace expresses genuine surprise but sees no way out and grants it. By then the bishop will have been too late to the party. At that juncture he can't justify moving the trial to civil court while still retaining control without creating a distraction of his own, for example, wading into the philosophical cesspool of *nos inter alia* as rationale for declaring himself judge of a secular trial. The upheaval in legal and clerical circles could only place him at the center of the ensuing controversy, drawing attention to himself and eventually, by reflection, to Mademoiselle Philipot. Any sensible cockroach seeks anonymity in darkness to avoid being crushed underfoot. I predict the trial stays in canonical court and that we'll see the resultant festivities reach new heights of absurdity." Révigny's eyes were blinding red, so bright I couldn't look at him. He was bent forward and rubbing his hands together. They slid and flowed over each other like lubricious eels in high passion. "I can't wait!" he said.

FRIDAY MAY 16TH—RÉVIGNY CORNERS HIS GRACE FORCING HIM TO ANNOUNCE THAT THE TRIAL WILL NOT BE TRANSFERRED TO CIVIL COURT

WHEN THE BELLS FINISHED TOLLING TERCE Révigny obtained permission to speak and immediately prodded the judicial vicar into a corner. "I bring to the court's attention that if His Grace decides to continue the trial following canon law rather than shifting it to civil court we shall face still another example of principal and accessory crimes discussed at length yesterday. I refer to Madame Truye having committed a venial sin in addition to the principal sin of homicide. Venial sins are typically private matters handled between sinner and priest inside the confessional.

"Secular courts rarely prosecute venial sins as crimes, leaving such matters to the Church. An ecclesiastical court is obviously empowered to investigate them, although doing so would be the equivalent of killing flies with a hammer. His Grace has noted that homicide is simultaneously a civil crime against mankind and a mortal sin before God. Without your having yet stated, I presume Your Grace intends to judge the mortal sin in this case as the principal crime, although unless secular authorities objected strongly—and it's unlikely they would—you could as easily decide to charge civil murder and after the verdict relinquish sentencing and punishment to a civil authority so as not to break the clergy's vow against spilling blood. Either way punishment will be handled by civil authorities for just this reason. Overlapping jurisdictions aren't uncommon, as when sorcery or witchcraft is practiced toward illegal ends.

"That isn't quite the situation here, of course, despite certain similarities of context, mainly because the defendant is an animal, not a human. Furthermore, the distinction between ecclesiastical and civil proceedings is more functional than causal, and precedents taken from one can be applied directly to the other without crossing legal boundaries. Regardless, the principal crime is homicide committed by a domestic animal, not *jejunium sextae*, which, once again, an ordinary citizen could expiate in private conversation with a priest followed by suitable penance. In canonical terminology this issue is conveniently resolved through the Church's 'internal forum' of the confessional.

"Canon law holds that accessory crimes like *jejunium sextae* committed incidentally in the course of carrying out the principal crime can also be treated as a principal offense, homicide in the case here; that is, if Your Grace so wishes, although as I said it seems trivial considering the alternative. From my end I intend to prosecute only the charge of homicide, Madame Truye's mortal sin, and pursue it as her sole criminal act, ignoring the fact that she subsequently ate her victim on a Friday, which, to restate yet again, merely requires confession to a priest or porcine equivalent. Some would hold there's little difference."

The gallery denizens demonstrated their delight by cheering and stamping. Révigny was charming them with his famous wit and irreverence, and I could see that even the judicial vicar, clearly bored at the start of the proceeding, was showing sudden interest and beginning to look kindly on his antics. I could be left hopelessly behind if these two developed a repartie. It was time to ramp up my game. I already looked ridiculous for being a pig's lawyer, and my clownish appearance and gnomish stature didn't help.

Révigny stood basking in the accolades. When the noise subsided he cleared his throat and continued. "In his *Metaphysics* Aristotle declared animals incapable of intentions, but that was long ago. Since then we've acquired ample proof of the opposite. Take, for example, the case of a sow condemned and executed for killing a child in the year of grace 1266 at Fontenay-aux-Roses. Witnesses swore before God they saw her running from the crime scene *with a guilty expression on her face!* Plus, consider the unusual color of her face, which was black, as witnesses reported prior to her capture, and most uncommon for a pig, whose face ordinarily is pink like the rest of its body. That it was this specific pig and none other who committed the crime was undeniable.

"We know from property law that domestic animals are chattel, but in modern times and especially here in Burgundy we presume these beasts to be sentient beings and punishable according to laws governing humans. Madame Truye's crime was extremely cruel, and it outraged and saddened an entire community. Consider the horror of her devouring most of the face and part of the head, the right hand and shoulder, and much of the chest of a baby boy of around three months *while he was still alive and lying helpless in his bassinette!* Name a crime more vicious, demonic, and deserving of death!" With this, Révigny quit the field and took his seat to huzzahs from the spectators.

His Grace, after waiting patiently for the cheering to diminish, said, "I'm somewhat confused by the opening part of your statement, Monsieur Révigny. If you're again asking if this proceeding will be transferred to civil court the answer is still no. The bishop prefers keeping it where it is. And if you're asking indirectly if I might contest your unwillingness to prosecute the sow for *jejunium sextae*, my answer to that is also no. The principal crime of homicide is more than adequate to convict. Your statements about legal overlapping and such entered these ears sounding like babble. Forgive me if I don't ask you to repeat them."

Révigny and I glanced at each other. His eyes were bright yellow, on the verge of turning orange. The excitement was mounting. Now it was my turn. I was hoping that at least a few spectators would pay me some attention after Révigny's finishing flourish. This crowd wanted blood and intended to have it. I said, "May I speak, Your Grace?" He nodded. I stood and yanked the robe over the curve of my belly.

"In rebuttal to Monsieur Révigny's statement, in his *Metaphysics* Aristotle indeed declares animals incapable of intentions, but in the case before us we're asked to presume the opposite, that Madame Truye set out to purposely commit the crime with which she's charged and therefore attacked the Philipot foundling with *intent*. I agree with my adversary's description of the crime. Her act was undeniably horrifying, and a community has been outraged. I don't dispute this, not even the fact of Madame Truye having committed it, but consider the issue logically: to which 'community' is a pig's loyalty pledged, that of humans or its own kind?

"Think about it. To try pigs in human courts presumes them to be sentient creatures. In their presence we argue cases before them in French, then afterward read the verdict and sentence to them in Latin. What's the point unless we presume they understand all this and are fully conscious? Nonetheless, the Church insists that the inferior mental state of nonhuman animals makes them incapable of perceiving and comprehending the world within the context of human intellect and human sensibilities. Don't these positions present an unresolvable contradiction? So, is a pig only a sensate, rational beast when on trial and at all other times a dumb brute?

Even assuming the first, how can we take for granted that a pig's moral and cultural values match ours?

"I remind the court that as early as the year of grace 1283, Philippe de Beaumanoir in his *Coutumes du beauvaisis*—in the vernacular known among scholars simply as *The Customals*—criticized the tradition of putting pigs on trial for murdering children, pointing out that dumb animals are unable to distinguish good from evil, making the purpose of punishment incomprehensible to them. Doing so to avenge a crime against mankind has no meaning to swine and thus is pointless. He recommended that the owner of any such beast, and I quote: *In any case if it is a bull or a pig or a sheep or an animal of whatever kind that has gone wild, it is better for him to kill it and take his profit from it, so that it will not do the same thing again. . . .*

"And we also have the wise and holy opinion of Saint Thomas Aquinas advocating in his *Summa Theologia*, in the vernacular *Sum of Theology*, the same position based on his view that an animal is incapable of committing wrong. He taught that both curses and blessings should be reserved for beings able to reason and understand, namely humans alone. Even in instances when God cursed the fields, orchards, and vineyards the intended recipients were humans who would be punished and consequently suffer if they failed to bear grain and fruit. The soil itself would feel nothing. In fact, haven't most ecclesiastics agreed with Aquinas that when animals turn on mankind it's the Devil directing their violence? Far better for the people to repent their sins than hold animals accountable.

"In societies of swine the devouring of human flesh isn't out of the ordinary, nor is it judged a crime. Have you ever witnessed pigs castigating one of their own for unacceptable dietary habits? Of course not! Name something a pig won't eat. Pigs have private lives apart from ours. It's highly doubtful that Madame Truye purposely set out to find and eat a child. More likely, she came across it unguarded in its bassinette and made good use of the opportunity. With pigs wandering untended through the streets and even entering our dwellings only neglectful parents and caretakers would leave a young child alone and susceptible to predation, so don't blame this four-legged beast in the dock for doing what any pig does naturally while foraging." I sat down to boos and curses, holding up my arms and turning away from the gallery to deflect the rotten fruit and vegetables thrown at me.

Révigny now rose to rebut, saving me further abuse. "My learned colleague's touching argument is irrelevant. Fortunately, in these modern times the law permits us to prosecute intent and liability separately. An animal can be held legally liable for its actions despite lacking any reasoning capacity. We have only to examine the writings of Flemish jurist Josse de Damhouder, who clearly states that liability remains attached to the perpetrator. He recognizes two forms of animal crimes, those perpetrated by malice and others resulting from excitement of the moment. In the former the animal is liable, in the latter the animal or person inciting the incident bears the blame. The renowned jurist Philippe de Beaumanoir agreed, classifying the former as murder, the latter as homicide. He considers murder a crime committed surreptitiously, homicide as spontaneous, often occurring openly.

"It's the prosecution's contention that Madame Truye acted alone and purely from malice; in other words, that she committed murder. I base this on two observations, one presumed, the other deduced from direct evidence. First, according to witnesses no humans or other pigs were present when Madame Truye was observed fleeing the crime scene, her snout smeared with blood and obviously having committed her evil act surreptitiously. Second, who or what could have driven Madame Truye to commit this abomination? The baby had been left untended. The caretakers are obviously guilty of negligence, but were not in the vicinity and so could not have incited Madame Truye's vicious attack. The child was a baby of three months, hardly of an age to tease or anger a pig or commit other acts that might encourage homicide by Beaumanoir's definition.

Furthermore, instead of merely plucking out the baby she overturned the bassinette and trampled it in murderous fury. My friends,
we have before us a clear incidence of murder! But of what use is
accusation without proof? What could be more convincing than wit-
nessing the murder yourselves?"

The crowd had become restless and noisy, as if anticipating something. Révigny raised his arms and shouted for silence. Suddenly, all
noise and movement ceased as if an evil wind had swept through.
Everyone felt it. There was not a murmur, not a whisper, no shuffling
of feet. The Théâtre Romain had suddenly become an echoless crypt
from which no sound escaped. Révigny wiggled his right index finger,
arms still raised. It was a signal. A man emerged from behind the
stand and emptied a bucket of bones into the dock, some with meat
still attached. Fresh lamb bones, I learned later in the tavern when
Révigny confessed with a smirk that he'd ordered Madame Truye
starved for three days. Madame Truye fell on the bones at once, mas-
ticating them with eager snorts and loud crunching sounds.

At that moment we noticed a small boy standing beside Révigny.
He had appeared spontaneously from who knew where. The right
side of his face had been ripped away, along with most of his skull.
His right shoulder and arm and the upper part of his chest and ribs
on that side were missing. Those closest could see a pink lung rhyth-
mically inflate and collapse as he breathed. The boy Madame Truye
killed had been three months old. This child was perhaps four
years, but the distinction went unrecognized.

The crowd's response was a collective gasp followed by a ground-
swell of murmuring. Some began to pray loudly, dropping to their
knees and grasping their beads. Révigny had his arm around the
boy's good shoulder. He again raised his hand for silence. "Is this
the sound of your face and skull being torn and eaten?" All heads
turned toward the dock, ears tuned to Madame Truye enthusiastically crushing bones between her powerful molars and snuffling in
the mud for leftover splinters.

"Yes," said the boy in a tiny voice.

"And is this also the sound of your arm and chest being devoured while you lay alone and helpless, suffering unspeakable pain and terror?"

The child looked at the crowd with his remaining eye then emitted an ear-splitting shriek, a noise so terrible it raised goose pimples on all present. Some spectators started to weep and wail as if possessed. Others stood or sat motionless and silent as if in shock; still others abandoned their places in the gallery and ran, covering their ears with their hands, not looking back.

"How could he be alive?" a man near the front asked no one in particular. Clearly, he couldn't. He must be a demon, and as Révigny also admitted to me that evening, what we saw had been a momentary satanic illusion of own conjuring.

Just a few spectators remained, too stunned or frightened to leave the bleachers. The judicial vicar was pale and shaken. "Court is adjourned until terce Tuesday the 20th of May," he said in a barely audible voice. "Monday will be an extra day of prayer." His gavel struck the sounding block, abruptly ending court.

I changed into other clothes and instructed the Innkeeper's wife to wash the fruit and vegetable stains from today's court attire and have everything clean, dry, and ready by vespers on Sunday. She looked at me with a smirk and said, "A bad day at the court, monsieur?" Then she looked away at once and added, "Of course, monsieur. As you wish."

Révigny was already seated at our table in the tavern when I arrived. He was surrounded by three beggars on all fours scrabbling for bits of bread he was dropping, watching with amusement as if they were barnyard fowl. On seeing me he kicked at them from his chair until they limped away.

"Having a good time?" I said. "You know what Jesus would think. Having fun when you should be baring your soul in the confessional, weeping over some sin or other. Yet here you sit teasing beggars and sipping the judicial vicar's wine."

"I like it!" Révigny said. "You're gradually moving over from the other side."

"I was never on the other side. I'm not on any side except the one offering the most reward for the least effort."

"Well said! I need a lift after today's tedious performance before the bar. What's more boring than debating the relative weights of mortal versus venial sins? And all because the fairy tale of Original Sin supports all other sins. It's a farce, Barthélemy. The questions Original Sin pose are unanswerable, yet there's always an answer. Why do innocent people die, for example? According to Saint Paul in *Romans*, chapter five verses twelve to twenty-one, death entered the world through Adam's sin. Earth was doomed forever the moment Adam and Eve fell from grace. The Italian theologian Bartolomeo Spina explained it this way: even saints die like everyone else, not because of any sins they committed but because they're guilty of Original Sin from birth, the same as everyone. Others later postulated why only humans can suffer. Having never eaten the forbidden fruit, animals are untainted by Original Sin. As irrational brutes and bestioles they are incapable of any subsequent sins too, and when they cry out they do so without pain or anguish."

Révigny refilled our cups and settled back, eyes pulsing bright orange. "Don't you find it odd," he said, "that considering the gravity of this matter, nowhere in the New Testament does Jesus mention either Adam or his sin? Could the reason be that it's unimportant? Now there's a novel idea."

I saw the extra court-free day as a gift because Tuesday was reserved for witness testimonies. There was no time to linger in the tavern with much work to be done, and I excused myself after eating. Now that Aufrey had arrived and was staying at the inn I set him to work. He was known and trusted by the town tradesmen and could procure what I needed without difficulty. I rounded up François and Alvin and gave them instructions to follow Aufrey on the mule when he was ready, probably not until Saturday night, and obey his orders. If additional muscle was required, they were to provide it. I promised an extra flagon of wine Tuesday night after successfully completing the mission and returning to the inn. This was all the motivation they needed; they would have followed Aufrey anywhere.

TUESDAY MAY 20TH—PIGS IN THE DOCK;
MADAME BIRCANN IN THE WITNESS CHAIR;
CHASSENÉE REQUESTS PURGATION FOR MADAME TRUYE

COURT RECONVENED AT TERCE AS SCHEDULED. The judicial vicar looked haggard, as someone does who sleeps poorly or spends excessive time on his knees in prayer. No sooner had the clerk finished speaking than His Grace, voice trembling with repressed anger, said, "Who's responsible for this outrage?"

"Your Grace?" said Révigny innocently.

"Was it you . . . or you?" His Grace pointed an accusatory finger first at Révigny, then me.

I stood and said, "It was I, Your Grace." Aufrey and I had made good use of the weekend and first day of the week when court was not in session. Through his contacts in the trades Aufrey had "rented" five adult sows from a local farmer. He also had "rented" their owner plus his farm cart and mule. Then assisted by François and Alvin these four had installed the sows in the dock the previous night where they were now milling around in tight quarters with Madame Truye. I said, "The additional pigs are necessary to defend my client. I promise to have them removed after court ends today and regret any disruption of the proceeding, but my motive will soon become clear."

"It had better," said His Grace, yanking at his robe as if the collar felt too tight. "They must be gone by this time tomorrow. Today has been reserved for prosecution and defense witnesses. First, Monsieur Révigny for the prosecution."

Révigny stared with bored somnolence into the distance, half-lidded eyes slowly pulsing green. "I don't have any witnesses, Your Grace. In the prosecution's opinion the facts of the case are obvious and sufficient in themselves to prove our case. We consider Madame Truye guilty of homicide—or murder, take your choice—without any need of qualification. The charges are sufficient as written."

The judicial vicar looked at me. "Monsieur Chassenée for the defense?"

"Thank you, Your Grace." I stood and bowed. "I call Madame Bircann to the witness chair." I descended from the stand and walked the few steps to the dock, then lifted my head and faced the spectators. A woman wearing a ragged tunic and a coif on her head emerged from the gallery, accompanied to the witness chair by a bailiff's assistant. She was short, even shorter than I, and stout, her bare feet heavily calloused and weathered to a dull purple, toenails rippled and umbered like old horn. She doubtless had been barefoot since birth and never known shoes regardless of the season. After she had been sworn in I asked her to sit in the witness chair and allowed her to settle down and become aware of her surroundings.

After a moment I said, "How many pigs do you see beside you in the dock?"

"I don't know, sir, I never learned to count."

"I can tell you. There are six. Which one is Madame Truye?"

She looked at me, startled and confused, not expecting the question. "Sir?"

"Which of them is the sow you saw running away from the bassinette on the day the foundling child was killed while you supposedly were guarding him?"

She paled and buried her face in her hands. "I'm so very sorry, sir. As I told the clerics who came to investigate, I went indoors for only a minute to grab a piece of bread. I hadn't eaten, and the hour was nearly sext."

"Yes," I said, neither kindly nor unkindly, "but which of these pigs did you see fleeing the scene, the one later caught, arrested, and is now on trial?"

She raised her head and looked at me. "You mean running away from the bassinette?"

"That's right. Which of the pigs in the dock beside you is the one you saw running away? Please identify it. If necessary, stand and look them over."

Terrified by her situation, she stayed seated and glanced at the dock without really seeing its contents. "I couldn't say, sir, they all look alike. Maybe my husband could tell."

"But your husband wasn't there. He was working in the fields well out of sight of the house. One of these pigs is a baby killer, and you are the only witness. Which is it?"

"I don't know, My Lord. They're all the same size, and one pig looks pretty much like another."

"Very well. You're excused."

The judicial vicar said, "Monsieur Révigny, do you have questions for this witness?"

"No, Your Grace." He looked my way, eyes barely transitioning from green to amber, signaling disinterest.

"Monsieur Chassenée, do you have any other witnesses?"

"No, Your Grace. Madame Bircann was the only person who might possibly identify Madame Truye as the guilty party, and she was unable to do so. Seeing as how there is only circumstantial evidence linking my client to the crime I ask the court to release her at once. Clearly, the prosecution has no case."

"Your petition is denied, monsieur. Do you have anything further?"

"Yes, Your Grace. Thank you. According to canon law purgation is a subordinate form of proof applicable in the absence of definitive evidence of a crime, such absence having just been dramatically demonstrated. Dissenting citizens may object by coming forth and producing evidence of guilt. Certain members of the Church hierarchy dispute whether a domestic animal can be tried in ecclesiastical court in matters of public purgation. So the audience understands, 'purgation' is defined as an oath of innocence by the accused and confirmed by oaths of several so-called compurgators who swear to its veracity as a group. These compurgators are neighbors acquainted with the accused, of good repute, and of similar economic and social standing. As to the basis of the controversy among ecclesiastical scholars I refer to the decretal *nos inter alios* of Pope Alexander III. Its broad philosophical implications were discussed earlier by Monsieur Révigny and are of no concern here. In practical terms oaths sworn by compurgators have nothing to do with the putative innocence or guilt of the accused; rather, these are testaments that they, the compurgators, believe the accused's oath to be truthful and not intended to deceive. Nor are the compurgators required to know the underlying facts of the case. Therefore, guilt and innocence, presumed or actual, are irrelevant. Only one thing matters: that the compurgators believe the accused's oath has been presented truthfully before God and man."

The judicial vicar looked at me as if startled. "Am I to understand from your roundabout posturing that you request purgation for a *pig*?"

"Yes, Your Grace," I said, "although Your Grace might be falling into Monsieur Révigny's trap of conflating the cruelty and viciousness of the crime with malice of intent. Monsieur Révigny, on his part, has conflated intent with liability despite acknowledging a legal difference in modern French law. None of the associations is relative to this case, the first because an unreasoning brute is incapable of intent, or of premeditation in any form, either evil or benign. Liability is irrelevant by not being a component of the formal accusation against my client. Even if it were, Madame Truye has no money with which to compensate the Philipots for murdering their foundling. Her life is her only asset, which she will ultimately relinquish to pay her debt. As Your Grace acknowledged earlier a legal distinction between homicide with and without intent does not exist in French law for either animals or humans. Consequently, homicide involontaire and homicide volontaire are prosecuted and defended the same way. To repeat, the mention of intent to commit homicide by Madame Truye is irrelevant, benefiting only my adversary who hopes to establish unwarranted bias in the public mind against my client.

"Would the result have been different if her behavior at table were refined and all elements of intent and cruelty banned from discussion? Not in legal terms." I paced back and forth on the stand in front of the main table, forefinger to my lips as if in thought.

"Suppose, in other words, if Madame Truye had formally asked the child's permission to be eaten would this case even be considered a homicide? And after receiving permission, could eating the child's remains still be described as vicious? Suppose further that Madame Truye sat down to a well-laid table sparkling with expensive cutlery and dined quietly, the meat before her carved into thin slices and presented on a silver platter surrounded, we might imagine, with accompanying servings of potatoes, onions, and carrots baked in the child's own lard. Try picturing Madame Truye with a silk napkin tied underneath her chin and a maître d'hôtel standing by to season the dishes properly with salt and pepper and refill her crystal glass with a fine red Burgundy." I raised my eyes to the gallery and was rewarded with howling laughter, cheers, and the stamping of feet.

The disruption lasted several minutes while the judicial vicar leaned back in his chair and looked hopelessly at the sky. Returning his gaze to me, he said, "Let's get back to the matter of purgation and the compurgators specifically. Who—or what—will they be, and who will select them?" Now I had him.

"I propose simply following protocol," I said. "There should be twelve compurgators based on the tradition of Christ having twelve apostles. Pretty standard in my experience, and doubtless yours too."

The vicar nodded, a quizzical expression on his lips. "Continue."

"Right." I turned and faced the spectators. "Because compurgators who swear by the accused are neighbors and acquaintances I propose that Madame Truye or a human surrogate choose a dozen porkers from her home sty and bring them here to court."

"Of course you do," His Grace said sarcastically. "And will they volunteer or must we conscript them into service? I state for the record that purgation is anything but dispositive. It stinks of organized lying and tribalism, although my opinion is irrelevant. It's certainly a legal option to you in defending your client, monsieur." The judicial vicar was twirling his quill and studying me as if I might be a curious natural history specimen, and he was considering how to pin me to a board.

I ignored these signs of annoyance and trudged on. "I suggest we assign this task to the swineherd who daily interacts with Madame Truye and her colleagues and knows them best as individuals. Madame Truye is presently incarcerated and eating the king's bread when she isn't here restrained in the dock during court. We could achieve our objective and save the Crown some expense by returning her temporarily to the herd where her interactions with fellow pigs could be observed. The swineherd will interpret the group's behavior and choose the dozen with whom Madame Truye is most friendly. I further propose that I, Monsieur Révigny, and Your Grace be present for the selection to avoid any later rumors or accusations of skulduggery."

"I object to this, Your Grace," Révigny said. "What if she runs away, knowing herself to be guilty, or kills another child?"

"Then," I said, "Monsieur Révigny might make his case for my client's guilt even stronger. However, if she does neither and simply stays with her companions this could be interpreted as evidence of her innocence, seeing as how a guilty pig would be likely either to flee or kill again. Of course, it could also be interpreted as her being just a dumb beast having no notion of participating in a trial or even committing homicide, thus rendering this trial comical.

Which is it, Monsieur Révigny? Under what argument are you specifically protesting my request for her temporary release?"

"He's right," the judicial vicar said. "I have no problem with releasing the defendant into the custody of her owner and swineherd. "More seriously, I anticipate legal difficulties with designating pigs as compurgators. What about the speaking then signing of oaths and, needless to say, lack of a precedent?"

I said, "Consider two facts, Your Grace. First, Madame Truye has yet to swear an oath of purgation—an 'oath of innocence' in the vernacular—declaring she isn't guilty of homicide. Most legal scholars consider it a step onto friable legal ground when the defendants are irrational brutes and the issue is therefore without precedent. However, an oath of purgation establishes *de facto* proof of an animal's status as a defendant and a record of its plea in a court of law. In cases of homicide animals and humans are supposed to receive the same considerations. In addition, His Grace's concern about whether pigs can swear oaths of compurgation is subsumed in the dispositive fact that Madame Truye's oath of purgation must precede those of her compurgators."

"Second, few citizens of France can even write their names. In ecclesiastical courts a judicial vicar not associated with the trial, or a designated lawyer associated or not, prepares the standard oaths of purgation and compurgation, which are approved by the presiding judge prior to being proffered. By power granted from the bishop the judge then signs on behalf of the participants. In practical terms we choose twelve pigs identifiable as individuals from Madame Truye's herd qualified to testify as to her good character, then proceed with preparation and carrying through of the oaths. As for precedent, this very trial will establish it. Your Grace's name will appear in the canons for eternity."

"My worst fear," the judicial vicar muttered.

Révigny rose from his chair. "Noting that swine have cloven hoofs I can't think of a reason why they couldn't grip quills and sign for themselves." He sat down smiling like a death's head as the gallery erupted in hoots and laughter.

The judicial vicar pounded his gavel on the sounding block. "Enough!" he shouted. "Monsieur Révigny's disruption aside, even assuming someone legally signs on behalf of these pigs the oaths must also be spoken."

My adversary rose again. "Why should pigs take oaths of any kind when they don't have souls and automatically are denied entry into Heaven?" He waved his hand as if warding off a bad odor. "But if protocol must be followed . . ." Révigny paused and sighed, seemingly resigned to pursue some foolish path. "If protocol is required I offer a sensible recommendation. The pigs could be tied to stakes in such a way to keep them standing on their hind legs. Then one at a time, with the left front hoof placed on a Bible and the right one raised and held upright by a bailiff's assistant, the judicial victor who signed the oaths and now is wearing a pig mask as if dressed for a masquerade speaks the oath for them." He sat down once more to the gallery's raucous amusement.

This time the judicial vicar ignored Révigny. He turned and nodded at me to continue. I stood. "To conform with the first requirement of purgation under canon law that there be 'pre-existing public fame' of Madame Truye's supposed crime—publicity, in other words—the court is duty-bound to make the announcement not just to all humans living in the district but also all the pigs. This is because pigs will serve as compurgators. Without the public's—and barnyard's—full knowledge of the proposed crime and charges against Madame Truye she can't legally be put to purgation. I therefore emphasize that pre-trial public awareness of the imputed crimes be elevated to 'openly disseminated rumor,' the law's exact words. As Madame Truye's legal representative I shall require in due time a sworn inquest and letter from the court on her behalf—and to which she's entitled—that the public fame requirement has been fully met. Finally, if Madame Truye is eventually restored to good fame I trust the court will issue a testimonial letter as proof that her name has been cleared in the law's eyes."

"So be it," said His Grace. "I hereby order that notices of accusation against Madame Truye and a description of the charges against her be posted on all public buildings and squares, places of worship, and pigsties in the district, and that the prisoner stop being fed the king's bread at once and released into custody of her owner and his swineherd. The two lawyers and I shall meet at the hour of sext three days hence at Monsieur Philipot's pig farm to observe selection of the compurgators." He looked at the clerk, who consulted his calendar and said, "That will be this Friday the 23rd of May."

"Let's make it the following Monday, the 26th," the judicial vicar said. "Afterward, I propose a day of rest, meaning court will next convene here at the Théâtre Romain at the usual hour on Wednesday the 28th." With this pronouncement his gavel fell and the gallery began to depart.

I was feeling good. According to the law there was no specific requirement that potential compurgators address the crime itself, although anyone objecting to the process could be punished if found to hold malicious motives. The court's duties were to offer citizens a chance to present valid proof of the crime and assure adequate public knowledge of the impending purgation so dissenters might have the opportunity of coming forth. At every step canonical purgation is a public act. Those claiming to have affirmative evidence of a crime—not simply hearsay—and petition to testify against granting purgation, in legal language *causa reclamationis contra purgationem*, can cause suspension of the proceeding until their statements are heard and assessed. Such cases are a minority: there's considerable risk to an objector whose proof is shown to be false, flimsy, or demonstrably malicious.

On returning to the inn and finding no sign of François and Alvin, I went around back to the stables. Loud snores emanated from one of the stalls. I looked inside and there they were sprawled in the hay, drunk and snoring and sounding like hogs rooting on a forest floor up to their hocks in autumn mast. Scattered around were several empty flagons. I kicked François in the ribs several times, but he only groaned. I hoped the animals had been fed and watered before their caretakers had passed out. To be certain I went inside and rousted the innkeeper from his afternoon nap, ordering him to do it himself if they had not.

Révigny and I had scarcely settled into our chairs when the innkeeper appeared with the wine. After setting it down he hovered around as if wanting to say something but reluctant to speak. Finally, I said, "Do you want something, monsieur?"

"I hate to bother you, My Lord, but it's about your footmen. I took care of your animals as you asked, but someone must pay for the wine they drank."

"I told you in the beginning I would be responsible for one flagon with their evening meal, no more. Now leave us."

"I remember, sir, but the older one convinced a serving girl to fetch him however much he wanted on promise of marriage."

"This would be one of the girls who also works here as a whore?"

"That's right, monsieur, but what they do on their own time is none of my business. So you will pay for the wine they drank today? My wife tells me it was four flagons, starting about terce."

"Don't be a fool, monsieur. François already has a wife, and Alvin, his drinking companion, is their son. If the girl believed what he told her it's her problem. And if she gave away your wine that's your problem. Now don't mention it again or I'll see you scourged and jailed, am I clear?"

"Yes, monsieur." He left walking backward, bowing several times. A few minutes later we could hear him in the scullery shouting at the women and berating their gullibility.

"This is truly scandalous," Révigny said with faux rectitude. "A man of your standing employing adulterous footmen who frolic with prostitutes. What would the Church think if word got out? On the contrary, quirky episodes like this are widely admired in Hades. Satan especially appreciates a good laugh at the expense of the establishment. You'll be applauded down there."

I said, "Why are you so intent on hustling me down to Hell? I'm an ordinary man and passive sinner, hardly worthy to be Satan's companion. In one sense I'm intrigued, in another the whole idea is terrifying."

"You don't really think you're going to Heaven, do you Barthélemy? How droll. Your sins . . . let's see. I'll merely scrape the surface. You haven't attended Mass or confessed to a priest from the sinner's side of the curtain within the expanse of your own memory. Little wonder, considering most of the priests of Saône-et-Loire owe you money. Good thing they haven't confessed as much to His Grace because he would surely deny your participation in canonical disputes. You've committed adultery and lie whenever it's to your advantage. As to pride you dress like nobility despite being short, obese, ugly, and bourgeois. You regularly fantasize about scourging your peasants, masturbate ferociously, lust while asleep and awake, and shamelessly ogle pre-pubescent girls.

"As to envy, although you don't covet your neighbor's ass, as the Bible admonishes, you surely covet his wife's ass. And this woman is a dear friend of your demure spouse, the fetching Madame Chassenée. Goodness, how close to home you sin! You acquired your estate by cheating a senile widow and gaining a court order to incarcerate her in a poorhouse where she was forced to dress in rags and survive on stale bread and congealed porridge through her remaining years. You routinely overcharge your clients, billing them for time not spent on their behalf. Even the palfrey you ride and of which you're so proud was stolen from an estate near Levallois and given to you in partial payment by a thief whom you represented in court and somehow got released, God knows how. I'd continue, but you see the picture."

Révigny reached across the table and gave me an avuncular pat on the shoulder. It carried the weight of a kitten's paw. "No need to worry. We're lawyers. We scrabble viciously over the backs of our colleagues and clients oblivious of their ruin. Didn't Thomas Basin describe his fellow attorneys as 'beasts who hunt, stalk, gnaw, suck, and consume their prey,' clients and opponents alike as primitive and predaceous as themselves? If not a direct quote, certainly words to that effect. We're creatures who live only for new trials and to pass their foul, disruptive contagion to younger recruits just joining the guild then test how quickly we can flense the meat from their bones. It's dog eat dog with the smartest and hungriest destined to emerge victorious, sending adversaries whining into obscurity, tails between their legs.

"We prosecutors feel the necessity of intimidating the accused by assigning them elements of our own carnivory and propensity to scavenge. You who represent them are no more humane. Each camp expresses outrage at the crimes of these degenerates or paradoxi-cally touts their innocence, painting them as specimens of deranged mankind unfit to ever see daylight, or alternatively to be pitied, declared harmless, and released into society. It's la raison des plus forts, and the only question is, who's truly the stronger? A prosecu-tor's duty—no, his *passion*—is to project onto judge and gallery the law's own thirst for blood and retribution; in a setting like we now occupy here at Autun, to emulate the rampaging pig that I prose-cute and you defend, a cold, mindless killer unable or unwilling to distinguish God's children from garbage.

"Are we adversaries, you and I? No, just fellow members of a select brotherhood. We could switch sides and continue the charade effort-lessly. Yes, in viewing the present festivities, revenons à nos cochons! In terms of retributive justification the greater the moral outrage the more severe the punishment. How can we not love it? And who lever-ages the moral outrage at a trial or tribunal? Who plays the spectators like stringed instruments? Why, the lawyers, of course."

Monday May 26th—The Court Visits Jean Philipot's Pig Farm; His Grace's Shoes Are Submerged in Pig Shit

THE JUDICIAL VICAR EXPLAINED TO THE swineherd that twelve of Madame Truye's associates would be chosen to swear to her good character, specifically to the truthfulness of her oath of purgation. He emphasized that canon law requires prospective compurgators to be of upstanding reputation, not associated with crime or public defamation. They must be neighbors of equivalent social status as the accused and attest to the honesty of the latter's oath of purgation—not her actual innocence, but her oath that she believes herself innocent of the accused crime, or at least not responsible for her act.

"But isn't she guilty?" the swineherd said. "Everyone in Saône-et-Loire knows she ate the baby staying at the main house. But if you're telling me that an oath of purgation is the same as an oath of innocence, how can she swear to be innocent?"

"It's a good question," I said. "The court is still working on a solution. Madame Truye's oath will be written for her, of course, and worded in such a way that she won't be required to lie." The swineherd wrinkled her brow but stayed silent.

The judicial vicar asked her if any of the pigs had ever been arrested for a crime.

"No, Your Grace," she said. "All are law-abiding citizens, so far as pigs go."

"What about the cripple?" His Grace said. "The one hobbling toward the far corner of the sty? He has squinty eyes and looks guilty of something."

"Oh, that's Lame Loois," said the swineherd. "He's one of Madame Truye's dearest friends. In fact, these two showed up together one night several years ago. No one knows where they came from. They just appeared and joined the herd."

I added, "If you want him as a compurgator the trial had better happen soon. Crippled pigs usually aren't kept around, and he's probably destined to become hams and bacon in the fall."

"That's true," said the swineherd, "but Madame Truye will still be here, assuming she isn't hanged. She's one of our best breeders. Whether any of the other boars will interest her after Lame Loois is gone is the question."

The judicial vicar asked if Madame Truye had ever married, or were we to attribute her fecundity to sluttish behavior. Which boar in this group was the lucky father, His Grace wanted to know, and were Madame's offspring legitimate or bastards?

The swineherd looked pensive as she studied her charges. "It's hard to say. We have three boars and seven sows in this sty. The rest of the herd is foraging in the fields with my husband watching them. He's a swineherd too. The sows definitely can be promiscuous when they come into their time, but as I've said I don't think any but Lame Loois fathered Madame Truye's litters. I saw him mount Madame with my own eyes. He was clumsy, but she stood for him patiently. I think it's true love. Ordinarily, a sow in the moment of passion won't maintain her wide mating stance for a fumbling boar."

I whispered to Révigny, "I've heard of a fumbling bore, but a fumbling boar?"

"Yes, but are they married?" The judicial vicar was becoming impatient, perhaps from looking down and seeing his shoes sunk over their tops in a soup of mud, pig shit, and urine. The supernatant liquid was wicking up his white haut-de-chausses, threatening to yellow them to the knees. Doves called sadly from the nearby bushes.

"Married?" The swineherd seemed puzzled. "You mean joined by a priest in a ceremony?"

"Exactly." The judicial vicar glanced again at his shoes and trunk hose. He seemed melancholy. He had worn a long-sleeved tunic despite the warm day and was sweating heavily. It was obvious he considered our interview with the swineherd a fool's errand and would rather have been sequestered inside the cool stone walls of his Cathédrale quarters, perhaps napping or sipping wine.

"I couldn't say," the swineherd said, "except that swine have their own piggy rituals, and marriage might be among them. If ever two porkers were married, it's these two. I'd vouch for it."

The judicial vicar said, "So, we don't know if Madame Truye is married, widowed, or merely a whore."

"We might have a priest marry them, then we could be certain," I said.

His Grace looked at me tiredly. "How would they understand the ceremony? They're only pigs."

"The same way Madame Truye will understand the court's accusations, by having them read to her. If we expect her to understand the profound subtleties of law expressed in Latin and French she can surely decipher the meaning of a short, simple marriage ceremony."

"And under what aegis would you advise, Monsieur Chassenée, civil or clerical?"

"I leave that to Your Grace," I said.

The judicial vicar studied the milling herd before saying, "Clerical, I should think. God obviously is Catholic."

"If you say so, Your Grace," said Révigny, "but are His pigs? I've yet to see a member of the swinish race finger a rosary. Perhaps this is done in the privacy of the sty where confessions are also heard and forgiveness delivered through the wooden slats."

"Please, monsieur," His Grace said. "Don't make this more painful and ridiculous than it already is."

"Sorry, Your Grace, it's just that they look and sound more Calvinist than Catholic."

"I regret that the marriage ceremony must be part of the official record of this proceeding," His Grace said, "but it seems I'm left little choice." He turned to the clerk, stoic as always despite his own discomfort. "Monsieur, see that Madame Truye and Lame Loois are carted to the Théâtre Romain, installed in the dock, and put on a diet of the king's bread until further notice." To the swineherd, he said. "Young lady, are you married?"

"Yes, Your Grace. My husband, as I said, is a swineherd too. Monsieur Philipot has lots of pigs, more than one person can handle."

"You and your spouse will be summoned in time for the marriage ceremony, he to stand in and speak on behalf of Lame Loois, you on behalf of Madame Truye. Do you understand?"

"I think so, Your Grace. Do you mean that afterward my husband and I will be twice married?"

"No, madame, still just once. It's the pigs who will be married on that day. You and your husband will merely speak the necessary words for them, unless by a miracle they learn French in the interim."

WEDNESDAY MAY 28TH—CHASSENÉE ARGUES THAT
BECAUSE THE CASE IS BASED ON CUSTOMALS IT SHOULD BE
DISMISSED; RÉVIGNY REBUTS

WHEN COURT RECONVENED I ASKED AND was granted permission to speak. "Your Grace, I submit that this entire trial is illegal, being based on customals that vary from place to place. Murder and other high crimes warranting the death penalty can be properly charged to humans alone. A maxim of Roman law is *hominum causa omne jus constitutum est*, in the vernacular 'all law is created for the sake of men.' There's no allowance for trying animals in Roman law, which instead relies on the principle of *noxae deditio*, in the vernacular 'surrender to satisfy damages.' In such instances the animal committing what in human society is perceived as a crime—including homicide—is relinquished to the offended party. Thus, the matter ends with no expense to the state for trials, board for the animal while awaiting its fate, payment to the executioner, and so forth. Instead of punishing an unreasoning beast without a soul the brute is treated for what it properly is, and that is chattel.

"Under Roman law action can't be taken against insensate, unreasoning animals. An animal can be neither summoned to trial nor tried. Animals are subject to laws of nature, making them immune to manmade laws, both canon and secular. Roman law also holds that an unreasoning animal can't be punished for a past misdeed, yet Madame Truye resides in the dock before us. Like insane humans such an animal can be prevented only from committing future crimes, which is easily accomplished by restraint, in this case incarceration in a pigsty or perhaps tight supervision while foraging."

"Your Grace," said Révigny, "I wish to rebut my colleague's argument. His points have superficial merit, except for two fatal flaws. First, although we in France are attempting to implement Roman law, the day hasn't come when it or any other is the law of the land. In the case of animal trials we continue to follow customals under the guidance of which are perfectly legal. My colleague's position is therefore refuted as being irrelevant. Second, we find a common precedent for such trials in *Livre de justice et de plet* (*Book of Justice and of Pleas*) from the Orléanais region, which addresses the problem of responsibility when a domestic animal causes damage. This clearly states that an owner who neglects to keep his animal confined bears responsibility for its actions. Otherwise, the animal is to blame. Nowhere have we encountered a trial in which a pig led to the gallows has been granted a reprieve and its owner hanged. No law says pigs aren't allowed to range freely wherever they wish. Until one is enacted it's the pig's responsibility not to attack and eat humans."

I rose from my chair. "Ah, but Monsieur Révigny has cited only part of this law and in doing so presented it out of context. The section he mentions from *Livre de justice et de plet* is actually a blend of customal and Roman law. It indeed holds the beast responsible for its damages, but never claims it should be tried and then punished in a conventional sense. Instead, the author recommends *noxae deditio*, in the vernacular 'surrender of that which caused the damage.' The animal is 'punished' adequately by requiring it to switch ownership, forfeiting itself to the plaintiff, who may then do with it whatever he wants."

Révigny rose and spread his arms in disbelief, turning first to His Grace and then the spectators. "And how, Monsieur Chassenée, does this change of allegiance come about? Do we assume that a pig having recently been charged with homicide and feeling remorse leaves its home herd and joins another owned by the victim's family? Assuming such a preposterous thing is even possible, how is it determined that the accused's decision was voluntary and not coerced? These ancient Romans of yours envision on one hand that animals are subject only to their own laws and on the other hand demand they forfeit themselves voluntarily to be turned into bacon and hams." The gallery shouted approval.

"That's enough, monsieurs," the judicial vicar admonished mildly, although he was clearly enjoying the debate. "I have unfinished business elsewhere. Take the remainder of the week to rest. Court will reconvene Monday the 2nd of June. At that time we shall revisit the matter of purgation."

Later in the tavern Révigny was in a playful mood. "I've never visited Heaven," he said, "but the rumors aren't interesting. Imagine a place where everyone is high on a soporific drug and experiencing only bliss. There's no wine, no fornication, no hijinks, and no song unless you count hymns. What an awful bore. Skipping from cloud to cloud strumming harps? Really? And the hierarchy is exceptionally dreary. Erudition and creative evil tendencies count for something in Hell, but the saints, those human spirits closest to God, suffered excruciating pain and needless guilt on Earth. Don't expect a sense of humor from souls like theirs. A life of endless physical pain, self-denial, and living in constant fear of Judgment Day gained them only one advantage in Heaven: residency on a cloud with superior views. Heaven is already 'up there,'" Révigny said, jabbing a forefinger at the sky. "Nonetheless, in celestial real estate your level of elevation determines status, and saints occupy Empyrean. Only God floats higher. Anyway, Satan could tell you remarkable stories about Heaven and how every soul is zoned out, eyes staring blankly, a moronic smile on its cherubic face. Satan, as you know, was a resident angel there until God kicked him out.

"Ah, my friend, there's no guilt the equal of Catholic guilt for those who strive to emulate the saints. Not even confession can hold back the flood of irreversible melancholy and paralysis of scruple driven by despair of the Last Judgment, of solitude, recounting personal sins, prolonged fasting and meditation, food and sleep deprivation, relentless repetition of the breviary, kneeling in prayer for hours on rough stone floors, lamenting the unfulfilled desire for pain and humiliation reinforced by asceticism, thinking up creative acts of self-denial, the anguish of self-loathing and regret, and the endless worry about the length of eternity if God ultimately consigns your soul to fire and damnation. We're born, suffer, die, and are judged. There's nothing else. For confirmation think of history's tragedies and the risible behavior of those keepers of the Holy Writ in modern times.

"Aren't the Hundred Years' War, the Great Schism, and the latest wave of the Black Death snapping at our heels sufficient to make even the most devout howl for mercy? Then look around today. What about a clergy gone mad on consumer luxuries, raising tithes on the already destitute peasantry and selling indulgences to the wealthy to pay for them? Don't forget their habit of collecting fair boys with wavy hair and feminine manners and passing them off as 'initiates.'" He snorted. "Initiates into the rites of sacramental sodomy? These toys aren't cheap, especially those with blue eyes and angelic smiles. There was never a Golden Age, Barthélemy. Underneath the glitter was the blandness of lead. It was all failed alchemy."

Révigny's initial light mood had darkened. Now the flashing red of his eyes was so bright I had to look away. "Mankind's guilt and

the shame derived are boundless. The result is wariness and constant anxiety. Malice and the subaltern cruelty it spawns are nowhere
present in the list of deadly sins. This was no accident. The Church
requires both to control the populace, and their deployment under
the guise of Christian rectitude is remarkably effective. We live in
perpetual fear—terror, even—of the night; of goblins, demons,
witches, and werewolves prowling the darkness. We fear for our
physical selves and the pain of this life, but we truly dread and think
always of the afterlife and Judgment Day when our sins will be
counted and the soul's place in the final hierarchy is decided. Will
mine live blissfully in perpetual grace near God's hand or in endless damnation burned in fire stoked by Satan? This unease is
reinforced by clerics who remind us daily how our sins are more
numerous than the sands in the sea, that mankind is a superfluous
excrescence polluting Earth's surface; that humans are the Devil's
playthings, capable only of ingratitude and iniquity.

"God reminded the Israelites repeatedly that if they turned away
from Him He would deliver them into the hands of their enemies,
subject them to horrible plagues, starvation, torment, and death
without possibility of salvation. In *Leviticus*, chapter twenty-six verses
sixteen and seventeen, He warns about breaking His covenant:

> I also will do this unto you; I will even appoint over you terror,
> consumption, and the burning ague, that shall consume the
> eyes, and cause sorrow of heart: and ye shall sow your seed in
> vain, for your enemies shall eat it. And I will set my face against
> you, and ye shall be slain before your enemies: they that hate you
> shall reign over you; and ye shall flee when none pursueth you.

"The Israelites' only hope was worshipping Him and no other
god with slavish devotion. If their penitence lapsed even for a
second Satan would swoop in and capture their souls. He's everywhere and lurks in everyone's corrupt heart ready to pounce.

"Is it any wonder that modern man suffers from never-ending
melancholia and despondency? What remains to live for? What

assurance is there that existence after death won't still consist of pain and misery more terrible than life hands us? We can never be guilt-free regardless of how many sins we expiate. Sadness has ruled mankind's emotions from the start. Saint Hildegard of Bingen wrote that the instant Adam fell from grace the Devil breathed melancholy into him, coagulating his blood. Consequently, all mankind has become 'fainthearted and unbelieving.' Humans are creatures of sadness, Barthélemy, and always will be. Paradoxically, mankind attained his apotheosis only after tumbling from grace.

"Le Père Bougeant's theory that every living being from gnat to elephant is a demon's potential dwelling had a serious hurdle, one of magnitude, specifically. It didn't require mathematical prowess to realize that even assuming every living human not a baptized Christian is infested still could not account for all the demons thought to out there roaming the forests and fields, the cities, towns, and villages seeking suitable homes, a place to sit back, put up their feet, and enjoy behaving devilishly. Furthermore, potential individuals ripe to parasitize were diminishing rapidly as more humans heard the Word and converted to the path of Christ. Having been evicted from the bodies and souls of these new converts was making thousands more demons destitute and homeless by the day. Eventually, they would band together in protest, and Satan might have a full-fledged revolution to deal with. A demon without a domicile is like a flea without a dog, a bedbug without a peasant. This situation, already orders of magnitude out of balance, could be remedied easily if every insect, crustacean, fish, amphibian, reptile, bird, beast, and bestiole were made available for demonic habitation.

"There was only one caveat, and it was a big one. Le Père Bougeant realized that to implement his hypothesis meant extending human qualities to all these creatures. They must be reinvented as less bestial and more spiritual, rational, and sentient, but still within the conceptual boundaries of Catholic dogma, not reaching the heights of creation in God's image like man and thus remaining imperfect in comparison. And humans, realizing the new status of animals as near-equals, must pray humbly for their souls—*yes, their newly acquired souls*—sympathizing with their awareness of being trapped inside the bodies of houseflies, catfishes, and field mice, yet conscious of this inescapable embodiment as Hell's infinite anterooms.

"Do these creatures feel pain? It depends. Some theologians have claimed that only humans can suffer. Having never eaten the forbidden fruit, animals are untainted by Original Sin. Irrational brutes are incapable of any subsequent sins too, and when they cry out they do so without pain. Others hold that an animal's screams aren't those of the animal but rather from the demon inside. When you beat a dog it's the demon that suffers. Although the dog yelps, it feels nothing. Similarly, the lamb going to slaughter experiences no pain or emotion; it's the demon that bleats, fearful of being evicted from its place of habitation. Thus, when man mistreats an animal he aids God by punishing the devil within. Some say all living creatures excepting a select few humans will tumble ultimately into Satan's fiery realm. That isn't true, of course. We don't have any animals in Hell, or any demons disguised as animals.

"When the animal dies, what becomes of the demon inside it? In Le Père Bougeant's ecclesiastical model it effectively jumps ship and enters the egg or embryo of another animal, perhaps of a different kind. A devil that once tormented a rhinoceros in the body of a tick might next enter the egg of a little bird that plucks ticks from a rhino's hide; it might enter one of the ticks or perhaps a grasshopper underfoot. If the tickbird houses a demon we have a situation in which one demon devours another. Demonology can get very complicated. Demons inhabiting animals have unlimited options. According to a certain logic yet to be demonstrated, this explains why animals of all kinds ordinarily produce many more eggs or offspring that ultimately survive to adulthood: only those infested by demons make it all the way.

"Intermittent plagues of grasshoppers, weevils, caterpillars, and rodents can be explained by a sudden availability of an equally large plague of invisible demons to infest them. A close investigation of the surrounding countryside will undoubtedly turn up evidence of many recent animal deaths, which made them available."

Révigny leaned back and looked my way. Yellow fog passed across his face separated by little pockets of clear air near his nose and mouth when he exhaled. "But the deadliest demons of all inhabit mosquitoes. By the year of grace 2019 learned men will conclude that half of all humans who ever inhabited Earth will have died of mosquito-borne diseases. I find this both wonderful and remarkable. Just imagine! Sum all the deaths caused by man-eating lions, crocodiles, sharks—even the carnage left by wars, plagues, and acts of God and they're nothing in comparison.

"Despite all these theological barriers placed before them the holiest have always found creative ways of making guilt work in their favor. The Dominican monk Heinrich Seuse died in 1366 at age seventy-one. His penance became a model to many suppliants who read his biography *Life*. Seuse described having spoken at table only once in thirty years and no doubt regretted that incident through all his subsequent waking hours. He wore an iron chain and a hairshirt that he never removed. This self-crafted device of torture was fitted with leather strips containing one hundred-fifty nails turned inward. The coarseness of the material in combination with his sweat and blood attracted vast hordes of lice, fleas, bedbugs, and ticks. In addition, he wore between his naked shoulder blades a cross with thirty nails and seven needles facing inward.

"Angela de Foligno considered the flesh of lepers and of Christ to be the same. After washing the feet of lepers she drank the water (Christ's blood), and any scabs and pieces of flesh ingested with it became part of the Host (His flesh), the whole experience a Eucharist. At Manresa, Ignatius of Loyola stayed awake for nights at a time, often refused food for a week, prayed seven hours each day on his knees, whipped himself with studded chains, beat his chest with a rock, and to a leper gave the 'Franciscan kiss,' directly sucking the pus and rotten flesh from the poor man's sores. The reason for all this self-inflicted torture was the belief that the degree of suffering in this life would be reduced proportionately in Purgatory.

"The Church teaches that fun is sinful; join instead in fun's abnegation. The pious are advised to avoid plays, concerts, parties, carnivals, dancing and wearing masks, gambling, singing (except hymns), and every sort of festivity. It's been noted many times that Jesus wept. He wept for Jerusalem and for Lazarus and on other occasions too, but nowhere in the New Testament does it say he ever laughed. No, Jesus was all business all the time. Fun was not a word in his vocabulary. If we hope to be like him we must never laugh, but instead remain in a state of constant lamentation and grief. Abase yourself at every opportunity. If you must laugh do so moderately and for spiritual reasons, not entertainment.

"Remember what Bishop Guillaume Briçonnet told the citizens of Meaux? He said that holidays aren't for pleasure and celebrating, but for weeping, that the greatest pleasure is the abhorrence of pleasure. As for celebrating the birth of a child or birthdays generally, what for? Have you examined the state of the world lately, this 'vale of tears' in which we fight daily not to drown? No, you should weep and expiate your sins. Celebrate death instead of earthly life for its possibility of eternal salvation. If you are poor, take solace in knowing that the rich and fat will be consumed by the worms before the impoverished and thin. And never forget that no sounds are more pleasing to God than pitiful wailing, sobbing, and gnashing of teeth emanating from the confessional. And to think how easily the Church has inculcated everyone. Most believe the confessional has been with us since Adam and Eve, but only since a decision by the Fourth Lateran Council in the year of grace 1215 has confession been mandatory. It's all a ruse. Why confess to God what God already knows? Praying for His forgiveness makes a certain sense, but confessing to another human being what has already been recorded in the Holy Ledger seems superfluous."

So this night ended. I ascended the narrow stairs to my bed in a melancholy state.

Monday June 2nd—The Purgation Decision Explained; Chassenée's Dream Goes Awry; Madame Truye and Lame Loois Are Joined in Marriage

❀

Court reconvened at the usual hour of terce. Since it last met Madame Truye and Lame Loois had been carted from the Philipot pig farm east of Autun and moved into the dock at the Théâtre Romain. On this fine morning in early summer the bleachers were mostly filled, the spectators eager for a show. No one could have anticipated what was about to happen.

The judicial vicar rose from his chair behind the long table, reluctantly it seemed, and began to speak. "After extended and justifiable deliberation, not to mention prayer, I've made the difficult and controversial decision to grant the defendant, Madame Truye, her lawyer's request for purgation. I realize this is extraordinary, having never occurred in the history of French jurisdiction. It will set a precedent that only time will decide has been harmful, benign, or neither. For the present our immediate concern is the veracity of Madame Truye's oath in which she acknowledges guilt of the crime of homicide but pleads mitigating circumstances, specifically, her status as a pig. Lacking *mens rea* she was unable to resist attacking and eating the Philipot foundling, her claim being that any true member of the swinish tribe would do the same, given a chance.

"In debating whether pigs are entitled to such a legal defense that until now has been available only to humans, the two lawyers and I encountered a dilemma. Put plainly, how can an oath of purgation be accepted as truthful in a canonical court if the being swearing it is of low moral character and therefore untrustworthy? Madame Truye has given birth to several litters, and the question naturally arises whether they were conceived and born legitimately or out of wedlock. Is Madame Truye an upstanding sow and respected matron in the swinish community or nothing but a barnyard slut? One of the Philipot's swineherds has partly answered the question by swearing that only a single boar has fathered all her piglets, namely Lame Loois now in the dock with the defendant. However, to leave no doubt that the purgation will be conducted honorably the court has decided to join Madame Truye and Lame Loois in a simple marriage ceremony, which should dispel any controversy about her moral character once and for all. We intend to make an honest sow of Madame Truye. Monsieur Chassenée?"

I stood and as usual walked around the table to the front so the spectators could see me clearly. My short stature left only my upper torso visible if I stood and spoke after pushing back my chair and stayed behind the table, as His Grace and Révigny often did. I spread my arms to quell the rising disturbance. Early murmuring after His Grace's opening remarks had swelled to a cacophony of loud muttering and surly curses. I was forced to raise my voice. "My friends, I realize the proceeding has turned unorthodox, perhaps even blasphemous to some, but I assure you the judicial vicar, a learned man in all ecclesiastical matters, has thoroughly reviewed the canonical statutes and found nothing that decrees marriage between pigs either illegal or offensive to God and the Church. The purpose of this impending ceremony is to make certain that when the time comes my client's oath can be accepted as truthful by her compurgators; otherwise, their sworn trust in her veracity has no meaning."

While I was speaking three mimes gathered between the stand and dock. Two dropped to all fours and commenced snuffling around like pigs. After a minute or so of this, one tried to mount the other from behind. The third stood as if impersonating a priest, pretending to leaf through a nonexistent Bible. The two on the ground then stopped their antics and looked up at the third with beatific expressions. The standing one mimicked a marriage ceremony, holding out his right arm above the heads of the two below as if bestowing a blessing and moving his mouth silently. The crowd loved it, and soon rotten fruits and vegetables started to fly toward the stand. Before I could turn my back a foul-smelling apple struck me directly in the belly, an onion in the temple. Some of the missiles landed in the dock, much to the delight of its occupants. His Grace and Révigny ducked under the table to avoid the barrage. The clerk also ducked under his, although he wasn't a target.

Order was restored when the bailiff's assistants rushed the bleachers armed with truncheons and began cracking heads. A low-level priest wearing a standard black cassock had been summoned from the Cathédrale to conduct the marriage ceremony, and he now strode to the dock where the two swineherds stood ready to speak on behalf of their charges. The priest read from his book, but first asked Lame Loois if he was ready.

"Yes, Father," said the male swineherd.

The priest said, "Repeat after me. I, a boar named Lame Loois, take you, a sow named Madame Truye, to be my wife. I promise to be true to you in good times and in bad, in sickness and in health. I will love you and honor you all the days of my life." The swineherd repeated it. Next the priest asked Madame Truye if she was ready, and the female swineherd said she was. Repeat these words. "I, a sow named Madame Truye, take you, a boar named Lame Loois, for my lawful husband, to have and to hold, from this day forward, for better, for worse, for richer, for poorer, in sickness and in health, until death do us part." The woman repeated it.

The priest said, "I now ask you both three important and binding questions before God. Please grunt or squeal assent, or have your human surrogates answer on your behalf. Lame Loois and Madame Truye, have you come here freely and without reservation to give yourselves to each other in marriage? Will you honor each other as boar and sow for rest the of your lives? Will you accept piglets lovingly from God and raise them to be good Catholics according to the laws of Christ and his Church?" All were answered in the affirmative by the two swineherds.

"Very well," said the priest. "Through authority vested in me by the Holy Church, I pronounce you joined by wedlock in the eyes and laws of God and by the secular laws governing Christians and all members of the swinish race. May the Lord bless you. All present, please bow your heads and remain silent while I recite the *Pater Noster.*"

As the prayer was ending and the priest intoned *et ne nos inducas in tentationem, sed libera nos a malo* I felt the familiar onset of light-headedness, a prelude to being engulfed in one of my dreams. I believed I was talking, although I stood silent, head bowed. I thought I heard my voice—entirely imaginary—turn inward and echo back instead of projecting, tickling my heart with its changes of pace, frequency, and amplitude. The sky darkened momentarily, or did it lighten? The space where I stood expanded, and I spread my legs to brace myself as if balancing on the deck of a pitching ship. The whirlwind swept me up, and I rotated at dizzying velocity. My voice, entirely self-contained, still reverberated, clear if incoherent in the roaring maelstrom. I heard it as an echo deep inside my ears. Details of faces in the gallery faded, merging into splotches of color and form, whirling faster and faster. I felt eternal, coeval with the Universe. Everything seemed infused by an enormous weight, and I felt the ground grip me more tightly. Putting one foot before the other became impossible.

My self, or perhaps my soul, separated from its fleshy prison and drifted upward. By now I'd stepped outside the storm and hung motionless in a vacuum, Plato's featureless void, gazing down at my body with its appendages outstretched, its open but unseeing eyes. I heard myself still talking, the source mysterious and without definition or form. Images of the present had disappeared, then miraculously I was standing in a familiar place above a cauldron of bubbling stew watching chunks of meat and sliced vegetables rise and sink with the regularity of a symphony. Mermaids started surfacing, flashing glimpses of their anatomies: a thigh, a foot, a face in profile, a splay of hair looking wind-blown through the roiling broth. Fingers beckoned. I poised to join them despite my inability to swim. The dream, I knew, would culminate in erotic sex on the bottom of the empty cauldron after the woman and I consumed its contents, a familiar woman, yet a stranger.

I stepped forward but was stopped from jumping by an unseen hand. A disembodied voice said, "You aren't permitted here." Instead of plunging into the stew I was pulled gently back.

Startled, I said, "Who are you?"

"It doesn't matter," said the voice from somewhere behind. "Suffice to say you are contaminated beyond redemption, body and soul."

"What have I done?"

"That doesn't matter either. The dice have been tossed and their numbers revealed. There's no going back. You are dead to the world despite still drawing breath among the living."

"I don't understand," I said, confused and frightened.

"You're a leper, my son, no longer a member of the human race but a perpetual outcast for however many more years God grants you."

"Is there a cure?" I said.

"Yes, but not one you will likely encounter. The known remedies are to be brushed by an alchemist's gold, touch water in which the baby Jesus was bathed or His swaddling clothes had been washed, and feeling the direct touch of the adult Jesus. Some of these remedies are obviously more elusive than others, but everyone knows that the power of a charm is proportionate to the difficulty of obtaining it. Follow the mantra to take heart and pray often. Bear the pain knowing you will avoid Purgatory as compensation for your earthly suffering."

Then the hand was lifted from my shoulder, and I was standing in a graveyard. To the side stood solemn people dressed in black. Among the mourners was Madame Chassenée, a head taller than anyone else. She leaned away from the others, neck bent forward like a vulture's, hard-eyed, mouth expressionless.

A priest in an alb stood nearby. He licked a forefinger and raised it to test the air, trying to gauge which way the breeze blew so he could position himself upwind and not catch my contagion. I was vaguely aware of him speaking directly to me in a low voice. "You have brought this on yourself, Monsieur Chassenée. You couldn't ignore the swollen, itching blood vessels under your tongue that drove you into fits of satyriasis and subsequent moral incontinence. Can there be a difference between leprosy and the French pox? The Italian polymath Girolamo Fracastoro teased us with this question in his opulent rhymes. Obscenity drips from your open sores, your rotten breath. God blesses you and simultaneously shuts His eyes to your foulness.

"Haven't you read the fifty-nine verses of *Leviticus*, chapter thirteen? At the first sign a leper must report his disease to the priests, who will then decide his fate. In verses one and two it's written:

> *And the Lord spake unto Moses and Aaron, saying, When a man shall have in the skin of his flesh a rising, a scab, or bright spot, and it be in the skin of his flesh like the plague or leprosy: then he shall be brought unto Aaron the priest or unto one of his sons the priests.*

"Why did you ignore us? There are many in Saône-et-Loire eager to burn away your disease by fire, who in an instant would gladly erect a stake where we stand and surround it with dry kindling for a pyre. The only items then required would be a rope, a flaming torch, and your suppurating body. Instead, a tribunal has decided to legally isolate you from society, casting you out and thereby sparing your life, such as it is. We're here today for the ritual ceremony of *separatio leprosorum*, in the vernacular 'the separation of lepers.' I'm about to say Mass. Please climb down into the newly dug grave beside you and stand in it quietly. Think of the grave metaphorically as your new dwelling."

I did as ordered, trembling and in considerable pain from my malady. When Mass ended another leper crawled forward, leaned down, and draped a black cloth over my head covering my face. Three times the priest pitched a spadeful of earth excavated from the grave onto my head. After each he intoned, Il est mort quant au siècle, renaître à Dieu (be dead to the world, reborn to God). My paradoxical new existence among the living dead had begun: although leprosy is a legacy of sin and heresy, it nonetheless set me on a direct path to Heaven, bypassing Purgatory as ordained by Him Above.

I stood as erect as possible while the priest read the many rules to be followed. From this moment forward my only companions would be other lepers; even God had disavowed Himself of me. Everything I owned of value was forfeited, and I lost all right to future ownership of property and goods, although I might be accorded usufruct during my lifetime. Like infants and lunatics I had no rights of ownership or to make a will. I could neither bequeath nor inherit. My wife, now officially a widow, was free to marry again, and what I once owned was now hers. As a warning to others I must wear a gray or black robe bearing the red letter *L*. At physical death I would be buried in a lepers' graveyard after a brief ceremony read by a priest, himself likely a leper, and mourned by no one. When walking in a public place I must carry a bell to alert healthy citizens of my approach and position myself downwind of them. I was forbidden to touch any living thing that risked being touched by someone healthy. I must never drink from public fountains or streams that flow through inhabited locations, nor could I wash in them.

Everyone feared my touch and polluted breath. My misery and I would dwell in a one-room peasant hut with an earthen floor and porous thatched roof. I was excluded from public places such as markets, churches, inns, taverns, mills, squares, and anywhere food or drink is prepared. In isolation I could plant a small garden, keep some chickens, and barter with other lepers for any necessities they had that I lacked.

The ceremony ended, and I was instructed to remove the black cloth. When I looked around the mourners were gone; only the priest and the leper remained. The priest left abruptly without another word. The leper attempted to say something, but his vocal cords had been ravaged beyond repair. He blinked back tears, emitted a feeble groan, and waved one claw as if saying goodbye. I climbed painfully to the ground above and limped away in the opposite direction from which the others had arrived. I thought, le monde est perdu pour toi (the world is lost to you).

Révigny and I had entered the tavern together. I still felt weak and unclean and examined my hands and forearms for bright spots and pustules. "It was terrifying, Humbert, truly terrifying." I shivered involuntarily as if licked by a foul wind and downed two cups of wine in quick succession.

Révigny turned and hailed the innkeeper. "More wine, and quickly!" To me he said, "The bailiff revived you with damp cloths applied to your forehead. Fortunately, this time you toppled off the stand onto the grass and avoided cracking your skull on the stand's flagstones. Court has been cancelled tomorrow and Wednesday so you can recuperate and also allow time for transporting the compurgators to court. Thursday ought to be quite amusing." He grinned and took a sip from his cup.

For some reason relaying a description of my leprous condition seemed necessary, despite most people having seen a leper at one time or another. Certainly, they weren't novel sights to anyone as worldly as Révigny, but he waited patiently while my ruptured nerves reconnected and fused. "Strands of putrid flesh were all that held me together," I said mournfully, "and from their interstices oozed the vilest putrescence imaginable. Patches of skin were visible through holes and tears in my disintegrating clothes, their surfaces shiny and coarsely textured like tree bark. My arms and legs resembled the limbs of a newly skinned lamb. In addition, they were swollen, outsized, and oozing pus. My nose had rotted off completely leaving a pair of open holes leaking snot. I breathed through these in ragged puffs. My hands and feet were clawed and useless, the phalanges grotesquely deformed and blackened from decay, and trailing me everywhere was the odor of a rotting corpse, sitting where I sat, lying where I lay, like a persistent shadow. Any movement, no matter how small, was exceedingly painful. The disease had eroded the mechanisms of speech, reducing my voice to weak croaks and grunts, and I deeply regretted having lost that eloquence once deployed in court. I was dead, Humbert, dead and yet alive. I thought of Job, that most famous of lepers, where in chapter eighteen verse thirteen of his eponymous book are the words, *even the first-born of death shall devour his strength*. And I'm more than a little peeved on remembering it was Satan, one of God's angels at the time, who had been dispatched to pile on Job's miseries. *Your associate*, Humbert. How can I be sure he doesn't have something like that in mind for me when we meet?"

After a moment's pause, Révigny said, "God was testing Job. Satan doesn't do that. He takes all comers as they are, and I know he's keeping an eye on you as a potential member of the inner circle, so don't worry. Interesting experience, your dream." He was looking thoughtful, eyes idling at dull amber, then suddenly he smiled evilly. "What a shame. I'd have missed looking at your considerable Gallic nose cratered by pockmarks. It was gone, you say? Through a strange quirk of Church reasoning lepers are allowed to partake of only half the Eucharist. Did you know this? They can consume the Host and thus Christ's metaphorical flesh, but are forbidden from drinking the wine and ingesting His blood. And those tribunals that decide whether someone is leprous or not are laughable. Sometimes the group pronouncing the diagnosis includes one or more lepers, apparently based on the lurid belief that anyone with a disease is qualified to diagnosis it in others. This is the case at Lille. Tribunal duty at Amiens to decide who is and isn't a leper falls to the city magistrates; at Piquigny it's the bailiff; at Saint-Quentin the abbot decides. At other times and places porters, constables, priests, and monks have been conscripted as judges. Strangely, physicians aren't always included in these decisions, and when they are the lepers are often retained as their expert consultants. This should tell us that leprosy is viewed as more a disease of the soul than the body."

Révigny's scholarly musings and the wine were having a positive effect on my attitude. I felt the transitory fears dissipating. I said, "At least as a leper and having suffered so much on Earth I'd have been guaranteed bypassing Purgatory and entering Heaven directly."

Révigny's eyes flashed yellow. "Don't believe that tired horseshit, Barthélemy. Leprosy is a curse, not the 'divine mandate' the clerics claim. Look closely at a leper. Nothing is hidden. A leper's fate is Hell on Earth and likely the same prospect awaits in the afterlife. We have many lepers down below, and their tormented souls burn as intensely as anyone else's. Be grateful your experience was only a twisted dream and hope for happier ones.

"Want to know how leprosy became a heavenly blessing? The contradiction to be overcome was this: if leprosy results from sins and heretical acts intentionally committed, how can it then be the divine mandate we know from the story of Lazarus in *Luke*, chapter sixteen verses twenty-two to twenty-five? A practical rationale arose when participants who had risked their lives in the Crusades returned from the Holy Land afflicted with leprosy. They had fought in a holy war trying to recoup Jerusalem. These men weren't sinners and heretics but heroes to be admired, especially by the Church, so surely their disease must have been divinely bestowed. Ha!

"But back to dreams. Truly, my friend, Christian dreams, no matter how sordid, are delivered by Satan's couriers to induce sin. Since we seem inclined to quote the Holy Writ this evening, remember that *Leviticus*, chapter nineteen verse twenty-five, and *Ecclesiasticus*, chapter thirty-four verse seven, warn against the *somnia*, or dreams in the vernacular, and for good reason if you subscribe to Catholic superstitions. A moment after you swooned His Grace dropped to his knees, hands clasped and gaze directed heavenward, claiming to have seen the five temptations—infidelity, despair, impatience, vainglory, and greed—gathered around you. Luckily for your soul he managed to summon five angelic 'inspirations' in time to drive them away. You had a close call, my friend, coming within a hair's breadth of a chthonic eternity in the Underworld without my guidance." His laughter was like a cluster of defective bells ringing asynchronously, and its echo stayed with me until eventually silenced by the wine's effects.

THURSDAY JUNE 5TH—THE TWELVE PIGS SELECTED AS COMPURGATORS HAVE BEEN CARTED TO AUTUN AND CONFINED IN THE DOCK; MADAME TRUYE TAKES THE OATH OF PURGATION; THE COMPURGATORS TAKE OATHS STATING THEIR BELIEF THAT HER OATH IS TRUTHFUL; COURT ENDS IN PANDEMONIUM

THE JUDICIAL VICAR HAD USED THE days off to arrange for twelve pigs serving as compurgators to be carted from Philipot's farm and herded into the dock. It was barely large enough to hold them. They squealed and grunted, clearly distressed.

On the day when members of the court visited the farm and spoke to the swineherd, His Grace, plainly irritated by the prospect of purgation for a pig, disgusted by the filth of the sty, and overheated in his long-sleeved tunic, had departed with the clerk leaving

Révigny and me to select the pigs to be conscripted for service as compurgators.

It must have been near the hour of nones, and our swineherd's husband, Monsieur Philipot's other swineherd, arrived from the fields driving a huge group before him. She ran to help corral them inside the main sty and then force Madame Truye, Lame Loois, and the rest of their group into the main sty too. After they were all confined in one place and the gate secured, we asked the woman if she was able to tell the pigs apart and were assured that she could. She had names for all of them, probably fifty or so in total. It was an amazing feat. We asked her if she knew how to count. Up to twenty, she said, the number of digits on her hands and bare feet now immersed beneath the soupy pig shit. She reminded us that no two toes look alike. Similarly, pigs are easily distinguished as individuals if you watch them closely. Each has peculiar habits and markings setting it apart from the others. It was no different from recognizing your child from a group of children as they ran around and mingled.

We decided to test her prowess. Révigny chose two pigs from the milling mass; I selected two others. Each watched his pigs carefully. We asked the swineherd their names, then after a few minutes of waiting until they had blended with the others we asked her to point out the four. She executed the request flawlessly. We were convinced. We then wanted to know which twelve, in her opinion, were friendliest with Madame Truye, and she rattled off their names, pointing to them as she did. Of course, Lame Loois was at the head of her list, but in a private discussion we members of the court had decided to recuse him for reasons of bias, he and Madame Truye having been acquainted prior to joining the Philipot herd and also because they were now married. The other twelve chosen by the swineherd were the pigs destined to be compurgators and would be present in court at Autun when the day arrived.

Now it had. The gallery was buzzing. Révigny was right: a trial is nothing but a play, and this time some new actors had appeared in the guise of additional pigs. Also back were the two swineherds to offer advice and assistance in handling them. The bailiff's six men would provide most of the muscle needed to catch and restrain each pig individually when its time came to swear the oath of purgation. I also donated the services of François and Alvin, who had nothing else to do back at the stable. At the moment everyone was standing around the dock awaiting orders from the judicial vicar.

His Grace stood and asked if the lawyers might suggest how to proceed. Révigny said, "I think we should let the swineherds supervise the bailiff's men when separating and handling the pigs."

His Grace said, "So be it. The clerk of the court and the bailiff will take note. Now to three sticky legal matters. First, it's my understanding that we could accept just a single oath from the compurgators as a group, which is sometimes done for convenience with human compurgators, but I don't want our methods questioned in the future. Therefore, each pig in the dock with exception of Lame Loois and Madame Truye will swear individually, no matter the difficulty.

"Second, I considered substituting affirmations for the oaths of purgation and compurgation, thinking pigs aren't Christian and might have religious beliefs unknown to us, but such speculation led nowhere. I concluded that God created the animals to service mankind's needs and that animals lie well below us in the earthly hierarchy. Therefore, if man follows God's laws then animals must obey man's, which in ecclesiastical courts are also God's. I reviewed the canons and it seems a judicial vicar in a tribunal such as this likely retains authority to designate humans as spokespersons for animals when the latter are defendants, although the matter is foreign ground, and our court will be the first to test it. This is my conclusion and consequently my ruling, leaving open the possibility that a future judicial cleric who outranks me might someday overturn it.

"Third, assuming my authority in the second matter is valid, I also waived the requirement that this defendant and her compurgators must sign their names or be required to speak French. After all, clerks and clerics may be authorized to sign legal documents on behalf of illiterate citizens and speak on their behalf if the person represented is mute or a foreigner ignorant of our native language. How is this situation any different?"

Monsieur Philipot's swineherds had evidently discussed beforehand how the procedure should be handled. They worked with the bailiff's men to herd the pigs into two-thirds of the dock, reserving the remainder as open area. This was done by roping off the bigger section, the swineherds shouting at their charges and prodding them with staffs until they had been squeezed into the vacant space, grunting and squealing in protest. Madame Truye was singled out and released through the ropes into the open area. The bailiff's men then jumped on her and flipped her onto her side. Following the swineherds' instructions they tied her hindlegs together, leaving the forelegs free. They then rolled Madame Truye onto her back and the three biggest men draped themselves across her abdomen, keeping her pinned to the ground and unable to roll. From his desk the clerk asked the swineherds to verify Madame Truye by name and wrote it down. A priest approached. One of the three unoccupied men lifted the sow's left forehoof and held it on a Bible while the other two stretched the right foreleg up and out in a raised position. Madame Truye would swear her oath while lying on her back, as would the rest of the pigs.

The priest then read Madame Truye's oath of purgation, which Révigny and I had composed and His Grace approved:

> I, Madame Truye, now on trial before the Session of the Congregation of God's Church at Autun for the mortal sin and capital crime of homicide having been committed by me, do say the following. To end the proceeding and satisfy all, man and beast alike, I declare before God and my associates and this Holy session that although I avow the criminal deed of homicide I disavow the free act of having committed it by reason of mitigating circumstances I could not control, these involving my status as a pig. And so I entreat God Almighty, judge and

avenger of lies, to be my witness if He deigns lower His gaze to a being not created in His image but who walks on all fours with nose and eyes directed at the ground instead of Heaven, a mere sow and chattel, and finds mercy in His heart to pity me so if I must die for killing a child that I be executed humanely. Out of my mouth comes His blessed name, and I swear by Him who knows all hearts great and small, and in sincerity do recognize my status as a lowly, unreasoning brute. I understand I shall be excluded from that wondrous Judgment Day when mankind gathers humbly before Him and answers in the flesh for all earthly deeds, being as I am a soulless beast, ineligible to witness His glory in Heaven after my earthly life has fled.

Madame Truye was an exceptionally large sow, and she tussled fiercely with the bailiff's men. Fortunately, the past few days had been sunny and dry. Nonetheless, by the time she had sworn the oath of purgation and been released they were sweating and the dust sticking to their clothes was turning into mud. Now the same maneuver was necessary for the twelve compurgator pigs, and obviously they weren't happy. Luckily, these pigs seemed weaker and less inclined to resist, and the process was over in about three hours.

Révigny and I had also written a suitable oath of compurgation, which was approved by His Grace, and I reproduce it here. A blank space has been left for the names of the twelve pigs. As each was sworn to the oath in the manner of Madame Truye its name was filled in by the clerk of the court. The clerk also read the oath to each pig. All answered in the affirmative, as agreed unanimously by the four members of the court. The oath read:

> Do you swear to tell the truth, all the truth, and nothing except the truth? Have you been advised of the meaning of an oath of compurgation, which you are about to take? Is your name _____ and do you reside on a pig farm east of Autun owned by Monsieur Jean Philipot? At that farm are you a companion of a sow who goes by the name Madame Truye and is currently on

trial at the Théâtre Romain, City of Autun, Département de Saône-et-Loire? In your experience is Madame Truye an honest pig admired by her peers and of good character? Do you swear by Almighty God who seeks to protect and avenge all creatures great and small and His son, our savior Jesus Christ, to the truthfulness of Madame Truye's oath of purgation given earlier this day, the 5th of June, year of grace 1511?

Immediately after the last pig had sworn its oath they were herded into carts for transport back to Monsieur Philipot's pig farm, and that was the last we saw them. The day had been long and trying. The spectators had immensely enjoyed watching the bailiff's men wrestle their weight in writhing pork and often coming up bloody, cheering in every instance for the pig. Near vespers when the judicial vicar's gavel had struck signaling the end of court on this momentous day, some peasants in the bleachers started a riot. The bailiff's men were exhausted, and the bailiff ordered them to stand down and go home, telling them to let the riffraff sort it out. They could kill one another for all he cared. Meanwhile, we court officials gathered our papers and sneaked from the Théâtre Romain out the back way.

Our wine arrived, and Révigny and I settled into our chairs. The ruckus of the tavern seemed tame compared with our day in court. We had each taken a sip or two when my companion said, "You realize they're all demons, don't you?"

The question startled me. "Who?"

"The two swineherds and all the pigs except Madame Truye and Lame Loois. Their eyes are phosphorescent green; rather, that's how they appear to me. To you they look normal. Have you noticed anything unusual about the swineherds?"

"Only that both are very thin. In terms of opposites, as thin as their pigs are fat."

"True, but demons can be any shape and size. What I meant was, did you notice how they moved fearlessly among the pigs, and the pigs appeared to anticipate their instructions and obey them? I'd have expected a bunch of swine recently carted to an unfamiliar location to charge the ropes and try to escape, but each time the woman summoned one by name it responded and the rest stayed huddled in the segregated area. Also, compared with Madame Truye's performance they mostly succumbed with only a little resistance when grabbed and restrained by the bailiff's men. It wasn't that the men became more proficient as each animal passed through their hands, although they no doubt thought this. No, the pigs had been ordered by the swineherds to stage just the appearance of a struggle."

I sat back. "You're right. I see, now that you mention it. Remarkable. The woman was particularly adept."

"Yes," said Révigny. "She was indeed. Adept and clever." Later that night a courier from the judicial vicar delivered a notice to us in the tavern that he was in process of preparing his verdict. Court would not reconvene again until Friday the 20th of June. That was fine with me. I would use the time to prepare my next strategic move, one even more outrageous than petitioning purgation for a pig.

Friday June 20th—Chassenée Makes a Final Plea yo Save His Client; The Judicial Vicar Pronounces Sentence

Court reconvened, and the judicial vicar spoke. "Whether the perpetrator has two legs or four the crime doesn't change. Homicide demeans the laws of both God and man. Based on the cruelty and ferocity of the crime, I sentence this sow called Madame Truye to be hanged upside-down until death. That is my verdict."

I rose and said, "May I speak, Your Grace?"

"You may, monsieur."

I walked to the front of the stand and addressed the gallery. "Humans place themselves on a higher plane than animals when the separation is at most a low curb. They look down on pigs because pigs don't speak French, but then neither do the English or Germans. Not surprisingly, citizens of these nations are considered by the French to exist on a level with animals.

"After the Flood it was Noah who spontaneously introduced the practice of animal sacrifice to honor God. In *Genesis*, chapter eight verses twenty and twenty-one, we're told, *And Noah builded an altar unto the Lord; and took of every clean beast, and of every clean fowl, and offered burnt offerings on the altar. And the Lord smelled a sweet savour; and the Lord said in his heart, I will not again curse the ground any more for man's sake.* . . . And what was that 'sweet savour' God smelled? The odor of burning fat, which no man or deity can resist. Because life of the flesh is contained in the blood, to consume blood was forbidden, so stated *Genesis*, chapter nine verse four.

"By this time God approved of Noah's sacrifice to Him, but He still had other reservations. God then prohibited the spilling of human blood by both humans and animals and says in *Genesis*, chapter nine verse six, *Whoso sheddeth man's blood, by man shall his blood be shed: for in the image of God made He man.* Animals, however, were free to devour each other and spill blood in every direction. In other words, God noticed that animal sacrifice comes dangerously close to the murder of humans and spilling of *our* blood, and therefore the explicit demarcation became necessary. Murder and sacrifice have always been associated closely, but the distinction becomes apparent only after intervention and consent of a deity. Then their separation reinforces where man and beast rank in God's earthly hierarchy. These days we rely on judicial procedures to put us apart from the animals when the dichotomy becomes blurred and occasionally confusing. This is one of those instances in which clear thinking is necessary."

I immediately stopped rambling on seeing the judicial vicar start to fidget. "This proselytizing is best left to the clergy, Monsieur Chassenée," said His Grace. "What's your point?"

"My point, Your Grace, is that mankind's dominion over the brute beasts is far from absolute. As we can see in *Genesis*, chapter nine verses four and five, and reinforced in the Holiness Code of *Leviticus,* chapter seventy verses eleven to sixteen. Violation of these admonitions made blood-guilt a major concern. Would you like me to read the Holiness Code?"

"That won't be necessary. As a priest I believe I'm sufficiently familiar with it. Please try to stay focused."

I bowed. "Yes, Your Grace. I apologize for the distraction. As these sections of the Pentateuch make clear, the shedding of human blood by either animals or humans is folded into those prohibiting consumption of animal blood by mankind. The divisions are clear: man can eat the flesh of certain animals, but the blood and fat belong to God, as stated in *Leviticus,* chapter three verses sixteen and seventeen. During a sacrifice the fat is burned until rendered into smoke and the blood thrown against the sides of the altar, as decreed in *Leviticus,* chapter seventeen verse six. These acts confirm two things: the Lord's interest in all his creations, and recognition that man's dominion over animals doesn't include control over their life and death, at least not without qualifications.

"Going back in time to the ancient Greeks, pagans all, we learn from the story of an immigrant named Sopatrus, who was farming at Attica. He built a sacrificial table . . ."

The judicial vicar pounded his gavel. "That's enough, Monsieur Chassenée! Your tactics are nothing more than a frivolous delay of this proceeding. Monsieur Révigny, do you want to say anything? I regret that your opinions have been crowded out."

Révigny was clearly enjoying my dressing down. He said, "No, Your Grace, I bow to my adversary's erudition and wish to hear more of his foolish soliloquy. He's truly the suzerain over bluster and bloviation."

"Indeed," said the judicial vicar.

I saw this exchange as permission to continue my rant. "Then I appeal to His Grace's well-known fairness and humility and ask that my client be allowed to appeal the verdict to a higher court. I realize that granting it would be unusual and cite as precedent the case of a sow and a she-ass sentenced to be hanged, but after re-trial were executed instead more humanely by a knock on the head with a heavy mallet."

The judicial vicar said, "Monsieur, the precedents you cite are from secular trials. This is an ecclesiastical tribunal, and you well know appeals are precluded. My verdict is final."

I said, "Then at the least issue a decree that orders all swineherds within the Département de Saône-et-Loire bring their charges to the public square on execution day so they can witness the guilty pig pay with its life. We can only pray they learn a lesson."

Révigny now rose. "Your Grace, I accept your offer to speak. I hold that such a spectacle is unnecessary."

"So do I," said the judicial vicar. "Now, Monsieur Chassenée, please take your chair and allow me to relay the verdict to the defendant."

After I was seated his grace descended from the stand and walked the few steps to the dock where Madame Truye was incarcerated. There he announced the verdict and sentence in Latin. It read in the vernacular:

> Because the wounds inflicted by the pig on trial before me have caused a child in this century to pass away (de ce siècle trépassa), we, the ecclesiastical court of Autun, in detesting the horror of the crime, and to establish an example that justice may be upheld, have determined, judged, sentenced, and pronounced said sow who goes by the name of Madame Truye, now in detention as a prisoner, shall be by the bourreau, known colloquially as the master of high works (maître des hautes oeuvres) hanged upside-down from a gibbet of wood until dead. The date of execution will be announced and posted in public places throughout the département.

"I have one addendum," the judicial vicar said. "I shall personally escort this guilty sow to the gallows. Being a pig, it will take its final stroll toward limbo unclothed, wearing only the skin in which it was wrapped at birth and destined to be pork cutlets that no human mouth will ever taste. Some districts—Saint-Diez and Moyen-Moutier, for example—confiscate the clothes of condemned men and women on the day of execution and later give them to charity. The prisoner then suffers a final public humiliation by dying naked. However, the definition of 'naked' was not always clear. Some clerics claimed that ropes used to drag an obstinate pig to the gallows and another used to hang it constitute clothing. Opponents, of course, argued that ropes are simply ropes, not clothes. The matter came to a head after a pig was hanged at Moyen-Moutier for killing the infant daughter of Claudon François and the abbot feared that a man dangling from a rope in his birthday suit might then be considered as 'dressed,' rupturing for all time the local practice of hanging prisoners naked. If ropes are clothes how could anyone be hanged ever again? To the relief of all a commission of clerics appointed by the pope declared ropes to be articles of restraint and execution, not clothing, thereby upholding tradition."

The judicial vicar returned to his seat. "Court will reconvene Monday the 23rd at the usual time to discharge any unfinished business."

MONDAY JUNE 23RD—THE BISHOP IS CALLED
TO PARIS; CHASSENÉE ANNOUNCES HIS INTENTION
TO WRITE A REMISSION LETTER TO THE KING
ON BEHALF OF MADAME TRUYE

COURT RECONVENED ON SCHEDULE. WHEN WE were all settled in our chairs and the proceeding was officially in session His Grace announced that the bishop had been called to Paris unexpectedly on confidential Church matters leaving all final decisions about Madame Truye's trial to his discretion. Therefore, unless one of the lawyers raised a new issue he considered the proceeding closed. Notice of the execution date would be posted when he got the time. The executioner had been notified and was awaiting orders.

I asked to speak.

"Of course, monsieur, but let's be quick. I have other business needing my attention, especially with the bishop gone."

"Thank you, Your Grace," I said. I rose and stood behind the table. There were less than a dozen spectators now that the verdict had been read, and my principal audience comprised members of the court. "I'm issuing notice to file a letter of intent to His Majesty King Louis XII on behalf of my client, Madame Truye." I glanced at Révigny, who nodded almost imperceptibly and grinned.

"You're *what?*" said His Grace.

"I'm petitioning the king to remit my client's death sentence. I've written a Letter of Remission identifying her as the suppliant, along with the requisite Pardon Tale in narrative form explaining the circumstances of her crime, subsequent accusation, and reasons she ought to be declared innocent and released. Any convicted criminal has this right under French common law."

"Surely, you're not serious, Monsieur Chassenée," His Grace said.

"I am," I said. "The letter and tale have been prepared and need only transcription by a clerk. As addenda I shall require a complete transcript of the trial once you have approved it, along with copies of the oaths of purgation and compurgation bearing your stamp."

"This has never been done," said His Grace. "A remission request for a pig? It's outlandish."

"The pig is my client," I said, "and it's my duty to explore every avenue of possible exoneration."

"I'll approve your request, monsieur, but let the record show that I do so reluctantly. If your wish is to become a butt of jokes in the King's circle it will doubtless be granted."

"My client and I thank Your Grace for such generosity. I shall deliver the Letter of Remission and Pardon Tale to the clerk of the court within three days. He can date and notarize both documents. In the letter I have stated June 20th, year of grace 1511 as the date of your verdict. I trust the clerk of the court to forward the letter and enclosures to the nearest Royal Chancellery, this being at Dijon, eighteen leagues northeast of Autun, and arrange for the package to be sent by courier with other legal documents routinely dispatched to the court of His Majesty."

"That will be done, monsieur," said His Grace. "I have two questions. First, how did Madame Truye transmit her tale orally; second, how was it transcribed?"

"As Your Grace is aware, that animals can talk to humans on certain occasions is common knowledge. The details of its occurrence in this specific case are revealed in the documents. For the transcription, I did that myself, Madame Truye being too shy and embarrassed to relate private aspects of her life to a stranger."

At this His Grace broke down in laughter, joined by Révigny. He began gathering documents from the table in preparation to leave. "I hope for your sake the king shares our mirth. I'm told he enjoys a good story or joke on occasion. Court is dismissed."

"One more thing, Your Grace. Once ratified by the court of law, in this instance where the trial has been held, the defendant, now legally a suppliant, can't be executed without the king's reply denying the pardon and allowing the sentence to be carried out. I therefore request that she be returned to her herd."

"I understand, Monsieur Chassenée. With the bishop gone the approval falls to me, and I shall take care of it." He turned to me and bowed, then to Révigny. "Good day, gentlemen. The clerk will stay in touch."

My Letter of Remission and accompanying Pardon Tale read as follows:

1st of July in the year of grace 1511

To King Louis XII, Our Most Serene and Mighty Lord, Royal Highness by the Grace of God, Sovereign of all France, Defender of the Faith, Etc., Please Accept For Consideration This Letter of Remission, Pardon Tale, And Other Pertinent Enclosures

Letter of Remission—I, an adult sow known as Madame Truye and your humble suppliant, submit this Letter of Remission, accompanying Pardon Tale, and other supporting documents from the ecclesiastical court of Autun. In them I petition Your Highness to overturn my death sentence handed down on the 20th of June in the year of grace 1511 for the crime of having killed and eaten a child of three months, or thereabouts. I also request that you spare from slaughter my legal husband, a boar known as Lame Loois. All documents have been duly and properly notarized by a clerk of the court of the ecclesiastical tribunal of Autun. I swear that the contents of my letter and tale have been transmitted with what truthfulness memory can permit, and that the words are mine as spoken straight from my own porcine lips and recorded faithfully by Monsieur Barthélemy de Chassenée, my trusted lawyer. Meanwhile, the court has ratified an agreement to hold in abeyance my execution and the slaughter of my husband for table meat until a written decision from Your Majesty has been received and reviewed by the ecclesiastical authorities at Autun.

As addenda I have included (1) a Pardon Tale describing the situation and circumstances of my crime and subsequent accusation, (2) my Oath of Purgation as the suppliant, (3) oaths of twelve compurgators chosen from among my sty-mates, (4) a copy of the record of the trial, (5) a copy of the verdict of the 20th of June in the year of grace 1511, and (6) a document offering proof of the joining in marriage of Lame Loois and me by an ordained priest of the Catholic faith on the 2nd of June in the year of Grace 1511.

In my Oath of Purgation I have not declared innocence of the crime, but innocence of intent, fully understanding that homicide involontaire and homicide volontaire are indistinguishable legally. Note too that twelve compurgators, all fellow swine who know me well from my herd at the farm of Monsieur Jean Philipot, have attested that my oath was given truthfully. I therefore ask His Majesty for exoneration and by separate mandate to spare my lawful husband, Lame Loois, from future slaughter so that we may enjoy what years God may allot us while wallowing in the bliss of our home sty and dining on slops and mast with our friends and associates.

Pardon Tale—I pray Your Highness will not be insulted that my Pardon Tale is communicated in the vernacular French instead of formal Latin. I apologize profusely for this indelicacy, the disruption my petition might take of your time more precious than gold, and other inconveniences caused by this intrusion. I apologize also for my tale's brevity, but I did not want to bore Your Highness. As I shall explain, I was a woman until one night evil demons changed my husband Eudes and me into pigs, and we later found ourselves held captive on a swine farm east of Autun, a situation persisting to this very day. My husband, rendered permanently lame that fateful night, will be slaughtered and butchered this autumn, and I have just been declared guilty of homicide at ecclesiastical court in the city of Autun. I have subsequently taken an oath of purgation at which I allocuted to my foul deed but disavowed the act itself based on mitigating circumstances brought about by having been turned abruptly into a sow.

You might wonder how a pig could write a Letter of Remission and a Pardon Tale, given our status as dumb brutes with cloven hoofs incapable of holding a quill. This too can be explained. Put simply, my words have been dictated. Direct conversations between animals and humans are well documented, and my being a woman in a pig's skin explains the even greater likelihood of communication in my case. Such conversations mostly take place during the Christmas season when miracles are to be expected and involve only farm animals, horses in particular, but pigs are farm animals too, and nothing rules out animals and humans conversing at other times of the year. To my knowledge no one has yet reported a conversation with a pig, rat, or insect. Nor has any pagan god granted this gift to any but a few special animals, notably Achilles' horse Xanthos. Perhaps I'm the first porker to step forth and speak to a monarch, and I do so through the kind graces of my trusted and sympathetic lawyer Monsieur Barthélemy de Chassenée, who listened to my words and wrote down my story.

For another well-known illustration of animals talking to humans I direct His Highness to the case of the prophet Balaam and his donkey. The incident is described in the Old Testament, specifically Numbers, chapter twenty-two verses twenty-three to thirty-three. In brief, Balaam, on an errand for God, encounters an angel in his path holding a raised sword. This heavenly being was invisible to Balaam but not to the donkey, which tried to avoid it by leaving the road. Angered and confused by her behavior, Balaam struck the beast three times with his staff. The donkey, suddenly able to speak, asked Balaam why he was mistreating her, at which point the angel became visible to him too. The donkey not only spoke, she had suddenly been granted rationality and was, at least in that moment, no longer a dumb brute.

Monsieur Chassenée and I met several times alone when court was not in session and I remained imprisoned in the dock at the Théâtre Romain, City of Autun, he listening and transcribing my words while sitting in the witness chair nearby. Anyone eavesdropping in the vicinity heard only pig sounds, but my heartfelt squeals and grunts entered Monsieur Chassenée's mind as a truthful record of my sorrow and woe and a detailed description of the events bringing them about, the sum hereby presented in legible French directly before your royal eyes. Thanks to Monsieur Chassenée's willing assistance I once again have a voice. Monsieur assures me he has transcribed the words with the accuracy of a trained clerk of the court, omitting no important detail. To Your Highness alone has the august power of remission been granted, and on your mercy do I bare myself and tell my tale.

The horror began at a Christian gathering of villagers to celebrate the Feast of Mary, Mother of God. It was the evening of January 1st in the year of grace 1509. I suddenly was defending my honor and that of my husband Eudes by rejecting the crude advances of a drunken woodcutter. The man had been sorely surprins de vin (surprised by wine). He lurched at me trying to force my lips to meet with his, emitting his foul breath in my face and cupping my breast in his filthy hand. I turned away screaming and trying to escape, but he wrapped his other arm around my waist and pulled me against him. Rape was clearly in his eyes, nothing less than the evil intention of despoiling my body and spirit. Eudes immediately rushed to my aid and slapped the aggressor hard across the face, demanding that he release me or pay with his life. Eudes, a schoolmaster who often tutored his students past the hours of daylight, carried a dagger to protect himself from highwaymen. He pulled it from its sheath, touched the point to the man's throat, and I was let go at once.

In all modesty I was considered a comely woman and a loyal, obedient, and faithful wife who attended Mass regularly and was liked and admired by everyone who knew me, any of whom would gladly give me an entérinement. My only fault was infertility, for which I received much sympathy, including from Eudes who promised always to love me anyway. I wore my burdens lightly with a smile, willing to lend a helping hand or dispense a kind word to another less fortunate soul in the name of Jesus Christ, our Lord and Savior. That was, of course, before the terrifying event that overtook my husband and me that night.

We left the gathering immediately, but the crétin was hiding in the bushes with an axe and swung it as we passed him in the dark. He struck blindly, but the blade still caught Eudes' leg, hamstringing him. He fell in pain but rose quickly, grabbed my hand, and we hobbled into the night, Eudes spilling his blood along the way, the attacker apparently too drunk to pursue us.

We ran into the dark forest nearby, tripping over roots and rocks, unable to find a path in the inky blackness. Branches tore at our faces, vines grasped at us like evil serpents. When we tumbled and struck the frozen ground the sudden pain caused us to yelp and groan. We stopped running on emerging into an open field where dozens of milling pigs revealed their shapes under the weak moonlight. Two hunched swineherds thin as death approached us wearing hooded cloaks and carrying wooden staffs, faces invisible but eyes glowing phosphorescent green. Then we noticed that the pigs had stopped grunting and shifting about and were looking up at us in silence, their eyes the same as those of their captors. The frigid air above them should have been misty with their exhalations, but not so. It was as if the swine and their keepers had no need of air. We had stumbled into a coven of demons and were surrounded and trapped by these evil beings. Eudes could barely stand, much less run. There was no escape.

Theologians have proved many times that animals lack Christian souls, although their bodies are always amenable to occupation by demons, and swine as demonic habitations are named specifically in the Holy Writ. In Matthew, chapter eight verses twenty-eight to thirty-four, Jesus ordered devils into the bodies of some swine at Gadara, driving them mad and inducing them to plunge over a precipice into the sea. Thus Le Père Bougeant's theory had been right: every creature great and small is potentially a demon's habitat because suddenly we became swine, an experience nearly too lurid to recount.

Suffice to say, we were transformed starting when our noses changed instantaneously into snouts. A feeling like a shock-wave passed over us, probably lasting just a few seconds but seeming much longer, as if time had slowed. We felt our different muscles and bones shrink or lengthen as the transformation progressed, sensed a tightening of the skin, an overall heaviness from an unexpected weight. Every muscle, every tendon and sinew, was being pushed and pulled into a new configuration, yet because they remained anchored in place the sudden forces of change as they rearranged themselves made us twitch and whirl around dizzily as if gripped in a terrifying Saint Vitus dance. Our faces twisted and contorted as hands and feet morphed into cloven hoofs, heads and backs were yanked forward; we toppled onto all fours, no longer able to stand erect. We had sunk in the terrestrial hierarchy from exalted to excluded, no longer representatives of God's highest achievement so carefully crafted in His image. The swine had formed an open circle around us and watched in silence as we became . . . them.

Consider the consequences of my fate and that of my beloved Eudes, Your Highness, the terrifying metamorphosis, the horror of the maggot becoming the butterfly except in reverse.

If at all possible imagine my stultifying existence ever since that night. Imagine if you and those you hold dear had swapped places with Odysseus' men at the instant Circe transformed them into swine. Yes, that very Circe, high priestess of witches, herbalist par excellence, and since the beginning of the Christian era inarguably Satan's disciple. Those poor souls. Close your eyes and try to experience their sudden urge to devour one another in the onrushing flood of esurience that dominates a pig's existence, a life in which everything organic is food and nothing more. Be one of them and watch in horror as your sailors' boots become a pig's feet, your curses and exclamations of alarm are smothered in frightened grunts.

That night we were conscripted into the herd at a pig farm owned by Monsieur Jean Philipot of Autun. You know what happened then. The record of the trial recounts how I was accused of eating a foundling child being cared for at the farm, causing his death. The transcript mentions how I was tortured in the hope of wringing a confession of my guilt, which I readily admitted. Then what had been the point of inflicting such pain? None I can conjure.

Nonetheless, beneath the Cathédrale Saint-Lazare d'Autun is a dungeon, a place of horror and perpetual night where daylight has never penetrated, where thoughts of God can't be distinguished from anguish, where Lazarus lies in his casket somewhere nearby in a niche along a dank passageway, one of several. The walls of the dungeon are poorly caulked, purposely so, it seems. In winter the cold seeps in from the frozen earth; in summer the stones perspire from the suffering all around. The floor is slick with an evil broth of congealing blood mixed with vomit, shit, urine, and saliva expelled into the open by fright and pain. It flows in a thin stream, pooling here and there on the flagstones, diluted by tears and sweat. The dungeon's stale air reeks of these internal fluids and exudates, filling the bleak space left where love and kindness have never visited. Disembodied screams like the echoes of souls departing reverberate, attenuate to whispers, and begin again. The sounds that reach me are rapid breathing, muttered curses and prayers, weeping, pleading, the soft thud of iron-tipped scourges on flesh. Banks of torches stuck in wall sconces cast flitting, demonic shadows. Can Hell be worse than this place?

The tormentors are masters of their craft, knowing when a tiny flick of the rack's wheel can almost but not quite disarticulate bones, pop tendons, stretch muscles nearly to the separation point. They understand how to bring a victim to the precipice of fainting before pulling back; they hate that unconsciousness is solace. The engineers who build these machines and keep them tuned like clocks are equally adept at their calling: oiling the moving parts on schedule, making intricate adjustments to keep the wheels and gears lubricated and spinning smoothly. What marvels of technology, these torture devices! Exempla of mankind's relentless advances over the material world. We can't feel anyone's pain except our own, and pain has a voice only the person experiencing it can hear. We exist inside individual envelopes, isolated and unbridgeable to others. My envelope of reality of which pain is a part is inaccessible to you, and yours to me. True suffering is unsharable.

My geôliers took me to this place of irrevocable sorrow and shame hoping to wring a confession of guilt by exerting pain on nerves and flesh that were only borrowed and not my own, yet I felt them. What did they expect to gain? What was the purpose? They put a rope around my neck, and I followed passively as a puppy. To resist was futile. I knew the outcome. As a sow I had fewer rights than a woman, who has few enough. Women are treated as chattel too in these misogynist times.

The handlers strapped me on the rack and set to work, and in a short time they got the anticipated response: in the presence of the judicial vicar, clerk of the court, and the two lawyers I squealed like a pig, which I simultaneously am and am not. To Monsieur Révigny and the judicial vicar my vocal display was clear evidence of guilt. Monsieur Chassenée, however, argued that if irrational animals are devoid of mens rea then how was it possible for me to confess either guilt or innocence? He argued that I instead should be treated as an insane adult human or minor and acquitted. If this was still unacceptable the court might consider that its logic is faulty, he continued. If dumb animals indeed are incapable of lying then my squeals could just as easily be declarations of innocence, in which case I was not guilty and ought to be freed. The three men debated for what seemed eternity before my lawyer agreed to relent and also consider me guilty so the torture would cease.

Everything had become backward, you see. Typically, a demon gains entrance to a dumb beast or bestiole and from that moment forward controls its every impulse and movement, but here was a sentient being, not a demon, forced to take up residence in a pig, although not to the extent of completely controlling it, and certainly having no influence over its host's impulses. I remained a human only in terms of the sensibilities conferred by God to every man and woman and His concomitant blessing of rational thought; otherwise, I was a pig in every way, an animal intent only on finding its next mouthful of food and not much caring about the source or consequences.

And thus my dilemma, Your Highness. I committed homicide—or murder, if you like—by killing a child, a mortal sin, and in addition the venial sin of *jejunium sextae* for devouring its flesh on a Friday. Is my crime excusable? Not according to the jurist Jean Papon's list of thirteen extenuating circumstances, none of which applies in my case. If

Eudes or I had possessed the presence of mind to wrestle that axe from the woodcutter's hand and split his skull with it we surely would have been exonerated and spared this predicament. Ah, l'appel du vide.

Our experience has been a blessing in one respect: I am no longer sterile, having now borne several litters sired by Eudes to whom I remain ever faithful, and he to me. I weep piggy tears each dreadful day my young ones are taken to Autun and sold at the livestock market. Losing them is painful beyond belief. What more can be said? Eudes watches helplessly with rheumy eyes and a melancholy air as they're loaded into the cart. We have no means of comforting each other, a pig's grunts being only affective noises devoid of the vocabulary of reason and revelation. Our metaphysical concerns are trapped inside, unable to be expressed. Sadly, Eudes too will soon depart, butchered this autumn slaughtering season to provide winter meat for Monsieur and Madame Philipot's table. And I? My corpse will be forbidden flesh buried in a field somewhere, the site unmarked and soon forgotten. For a human to eat it would be cannibalism, for the Philipots to do so even worse if they were raising the foundling as their own flesh. How so?

In peasant dwellings the pig being fattened might be confined in one of the rooms. It's important to keep the door to the room barred, especially if children are around. From an early age children are taught not to approach the pig. In effect, a bogeyman lived among them with a taste for tender meat. The ominous creature being raised for food must never come too near; if the flesh and blood of the child were to fatten the pig, how would this be different from devouring their own lineage? Cannibalism comes full circle: the pig living and sharing food with the family is then a de facto relative who eats a child and is eaten in turn by the child's survivors. It's the final metamorphosis when the family members turn the child's flesh into themselves.

I wasn't born to this craving; rather, the urge inherent in my adopted species overcame Christian sensibility on smelling the fragrance of the Philipot foundling's flesh and the breast milk recently dribbled from its lips. The urge simply was too powerful. All contemplation became blinded by esurience, and animal instinct reigned. I could easily have lifted the child from its bassinette, but in swinish eagerness I tipped it over, trampled it, and began to devour the living contents. Even the clothing tasted sweet, but before I could complete my grim task the caretaker appeared screaming and waving her arms, and I ran away feeling waves of guilt mixed with frustration at leaving those succulent remains behind. I ask no mercy for myself because I deserve to die for this appalling crime. I ask only that my loving husband be spared the slaughterer's blade and allowed to live his remaining years in peace.

And so, Your Highness, this is the story of my travails as relayed to Monsieur Chassenée and recorded by him with honesty and care. Do with me what you will.

Be assured I shall pray until my moment of death to Saint Antony, patron saint of swineherds and pigs. May the great and good God long preserve Your Majesty in safety and prosperity.

Your devoted and loyal servant,

Madame Truye (née Madame Amée Clavel)
City of Autun
Département de Saône-et-Loire

TUESDAY AUGUST 19TH—
A LETTER FROM THE KING ARRIVES; RÉVIGNY
REVEALS THE BISHOP'S FATE TO CHASSENÉE

FRIDAY THE 15TH OF AUGUST HAD been Assumption Day. The city was recovering from a festive mood, although for unknown reasons I felt melancholy. Madame Chassenée and I had come to Autun for the feast during which Madame celebrated with her relatives. I stayed at the inn with Aufrey, François, and Alvin. Aufrey and I shared a bed while François and Alvin stayed in the stable as usual to keep an eye on my animals and coach. After Mass on Sunday Aufrey returned to the estate with Madame and the coach. It was nearly sext, and I was waiting in the tavern for Révigny to come back from the judicial vicar's office at the Cathédrale.

The previous night while I was dining alone a courier arrived with news that a letter from the king had been received with a decision on Madame Truye's request for remission, and His Grace requested an audience with Monsieur Révigny at his earliest convenience. I told the man I would relay his message when next I saw Révigny. I had no doubt he would appear any minute, knowing his habit of showing up right at the proper time without having been summoned. Just as I was ordering wine he walked through the door.

"Where have you been?" I said.

Révigny flopped into the opposite chair and waved to the innkeeper's wife to fetch him a cup. "Here and there," he said, "but mainly there."

"And where might 'there' be?"

"Paris, mostly. I listened discreetly as our bishop was excoriated by Church leaders for his unseemly behavior, then told his fate, which is to live out the remainder of his days as a monk at Monastère Saint-François d'Assise, a bleak outpost in Le Trévoux in the far northwest where the people speak Breton. You could scarcely be more distant from Paris and still reside in France. Not really unexpected.

"In his defense our bishop brought up the concept of spiritual hearing, claiming a demon had whispered in his ear and taken over his mind, but no one bought it. Spiritual hearing is far more powerful than its corporeal counterpart because it detects the mind speaking and eavesdrops on the monologues of the soul. The corporeal ear is a selective filter, often hearing only what it desires. However, the spiritual ear hears and knows everything. Nothing remains hidden from it. But demons can nonetheless insert themselves, crowding out and disrupting holy thoughts and replacing them with illusory images of avarice and lust. What the physician discerns of the heart's thoughts by checking his patient's pulse, so can demons judge a person's susceptibility to evil deeds from listening to what the mind is saying as it converses with itself.

"I've mentioned before that Hell has its share of clergy, ranging from rural priests to cardinals and popes. As you've no doubt noticed, sin is rampant among ecclesiastics. Name a holy vow and I can show you the soul of a cleric who postponed penitence and is now paying the awful price. We have uncountable examples of God's 'representatives' suffering the searing heat without a drop of water to cool their hypocritical tongues. They never realize that praying won't help once ensconced in Hell. Their earthly crimes? Those you might expect: simony, lust both expressed and repressed, fornication in all its manifestations—pederasty, sodomy, incest, masturbation, adultery. Now add pride, selling indulgences and pocketing the fees, gluttony, drunkenness, calumny, avarice . . . The list is nearly too long to recite. Ah, the flesh is weak, isn't that so?

"Well, a cup or two with you, and I'm off to the Cathédrale and His Grace. He naturally summoned the prosecutor as representative of the Church's interest, rather than the defense attorney. Don't feel regret. Better to be nearer the wine anyway."

I had been controlling my wine intake but was slightly drunk nonetheless when Révigny returned. He sat and waved for a cup.

"Well, my friend, your Letter of Remission and attached Pardon Tale made quite an impression on His Majesty." He grinned, eyes pulsing red, and stuck out his forked tongue, letting it crawl halfway across the table. I made a show of pretending not to notice, but confess that the little snake eyes on the two tines of the fork always unnerved me.

"Let's hear it, Humbert," I said.

"As you probably surmise I was there in the king's chambers when his personal secretary delivered your letter. Nobody knew, of course. Who notices a green-eyed fly clinging to the ceiling upside-down? Anyway, the king ordered the man to open the letter and read it aloud. With each sentence he became more fascinated, interrupting and asking that the previous bit be read again and making comments like, 'Purgation for a *pig*? The bishop actually allowed it?' This confirmed one of our original questions about whether the bishop had informed the judicial vicar of his tendentious relationship with the Church hierarchy in Paris over the Philipot daughter. He obviously had not, thus giving His Grace freedom to approve your outlandish requests for purgation and later remission.

"I must credit you, Barthélemy, your strategy was brilliant, disrupting the blind legal machinery of the Church so cleverly. And your letter on behalf of Madame Truye was dazzling, filled with sadness and pathos. It nearly brought tiny fly-tears to my compound dipteran eyes. Fortunately, there were six appendages available to rub them."

Disturbing the Church's order had not been my specific intention, but the wine rendered me amenable to a compliment. "Thank you," I said sincerely.

"The king found your Letter of Remission, Pardon Tale, and appended materials enormously entertaining. He laughed so hard at the wedding scene that he pissed his breeches. After departing the room briefly for a change of clothes he asked his secretary to read it again. 'Who is this lawyer, Chassenée? He should give up the law and become a novelist.'

"After the third reading of Madame Truye's Pardon Tale the secretary asked His Majesty how he wanted to reply. That's when I heard the decision straight from his mouth, essentially the same words transmitted in his letter I've just seen. In my view King Louis did the right thing. His decision was to carry out the verdict and hang Madame Truye from a stout gibbet, as the public expects. A murderer can't properly be exonerated. The Church is to pay Monsieur Philipot the market value of Lame Loois as pork on the hoof and allow him to live out his days unmolested at the pig farm, never to be slaughtered and butchered. In the king's opinion this outcome made everyone a winner, including you, monsieur!" Révigny raised his cup to me in a toast.

Perhaps fittingly, supper that evening bordered on the regal: crispy bacon sliced thick with freshly baked bread and lentil soup that was actually hot. A couple of hours had passed since the bowls and cutlery were cleared away, and we were left with our cups and a fresh flagon.

"Being a demon exempts me from most postprandial issues, as you know," Révigny said. "However, eating and drinking can still lead to indigestion." He paused to hold his stomach and belch. "Fatty pork always gives me gas." I immediately smelled something dreadful and realized Révigny had farted. I expected green smoke to seep up from underneath the table but instead saw a vaporous cloud the color of brimstone. How could he generate gas while bypassing digestion? There must be an unknown mechanism of physiological combustion known only to experts in demon anatomy.

While I tried not to gag, Révigny said, "I ordered the innkeeper to prepare this meal especially for us on this evening of celebration. Notice that everyone else is spooning up the usual swill. I'll naturally pay the extra charge. What else is a demon to do with his money? Anyway, the bacon is a gift of Monsieur Philipot. He says it's special and that the court will never bother to check the source. He wants nothing more to do with the court or the memory of Madame Truye."

"Bacon is bacon," I said. "Why is this so special?"

Révigny leaned forward and wiggled his eyebrows. "Because it's Lame Loois."

PART III

Le Loup-Garou In The Dock

"For Little Red Riding Hood,
the real world is the one where wolves speak."

—Laurent Binet—
The Seventh Function of Language: A Novel

Monday September 10th, year of grace 1515—
Chassenée, François, and Alvin Depart the Estate
for Magny-Cours Where Chassenée
Will Defend a Purported Werewolf

During late summer in the year of grace 1515, on a date I can't recall, I received a courier at the estate bearing a document signed by the secretary to Andrew Forman, a Scot who had recently been appointed to the archbishopric of Bourges by King Louis XII. The document asked if I would represent a man accused of being a werewolf now incarcerated at Magny-Cours. Opposing me as procurator would be my old adversary Humbert de Révigny.

I signed the document agreeing to take the case and sent the man on his way, suspecting that Archbishop Forman doubtfully even knew about it. He was a revered diplomat, not a cleric, never passing up a title or sinecure when offered and gladly accepting the associated lands, prestige, wealth, and other entitlements. For me the appeal was once again opposing Révigny and renewing our friendship, visiting a city I had never seen, and representing a werewolf for the first time in my career.

Since defending the rats and Madame Truye my law practice had grown considerably, and I was now famous throughout Saône-et-Loire. Not long after Madame Truye's trial I opened a bigger office at Autun staffed with a secretary and an eager young attorney to whom I left such mundane matters as wills and title searches, saving the more interesting work for myself. Our arrangement was going reasonably well because from the start I anticipated and quashed his amateurish attempts to cheat me. Fear of losing his livelihood now kept him circumspect, allowing me to retain his services at a lower salary than he probably deserved. I'd hinted that if he solicited and defrauded unimportant clients on his own time I would show him the respect of our profession by looking askance. However, if he cheated me or my regular clients in any manner he would quickly find himself shackled in the stocks and displayed in Autun's public square, and I would see that his law license was revoked permanently. This threat was proving adequate deterrence, at least for the present time, and I had no qualms about leaving local affairs in his hands for several weeks. As for Madame Chassenée, no doubt she would relish my absence. Her new coach had arrived recently from Paris, the first contraption having broken down from nearly continuous use, and Aufrey was presently squiring her all over the countryside so she could flaunt its unrivaled finery.

Magny-Cours is a city of modest size about twenty-five leagues directly west of Autun. Having never been there I was allowing ample time for travel and acclimation. A leisurely pace would allow me to enjoy the scenery along the way and become acquainted with local conditions before court convened. I would need to find suitable inns with taverns while in transit, and on arrival make arrangements for my men and animals and learn my way through the streets. Fine autumn weather was setting in, the leaves were changing from monotonous green to fiery oranges and reds, and I looked forward to days of pleasant weather and avoiding Madame Chassenée.

The morning of departure had started with the usual unpleasantries, Madame insulting my appearance and I making equally sharp retorts. She had become increasingly obsessed with Judgment Day when the dead scrabble out of their graves and the living assemble beside them to be lifted into Heaven. I offered the sarcastic advice to pray that she not die deaf and miss hearing the trumpet's blast. Madame now kept a small valise under the bed with a change of clothes and certain female accessories, and her bedside table at night held not only her dentures but a freshly baked loaf on a silver plate. Her reasoning was that Heaven is a long way from Earth, and she might need a snack along the way. And so went our parting.

I rode the palfrey; François and Alvin followed sitting double on the mule and leading the donkey loaded with baggage, the latter now suitably docile after his long-ago appointment with the cas-traire at the livestock market in Autun. I expected the way to be slow and arduous, and it was. We trundled along making some three or four leagues a day, departing after breakfast well before terce and starting to seek lodging as afternoon slipped past nones. A midday meal was eaten by the roadside or sometimes skipped.

The way was poorly marked. We often lost time by choosing a wrong fork, traveling a considerable distance before discovering the mistake, and then backtracking to the site of the error and taking the other road. We passed only a few fingerposts, but these are notably unreliable. Shiftless peasants often twist them so they point in the wrong direction to purposely lead innocent travelers astray. At first I tried asking directions from rustics we encountered shuffling along under their burdens, but found their instructions useless. Most never venture more than four leagues or so from their place of birth and consider any location outside these self-imposed boundaries to be a distant country. François and Alvin were no help, the former nearly mute and contributing only his permanent smirk, the latter babbling about birds while excitedly tracing their aerial maneuvers. My only consolation was congratulating myself for having allowed ample travel time.

We rode through copses becoming leafless in the autumn chill, among rolling hills partitioned into fields of drying hay. The road was congested at times with the carts and wagons of farmers and merchants and an occasional coach bearing a wealthy lady. Most of the travelers were pedestrians of the lower classes: orphans and beggars, peddlers, tinkers, monks, and entertainers of all sorts.

Sometimes a curé riding a bony mule passed and tipped his hat. The roadside held the immobile and squalid, notably lepers in various stages of decay, their grotesque twitching torsos rotting slowly. There they sat or lay barely mobile, these wretched scarecrows, some praying to die, others pleading with passersby to kill them and end their misery. Although I felt a twinge of compassion and occasionally dropped a coin, their fate was not in my hands, and I rode on trying to erase from my mind the indelible images of their limbless trunks, the memories of their pungent odor and hoarse croaks of anguish.

The establishments where we hoped to lodge would be unmemorable except for a certain consistent squalor and the clumsy criminality of the proprietors. Our needs were hardly extravagant. Nonetheless, each morning when trying to settle the bill amicably it would be necessary to remind the innkeeper of my exalted standing as a lawyer in the king's legal courts. It required telling him sternly that if he overcharged or otherwise tried to cheat me I was prepared to see him stand a day in the stocks in the nearest village open to public ridicule, possibly followed by forfeiture of his property to the Crown.

On hearing these threats his surly attitude changed abruptly, and he then addressed me as "My Lord," hovering obsequiously as I carefully checked the list of items for which I had been charged. For myself a night's lodging under a leaky roof in a louse- and flea-infested bed shared with another traveler. A supper of moldy bread kneaded by his wife's grimy fingers and bowl of gristly meat and a few limp vegetables bobbing in tepid broth, the revolting whole washed down with a flagon of unpalatable green Spanish wine, or, with luck, the same wine adulterated with a slightly better local vintage. Added to the bill on chilly nights would be a few sticks of firewood to relieve the dampness, the cost divided evenly by all sharing the room. Then the purchase of a candle for any needed trips outside to the latrine after dark (I carry my own flint and steel); fodder for the animals; barley bread, cheese, a flagon of green wine, and a night's lodging for François and Alvin in the stables, plus their breakfast of barley bread and a bowl each of small beer. Breakfast for myself: a similar bowl of small beer, a pot of tea, barley bread with cheese, and maybe a piece of spiced cake soaked in wine.

Sometimes the inn is also a brothel, the prostitutes doubling as serving girls during supper when arrangements for later trysts are made with travelers and fees negotiated. One of them would deliver breakfast and supper to my men in the stables. If François took a tumble in the hay with her he would somehow have to pay for this pleasure (or grief), a sticky situation considering he has no money, and in such instances I refuse to reimburse the innkeeper for whoring services based on François' false promises. These conditions all held true when we stopped that first night.

By afternoon of the second day, Tuesday the 11th of September, traffic had become sparse, as if most of the travelers had arrived simultaneously at their destinations. Where these places might have been was puzzling. We hadn't passed through a village since early morning, yet by nones we were alone and the sun was starting its downward trajectory toward the horizon. A wind kicked up causing the fallen leaves to momentarily levitate in miniature devil's spirals. Clouds now occluded the sky. I stopped and ordered a dismount so we could rummage in the baggage for our coats and let the animals drink from a stream, which was sufficiently swift to turn the wheel of a small mill. In a window of the miller's house the glow of a lone candle competed with the dying sun's reflection.

We rode on through the hour of vespers, still without encountering an inn, farmhouse, or other sign that the countryside was inhabited. It was as if we had reached the end of the world. Behind me Alvin began to whimper, and François muttered something about needing his supper. It was now well past dusk, and continuing much longer as darkness descended would be folly. We might be set upon by highwaymen, or one of the animals could stumble, injuring itself or one of us. We carried blankets, bread, wine, cheese, and sausage, so bedding and food weren't issues. The animals had been watered, and there was plenty of grass beside the road. We could hobble them and let them graze in the dark. We needed only shelter and safety for ourselves—and light. Man is a diurnal and social creature, and to feel comfortable he needs illumination and the company of others. While I was musing about why this is so, most of what little light remained vanished abruptly. The road had narrowed and we were entering a forest. I could vaguely discern the outlines of trees on either side and became aware of their dry leaves rattling in the wind, their trunks stirring and creaking. Was this a haunted place? Behind me Alvin's whimpers became moans. Without having to look back I knew François' head was swiveling in growing terror. An unknown woods in darkness is no place to be.

Intermittent streaks of moonlight wavered on the road ahead as the wind rearranged the canopy. Above us branches writhed and scraped across the moon like angry hydras. Objects of uncertain size and shape scuttled back and forth across our path, disappearing and reappearing from the tree lines. When they turned toward me their eyes glowed phosphorescent green. I muttered a protective blessing and crossed myself three times: disappear evil spirits, go haunt elsewhere, your powers are blunted while I wear the cross against my heart. Suddenly the donkey brayed. I turned to see its hindquarters prancing like a pram yawing at its mooring. The mule reared, dumping François and Alvin on the ground where they lay howling in fear, clutching each other and rolling to avoid being trampled by the mule's hoofs. Something was attacking the donkey, causing its evasive movements. I turned the horse around, grabbed my whip, and began beating the attacker with all my strength, not knowing what manner of beast it could be. A wolf, perhaps? A werewolf? Then it spoke: "Please stop, My Lord! I'm so sorry!"

Hearing a human voice was startling, rendering me momentarily speechless. After gathering my wits, I said, "Who—or what—are you? Stand still and reveal yourself or this beating will continue. Tell me your name and estate at once."

"My name is Jamet Ruisard. I'm merely a hungry man and a mendicant, My Lord, and don't mean you any harm."

"What are you doing in these woods? Are you a robber?"

"No, My Lord, just a beggar. I've never robbed anyone in my life."

"Then why did you attack my donkey? Surely you didn't intend to eat it."

"I smelled the victuals it's carrying in the saddlebags,, the bread and cheese. It's been nearly a week since I last touched food, a hunk of moldy bread begged from the wife of the miller whose mill you must have passed. She was about to throw it to her chickens."

"Is there an inn ahead?"

"Not nearby. The wind is softening, and the night is turning clear; it would be best to camp by the roadside."

"Is it safe?"

"Yes, My Lord. No one dares enters these haunted woods at night."

I dismounted. The mule had ceased stamping, which allowed the donkey tethered to it to stand in place. I told François to unload the donkey, unsaddle the horse, and hobble all three animals. They had been trained to raise and bend back whichever foreleg is tapped so they can be hobbled quickly. My instructions were to station them well apart where the grass seemed plentiful, allowing them ample rope to prevent entanglement.

I set Alvin to collecting what firewood he could find nearby, knowing he was too frightened to wander far. I ordered Jamet, the new man, to range deeper into the darkness and collect all the dry wood he could carry. He did this and then made several more forays without being asked. Soon we had a cheery fire on which François made tea. I always traveled with an extra cup and plate in case a set was lost or damaged. Jamet, smiling happily, joined us in what for him was a feast of hot tea, wine, and hunks of bread with slices of hard cheese and summer sausage.

After filling our bellies and calming our mutual fears with wine, Jamet told me his story. He was an educated man, a former priest who had fallen into a carnal relationship with a married woman of his parish. On learning of the scandal the bishop had defrocked and expelled him. His options were entering a monastery and spending the rest of his days copying holy documents or traveling random roads and begging. The second choice seemed the more interesting. He had recently come to this forest and found it quiet and pleasant. Being haunted, it was unnaturally empty of humans, and he was thinking of staying a while. I asked if the demons I'd seen were dangerous.

"No," he said, "although they try hard to make travelers think so. Most are common forest hobgoblins, which are naturally mischievous and more a nuisance than evil, and in a place like this with so few people passing through they get bored quickly, especially at night. Nothing depresses a hobgoblin more than losing the capacity to scare someone. They don't speak, of course, except in grunts and shrieks, and they don't eat, so trying to beg food from them is useless. Everything considered, these creatures are harmless and make irritating companions. Trying to converse with one is like talking to a squirrel. If I someday get too lonely I'll move on. Trouble is, where people gather you'll also find more beggars, so the competition can be intense."

We arose around prime the next morning, Wednesday the 12th, and breakfasted on tea, bread, and cheese. Jamet proved himself a man of energy and quick intelligence. He rapidly organized the gear into the correct saddlebags despite having helped unload everything in the dark. Before I could instruct François and Alvin to unhobble the animals and untie and coil the ropes Jamet had undertaken and completed these chores. He discharged them without instruction, whereas my footmen required daily orders to carry out the same quotidian tasks they should have known by rote.

In appearance, Jamet was disheveled and slight to the point of boniness, as might be expected of someone who lives in a haunted forest and earns his bread by begging. At least he was honest. He could easily have slipped away in the night with some of my possessions and vanished among the trees.

When we were ready to depart he made a step of his interlaced fingers to help me onto the palfrey without being asked while François stood stupidly nearby. "Goodbye, My Lord, and good luck," he said.

In that moment I was struck by an idea. "Would you care to be employed as my personal servant? As you can see my footmen are shiftless, yet they're lifelong members of the estate and I feel a certain responsibility toward them. Your duties will be to serve me and carry out whatever orders you're given. In return you may reside on my property near Autun and receive shelter, food, and clothing. I'm a prominent attorney in the Autun region on the way to a trial at Magny-Cours. How long will we be away? Who knows? Answer quickly."

"Yes, Master, by all means I'll serve you faithfully! It's a great honor!"

"Good," I said, dismounting. "Then take the feudal oath of loyalty by kissing my left hand." Jamet immediately dropped to his knees and did so, then scrambled to his feet. "I haven't introduced you to my footmen, François and his son Alvin. You two," I said looking at them, "are to obey me, as always, but also Jamet here and assist him in any manner required. Is this understood?" François gave me his smirk, looked past Jamet with his wandering eye, and nodded. Alvin giggled then pointed to a bird overhead and flapped his arms. "Je suis un oiseau! Regar de moi voler! Regar de moi voler!"

"You three lighten the donkey's burden so Jamet can ride it," I said. "Put some of the leftover baggage behind me on the horse." I watched Jamet swing into action, quietly directing the others, and in a matter of minutes the task was completed, a small miracle.

Jamet seemed unduly excited. "I've never ridden on the back of an animal. Wherever I went I walked. This is a new experience, one I greatly appreciate, and a donkey, no less! Now I'll have some notion of how Christ felt." He glanced at Alvin, then at me. "The smaller one looks very much like you, Master," he said with an impish grin.

"I noticed that too," I said. Unfortunately, it was becoming truer each day. We were both short as gnomes and totally bald with pointed heads shaped, indeed, like the small end of an egg set upright in an egg cup. We sported dark beards, and our heads seemed to have been hammered down between narrow shoulders until our necks all but disappeared. Neither of us could properly turn his head without also turning his shoulders. Alvin's stomach was still not a match for my extravagant paunch, but that would come eventually.

The road continued through the forest, which began to thin toward nones. We saw no other travelers, nor did we come upon a dwelling, even a hermit's hut. The weather remained pleasant and intermittently overcast, the trees unmoving, dropping their leaves solemnly in the still air. The forest was unnaturally silent, and the only sounds were those we made: the squeak of leather, footfalls of the animals, and our combined exhalations. Just as the light was fading we emerged onto a meadow and saw only isolated trees in the distance, indicating open country ahead. With no inn in sight we again bedded down beside the road. Jamet quickly organized everything, and in record time the baggage had been unloaded and unpacked, the animals hobbled, sufficient firewood to burn through the night collected, and I was leaning against a tree trunk sipping hot tea while Jamet sliced sausage and cheese, broke loaves, and readied the wine. He had been a remarkable discovery, and I congratulated myself for recognizing his redeeming qualities and taking him into service.

Thursday September 13th—Chassenée's Retinue Arrives at Magny-Cours and Finds an Inn; Révigny Joins Chassenée in the Tavern Near Vespers

⌘

SHORTLY AFTER SEXT WE BEGAN TO pass shabby huts and small houses, indications that Magny-Cours was not far. Many had adjacent or attached makeshift stalls offering goods and services. As when nearing any French settlement these rickety structures would become increasingly numerous, eventually piling up like flotsam against the city's walls, which stand as both a physical and a social barrier separating the indigent from the more prosperous tradesmen and merchants who own permanent, sturdy houses and shops within the walls and constitute the urban bourgeois.

The road led directly to a merchant's toll gate where I paid the fee and received directions to a recommended inn with a tavern. Once inside the city we proceeded carefully down the narrow streets. Citizens commonly build private latrines that project out from their houses above rights-of-way, allowing piss and shit to rain down on passersby. Sequestered inside, residents can expunge bladder and bowel in anonymity, pedestrians below beware and be damned. From these domiciles there would be no gay warning cry of *gardez l'eau!* before emptying a chamber pot out a window into the street.

I followed the toll taker's directions to the inn and made the usual arrangements, except now I was paying for three men's food and lodging. As before I asked to share a bed with Révigny, who had not yet arrived. The men would be ensconced together inside the stable in a dry stall with clean hay. The innkeeper seemed more sophisticated than usual and listened to my instructions politely. When I asked that a table at his tavern be reserved for my colleague and me to take breakfast and supper and that the wine be an acceptable local vintage he gave a knowing nod.

And on hearing that Révigny and I were lawyers for the Church and Crown who countenanced no cheating on bills, doctored wine, bad food, and unclean bedding he bowed graciously and assured me I could trust the services provided by his family unequivocally. If either of us had a complaint we needed only to state it and he would act immediately to rectify the situation. He added that he and his wife were available to serve our needs day and night.

I next gathered my men and held a brief meeting. I told them that I was increasing their ration of wine to two shared flagons per night. This was partly because I now had another man, but also to assuage any resentment François might hold against Jamet for supplanting him in the traveling hierarchy. And, in fact, I said as much, congratulating François and Alvin for welcoming Jamet into the fold despite no evidence they had done so. Knowing they would be idle most of the time, I insisted that the animals be groomed regularly, their stalls kept clean, and that they receive adequate hay and water. Not knowing Jamet's sexual proclivities, I reminded all three that they had no money; consequently, if anyone solicited whores the fees would not be paid by me, nor was any additional food or wine to be charged to my account with the innkeeper. When asked if these terms were clear, they nodded affirmatively. I then ordered Jamet to ask the innkeeper where the lamps, pitchforks, buckets, and shovels were stored and arrange any other matters relative to our stay as he saw fit. Afterward, I trundled off to my bed and napped through the afternoon.

Near vespers, as I was just settling into my chair in the tavern, Révigny shuffled through the door looking no different than when we had parted after Madame Truye's trial. "Monsieur Révigny, where have you been?" I said, gaining my feet. I was happy to see him.

"To Hell and back, monsieur!"

"You seem no worse for the wear," I said. "Hell must be a salubrious place."

Révigny plopped into the opposite chair. "Indeed so, and soon I shall be missing the warmth. I anticipate this proceeding lasting at least into early spring. By then you might be begging me to take you there on a teensie vacation to check out the climate."

"Ha! Not on your life! Oops! Pardon the slip." I signaled the innkeeper to bring wine.

Révigny exploded in laughter, vitiated almost immediately by the usual coughing fit as the acrid brimstone smoke inside his cocoon flooded his spectral lungs. "I see you haven't lost the gift of sarcasm," he said when the spasms finally ended. "Even Satan might be intimidated by your quick wit."

"Has Satan ever feared anyone?" I was curious.

"This wine isn't bad," said Révigny, taking a hesitant sip. "But to answer your question, very few, although a certain crone stands out. Have you heard the tale of Skoella?" I shook my head. "It's of Nordic origin. One time Satan tried and failed to break up a married couple. It irritated him that they were so much in love. One day he met an old peasant woman who lived nearby, quite an evil crone. She was barefoot, and winter would soon arrive. She said she would separate the couple if Satan promised her new shoes. Satan agreed.

"Skoella went first to the wife and told her that her husband was unfaithful, but if she cut a few hairs from his beard while he was sleeping he would immediately love her again and put away the other woman. Then she went to the husband and told him that his wife was unfaithful and planned to slit his throat while he slept. She advised him to feign sleep and have his own knife at the ready. That night the wife crept into bed and the husband saw the knife in her hand. Not knowing she meant only to harmlessly remove a few hairs from his beard he sprang up and stabbed her to death. As you might expect, Satan was extremely pleased. However, the old woman's cunning and malice alarmed him so much that he stood some distance away from her and extended the promised shoes attached to the end of a long pole."

"That's hilarious!" I said. "But is it true?'

Révigny spread his arms and widened his flashing orange eyes in a gesture of disbelief. "Isn't everything I say?"

I turned my head and waved a hand dismissively in good cheer. The comradery renewed, it was time to discuss business. The food arrived, and we commenced breaking loaves and spooning up the stew set before us, which if not exactly delicious was at least pleasantly hot. The innkeeper kept our cups filled, and over a leisurely evening we reviewed what we knew about the upcoming case.

My client, Marcel Plonta, presently incarcerated here in Magny-Cours, was accused of being a loup-garou, or werewolf. The documents said he lurked in the city's graveyard at night, howling and sometimes attacking passersby who took shortcuts along the paths. His presence was greatly feared. When reading the charges the man's case seemed straightforward. He hadn't killed any of his victims, just nipped them in the neck and shoulders. The wounds had been superficial, and he readily admitted guilt, claiming he was unable to resist the strange transformation that overcame him suddenly, including nights of a full moon, or plenilune. At such times the urge to become a wolf was overpowering and nothing, not even the threat of arrest and trial, could quell it.

The case would be tried in inquisitional court under the rubric of heresy with Révigny assisting the judge in procuring and evaluating the pertinent evidence and serving as prosecutor. Werewolfery is considered to be heresy, and convicted heretics are sentenced to die at the stake. Because an inquisitional court is under ecclesiastical jurisdiction, carrying out a death sentence is delegated to a secular jurist, saving the clerics involved from possibly violating their vows by having blood on their hands, if only metaphorically.

Friday September 14th—Chassenée Visits His Client, Le Loup-Garou, in His Jail Cell and Listens to His Story

THE NEXT MORNING, A MORNING OF sunshine and birdsong when the furthest thoughts from anyone's mind could be of werewolves and demons, I visited my client. The jail was a street away from the market, the cells in a dungeon beneath a public building that housed the city's administrative offices and accessible by a dank, narrow stairway. It was a gloomy place fit only for cockroaches, rats, and, apparently, werewolves. Despite the stone walls and iron bars the poor man was shackled hand and foot and tethered to a wall by chains. Thus restrained, he could shuffle about his cell only with the greatest difficulty. The guard told me this was a necessary precaution. Werewolves were said to have superhuman strength when the frenzy of metamorphosis came on them and that four strong men could not subdue a specimen of even modest size. The courts weren't taking chances of his again running loose in the community. Going to such extremes seemed absurd, but then I was new to the case and withheld comment.

Monsieur Plonta was not a big man, although neither was he small. I would call him average. His clothes were ragged and filthy, and through their holes I could see much of his physique, which was sinewy and muscular as you might expect of someone who had labored hard for many years, a history soon confirmed. Every movement involved pulling against the weight and forces of the chains seeking to keep him immobile, and although he didn't seem to notice the effort his muscles did, bulging and rippling like subdermal serpents seeking to escape confinement. There appeared to be no fat or soft places anywhere on his body, and I began to wonder whether the chains could indeed restrain him if he made a violent effort to pull free of the wall and twist apart the bars of his cell.

As I do with all clients—the human ones, at least—I asked him to relax and tell me his story, assuring him I was there to represent him to the best of my ability, that my expenses were being covered by the Church and Crown and my efforts would cost him nothing.

I said to him, "Should I address you as Monsieur Plonta?"

After a moment's hesitation, he said, "No, please refer to me as Le Loup-garou. It's how I'm known in these parts."

"Very well, Monsieur Loup-garou, please tell me your story and how you came into this predicament." He sighed and settled into a corner, graciously offering me the crude pallet that served as his bed and chair. This is what he told me.

Some years before (he couldn't recall how many), he had been a farmer near a tiny village in Sens Joigny. Life was difficult, of course, as it is for all peasants who work the land of a nobleman, receiving a pittance in return. However, each spring he and his wife had been allotted three piglets to raise for sale. One was the nobleman's, and money from its sale would go into his coffers; the other two were theirs. This was a generous arrangement because it gave them a pig to slaughter in autumn for the winter's supply of smoked meat and another to sell at the market. Ordinarily, most of the money would be spent buying a replacement piglet, but because of their benefactor's generosity they could put the profit from the second in their pockets. All in all their lot was better than most, and they had few complaints.

Then suddenly his wife fell ill. Aflame with fever she became delusional, shouting nonsense, not recognizing either him or their young daughter and slipping into fits of uncontrollable weeping. A midwife who doubled as a healer was summoned. None of her broths, teas, or unguents had any effect, and the wife's condition worsened. The midwife asked him and his daughter to leave the room while she put cold cloths on her patient's forehead. Soon thereafter she ran out, reporting in a terrified voice that steam was rising from the cloth and visible in the vapor were tiny imps and demons the size of large insects. They had cackled and grinned at her. She said she was afraid and promptly left, never to return.

Le Loup-garou tended his wife as best he could, but she died that night after a series of convulsions. In the candlelight he watched her thrashing, saw her sweaty nightshirt pasted to her body. He saw her eyes roll up until the blue disappeared leaving only the white sclera. Suddenly, she sat upright and bared her teeth at him like a mad dog, drool covering her chin, before giving a final spasm and toppling over dead. Two nights later his daughter died the same way.

These events happened so quickly that neighbors feared a return of the Black Death, except none of the symptoms fit. Buboes hadn't appeared in the groins of either the wife or daughter. Neither had coughed up bloody sputum, nor had their fingers turned black. Furthermore, the husband and midwife had remained asymptomatic longer than a week following exposure, which seemed to rule out a contagion of any sort. However, demons had been seen, leaving bewitchment the most logical explanation. Someone had cursed this family and for unknown reasons spared the husband. He must somehow have brought on the tragedy, or at least been an accomplice.

There ensued ugly accusations that might have led to his conviction of witchcraft and subsequent execution by fire except for one thing: he demonstrated no evidence of guilt, nor could anyone think of anything unsavory about his life. He had been a true and faithful husband, attended Mass regularly, gave what alms he could, doted on his daughter, and was widely admired for his diligence and honesty. The man had no detractors.

Nonetheless, he was eventually accused of witchcraft and taken before the court, where the lawyer assigned to defend him requested an order of purgation. This was granted, and a dozen suitable compurgators were found among his neighbors, who testified unanimously to their belief in his oath of innocence.

Persons accused of theft, murder, and other secular crimes often fare better in ecclesiastical than secular courts. This is especially evident in cases when the accused requests purgation. Clerical judges are generally more interested in community harmony than in punishment. Leniency in the form of a fine or public apology is common. A defendant who denies a false accusation might petition for a canonical purgation hoping to restore his reputation. Even if found guilty, sentences ordinarily are lighter than those issued by civil courts, often just public penitence.

The judge presiding over this case, however, was Institoris, celebrated author of the *Malleus maleficarum* (*Witch-Hammer*) and arch enemy of witches everywhere. I need emphasize that the testimony of a list of credible compurgators is nearly always sufficient to exonerate someone accused of a crime, particularly a person who has never in his life stolen even an egg or knowingly told a lie. Le Loup-garou's lawyer had done his job, and by all rights his client should have been released from custody immediately.

Institoris found himself in a difficult position, surely knowing he ought to do the right thing but evidently reluctant that his reputation as a relentless hunter and destroyer of witches might be tarnished. He therefore compromised. He spared Le Loup-garou's life, but sentenced him to perpetual banishment and to be chained for the remainder of his days in the bowels of the king's galleys among former runaway slaves and vicious criminals. Subsequently, the poor man was dragged from court and tossed into an ergastulum with others of the condemned where they wallowed for weeks in their own filth and supplemented the moldy bread with the roaches and rats that crawled over their bodies.

At last he was transferred to a galley. There he languished, little better off than in the foul cell. His oarmate was an outsized Greek slave with wild eyes and a runic symbol burned into the middle of his forehead. His long incarceration had loosened his wits, precipitating intermittent fits of rage during which he viciously attacked

Le Loup-garou and the oarsmen behind and in front of them until the rowing master descended from the deck, scourge raised, and beat the Greek bloody.

The food was so vile that men puked even when not seasick. It consisted entirely of moldy bread, often wet from seawater, and salted fish, more often rotten than not. The men shit in pails passed up and down the port and starboard ranks and emptied by a bent old man no longer useful as a rower, or they simply shit where they sat. When sleep was permitted they took it slumped over their oars. The Greek spoke no French, Le Loup-garou no Greek.

Until now the sea had meant nothing to him. Like sky, earth, and desert it was simply a concept, not a place. He had always been a landsman and was seasick during the first few days. This naturally annoyed his oarmate, who took to punching him in the face and ribs. At first the rough oar tore even his farm-hardened palms. Each wetting from seawater splashing through the oar ports raised the grain of the wood, making it a little rougher. Eventually, he grew callouses adequate to compensate, but his lower body was always soaked. This and the coarse wooden seat kept his buttocks, crotch, and thighs in a continuous state of inflammation.

Months went by, how many he didn't know. As men died their bodies were taken up to the deck and tossed unceremoniously into the sea. The galleys always carried extra deckhands, and soon a new man was shackled in the dead man's place. Nothing changed. The rowing master set the pace and gave directional commands. If the vessel was to turn right, starboard rowers momentarily shipped their oars, then on a command dropped them again but now rowed backward. Meanwhile, the port rowers continued apace rowing forward.

The rowing master was a cruel Frenchman, a criminal himself sentenced to the galleys and once chained to an oar. He took special delight in tormenting his French captives. Le Loup-garou's back, neck, arms, and shoulders were soon striped with festering whip lashes, and he once lost part of an ear when inadvertently neglecting to protect his head with his arms during a scourging. Their bare feet, which never dried, turned pale and wrinkled from the endless soaking in a slop of vomit, piss, shit, and swirling sea-water. In summer they sweltered below decks; in winter they shivered from cold and food too deficient to warm the blood. And always there were the beatings, either from each other or the rowing master. Always there was pain, discomfort, and the stench of effluvia and unwashed bodies. Men sometimes went mad, screaming and babbling incoherently, at which point they were unchained, dragged topside to the deck, and pitched overboard to drown.

One day when his Greek oarmate attacked him Le Loup-garou too went insane. He grabbed his tormentor by the testicles until he howled, then sank his teeth into the man's neck, ripping open the carotid artery. His adversary howled louder. The rowers stopped, everyone craning to see what had happened. The Greek's eyes were wide and staring, on his face was a look of surprise. He pawed absently at his neck as if searching for a spot that itched. Le Loup-garou watched without compassion as he slumped down, curiously shrinking as death approached. A pool of dark, thickening blood flowed onto the bench and spilled down to the deck. The rowing master looked at Le Loup-garou with something akin to respect. He calmly unshackled the corpse and called topside for assistance. Another man, quaking with fear at seeing the evidence of carnage, was soon chained to the oar and looking warily at his new oar mate. Le Loup-garou wasn't taken to trial or even admonished. How do you further punish a man already considered dead to the rest of the world? And who cares if a slave is murdered? It was soon afterward that his shipmates gave him his name.

The misery and monotony never varied, nor did it wane. By now he'd become rock-hard. On an afternoon in winter the rowing master told them to prepare for a storm. The sea was becoming noticeably rougher, and they were chilled by water sloshing in and out of the oar ports. From their location below deck there was no telling whether night had fallen when the storm struck. They were ordered to ship oars and stand by, realizing only that if the ship sank they would die. Some begged the rowing master to unchain them. He refused, probably fearing the men would kill him for his cruelty. We all drown if the ship sinks, he shouted at them above the wind and crashing of the sea, adding his doubts that any of them could swim, and in such a violent storm it wouldn't matter. No one can swim when the waves are the height of mountains and the water is near freezing. And anyway, to where would you swim? It's night, the rain and sleet are horizontal. Even the moon and stars have run away. No one knows in which direction land lies, much less how close it might be.

As it happened, land was very close. Shortly after the rowing master's remonstrance a towering wave lifted the galley, held it poised for a moment at the apex, then sent it slaloming down its shoulder to its very base, now sucked out and undercut by backwash nearly to the sea floor. Partway through its versant trajectory the vessel overturned and swung sideways, parallel with the unseen shore. The men on deck were thrown overboard; the rowers below, tethered in place, became airborne, yanked violently in all directions like windblown leaves. Arms were torn from their bodies when the chains stopped abruptly and rebounded with unthinkable force. The wave's full mass now landed on the vessel, having at that instant reached its nadir, and it was practically lying on the substratum. It shattered like glass, contents surging forth and disappearing as if the Great Flood had reappeared to wipe Earth clean in preparation for a new beginning.

But one living object survived, if barely. Le Loup-garou awoke from a daze on a cobble beach beneath a sun he hadn't seen in years. He was bruised and beaten, but with all extremities intact. Miraculously, no bones were broken, although his shackled wrist throbbed painfully; attached to it was the inevitable chain.

Directly before him a snow-white cliff rose abruptly. It was unlike anything he had ever seen. He found himself squinting in its reflected light. Could rocks really be this white, or had his eyesight been damaged by the years of semi-darkness? He staggered along the beach in search of a way up, passing a small group of wary sheep feeding on seaweed along the tidal wrack. He walked on until finding their path to the top. The sky was darkening, indicating foul weather on the way. He wrapped the chain around his neck and shoulders to relieve its weight on his injured wrist and climbed laboriously to the top, his tender feet feeling every pebble and thorn. In the distance he saw a farmhouse constructed of stone, the windows blocked by crude wooden shutters. Beside it was a stone barn and paddock for livestock, probably the sheep on the beach. A sliver of smoke rose from the chimney. He stumbled toward it, but before reaching the door a man and woman rushed out and helped him inside. Who was he? Where had he come from? What had happened to him? This was undoubtedly France, but their accent was strange. He answered as best he could before fainting.

He came to on the floor, his head pillowed on the woman's lap, and she was offering a spoonful of hot broth. Nothing in his life had ever tasted so good. After he was able to sit up her husband brought a cup of wine, a beverage he couldn't imagine ever tasting again. They told him he was near Étretat on La Côte d'Albâtre in Normandy and had just climbed their remarkable alabaster cliffs. He admitted to not knowing Normandy even existed.

They repeated their questions, and he answered them truthfully. They were stunned by his tale and sympathetic at his unfortunate luck and years of hardship and offered to help him reach wherever it was he was going. He said he wasn't going anywhere in particular, and that he surely wasn't going back his home village. That would be suicide. The farmer said he operated a small smithy and the two of them went to the barn to remove the shackle and chain. The man was about his size and offered some threadbare clothes, which he accepted gratefully. He stayed there a month recovering his strength and helping with the farm work for his room and board. Then they packed him a sack of bread, cheese, and smoked meat, and he set out for Paris, which they told him was some forty-five leagues east.

After exhausting the food he tried begging along the roads, seldom successfully. People noticed his quirky mannerisms and avoided him, thinking he was dangerously insane. For example, he told me, he sometimes growled deep in his throat, causing even the most aggressive feral dogs to slink away, ears folded and tails between their legs. It was an effective way of being left alone. Women and children huddled together for mutual safety as he passed, this strange ragged man with the long, tangled hair of a lion. At a roadside stand he stole a loaf and ran, but a pack of vendors chased him down, beat him, and cut off his ears leaving the healed earholes rimmed with pimples of hardened flesh that now stood stiffly like remnants of a stubbled field. The result made him appear even more frightening and mysterious.

I felt upbeat that evening on entering the tavern, this despite having listened to my client's lengthy and depressing story. I reminded myself that his sorrows weren't mine, that my role in this play was to help him, not feel his pain. What could be more pleasantly distracting than hearing one of Révigny's unholy tales?

He was waiting when I arrived and had already ordered the wine. I reached for the flagon and filled the waiting cup. An inane question came to me at that moment, and Révigny's reply was sure to be entertaining. "You said you might take me along on a vacation in Hell sometime. I was wondering what the job prospects are for lawyers."

"Hell is overcrowded with lawyers, Barthélemy. Far more than we can profitably use. Criminals up here hire lawyers to postpone Hell a few months or years, then both client and defender end up there anyway. What we need is engineers. Satan is always expanding his empire, digging tunnels and passageways through the subterranean rock, adding torture chambers, constructing new bridges across fiery chasms, igniting thousands more flaming pits each with its own stake to serve those arriving daily from Purgatory. At the gate a demon greets every soul, leads it to a stake, binds it, and lights the personal flame, the one that burns forever but doesn't consume.

"Shift-work down there is endless. Never a minute passes without the ringing of steel on stone. The forges and brimstone mines operate around the clock. To this cacophony add the piercing screams of the damned and shrieks of delighted demons, and it's a goddamn wonder everyone doesn't go deaf. It could certainly be more peaceful, but that's partly the helluva it, so to speak." He flashed that death's-head grin and spread his arms in faux apology, as if even the feeblest of witticisms deserves applause.

He lowered his arms and continued, "But engineers are so boring and staid that most find themselves in Purgatory for close to eternity, however long that might be. Ha! Only our Heavenly Father can imagine eternity, right? Anyway, Heaven has little need of engineers. Clouds can be shifted and transposed with a mere push. It's like rearranging fluffy furniture. The weakest, stupidest angel can do it. According to Satan, himself once a citizen of Heaven, the saints contribute nothing. They lounge around looking down on everyone else from Empyrean and acting superior. Most were insane in life and probably remain so up there. That's a bonus of elevated status: entitled sloth and access to Heaven's mezzanine where the clouds are padded." He made a show of bouncing off invisible walls. "Boing! Boing!"

TUESDAY SEPTEMBER 18TH—THE TRIAL OF
LE LOUP-GAROU BEGINS; DESCRIPTION OF THE COURT SETTING;
MEMBERS OF THE COURT AND THE DEFENDANT ARE INTRODUCED
TO A LARGE AUDIENCE OF CITIZENS AND TRANSIENTS GATHERED
IN THE TOWN SQUARE; RÉVIGNY PRESENTS A THEOLOGICAL
OVERVIEW OF WEREWOLF CORPOREALITY FOR THE
ENLIGHTENMENT OF ALL PRESENT

THE INN FACED THE TOWN SQUARE directly catercorner from the site where the court proceeding would be held. Révigny and I could walk there in minutes. The way across required traversing a system of narrow paths that snaked among the stalls and dodging the usual crowds and livestock on the move. During such forays into gathered masses of humanity the alert man grips his purse tightly: any slight bump or jostle could signal an accomplished pickpocket practicing his craft.

We arrived early that first morning, introducing ourselves to the presiding judicial vicar and assumed our places on either side of him behind the table. Court took up its business after the bells of Cathédrale-Saint-Cyr-et-Sainte-Julitte in the nearby town of Nevers finished ringing the liturgical hour of terce. The clerk then stood to announce that court would convene at this hour each day until the trial ended, exceptions being weekends, holy days, or if postponed for any reason by His Grace. The clerk then introduced Révigny seated to the judicial vicar's right, me to his left, and the defendant. The clerk himself, by tradition, declined to give his name. He was a scribe and keeper of the records and calendar and meant to be largely anonymous and invisible.

The layout was not unusual. A raised platform accessible by a half-dozen stairs had been erected in one corner of the town square apart from the markets, although not so distant that our voices would not be competing with the cacophony of daily commerce. At times our sage words would be erased by the cries of peddlers and entertainers, the bleats and squeals of frightened livestock herded down the narrow lanes between stalls, and from the side streets the rattles and creaks of wagons directed by shouting drivers.

At the back of the platform was a long table with three chairs. The clerk of the court sat at his own small table in front at ground level, to the right side of the platform as it faced the square. In place of a conventional dock a stout post had been inserted permanently into the floor of the cobbled square. There stood the defendant, shackled by one wrist to a meter's length of chain. The post was positioned several meters directly in front of the judicial vicar; three meters or so to its left was a witness chair. The area around was roped off and guarded by the bailiff and a half-dozen of his men, stout burly fellows carrying truncheons for crowd control.

The clerk of the court asked for silence, and when the noise had subsided to a buzzing murmur the judicial vicar rose to speak. "Trials of those accused of witchcraft in any of its devious forms involve more than a formal proceeding followed by a judge's sentence. Gathering evidence is of utmost importance to assure fairness both to the defendant and the court. Demonology is a complex subject, mysterious in many ways despite having been studied for centuries by brilliant scholars. My preference has always been that prior to the start of a proceeding in which an element of the theological is put on trial it's best that the court and audience receive a short overview of the issues. In this case the hope is that a thorough understanding of the meaning and implications of heresy within the context of demonology will lead to a calm and rational outcome. To this purpose I have asked Monsieur Révigny to provide a brief oration on the status of Christian theology pertaining to werewolves." Before sitting he turned to Révigny and held out his hand palm up, a signal for him to take the stage.

Révigny rose, looking tall and dignified. He organized a sheaf of documents on the table before him and began. "The defendant, Le

Loup-garou, is charged with the crime of being a heretic, having made a pact with Satan who in exchange gave him metamorphic powers. Everyone knows that werewolves are real entities. The existence of Satan and his demons are important elements of Christian belief, and to deny them reality is heresy. The reality of werewolves isn't at issue, but rather the forms they assume. Therefore, the presence of the defendant shackled to the post poses two questions. First, is he a werewolf or simply a man? Second, is any werewolf corporeal and thus a material being or an illusion of one? Both incarnations represent different metaphysical facets of reality, so theoretically both are possible. Specifically, can the body of a human actually be transformed into a flesh-and-blood wolf? A man so changed undoubtedly perceives himself in a wolfish state, and so does everyone else. All see a corporeal wolf, but what is he actually?"

The judicial vicar spoke. "I must interrupt you a moment, Monsieur Révigny, to emphasize that the existence of loups-garoux, witches, demons of all sorts, and infinite other diabolical forms exist without a doubt. We've had ample proof in the Christian world since Augustine of Hippo. Emperor Sigismund, in the 14th century of our Lord, had the matter of shape-shifting investigated scientifically by a panel of eminent theologians. The conclusion? Certain humans are undoubtedly capable of transforming themselves into animals. In the panel's words, it's a 'positive and constant fact.' That it happens is irrefutable, and our objective in this court isn't to prove the known and obvious. We're here to ascertain whether the man on trial is one of these beings. Please continue, monsieur."

Révigny bowed to him. "Thank you, Your Grace. The great French jurist and philosopher Jean Bodin provides some guidance in the second volume of *De la demonomanie des sorciers* (*Of the Demonomania of Sorcerers*). Bodin's thesis is that a true corporeal change is possible, and for confirmation quotes Saint Thomas Aquinas: *Omnes angeli boni et mali ex virtute naturali, habent potestatem transmutandi corpora nostra*. In the vernacular these words say, 'All angels both good and evil have the natural capacity to change our bodies.' However, Bodin contends, the mind always remains human. Agreement on this point seems universal.

"Jean de Sponde, reminding us that Satan is a master of deception, says in his *Commentaire aux poemes homeriques* (*Commentary On Homeric Poems*), the following: *The general opinion is that the human frame cannot be metamorphosed into the animal bodies of beasts: but most hold that although there is no real shape-shifting the Devil can so cheat and deceive men's eyes that by his power they take one form, which they seem to see, to quite another thing from what it actually is.* Sponde considers a change in corporeal status to be impossible despite the seeming sacrilege of blatantly stating it. Then he equivocates by adding that a man's body can't be changed into the body of a wolf unless his soul metamorphoses into the wolf's spirit. Every Christian scholar starting with Saint Augustine knows this is impossible, as carefully explained by William de Auvergne, bishop of Paris, in his *De universo*, in the vernacular *The Universe*. A man's essential component is his soul, which is retained within the security of his body and can never leave to enter a wolf or any beast. Claiming otherwise is to profess belief in the transmigration of souls into animals or other humans, called metempsychosis, which is heresy.

"The physician Gaspar Peucer wrote of the 'essence' of man in a different context; that is, when his ego becomes temporarily folded into the body of a wolf during metamorphosis, acquiring its instincts and ferocious nature and making use of that creature's strength, cunning, and swiftness. However, the man's body remains unchanged, lying somewhere unconscious and inert and holding fast to the soul. This is the standard Augustinian explanation of shape-shifting accepted generally; in other words, as an illusion or a dream.

"In a painstaking investigation of werewolfism and metamorphosis the Jesuit Peter Thyraeus concludes in his *De apparitionibus spirituum*, in the vernacular *The Manifestation of Spirits*, that shape-shifting, while meeting the perceptual qualities of reality is nonetheless illusion, and a man can't be transformed physically into a beast. So what happens? Thyraeus considers the possibilities. In his opinion hallucination is insufficient to explain many of the documented cases of werewolfism. However, direct contradiction was offered by the physician Jean de Nynauld in his treatise *De la lycanthropie, transformation, et extase des sorciers* (*Of Lycanthropy, Transformation, and Ecstasy of Sorcerers*). Nynauld claimed not only is Satan incapable of transforming men into beasts, neither can he separate the soul from the body to the extent it can't return if the body still lives. Every known incident of metamorphosis, he posited, is entirely attributable to hallucination."

Here Révigny paused in his oration and looked thoughtfully at the spectators, then back at his notes. It was a marvelous bit of acting. The distracted buzzing stopped, and the crowd's focus returned. "Back to Peter Thyraeus. He dismissed other hypotheses, including the superimposition of one form onto another, in this case wolf onto man, and also the belief that the enchanted subject lying rigidly in a suspended state is transmuted to an animal that stalks the countryside making mischief. No, the origin favored by Thyraeus relied on demonic powers so strong as to delude everyone—the sleeper and the awake—into believing the vision presented is real. But how is this different from illusion, which he considered an inadequate explanation? Both illusion and hallucination result from false perceptions, but hallucination might be the more perceptively 'real,' able to incorporate more of the senses— hearing and taste, for example, and not just vision.

"We may conclude from this evidence that a person of the Christian faith should accept that metamorphosis in werewolfism does not entail corporeal change, but rather a transformation during which the boundaries of ego disappear and the shape-shifter *figuratively* enters the body of a wolf, in which guise he then behaves wolfishly, if not even more cruelly than an ordinary wolf.

"What if the transformative process were reversed, as some learned figures have postulated? The theologian Pierre Mamor, born at Limogues, wrote of demonic metamorphoses in his *Flagellum maleficorum*, or *Wizard Whip* in the vernacular. He agreed with Saint Augustine that a werewolf is an actual wolf possessed by a demon. Meanwhile, the man who had been transformed and now occupied the wolf's body lay somewhere concealed, entranced in an unconscious state and held fast in the grip of involuntary metamorphosis. Some say this state can be induced voluntarily by the man applying a special ointment to his wrists or temples and so drugs himself. This scene reprises Augustine's *phantasticum*, the phantom in the vernacular, a spiritual transformation in which the werewolf is the manifestation of a dream: the transformed man—we may rightly call him a victim—has fallen under the spell of a sorcerer in league with the Devil.

"Saint Thomas tells us in his *Summa Theologia*, or *Sum of Theology* in the vernacular, how Satan can mold any object, living or non-living, from ordinary air and make it appear real when in truth it's only illusory. Naturally, demons are included among his creations.

"Saint Bonaventura, in *Commentaria in secundum librum sententiarum*, in the vernacular *Commentaries on a Book of Sentences*, relates that demons themselves can manufacture additional forms under Satan's direction. Therefore, a demon inserted by Satan into a wolf isn't a new creation except in the sense of a manufactured illusion or hallucination of one believed to be real by the man transformed and any eidetic who perceives him in his metamorphosed state. Only God can make new forms of life, which He did at the Creation, and they remain immutable today. Yes, the work of the Lord is unalterable. He can change one form of nature to another, as He showed when turning Lot's wife into salt. In addition, He can alter the outside without disturbing the essential nature within or shift the essential while any change perdures, as in the Eucharist. Satan's powers are much more limited, including his inability to separate a man from his soul. In other writings Saint Bonaventura tells us that evil spirits can occlude and scramble our senses in three ways. First, presenting an illusion or hallucination of something not actually present; second, creating a delusion causing something to appear other than it is; and third, hiding a real object by making it invisible. Satan's workshop has all these tools available for his amusement and our suffering.

"This concludes my brief and hesitant disquisition on the theology of werewolfism with emphasis on the thorniest of problems, the ontological dilemma of their corporeality in the context of Christian belief. I say 'hesitant' because we shall never know the actual answer."

Révigny's presentation concluded the court's first day. After adjournment I went to check on my men and animals, and Révigny went wherever it was he went. Not to our room, certainly, but somewhere he never offered to mention. Around vespers we met in the tavern for the usual drinks and bland supper.

That evening he seemed subdued and less inclined toward conversation, absently dipping his spoon into his soup as if fishing distractedly for a particular morsel. Finally, he looked up and said, "These are trying times, Barthélemy, beset as we are by demons all around, ruled by a clergy that places itself on a higher plane than the rest of humanity and propounding a mission to chastise instead of cherish." His voice trailed off into something muddled. In the surrounding noise all I heard was ". . . hounded by the Black Death, a scourge recognizing no principle, humble or sacrosanct." Then he raised his voice so I could hear him clearly: "Look at us. Ten fingers, ten toes. Same as a salamander. Lungs and a heart. No different from a pigeon. We have four appendages? So do chickens and frogs. Does a weevil take an oath vowing to remain a weevil, no matter what? Have you ever come across a fox who believed itself to be a hedgehog? Only in your dreams do you wish for gills so you can pursue mermaids."

It was one of those times for introspection when neither of us was in a mood for conversation. It was a time when I learned that even demons can become despondent. We silently finished the meal and parted company. It was fitting: I needed a night's rest before my presentation the next day.

Wednesday September 19th—Chassenée Makes His Opening Statement Summarizing the Taxonomy and Nature of Werewolves

We awoke to the wind giving voice to the trees behind the inn. Rather, I awoke to it. Révigny, as usual, was absent. He never slept, and where he went during the night I dared not ask. No doubt an errand of demonic mischief while the local God-fearing Christians slept uneasily in their beds. By the time I finished my morning ablutions and stumbled to the tavern for breakfast still rubbing my eyes Révigny was already seated and berating a serving girl for having brought him lukewarm tea. In a twinkling the inn-keeper's wife was there with a steaming replacement, then cuffing the girl's ears and pursuing her back to the scullery with loud threats.

I sat down opposite and said, "Good morning, Humbert. I see you've given the day a propitious start."

Révigny smiled broadly. "Indeed so!" he said, letting his emerald-green tongue slide sinuously over his equally bright green teeth. "Indeed so! And good morning to you as well! Today you and your soliloquy play the starring roles in our little drama. I trust you're adequately prepared. It ought to be great fun."

When His Grace called for my opening statement I moved around to the front of the table and stood facing the crowded market. A dozen or so merchants and shoppers paused to look up and listen, but the rest went about their business as if I might be a benign ghost of no substance. Two acrobats were performing directly in front of me. I turned and asked His Grace if they might be removed. He made a motion to the bailiff, who ordered them to abscond or suffer a beating.

I gazed out over the busy market and began. "Consider the werewolf. As beings, werewolves are marked by a wolfish appearance, ravenous hunger and bloodthirst, ferocity, and, of course, the capacity to shape-shift between human and animal forms. Having transformed into his animal shape he is stronger, faster, fiercer, and more cunning than his companion wolves, quickly dominating them, becoming their leader (meneur de loups) and bending them to his will. He is smarter by retaining his human intelligence and capacity to reason, yet overcome by an irrepressible craving for wolfish food, including human flesh. He's truly a human in a wolf's clothing."

I extended my open hand toward the post to indicate my client shackled to it and continued. "Monsieur Loup-garou stands accused of having these traits, although here he is, obviously human. But isn't he presently a werewolf in disguise? Is he likely to change dramatically into a ferocious wolf before our eyes, tear his chain from the post, and rip out the throats of those nearby? I assure you, my friends, that such an event won't happen—can't happen—and on this you have my word. How can I make such an outrageous guarantee before God and man? Easily! Because Monsieur Loup-garou isn't a werewolf at all despite his nickname; he's an ordinary man falsely accused of essentially harmless crimes, which I intend to prove.

"Let's begin with a brief overview of werewolf taxonomy; that is, the different kinds, or species, of werewolves known to exist in the world. We can begin by stating that all werewolves are theriomorphic humans; in other words, humans in the form of wolves whether corporeal or illusory. We might say next that werewolves are overwhelmingly male, females being comparatively rare. My extensive investigations show them to inhabit many countries and behave similarly everywhere. Consequently, we may make general statements about them, assuming such beings exist, more or less."

The judicial vicar quickly admonished me: "Be careful, Monsieur Chassenée. You know that questioning or making light of the existence of witches, werewolves, and other devilish beings is heresy. The Church tolerates no superstitions."

I bowed to him. "Pardon me, Your Grace. I mean only to categorize this specific class of demons, the better to present my case for the defense. My point is that some seem more corporeal than others. By no means do I question their reality, which has been long established and is irrefutable. May I proceed?"

The judge nodded, and I turned again to face the spectators. "Distilling tales from different countries to their common properties reveals several ways in which an ordinary man—or occasionally a woman—could become a werewolf. The first type is a person skilled in magic or alchemy who might self-bewitch in some manner, thus putting himself under a spell when feeling the urge to transform. Perhaps he effects the change with the help of a wolf skin, magic ring, or other enchanted object. He might drink water from a wolf's footprint or from a haunted pool or stream, or maybe pin a werewolf flower to his tunic. A man who swims across a certain bewitched pond leaving his clothes behind might knowingly emerge a werewolf on the other side. To return to human form he swims back and puts on his clothes. Others have been born with the inherent gift of shape-shifting, requiring nothing extraordinary.

"Such metamorphoses are self-induced, and we may call these beings *voluntary* werewolves. Immediately after shape-shifting a voluntary werewolf sometimes urinates in a circle around his clothes and then howls. At this point the metamorphosis is complete, and only then does he dash into the forest and commence his lupine mischief. Voluntary werewolves, without exception, are evil because each chooses to be like this. And all are branded with the Devil's mark, a tiny crescent. Some go so far as to practice bestiality during which the man while in wolf form covers she-wolves in heat, enjoying it more than sex with women. In some cases a voluntary werewolf can return to human form by divesting himself of the spell or charmed article inducing it. These situations are rare: typically, application of a curse, charm, or other means of enchantment is necessary to restore the human form. According to Bodin, some need only to roll in the dew or wash in a stream.

"Second, we have werewolves of the *involuntary* kind, those who perhaps never fostered an evil thought or uttered a harsh word yet come into their status through the malfeasance of a sorcerer or plotting of an evil person. If the curse involves simple betrayal the source is usually a woman, occasionally a cruel stepmother but more often an adulterous wife who schemes with her lover either to transform her husband into a werewolf, or, once the transformation has happened, make the condition permanent by hiding his clothes without which return to human form is impossible. I shall mention this again in a moment. In many tales of werewolfism these afflicted men aren't conjurers in the sense of the voluntary kind, but actually victims deserving our sympathy. Depending on the nature of the enchantment many undergo involuntary metamorphosis and live as wolves for days, months, or years depending on the curse, surviving while in wolfish form on wild game, domestic livestock, and even humans, at all times avoiding hunters, who consider them ordinary wolves and seek to slay them. If such a spell has been assigned for a fixed duration it might include a caveat; for example, the accursed may return to his former life as a human after the curse expires, provided that while living as a wolf he never tasted human flesh.

"Third is what I shall call the *accidental*, or *constitutional*, werewolf. He appears in some of the earliest werewolf tales, like those told by Petronius, who, with his Roman contemporaries called such beings *versipellis* in reference to their shape-shifting. How this is effected during the metamorphosis of any werewolf species has been a matter of controversy, some recently positing that a werewolf wears his skin fur-side out and simply reverses it when resuming human form. In any event the accidental werewolf is relatively rare, mainly because no charm or magic is involved. The metamorphosis is straightforward and abrupt: one moment a human, the next a wolf.

"Accidental and voluntary werewolves have in common the requirement of becoming naked before undergoing transformation. In addition, the clothes have to be hidden carefully because to regain human form the beast must find his original garments and dress in them again. Both forms can shape-shift whenever and wherever the mood strikes.

"The fourth species is technically not a werewolf at all, merely a fanatical man obsessed with werewolfism. This condition, known in the medical arts as 'lycanthropy,' or 'wolf-madness,' is a variety of *insania zoanthropica* called *daemonium lupinum*, a delusion in which the deranged believes he's been transformed into a wolf but in reality has retained every appearance and trapping of humanity. Stated differently, he doesn't shape-shift like the other forms; rather, he's just a lunatic plagued by an abundance of melancholy.

"Not all such transformations involve wolves. In general, a shape-shifter acquires the attributes of the creature into which he is transformed. If a donkey, for instance, he remains a man who can carry heavy loads. A famous transformation was that of Nabuchodonosor, king of Babylon. But was he actually transformed into an ox as history claims, or did God punish him during his penance by taking away his sanity after which he merely *behaved* as an ox, living in the fields and eating grass? Although some theologians have argued for physical shape-shifting the consensus today is that God pulled a cloak of madness over Nabuchodonosor, forcing him to wander as a lunatic and graze in the fields, but not actually transforming him into a beast. This seems clear in *Daniel*, chapter four verse thirty-three, where Nabuchodonosor's plight is described: *and he was driven from men and did eat grass as oxen, and his body was wet with the dew of heaven, till his hairs were grown like eagles' feathers, and his nails like birds' claws.* A few lines later, in chapter four verse thirty-six, Nabuchodonosor's sanity is restored. He tells us, *my reason returned unto me; and for the glory of my kingdom, mine honour and brightness returned unto me . . .*

"The terms 'werewolf' and 'lycanthrope' were used interchangeably in the past, an example being Bodin's writings, particularly his *De la demonomanie des sorciers.* However, there is no justification for continuing the practice in modern times now that we can properly distinguish them. Furthermore, Bodin's argument seems built on shaky ontological ground. Paradoxically, he justifies that a wolf emerging from the metamorphosis is an actual animal because 'the real essence' of a human being isn't its altered form but 'the rational faculty' of mankind, a seeming contradiction by implying the change is entirely spiritual.

"Lycanthropy, according to its modern, purely medical definition, was first diagnosed by Marcellus de Sidé, a physician and native of Pamphylia who lived in the 2nd century of our Lord. Like true werewolves, victims of this strange malady skulk about in cemeteries and dark forests at night howling and sometimes attacking people and in rare cases murdering them, but with an important difference." Here I paused and raised my voice for emphasis: "*They never transform into wolves; the only metamorphosis is the manifestation of a delusional imagination.* Take note of this fact. In appearance they retain at all times a pale complexion, and their eyes are dry, sunken, and reputedly have an absent look, although others describe the eyes as unusually piercing. The eyebrows often meet forming an arch above the nose, and the limbs have numerous cuts and bruises from traveling about on all fours. In mood they seem overcome by melancholy. Their hunger manifests as 'lycorexia,' the wolfish desire for raw, bloody meat, which they rip apart in chunks that are swallowed whole. Many are inveterate tomb robbers, digging up corpses and feeding on them and gnawing the bones, sometimes in the company of fellow wolves. They are unable to weep and barely able to salivate because of a dry tongue and chronic, intense thirst.

"Some of these characteristics describe my client. Note too that Monsieur Loup-garou, who clearly falls into this fourth category, never kills his putative victims or even injures them except superficially. Instilling fear is his greatest offence, and this community would do well to recognize him for what he is, a mostly harmless nuisance.

"Finally, concern with werewolves in Christianity dates back more than a millennium, at least to Augustine of Hippo who discussed them in his great work *De civitate dei*, or *City of God* in the vernacular. Saint Augustine was greatly absorbed with demonic shape-shifting. He doubted that demons possessed the power to change either the body or soul of a human, attributing the provenance of the phenomenon to a phantom, the *phantasticum* to which Monsieur Révigny has alluded, an illusion of dreams and the imagination. Saint Augustine held that the *phantasticum*—but never the soul— could depart the body while its owner dreamed, and that it could become perceptible to witnesses. Its actions, however, were caused by intervening demons and not the dreamer himself. It was, in other words, *similitudinem corporis sui*, in the vernacular a 'semblance of his body.' A *phantasticum*, once on its own, could roam about dabbling in mischief while the body to which it belonged lay elsewhere, dreaming and unaware. This condition is sometimes heritable because we see it clustered in certain families. We find stories to substantiate Augustine's hypothesis across different cultures, from the Nordic countries in the west to far Cathay in the east. Even the poet Marie de France in her timeless ballad of the werewolf, *Le lai de bisclavret*, tells us that such creatures inhabit every country.

"In all three legitimate werewolf species the afflicted being remains intact and conscious of his actions while in wolfish form, able to think and reason, experience human emotions, and retain memories; they are, in fact, human in every way except body shape, although able to communicate only in growls and howls. Some rustics claim to have heard werewolves speak, although this is doubtful. The lycanthrope, in contrast, retains his human form and speech at all times.

"This concludes my opening statement. I trust my brief introduction to the nature and different kinds of werewolves puts the issue before us in relevant context, and I ask your patience and sympathy for my client while he undergoes the coming ordeal." With these words I bowed to His Grace and then to Révigny, sitting down to a chorus of catcalls and derisive admonishments to end the trial quickly so Monsieur Loup-garou could be tied to a stake and burned alive. The spectators cared only for an entertainment culminating in pain and death. They wanted to hear the poor man scream as the fire consumed him.

THURSDAY SEPTEMBER 20TH—CHASSENÉE OPENS HIS DEFENSE; RÉVIGNY OCCASIONALLY REBUTS

THE DAY DAWNED OVERCAST AND PORTENDED rain. An awning of waxed canvas had been erected above the stage the previous day in anticipation of a change in weather. Autumn chill was in the air, and doubtless the market would be less crowded than it might have been on a fair morning. We assembled as usual shortly before terce, listening in the still air for the bells of Cathédrale-Saint-Cyr-et-Sainte-Julitte. After the clerk reconvened court His Grace turned to me and said, "Monsieur Chassenée, you may begin your defense."

I thanked His Grace and stood, papers spread on the table in front of me. "We've heard this posited before, so it's nothing new, but what if the law is simply a simulation? And why not? After all, it's a human invention, unlike a tree or a stone. What beings surpass humans at devising simulations? Ghosts are putative simulations of living persons unless, of course, they're only simulations of ghosts. Faux simulations, in other words, assuming there can be such things. But if both real and faux simulations exist, how can they be distinguished? In the case here, when the law is transgressed has a crime actually been committed? Consider my client, accused of being a werewolf. Logically, how is it possible for a man to become a wolf? Clearly, it isn't. Then how would a man who never became a wolf commit a crime only a wolf could commit?"

The judicial vicar interrupted and said, "Once again, be careful, monsieur. The ice you're standing on is thin, the lake of heresy beneath it very deep."

I bowed to him. "Yes, Your Grace. I'm not suggesting there aren't werewolves, rather that some authorities have offered the impossibility of physical transformation."

"Continue," the judicial vicar said.

"So what does he become at such times? Not a real wolf, of course, otherwise we'd call him that instead of a 'werewolf.' Is he a wolf or a simulation of a wolf? The first possibility is confirmed by tangible evidence: a paw, say, or a skin; the second, only if he's seen and perceived as such by the senses. If he truly became a wolf and proved it we could then say that a physical transformation has taken place. The problem arises when he becomes a man again and we're forced to look at him as such without bias, without the qualification, 'I see that wolfish nature in his face.' But where's the truth in a physiognomic assessment, which is nothing but an unfounded judgment based on perceived appearance and likeness? Does my client look wolfish as he sits before you? I see a man, and so do you. I agree that he foams and snuffles on occasion, but it's easily explained: he's a mouth-breather and hoarse from a dysfunctional throat."

Just then a spectator shouted, "Hoarse from howling in the graveyard all night!"

I waited until the laughter died, then continued.

"Why does he not groan and growl instead of speaking? Because he's a human being. I agree that he's disheveled, but who doesn't become that way during imprisonment? Still, he has lost none of the qualities that define mankind. In the Nordic countries it's claimed a werewolf can be distinguished from a true wolf by his eyes, which are yellow and obviously those of an animal. But that is clearly false. A werewolf's eyes remain human at all times. Look into the eyes of Monsieur Loup-garou. Are they the golden color of a wolf's? Are they an animal's eyes? Are they either pale or piercing? No, his eyes are calm and wholly human. Look at them! *Look into his eyes, the windows to the soul, and deny he's a man!*"

Révigny rose slowly to his full height.

"May I speak, Your Grace?"

Said the judicial vicar, "Certainly, monsieur."

"Ah," said Révigny, as if exhaling a rare and noble thought, "but appearances often deceive. The most innocent looking sometimes carry great evil in their souls despite a pair of eyes able to melt the heart. Satan can assume any form he chooses, from kingfisher to Fisher King, and no human on Earth could perceive the difference. No, my friends, we can't go by appearances alone because the image someone projects outwardly might be a deceitful illusion. Never forget that Satan's infinite forms are the most accomplished illusions of all. Nobody does it better." With that, Révigny made a half-turn toward his chair and glared at the scattering of spectators. Then with a dramatic flair he completed the turn and sat.

I stood again. "Le Loup-garou suffers from lycanthropy, the delusion that he changes reversibly between a human and a wolf; to say this another way, that he's a werewolf. As with all delusions, this is impossible." I emphasized the last while turning and looking directly at the judicial vicar. "Lycanthropy is a disease, although not the transmissible kind like plague or fever. It's a disease of the mind." I stopped and put my forefinger to my head and held the posture a few moments for emphasis while scanning the spectators. Then I dropped my hand and resumed speaking.

"My client is clearly disturbed. After all, he skulks among grave-stones and howls at the night sky. Are these acts of a sane man? The common inclination is to round up such persons and burn them to rid communities of their putative evils, but my client isn't evil, his mind is simply unbalanced. Being evil and having a disturbed mind are very different conditions. The first might fall within the category of heresy, but not the second."

Révigny stood and addressed His Grace, asking permission to question my client. On receiving it he looked at Le Loup-garou and seemed to study him a moment. "Monsieur," he said, "do you nor-mally feel irritable and aggressive, and are you easily agitated? I see you wringing your hands and scratching a place on your wrist."

"Yes, I am," my client said.

"I would like to examine your wrist." Révigny descended the stairs and walked to the post. "Please show it to me." When Le Loup-garou complied Révigny said, "The skin around what looks like a bite mark is reddened and obviously itches. Were you bitten by an animal?"

"Yes, monsieur, by a wolf." The crowd began to buzz with curiosity.

"Tell me, monsieur," Révigny said, "do you have any friends, anyone with whom you associated regularly prior to your arrest?"

"Just a wolf I encountered in my travels. He was my only friend until one day he bit me and ran away."

"Please tell us the story of this friendship."

"I had found work at Kerhinet in Saint-Lyphard cutting and bun-dling rushes in the nearby marshes. The roofs of the cottages there are thatched with them, and enough needed repair or replacement that extra men were being hired. I was passing through, and having no particular destination I welcomed a few sous in my pocket. When the work ended I decided to take the long road back toward Paris. I had just reached the outskirts of Kerhinet when a large wolf bounded out of the marshes and jumped on me. He knocked me to the ground. Instinctively, I gripped my throat in my hands to keep it from being ripped out, and then a strange thing happened. This animal, which was huge even as large wolves go, stepped back and seemed to grin. He put his forelegs flat on the ground, began wagging his tail, and raised his rump in the air as dogs do when soliciting play. I sat up and pondered whether to run, in which case I risked appearing like prey. Then the wolf approached while I sat frozen and licked my face. I was dumbfounded. I stood and continued on my way at a leisurely pace so as not to alarm him, but he was anything but alarmed. He trotted beside me like a faithful dog, and a faithful wolf is exactly what he became. I called him Lupo, and he has been my only friend."

When Révigny asked him to continue his tale he said, "For two years or more we traveled the country, stopping a few days here, a few there, anyplace I could find temporary work. In late summer I picked crops and scythed hay, in winter I chopped firewood, in spring I helped farmers till the soil. There's usually work to be had if you aren't lazy. And always Lupo was beside me. I'll tell you, the thugs and hooligans along the road kept their distance. All it took to scatter them was a glance into Lupo's fierce yellow eyes and the flash of his teeth accompanied by a low growl. I didn't fear traveling lonely roads at night because even the demons avoided us.

"Then near a small, unmemorable village a large dog dashed from a copse and attacked Lupo. The fight was epic, and Lupo eventually killed the attacker, but not without suffering several deep bite marks. I tended him as best I could, washing the wounds at every opportunity with clear stream water and sharing my food with him half-and-half so he was well nourished and might heal. Nonetheless, he languished and had difficulty keeping our normal pace. He lost his appetite, becoming thin and agitated. He suffered seizures, developed a sensitivity to loud sounds, and carried a chronic thirst that made his tongue always dry. His beautiful golden eyes lost their luster. One day about sext as we were resting under a tree and I was stroking his head, he turned and bit my wrist. By now his spittle was thick and foamy, and he never stopped drooling despite the dry throat. He seemed as startled as I by what he'd done and whimpered a little, as if apologizing. Then he rose awkwardly and staggered into the trees. I waited until well after nightfall, but he didn't come back. Assuming he had died I continued along the night road with a broken heart, missing him more with every step. You see, monsieur, Lupo was the most loyal friend and companion I could have wished for, and now he was gone." With these words he leaned his head back and wept, shoulders heaving. Strangely, his eyes remained dry. His sobs brought tears to my own eyes, and to the eyes of not a few of the spectators.

For a long moment Révigny stood respectfully, head bowed, before turning to the judicial vicar. "I have no more questions for the defendant, Your Grace."

His Grace said, "I am adjourning court for the remainder of the day and tomorrow as well. Other business needs my attention." With this he gaveled the session to a close and held out his hand to the clerk. "Monsieur Clerk?"

The clerk rose. "Court will reconvene at terce on Monday the 24th of September."

MONDAY SEPTEMBER 24TH—CHASSENÉE PRESENTS AN AGGRESSIVE ARGUMENT FOR IMMEDIATE EXONERATION OF HIS CLIENT; THE JUDICIAL VICAR DENIES HIS MOTION

THE FOLLOWING THREE DAYS WERE UNEVENTFUL, and I spent the free time tightening my case. The instant court opened I requested and was granted the floor. I rose to speak with no documents before me. The immediate strategy was to present a streamlined, extemporaneous argument sufficiently powerful to overwhelm the court with the force of a lightning strike. By catching His Grace in a moment of startled confusion I might gain a whirl-wind verdict.

I descended the steps to the square and took the initiative in a strong, ringing voice. "Contrast the three valid species of werewolves with the lycanthrope, who acquires some of these same wolfish behaviors and appetites yet carries them out in his own body, not that of a wolf." Here I paused and looked sternly at the gaggle of curious onlookers as if they were the judges who needed convincing. My voice rising almost to a shout, I said, "*Therefore, I emphasize, a lycanthrope never becomes an actual wolf, but instead remains a man over-come by the delusion of having transformed into one!*"

I paused again to let this statement gain traction. The market crowd quickly lost interest and went about its business. After a few minutes only an old man remained. He stood with crossed arms gumming an apple, evidently more curious about my appearance than my words, which were nothing new, simply a reprise of my original argument. I was counting more on how they were pack-aged than their content.

I had hoped to surprise the crowd enough to consider its collec-tive sensibilities and evince a herd response. That now appeared futile. Pragmatically, the only person I needed to convince was the judicial vicar, but trials are more than legal jousts and play-acting. They involve politics that encompass the social consciousness, and a judge is more likely to be swayed if a trial lawyer has the backing of the rabble even though it has no legal say in the outcome. Some in my benighted audience stopped their activities and looked at me blankly. I noted their bovine gazes and continued. "The distinction, which should now be obvious, is striking and has considerable bearing on innocence or guilt when the charge is heresy by means of werewolfery. Clearly, a lycanthrope such as Monsieur Loup-garou isn't presently a werewolf in human form, nor has he ever been. He's just a man."

I paced back and forth with the platform above me to one side, the market and its occupants to the other. Experience had taught me that delivering a single message as simply as possible is always the best strategy if the intention is to persuade. Nothing surpasses redundancy when driving home a thought to the unsophisticated. I stopped, turned, and raised my right arm, forefinger pointed to the sky. "To repeat: my opening statement presented a clear and concise taxonomy of werewolves. There are three kinds. Then there is lycanthropy, which some have included as a fourth class and that I have demonstrated beyond argument isn't werewolfism at all but insanity, a disease of the mind. Professor Johannes Fridericus Wolfeshusius of Leipzig, in a lecture titled *Oratio pro lycanthropia*, in the vernacular *Address on Lycanthropia*, considered lycanthropy a disease with symptoms such as excessive thirst, itching, and a racing heart. Or it might be a demonic hallucination in which the afflicted perceives himself to be a wolf, as do those who encounter him. The case before us is straightforward, and I see no benefit in continuing. My client is undeniably a lycanthrope and therefore not a werewolf." With this I whirled dramatically and spoke directly to His Grace. "Considering these circumstances I request that Monsieur Loup-garou be released immediately with the court's apology."

True to my prediction the judge was startled. "So soon? On what grounds, Monsieur Chassenée?"

"That he was exonerated once by purgation but nonetheless sentenced to the king's galleys for life. The decision was a cruel aberration, and my client suffered many years from its injustice. As all can see, he still suffers." I turned and held out an open hand toward my client. "He has been cheated of a normal life. To no one's surprise he sometimes behaves abnormally. The present accusation against him is false. Werewolves are tried under the charge of heresy, but this only applies to *real* werewolves, not pretenders suffering from lycanthropy. My client, therefore, should not be on trial at all."

"You're saying, if I hear you correctly, that you don't believe he's a werewolf?"

"Exactly, Your Grace. What I've been saying from the start. He's a lycanthrope."

"Then you claim not to believe personally in werewolves, monsieur?"

I turned to face the spectators. "His Grace is clever," I said with a smile, "and seems determined to trick me into a statement of heresy. I shall therefore make both my beliefs and the status of Monsieur Loup-garou absolutely clear once again. I have never doubted the existence of werewolves and believe in them absolutely despite the misgivings of several respected ecclesiastics I should mention. Some in the Church have preached the reverse; that is, *against* the belief in witches and werewolves, considering it superstitious. Notable were Burchard and Saint Boniface, the latter stating his opposition to belief in *strigas et fictos lupos*, in the vernacular 'witches and imaginary wolves.' I, however, take the traditional view and accept the reality of these beings. In fact, actual werewolves compose the first three species in the system of classification presented in my opening statement. What I do *not* believe is that lycanthropes are werewolves, and for good reason.

"Based on the strongest evidence, experts in the medical arts have declared them to be insane humans, not shape-shifters by any-one's definition. My client is undeniably a lycanthrope, ergo, he isn't a werewolf but merely a man. He has already paid the price of mis-construed justice when sentenced to imprisonment in the king's galleys despite twelve compurgators swearing to the truthfulness of his oath of innocence for a nonexistent crime. Consequently, he underwent years of needless anguish and torture, relinquishing his best years, and to what purpose? None. By rights he should be released immediately with a pension for life and the court's apology." I projected these words from the deepest part of my throat with as much certitude as I could manage, then stood at full height awaiting the inevitable response.

The judicial vicar said, "I've read the record of that proceeding judged by Institoris and don't consider the case to hold relevant precedence. It occurred before Monsieur Loup-garou was accused of werewolfery. This present situation is different. If so inclined I could return him to the galleys to serve out his sentence, but the matter before us is more serious. Furthermore, you're trying my patience, monsieur." He slammed his gavel down. "Petition denied."

"Very well," I said. "My client and I are prepared to continue and see the trial through to the end."

Said the judicial vicar, "How very noble of you both."

Regaining my normal tone I said, "Perhaps, but there's more. Werewolfery is considered heretical activity by the Church because it involves a pact with Satan, isn't that true, Your Grace?"

"Yes, certainly," His Grace said warily. "Where is this leading, monsieur?'

"Toward the truth, which presumably we all seek, am I right?"

His Grace nodded hesitantly. "Be careful, Monsieur Chassenée. I won't be trapped into agreeing that a novel form of heresy you intend to propose is suddenly permissible."

"Not at all. However, my classification of werewolves into three kinds, or species as some prefer, is not the result of frivolous pursuit. During the many hours I spent reading, pondering, and evaluating the legal, medical, and theoretical ramifications impinging on werewolfery I vowed to stay unbiased and consider only the facts while discarding everything smelling of conjecture. I carefully read each report on the subject available to me and remained true to my vow. The lawyer's duty is to burrow relentlessly down through the ethereal musings of the misinformed, not stopping until reaching the hard substratum of facts packed tightly like cobbles in a well-laid street. Refuting my conclusions on ecclesiastical or legal grounds will prove difficult because—if I may boast somewhat modestly—of the tireless diligence invested on behalf of my client and truth-seekers everywhere."

His Grace interrupted to say, "I've never heard of a 'modest boast,' but please continue. I presume your actual closing statement will now be postponed, and we shall proceed through the usual course of first presenting evidence and questioning witnesses." The last was stated with lethal sarcasm.

None of what he said required an answer, so I proceeded as if deaf. "The facts have been laid out, sorted into a pattern of logical categories, and should now be obvious to all. Your Grace can surely see that only werewolves of the voluntary kind can be considered heretics simply because their pact with the Devil is enjoined with full and hearty cooperation, the accused willingly trading their souls for the gift of transformation at the times and places of their choosing. Professor Wolfeshusius proposed as a corollary that Satan casts the putative werewolf into a trance. Wolfeshusius wasn't the first to label the man undergoing transformation a 'sorcerer,' implying that if the factor instigating metamorphosis is not a disease then the sufferer might be a victim of his own foul play; in other words, a voluntary werewolf whose condition is self-induced.

"The situation of involuntary and accidental werewolfery involves mitigating circumstances too numerous to discuss here, except to state that such beings are also innocent of heresy, although the proof is less clear and their cases more difficult to defend. At any rate, neither describes my client's condition, rendering both irrelevant for our purposes. As to lycanthropes they are innocent of heresy beyond all doubt. Consider this: can the involuntary werewolf be held accountable for actions resulting from a curse placed on his head by an adulterous wife or evil stepmother? No more than a conscripted soldier who kills his enemy under orders of a superior or an executioner who carries out a sanctioned death sentence.

"For anyone still unsure, a voluntary werewolf has made a pact with the Devil, which alone is heresy. As Saint Bonaventura warns, seeking counsel or assistance from Satan is a sin. By definition, someone who interacts with Satan at any level is himself a sorcerer and evil in the eyes of God. For voluntary werewolves there is no cure and no redemption. They must be eradicated without exception.

"Involuntary werewolves are cured automatically when the afflicting curse placed on their heads by malfeasance is lifted. Potential cures for the accidental form are still debated by the experts, although amputation of a limb is said to reverse the condition by relieving the melancholy causing it, in formal language *membrum virile veneficio ablatum*. As proof I cite the case of Raimbaudus de Pineta, a knight from the diocese of Clermont d'Auvergne. After his estate was confiscated and he was banished by his lord, Ponce de Castres, he became a wanderer of forests and fields. Believing himself changed into a wolf, Raimbaudus terrorized the countryside dismembering and disemboweling old people and feasting on children. Then a woodcutter chopped off one of his rear paws with an axe, and Raimbaudus at once regained human form. Afterward, he confessed that he never wanted to behave as he did, but the urge that came on him was uncontrollable. He was grateful to have lost the foot because it resulted in return to normalcy.

"It's worth stating that in some instances lycanthropy can be cured and the victim returned to society. How is it treated by the attending physician? Because the disease is a form of melancholy, some recommend opening a vein and letting blood until the patient faints, then for three days bathing him occasionally in sweet water and offering him wholesome foods. In chronic cases the process includes inducing vomiting with hellebore. Afterward, purge with a decoction of the herb *Verbena officinalis* at least twice followed by a theriac of vipers."

Révigny, who had been quiet to this point, asked and was granted permission to rebut. Just then the rain started. Its drumming on the canvas overhead, combined with the normal market ruckus, threatened to swamp Révigny's commentary until he raised his voice and was nearly shouting. "You claim, Monsieur Chassenée, that lycanthropy is a disease of the mind, not the body, a subcategory of *insania zoanthropica*. Those were your words. It is, you say, merely a delusion in which the afflicted believes he's a wolf, a metamorphosis that occurs as a figment of the mind without shape-shifting. Nonetheless, your argument of innocence because of insanity is refuted by the very class of demonology into which lycanthropy fits, namely the eponymous *daemonium lupinum*. Stated simply, your client is still possessed by the Devil, a condition making his innocence—and his release back into the community—impossible. In practical terms a demon resides inside him. The only sure way of killing it is by fire at the stake, when we shall hear its dying shrieks through the very human mouth of Le Loup-garou."

"Ah," I replied, "but the naming of something doesn't automatically bring it into existence. We name many things of which we have no knowledge. Clouds, for example, and wind. They exist not because of the names we give them. Consider too that the heterogeneity of the issue must be maintained, specifically, the clear distinction between lycanthropy and werewolfery. Even conceding both are satanic in origin, folding together voluntary, involuntary, and accidental werewolves and calling the composite, say, 'natural lycanthropy' would erase the distinction between true lycanthropy, a medical condition, and werewolfism, which is not. Furthermore, Pietro da Piperno di Benevento, the learned physician and theologian, has argued cogently in his *De magicis affectibus*, *The Magical Emotions* in the vernacular, that lycanthropy is not caused by demoniacal possession at all but is strictly organic, a disease of the brain. If my client is burned, consider the likelihood of the shrieks we hear being his own.

"Is the crux of your argument, Monsieur Révigny, that because my client's condition is demonic in origin he must be burned regardless? Keep in mind that the accusation before the court is heresy by means of werewolfery. If my client isn't a werewolf he can't be guilty of heresy, the lesser being contained in the greater. The wording of the charge is specific. If he's afterward accused of demonology—a different crime entirely—this would require another trial based on the new charge. I detect nothing refutable about my argument."

I took my seat as Révigny rose and said, "Satan has skills in the art of illusion like no other, and even if he can't physically change humans into wolves his power to fool us into thinking he has is breathtaking. So far I have been a purveyor of history and philosophy, but it's now time to undergo a metamorphosis of my own into a prosecutor of werewolves. I therefore advocate we follow examples set by such judges as Henri Boguet and Nicolas Rémy, who considered ridding communities of werewolves their duty. As Rémy emphasized in his *Demonolatry*, this is necessary if only because citizens are put at a disadvantage. Even when werewolves retain their human forms Satan has endowed them with extraordinary strength, speed, and ferocity. Humans have no chance against them when attacked. Rémy ended his treatise with words applicable to werewolves of any sort, including a lycanthrope, which you claim isn't one of the species. I quote: *I have no hesitation in saying that they are justly to be subjected to every torture and put to death in the flames.* I can't disagree. Therefore, even if Monsieur Loup-garou is incapable of transforming into a wolfly shape he nonetheless poses a threat to the community and must be exterminated for the common good. It's the court's responsibility to battle all elements of evil. Christ has delegated to the Church's legal servants the duty to protect His flocks and see they are not harmed."

I jumped to my feet. "But you presume my client to be a werewolf, or if not at least a werewolf's first cousin. Your argument then distills to what one of a perceived kind deserves, so do all, circumstances and true differences be damned. That is too broad a premiss on which to convict, monsieur, not relying instead on actual proof to refute my arguments. In sidestepping my evidence you ignore the very core of the accusation: *guilt or innocence of heresy by means of werewolfery.*"

From beside me His Grace interrupted. "Monsieur, your intended disquisition has itself metamorphosed into a disturbance of the ether you seek to penetrate. I believe I hear God's angels clamping their hands over their ears."

"Yes, Your Grace, I understand."

Said His Grace, "Do you now." It wasn't a question. "Court is adjourned for the day." His gavel struck the sounding block. "Monsieur Clerk?"

Said the clerk, standing underneath his tiny personal awning: "Court will reconvene tomorrow at terce, Tuesday the 25th of September, at which time the defense will continue presenting its case."

Jamet was proving so honest and efficient that I had left him in charge of my animals and footmen, depending on him to make decisions as necessary on their behalf and mine. It was a relief, clearing my mind for the legal tasks at hand. Still, having not talked to him recently I decided to check and see how he was handling his responsibilities. After court I went to the stable and asked him for a status report. He was busily shoveling out a stall. A quick look around showed that my animals were well cared for, and François and Alvin were just then washing and preparing to groom the palfrey, who stood patiently in crossties appearing to enjoy the attention.

Jamet, on hearing my voice, turned and put down the shovel. "Good afternoon, Master," he said brightly.

I asked if everything was proceeding normally and if he required anything. He replied that everything was fine and thanked me again for the roof over his head, the regular food and drink, and my faith in him to carry out his duties responsibly. He said, "I shall never lie to you, Master," and raised his right hand in a pledge. "At night I sometimes visit the market where I perform some rudimentary magic tricks learned in my travels and accept a few small coins as gratuity. I regularly recount to François and Alvin my near-death encounters with demons during these excursions, which keeps them frightened and disinclined to accompany me. I often give them the extra flagon of wine you so kindly provide to assure they stay behind, and on returning at dawn I find them safely asleep in the hay. It keeps them contented and out of trouble. Occasionally, I've hired prostitutes from the inn to keep François and me company, paying for their services with my meager tips from the market. That's the extent of my wanderings."

He stood stiffly as if awaiting a remonstrance, but I merely warned him not to extend the boundaries of his activities any further, do anything that might shame me, and be careful not to contract the pox. "Incidentally," I said, "don't you or François become attached to any of these women. I don't intend to increase my retinue." He nodded, obviously relieved and grateful, remarking that his arrangement with the serving girls had also improved their diet without incurring additional expense. Not uncommonly, he and his mates found an extra piece of meat in their evening soup, the loaves baked evenly, proof of them having been selected from the center of the oven, and the flagons of wine not shorted but filled to capacity.

Révigny later greeted me at the tavern with an open Bible before him on the table and this puzzling statement: "Consider, Barthélemy, the pitiful eremites huddled in caves in the Judean desert awkwardly transcribing the books of the Old Testament. Think of them painfully depositing their desiccated scats across the baked landscape. Feel the anguish of being denied suitable receptables for their equally hot sperm except each other's anuses and the vaginas of a few spindly, recalcitrant ewes. The Old Testament is riddled with rib-ticklers. We have these dedicated monks to thank."

THE MORNING ARRIVED MISTY AND RAIN-SOAKED from the previous day. All was gloom, the clouds having arranged themselves in a surly crouch directly above the market from where they rumbled acrimoniously like empty stomachs. The shoppers and stall keepers, subdued and shivering in their thin clothes, eyed one another with the usual suspicion. I had worked into the night on my strategy and felt confident it was sound. When court reconvened and His Grace gave me the stage I responded with alacrity.

The clerk rose and said, "The defense calls Monsieur Loup-garou, who will not be allowed the witness chair but remain chained to his post throughout the interrogation. Afterward, the prosecution may ask him its questions."

I descended the stairs and stood with my back to the court facing Monsieur Loup-garou, who got to his feet and bowed toward me respectfully. I bid him good morning and began the interrogation. "Does the phase of the moon affect your nocturnal activities, Monsieur Loup-garou? The term 'lunacy' derives from a form of madness induced by the stage of the moon."

Le Loup-garou considered the question. "To some extent, monsieur. They say werewolves are most active during nights of the plenilune, but it isn't necessarily true in my situation. It's just that I see better under strong moonlight, so I suppose the stage of the moon has some effect. If I were a were*cat* and could see better in the dark then the moon's phase might not matter."

"Some claim metamorphosis to occur under a waxing full moon, especially if the shape-shifters are sons of priests. These lads—voluntary werewolves all—disrobe at the edge of an enchanted pond, swim across naked, and don wolf skins left for them on the other bank by Satan. After carrying out their nocturnal mischief they leave the skins where they found them and swim back before dawn to put on their clothes and return home, their families and neighbors none the wiser. According to others attacks are more prevalent on a waning full moon. Is it your preference to attack on the waxing or waning moon?"

"As I said, monsieur, I notice only whether the moonlight is bright enough to see. I don't like wandering among the tombstones on black nights when I might bump into one or trip on a low headstone and injure myself. Also, you can never be sure when vampires might be creeping around searching for victims among the living, and that would include me. My skin crawls thinking of a horrid caped figure leaping onto my back and sinking its teeth into my throat to drink my blood."

"So, Monsieur Loup-garou, you're telling us that you, by reputation a fierce werewolf, are afraid to be alone in a dark graveyard? That you believe in vampires and other demons?"

"Of course, monsieur. Like anyone else I'm afraid of the dark and the demons who use it to conceal their presence." At hearing this the crowd laughed. "And don't forget that I don't choose to be as I am. The feeling that sweeps over me is uncontrollable, and I become like those with the falling sickness who succumb to fits, which recently seems to be unsettling me more often."

"May we assume correctly that you aren't the son of a priest?"

"I never knew my father, monsieur, although I assure you he wasn't a priest."

I approached the post. "Do you wander about at night with the intent of ravishment and murder?"

"No, monsieur. The urge washes over me like a great wave, and suddenly I'm changed, having assumed the personality and manners of a wolf. There was no intent to harm others, much less ravish or murder them. I would prefer being the ordinary man I once was."

I walked directly to my client. "Please present your left hand to me." Monsieur Loup-garou complied. I clasped my own hands behind my back and examined his closely, including the digits. "Now turn it over, please." As expected it was dirty and calloused, the nails cracked and broken, the knuckles swollen and misshapen from accidents and fights, but otherwise the hand and fingers were unremarkable.

"Hold up both hands so those nearby can see." Some in the audience took advantage of the offer and stepped forward. "In some cases," I said, "Satan commands his acolytes not to pare the nail of the left thumb but let it grow into a horny claw as a pledge of homage. Notice that Monsieur Loup-garou's left thumbnail is perfectly normal." Three men and a woman were at that moment looking at it closely. I asked their assessment, and each agreed that the left and right thumbnails were of equal length.

My client dropped his hands, and I stepped back. "Some say a werewolf is hairy at all times, others that he wears his skin hair-side out when in wolf form and reverses it when appearing as a human." I turned and looked at the table behind me. "Does my learned adversary wish to cut my client and see if any wolf hair appears in the open wound? I assure him it will not." Révigny made no acknowledgment of my challenge. His Grace was silent too.

"They say a werewolf, whether in wolf or human shape, trembles when confronted by a crucifix or cross." I pulled out the cross I wear on a chain around my neck and brandished it at Monsieur Loup-garou, who viewed it calmly.

I tucked the cross back under my robe. "It's universally accepted among demonologists that a voluntary werewolf while in human form bears on his body a small crescent known as the mark of the Devil. I looked my client in the eyes. "Do you have such a mark?"

"No, monsieur. Just yesterday you made me disrobe in my cell and with two guards as witnesses examined me all over. The only marks on me are scars from wounds inflicted during years of slavery aboard the king's galleys."

"Yes," I said, "and we have the signed affidavits of the guards to that effect, do we not, Monsieur Clerk?"

Said the clerk, "That's correct Monsieur Chassenée."

"Were you born with a caul, otherwise known as a remnant of the birth sac, across part of your head or face?"

"Not that I've been told, monsieur."

"Were you born on Christmas Day?"

"No, monsieur. My birthday is in the summer."

"Some say that lycanthropy runs in families. Is this true of yours?"

"I couldn't say for sure, not having seen my family in years. I don't know if any are still alive, but when last I knew they were normal rustics trying only to survive. I would say it is not true and that I'm the only member of my family afflicted by this strange malady."

"I see. Let's move along to the confusing theological issue of metamorphosis. Please pay close attention to my words and answer to the best of your ability. The most fertile minds in Christian and pagan history have grappled with the problem, emerging still unsatisfied that it's been solved. Here is some of what we know. Those who have clandestinely witnessed a werewolf undergoing metamorphosis claim that as the moon waxes into a perfect sphere at plenilune the conjurer's eyes glaze over. He disrobes, urinates around his clothes piled on the ground, then collapses and commences to writhe fitfully as if suffering an attack of the falling sickness. The fit ends suddenly. The conjurer's face narrows and elongates, and his body becomes hirsute all over. The limbs contract into those of a canid, and a bushy tail sprouts just above his anus. He whimpers and moans pitiful animal sounds, but whether as the result of anguish, pain, both, or neither is unknown. After a time he rises on all fours, settles back on his haunches, points his muzzle at the moon, and emits several mournful, terrifying howls. When finished he trots away to do mischief. Any traveler encountered from this moment forward is certain to be murdered, abandoning his life's blood to the thirsty ground. Now, Monsieur Loup-garou, a so-called 'werewolf,' is this what you experience?"

"As you requested, I paid close attention to your words, and say this. Of those transformative events I experience only fits like the falling sickness. I don't become a wolf, nor have I ever believed that I do. What overpowers me is an intense anger at the world. To disrobe in public is potentially embarrassing if women and children should see me, not to mention rude. Running around naked in front of others isn't what grown men should do. I therefore retain my clothes at all times. Do my eyes glaze over? I couldn't say, being unable to examine them myself. Do I howl and commit mischief? Sadly, yes, although I've never badly hurt or killed anyone. The transformations seem to come over me more often on bright, moonlit nights, although I don't plan for them. One event seems connected to the other, that's all. I sometimes find myself transformed on moonless nights too."

"And toward dawn after these fits expire do you feel a sense of complete exhaustion, as if you can hardly move a finger or toe?"

"Exactly! All I want is to lie still for many hours, and I do this even to the point of near starvation."

"Do you become febrile prior and during these attacks? People sometimes hallucinate and lose sensibility for a time. Physicians tell us that delirium and monomaniacal behavior can result when the temperature of the brain becomes excessive. In your case it could bring on the delusion of wolfishness."

"I never feel feverish at these moments, but sometimes I do before their onset or afterward."

I said, "If a werewolf is wounded or some part of his body is amputated he returns instantaneously to human form, and the location of the wound or missing limb then appears exactly where it was on the wolf's body. This has been demonstrated numerous times at many places and is indisputable. So, monsieur, have you ever been wounded while under your delusional spells? If so, please show us the scars."

"I have never been wounded at such times, monsieur."

I turned toward the court, allowing Monsieur Loup-garou to answer behind me. "It's well known that shepherds are especially prone to becoming werewolves. Have you ever been a shepherd?"

"No, monsieur."

"Have you ever wished to be a shepherd or dreamed of becoming one?"

"Never."

"I ask you now, Monsieur Loup-garou, if during the day you occasionally fall into a deep slumber."

"You mean as drunkards do?"

"Deeper. So deep that a passerby shaking you might think you are dead."

"No, monsieur. I sleep fitfully at all times, so lightly that long ago I ceased to dream. My life at all hours is a waking nightmare. Recently, the bouts of anger, thirst, and foaming never leave. Who can sleep under such conditions?"

I turned now to face my client. "Have you ever practiced bestiality while in a lycanthropic state by covering she-wolves in heat?"

"Of course not, monsieur! What a disgusting thought!"

"Have you ever knowingly rubbed yourself with magical salves concocted by you or someone else? If so, did they contain such compounds as nightshade, aconite, belladonna, or opium?"

"I'm an uneducated man, monsieur, not an alchemist. And I have never applied salves to my body, nor has another person ever done it for me."

I continued: "Certain werewolves seem to prefer eating girls, young virgins in particular, a condition called 'parthenophagy.' Do you fall into this group, or are you indifferent to the sex and age of your victims when evaluating them for gustatory purposes?"

"I've never eaten a young girl or anyone else, nor have I ever wanted to."

"Then may we presume you frequent the town graveyard to feast on the corpses and chew their bones?" I looked directly at him.

"No monsieur!" He held his hands with palms up and backed away from me as if warding off an attacker. "The thought of doing that makes me nauseous. I can only imagine stray dogs feeding on the human dead. I would rather starve." He bowed his shaggy head and shook it in disbelief. With his head still lowered he said, "I go there because when these terrible feelings consume me I want a quiet place far from water where there are fewer people I might hurt."

"Far from water?" I was puzzled. "Why?"

"I can't explain the reason, but lately I've tried to avoid water, not from fear of drowning. I don't know. I'm simply afraid to be near a pond or lake, even a puddle of rainwater. When this feeling first took root I attributed it to the awful experience of the shipwreck, but this is a recent fear."

I didn't push this aspect of the questioning because it seemed irrelevant. "I explained in my opening statement that voluntary and involuntary werewolves, and probably accidental ones too, must disrobe prior to metamorphosis. To my knowledge wolves wearing human clothes have never been reported." This comment brought a cascade of laughter and hoots from the spectators. "Following transformation the shape-shifter forms a 'conjurer's circle' by urinating around his pile of clothes. The clothes left behind are then hidden or guarded because without them the shape-shifter can't regain his human form. I also explained how voluntary werewolves don't require a magical charm, unguent, girdle, or anything else to effect transformation. If a girdle is used, sometimes it's a wolf skin, sometimes a human skin, but in either case about three fingers in breadth. Monsieur Loup-garou, do you require a magic charm, lotion, unguent, girdle, or other such magical aid in your metamorphosis?"

"No, monsieur."

"We know too that a sorcerer can cast spells on others. This is accomplished in three ways. First, the evil eye, Second, muttering an incantation, and third, a touch or gesture. In all cases it's agreed universally that the person dispensing the spell can do so only with Satan's cooperation, the looks, chants, or touches having no power in themselves. Considering the true werewolf's inability to speak human languages and even to gesture as humans do it makes most use of the evil eye, which is peculiarly human. So, has anyone including another werewolf cast a spell on you causing you to behave as a lycanthrope?"

"No, monsieur. The feeling simply comes on me, that's all."

"Then you can't be a voluntary werewolf. And do you disrobe and urinate in a circle around your clothes as part of the metamorphosis?"

"I don't do either, monsieur. As I said, the last thing I want is to startle and embarrass women and children who might see me naked or pissing in public."

"Then you would say that even when behaving as a werewolf you suffer the disadvantage of shyness?"

"I suppose so, but your question is embarrassing and upsetting. I'd rather not discuss it."

I stopped pacing, forefinger to lips, and faced my client. Something about his adversity to water was niggling at me. "Monsieur Loup-garou," I said, "tell me again how you feel about water." The question seemed to startle him. "What are your emotions in the presence of a body of water, say, a pond or lake, or the sea?"

"I am terrified, monsieur. I never go near water. Even drinking it has become frightening."

"But you told me you were a seaman for many years. Surely, you must have overcome at least some of your initial fear, considering you originally had been a landsman."

"True, but as I said, lately that's changed and now even a rain puddle sends me running in the opposite direction."

I said, "Thank you. You will now leave the post under guard, unless Monsieur Révigny has questions."

"Do you wish to question the defendant, Monsieur Révigny?" said the judicial vicar.

"Yes, if Your Grace so allows." I heard Révigny push back his chair and descend from the platform. When he was beside me I returned to my own chair.

"Monsieur Loup-garou, please tell me if moonlit nights have a different effect on you than nights of blackness."

"The two kinds of night are very different, monsieur. During moonless nights I stumble about tripping over headstones and bumping into those that are erect. The delirium makes me unstable, and I sense the contents of the entire graveyard out to injure and consume me. God forbid I should fall into an open grave." He sighed and leaned against the post as if for support.

"And on moonlit nights?"

"Those are the nights prompting me to howl loudest and most often. The light of a waxing moon seems to pierce my eyes through to the sockets and beyond into my very brain. It's as if a spike is being driven through my head, which I squeeze between my hands and try not to go completely mad."

"Tell me about your recent wounds, not the scars from your days in the king's galleys, but those acquired during nights prowling the graveyard."

"As I said, monsieur, in my violent thrashing about and running blindly I bump into things. In wolf mode I gallop on all fours, doing considerable damage to my knees and elbows."

Révigny folded his arms and took another tack. He was obviously in pursuit of something specific. "Yes, but many of your wounds aren't from bruises and scrapes. They resemble dog bites. Are they?"

Monsieur Loup-garou looked at Révigny as if for the first time. "Why yes. I suffer chronically from dog bites. When I begin to howl the stray dogs of the town reply with howls of their own. Soon they gather in the graveyard. I try to run, but they form into packs and hurl themselves at me. Then my world becomes one of barks, yelps, and growls while we battle grimly as if execrating the dead slumbering under our feet. I manage to kill a few by breaking their necks in my hands, but inevitably I'm bitten all over before I've driven away the last of them."

"And you testified earlier that you were bitten by your tame wolf, a constant companion, which afterward ran away and presumably died?"

"Yes, monsieur. That was Lupo, the only friend I've ever had."

Révigny seemed satisfied. "You're unusually articulate and perceptive for an uneducated farmer, and I admire your directness."

"Thank you, monsieur. I spent years living inside my head while rowing the king's galleys. At first it was a frightening and confusing space, but I needed a refuge from the oars and the beatings, if only in my mind."

Révigny turned and looked at the judicial vicar. "I'm finished with my questions, Your Grace."

After the geôliers had unshackled my client from the post and taken him away it was time to interview witnesses and victims of putative attacks by my client. Finding them had been the combined task of the prosecution and defense. Few members of the community had answered our call. Four, two women and two men, admitted under preliminary questioning to having been frightened by my client's howls, although not attacked. Their evidence was inferential and irrelevant. Several street urchins who came forth thinking they might be rewarded had actually been abusers and not the abused, eventually admitting under threat of the stocks to pelting my client with rocks and rotten apples until he ran away. Still another man claimed Le Loup-garou had accosted him in the cemetery and torn his tunic. He showed us some minor scratches on his shoulder, claiming they were inflicted during the incident. His story pertained directly to the case, and we ordered him to appear before the court for formal questioning. Despite local rumors no one came forth with proof of having actually been bitten or otherwise injured. Our final interview was with a junk seller who said he had been scavenging in the graveyard for saleable items when Monsieur Loup-garou crept up undetected and bit his ankle. He also expected a reward and was unable to produce a suitable wound or scar as evidence. The ankle he showed us was unmarked, at which point he complained that the wound was internal, although no less painful than if the skin had been broken. We chastised him for being an avaricious liar and dismissed him.

This left one reliable witness, the man whose tunic had been ripped. His name was Gérard Voisin. The clerk summoned him from the crowd to be sworn in and sit in the witness chair. I stood in front of the table out of the drizzle and began the questioning. "Was the being who attacked you a man or an animal?"

"A man, monsieur."

"Was he running on all fours when you first became aware of his presence?"

"No, he jumped at me like a madman from behind a tombstone. I barely escaped with my life."

"Did you happen to discern, Monsieur Voisin, if your attacker had hands and feet or forepaws and hindpaws?"

"He gripped my tunic with hands, and when I stepped back I must have stepped on one of his feet because he grabbed it and howled in pain. That's one reason I was able to escape."

"Therefore, you conclude your attacker had human appendages and not paws?"

"That's correct, monsieur."

"Do you see your attacker now?"

"Yes, that's him chained to the post."

"When you look at the accused do you perceive a man or a wolf?"

"He's clearly a man, monsieur, but that night his fingernails felt like the claws of an animal. I suppose they haven't been pared in months, maybe years. And he smelled bad, like a wolf."

"Have you ever smelled a wolf?"

"No, but tradition says they have a foul odor similar to old clothes."

"Similar to a wolf who doesn't do his laundry?" The spectators shouted their delight. "I might agree that Monsieur Loup-garou emits a strong odor, but of an unwashed human, not an animal. What were you doing at the time of the attack?"

"I was strolling along one of the paths on my way home from a tavern where I had spent several hours with friends."

"I see. And you were walking alone?"

"Yes."

"Were you feeling the effects of drink?"

"I suppose so. A little."

"And what was Monsieur Loup-garou doing?"

"I don't know. He suddenly pounced on me from behind a tall tombstone, growling horribly. I was terrified and tried to run, but he grabbed my tunic and ripped it at the shoulder." He pulled down the shoulder of the tunic, now repaired. "See these scratches on my skin?"

Said I from the platform, "They're too tiny to see from here. Please leave the chair and come closer." When he did I descended to the ground and made a show of trying to locate them, a way of showing and emphasizing their insignificance.

I asked him to return to the witness chair and began pacing back and forth at the front of the platform, head down and forefinger to my lips as if contemplating a matter of deep concern. When directly before Monsieur Voisin I turned suddenly to face him. "Werewolves are said to lurk around cemeteries in the night where they dig up recent graves using their forepaws, then gnaw the flesh and bones of the dead. Such a being is often considered a subspecies of werewolf called a 'loublin,' known to feed exclusively on corpses. Had my client been engaged in molesting graves prior to attacking you? If you give testimony confirming his putative status as a loublin, think carefully about the consequences of perjury before answering."

Monsieur Voisin fidgeted in the chair and pulled on his nose. "I don't know, monsieur. As I said, he jumped out at me. I hadn't realized he was there, so how could I have wondered what he was doing?"

"Please describe his appearance in detail."

"It was night, and I mostly remember just trying to save myself. My mind was clouded with fear."

"Yes, and with drink," I said, drawing laughter from the spectators. "Speaking of drink, werewolves in the Baltic countries are famous for breaking into the cellars of taverns after their owners close for the night and consuming the beer and wine. Some authorities even claim they stack the empty casks neatly for easy removal the next day. Monsieur Bailiff, has this fair city reported any such activity lately?"

"No, monsieur, and I'd certainly have heard about it." The crowd roared, some urging that Monsieur Loup-garou be given beer and wine without delay.

After the noise abated I continued to address Monsieur Voisin. "As to your own drinking that fateful night, allow me to assist your somewhat fuzzy memory. The being who attacked you, was he human or animal?'

"You've already asked that. Human, definitely. The man chained to the post." He pointed without hesitation at Le Loup-garou.

"You say this confidently, as if you have no doubt whatever."

"That's true, monsieur. It was him. He even smelled the same as now, and if the rags he wears aren't those he wore that night they're very similar."

"Do you believe he's a werewolf?"

"I couldn't say for certain, but his nickname indicates that he is."

"Thank you, Monsieur Voisin."

The judicial vicar said, "Monsieur Révigny, do you wish to question the witness?"

"No, Your Grace. I'm quite satisfied."

"Very well, the witness is excused. Court is adjourned for today."

Without being prompted the clerk rose and said, "Court will reconvene at terce tomorrow, Wednesday the 26th of September."

That evening in the tavern as we put the third (or perhaps the fourth) cup to our lips, Révigny said suddenly, "The clues are legion and ancient, Barthélemy. They lie piled at our feet like cobbles on the seashore. Sometimes the commonest objects are the least visible." He leaned back and looked at me, eyes flashing pale yellow.

Puzzled, I said, "What do you mean?"

"Remember Ovid's description of the werewolf in his *Metamorphosis*, the scene where the beast swoops down on the flock?" My expression must have been blank. "Fine, then I shall quote: *His jaws were besputtered with foam* . . . A few lines further Ovid states, *Hoary he is as afore, his countenance rabid* . . . What does this reveal?" Again, silence from me and probably an imbecilic look.

Révigny leaned toward me across the table, always a slightly unnerving experience. "Consider the symptoms, Barthélemy: dryness of the mouth and tongue, a fierce thirst that can't be slaked yet too afraid of water even to drink it, saliva so thick it collects as foam around the lips, the fits of madness and delirium that encroach suddenly and without warning, agitation and confusion, the seizures and spasms . . . As you well know these are symptoms of a disease that here in France we call le rage, or 'the madness,' derived from the Latin *rabere*. Your client has rabies. He will die of it unless the flames reach him first, and his victims, no matter how superficially marked by his nails and teeth, will die of it too if his saliva has flecked their wounds. There's no saving any of them. Le rage in our country is most commonly caused by wolf and dog bites, ordinarily when a wolf bites a domestic dog, which then passes it along to its canine companions. Ultimately, a human is bitten. The contagion is transmitted by *semina*, invisible seeds inhabiting the saliva of the infected animal." Révigny looked at me without expression, depthless eyes still blinking yellow. He backed slowly away and resumed his normal sitting posture, obviously not deriving joy from the information just revealed.

My feet had gone numb, and I scooted back in the chair. The insipient alcoholic fog departed, and I was instantly sober. Révigny's words had stunned me. I should have guessed; no, I should have known soon after Révigny began his questioning of Le Loup-garou. All the signs were there, the ones Révigny had enumerated during the interrogation and just now, in addition to others. Recently, I was aware of being nervous when visiting my client in his cell. He seemed increasingly jumpy, distracted, and unreliable, often lapsing into incoherency. The guards had become blasé and could never have saved me in time if I'd been attacked. The thought of contagion was even more terrifying. I couldn't recall ever touching my client or being touched by him, although I had sat on his sleeping pallet, walked on the floor of his cell, and breathed the same air, never observing any specific hygienic practices. Could his *semina* have infected me? There was no way of knowing.

Then Révigny said, "You're free of the distemper, at least at present, but be careful."

I threw up my hands. "But what can I do at this point in the trial? I've plotted every step of my case, and tomorrow is the summation."

Révigny shrugged. "Proceed as you've planned and allow the pieces to land where they will. My strategy, and I'm alerting you in advance, is to ignore the trial's specific mandate of heresy and toss a red herring at His Grace's feet, namely le rage. Your insanity defense based on lycanthropy is quite compelling, assuming we continue traipsing the current path. The strategy has been brilliant, and no doubt your summation will be too. I shall argue in mine that all you posit is irrelevant, and the court's duty should be protecting Magny-Cours from the impending ravages of le rage. Saving Christ's flock should take precedence over all else. There's nothing quite like the prospect of an invisible contagion to panic an ignorant citizenry." His eyes now glowed a fierce orange. That toothy green grin spread the width of his face, and he waggled his forked tongue. Twin serpentine heads emerged on its tines and gazed about as if searching for a miniature Eve or perhaps their long-lost legs.

WEDNESDAY SEPTEMBER 26TH—CHASSENÉE PRESENTS HIS SUMMATION FOR THE DEFENSE

THE WEATHER CLEARED OVERNIGHT, BUT WHETHER this portended good news or bad was impossible to predict. My mood was certainly better. I felt more comfortable performing in open air than underneath a canvas awning. I thought we might even experience a little sunshine. When the gavel struck and court opened I announced to the judicial vicar my readiness to make a summation, at which point any pleasant thoughts were quickly doused.

He said, "By all means, monsieur, although I assumed you were already well into it. In light of this request I suppose your endless debate with the prosecutor has been the preamble. Please begin. A brief peroration would be my preference, although take what time you need, keeping in mind that my late afternoon and evening schedules are filled, and I have no idle moments for empty monologues. Furthermore, it will have to wait until after sext. The clerk and I have business that must be finished in time for my later meetings. You and Monsieur Révigny will have to amuse yourselves until then."

Révigny and I went to a nearby tavern for a bowl of small beer and a midday meal, watching as the morning slid relentlessly into afternoon. My summation had been prepared in such a way that breaking it apart over two days would dampen the effect: important points are quickly forgotten overnight and not easily reprised the next day, and this judicial vicar seemed particularly irked by redundancy.

When court reconvened the sky had darkened and a light rain was falling. This resulted in a further delay as the awning was erected. At last I was free to proceed. I straightened my robe, brushed some breadcrumbs off my stomach, and looked out at the spectators. It was well past sext. Many had already departed; others were packing their belongings in preparation to leave. A mime trying to stay dry was curled up and dozing underneath the clerk's desk, practically on top of that good man's feet.

"The wolf is the enemy of the lamb," I said, "symbol of our Savior, Jesus Christ. His purported evil arrives ingrained in us at birth, although we typically fail to see it as metaphor. From Christ's Sermon on the Mount we read in *Matthew*, chapter seven verse fifteen, *Beware of false prophets, which come to you in sheep's clothing, but inwardly they are ravening wolves.* And in Paul's address to the Ephesians he tells us in chapter twenty of *Acts* verse twenty-nine, *For I know this, that after my departing shall grievous wolves enter in among you, not sparing the flock.* In such statements the sheep are the Lord's children, the wolf symbolic of Satan's influence. Today, the wolf of Scripture also embraces a wolf-human hybrid. Believing such a creature exists straddles the line separating truth and heresy. How? By tacitly acknowledging Satan's capacity to transform human flesh into that of an animal and back again, a purview exclusively reserved for God."

"Be careful, monsieur," said His Grace.

"I'm speaking only in theoretical terms, Your Grace."

"Then continue."

"The testimony of the only victim of an attack by my client has been entered into evidence. During cross examination I demonstrated its lack of both practical and legal utility and now formally ask that it be stricken from the record. I shall say more on this matter shortly. I have also introduced enough doubt about the possibility of physical shape-shifting that even if my client were to be one of the three species of true werewolves in my taxonomic system a strong case has been established for his immediate release. However, that evidence is superfluous, not to mention irrelevant, simply because Le Loup-garou is assuredly a lycanthrope, not a werewolf, and we should no longer consider him such.

"What do we get when we combine the natural strength, speed, and savagery of a brute with the sensibility, intelligence, and moral capacity of a human? We get a hybrid that functions more competently in some ways, yet incompletely as either. We denigrate both. The wolf is not inherently evil, but simply one of God's creatures placed on Earth to help fulfill His purposes. And humans strive a lifetime to leave animalistic tendencies behind and accept what God offers us instead: the capacity for sublimity, humility, kindness, and the awareness that He is in Heaven watching over us. However, metamorphosis into animalistic states isn't necessary to their attainment. Insanity can achieve the same effect. Lycanthropy, a form of madness, is a horrible disease. It first depersonalizes then ultimately dehumanizes its victims, toppling them from the most exalted of God's creations to His meanest and most brutish. Not even Job was so afflicted."

I glanced at poor Monsieur Loup-garou huddled against his post in the chilly rain, then at my documents spread before me on the table. "I begin by reprising a key piece in Monsieur Révigny's introductory oration, promising to keep my assessment brief and pointed. Clerical and secular experts alike have long debated certain ontological issues of werewolf metamorphosis, separable into two general areas. First, can humans transform into actual flesh-and-blood animals and back again, or is such shape-shifting entirely spiritual? In other words, can a human physically become a wolf, or is metamorphosis strictly a mental event and its perception by the transformer himself and others just illusion? Second, if tangible shape-shifting actually happens does the soul accompany the human body as it transitions to a wolf, or does it hover apart awaiting the body's return to human form and then re-entering? Animals, of course, don't have souls. This being so, it seems impossible for a werewolf to obtain one even on temporary loan. Saint Augustine and other great thinkers have claimed that body and soul are insep-arable until the moment of death. Most who accept this viewpoint believe a demon enters a real wolf and that the soul remains behind still fused to the slumbering body.

"I understand how these problems and conflicts with regard to shape-shifting have troubled learned men for millenniums and still there are no definitive answers, but that situation remains unac-ceptable in a court of law devised and judged by humans with a human life and its short allotted time on Earth in the balance. The law, regrettably in some instances, must decide between exonera-tion or conviction unequivocally. Philosophy is not its purview; there can be no middle ground. And as Monsieur Révigny has emphasized, in our courts the facts are all that matter. On this he and I agree. And there are plenty here to consider. I shall lay them out face-up like playing cards, proving that the case for my client's exoneration is irrefutable.

"So, what are these facts? First and perhaps most obvious is the troubling lack of victims and witnesses. Their absences point directly to my client's innocence. The prosecution and defense, working together, could find only one victim of an attack by my client and no reliable witnesses who could verify having seen anyone attacked firsthand. Monsieur Voisin, our single victim, was asked if he believes Monsieur Loup-garou is a werewolf. His answer? That according to his nickname he is. Since when is a nickname used to define and categorize someone? Is a man nicknamed Le Cochon an actual pig? I once defended an accomplished thief whose surname was Bisset. He was so slippery and elusive that even the gendarmes called him L'Anguille with a hint of reverence and respect. But was he really an eel? No, certainly not. He was a man. A nickname is merely a signifier, another means by which someone is identified and distinguished from others. It carries no reality of its own, and certainly no transformative powers unless spoken as part of a sorcerer's incantation. For this and other reasons I consider the testimony of the witness Gérard Voisin, such as it is, to be worthless and request it be set aside. The only damage Monsieur Voisin suffered was a torn tunic, a few minor scratches, and the embarrassment of looking ridiculous in public for the triviality of his complaint."

"Your request is denied, monsieur," said His Grace.

I proceeded as if not hearing him. "Next, consider the matter of shape-shifting, of which much has been made. As I just mentioned, in Monsieur Révigny's opening oration on werewolfism he stated that most authorities accept Saint Augustine's theory that such a being is an actual wolf possessed by a demon, a supposition as ragged and full of holes as my client's breeches. How are we to presume this demon, created out of weightless air by Satan, acquires its human qualities and looks out at the world through human eyes pressed against the eyeholes of a wolf skin? How can a demon instantaneously gain and then retain the knowledge, memories, and cached experiences of a specific human who hovers elsewhere in a catatonic state, his shape unshifted? In other words, that Satan assimilates every aspect of the victim's conscious thought: his memories, experiences, and longings; his triumphs, failures, and regrets and stuffs them together inside a demon, itself embodied in a transient package of compressed air? Can Satan really do this? If so, where is the proof?

"To state simply that Satan has enormous powers and stop there evades the issue, snuffing out any possibility of further discussion. The basis is an unfounded assumption, a well-known logical fallacy called 'appeal to higher authority.' Stated another way, some perceived authority once uttered it; therefore, it must be true, terminating the debate without seeking a conclusion. Those who reason in such shallow terms consider actual evidence tendentious and superfluous and set it aside! Within this restricted arena any phenomenon can be brushed away simply by attribution to a supernatural power, thus rendering it forever unexplained and unexplainable.

"Monsieur Révigny listed other authorities and described the salient difficulties and contradictions their theories pose, concluding that the mystery of shape-shifting remains unsolved. However, considering that Augustine of Hippo's writings have gained the largest following for the longest time, let's unearth and examine a few nuggets. He postulated that a werewolf never advances to corporeal reality as an animal but remains in human form still fused to his soul after metamorphosis. The beast assuming his place is a real wolf whose actions are controlled by a demon. I've highlighted one flaw in Augustine's logic; now, consider another.

"What becomes of this hypothetical demon while the particular man it hopes will be blamed for its impending behavior as a werewolf is still an ordinary human traipsing around in his ordinary life? Does it wait patiently for a wolf to trot conveniently through the neighborhood, then dart inside it? How else to explain Augustine's reasoning? Demons, to my knowledge, aren't notable for lying dormant. To the contrary, demons are the apotheosis of hyperactivity, always running around freely in the guises of goblins and salamanders and cockatrices when they aren't inhabiting humans and animals and prodding them toward invidious mischief. If we consider these issues thoughtfully we must conclude that someone like Monsieur Loup-garou, chained before you to a post and shivering miserably in the damp chill like the ordinary man he is, must be demon-free and quite harmless.

"I have checked with the graveyard keeper of this parish and confirmed that no one has been buried in consecrated ground since . . . excuse me, I must check my notes." I shifted the papers before me on the table until finding what I needed. "Since Madame Oroye Chenery, who died the 17th of July at age fifty-two from choking on a chicken bone. She was interred two days later following a Christian ceremony. I was subsequently shown the burial site, which is undisturbed and already blanketed with grasses and summer weeds. The graveyard keeper assured me that none of the other graves has been disturbed either before or after Monsieur Loupe-garou's arrest and incarceration. Clearly, he isn't a grave molester and confessed under oath to frequenting the cemetery solely for its solitude and to graciously protect others from his violent fits.

"Let's consider the diagnostic characters of werewolves and determine if Monsieur Loup-garou is a good fit for the group and, if so, ascertain to which of the known species he belongs. I remind everyone that the facts—and the facts alone—should be weighed in determining his guilt or innocence. With this in mind, note that Monsieur Loup-garou is most similar to the involuntary werewolf in not having actually worshipped Satan or entered into a contract with him. Voluntary werewolves and occasionally some of the accidental species commit heresy by honoring Satan when such tributes should be reserved only for God. My client has done no such thing. He has been a pious man all his life, to which twelve compurgators at his first trial years ago swore under oath.

"During my public questioning of Le Loup-garou I considered all the known traits diagnostic of werewolves to see which might apply. And the result? None of them did! Not a single trait of werewolfism proved adequate to describe my client! I now review them." I picked up my sheaf of documents and began reciting. "The phase of the moon is immaterial to his so-called metamorphoses, meaning that plenilune isn't necessary for transformation, as is commonly stated. He fears vampires and like everyone else is afraid in the dark. Does this sound like the prototypical werewolf who stalks the night terrorizing man and demon alike? Our putative werewolf finds the thought of sex with she-wolves repulsive. He isn't the son of a priest, nor was he ever a shepherd, two factors known to predispose vulnerable young men to werewolfery. He says he does not sleep in a catatonic state during daylight hours, and Monsieur Révigny and I in our investigations failed to find a witness willing to swear under oath to the contrary. If we are to believe my client— and the evidence, or its lack, gives no reason not to—then he clearly isn't a werewolf in the Augustinian tradition, slumbering elsewhere while a wolf acting on his behalf under direction of a demon lays waste to the town's cemetery or attacks its citizens. We know for a fact that Monsieur Loup-garou takes his repose outside public houses hoping for a crust of bread, or under trees and in alleys. In other words, even during the day he can be found in places where all can see him either fully awake of lightly dozing.

"I've heard rumors in the market that Monsieur Loup-garou is a loublin who feeds solely on corpses and likely devoured one on a Friday at some point, thus violating *jejunium sextae*, or 'fast Friday' in the vernacular. However, the speculation is groundless considering my client has never eaten a corpse at all, and if he had eaten, say, a decomposing arm or a leg on a Friday his sin would be merely venial, absolution available at the closest confessional. My research reveals that a werewolf captured in Franche-Comté was indeed guilty of eating one of his victims on a Friday, although murder in this case was the inexcusable crime, not the violation of *jejunium sextae*.

"To his knowledge Monsieur Loup-garou was not born with a caul, nor was he born on Christmas Day. Either can be the sign of the werewolf, both together assuredly a double sign. My client's eyebrows do not meet in the middle of his face but remain apart, one above each eye as anyone can plainly see, another sign of the werewolf we can reject. Monsieur Loup-garou denies any intent to ravish or murder while in his wolfish state and swears never to have done so. And proof by refutation? Only one victim came forth bearing just a torn tunic and minor scratches, an incident my client doesn't deny. Further investigation revealed not a single reliable eyewitness to another attack. However, one point in Monsieur Voisin's testimony stands out. He stated that my client's appendages were human during the attack, not animal, which has two implications. First, he did not perceive his attacker as a wolf but rather as a man, which means that neither man was bewitched in the moment. Second, Monsieur Loup-garou has never claimed to undergo a physical metamorphosis, meaning he acknowledges he remains fully human during his episodes. Both facts reinforce my conclusion that he can be only a lycanthrope, not a werewolf.

"But there's more, much more. My client's left thumbnail has not been pared, as often ordered of his minions by Satan. His skin is entirely human through and through, not a wolf skin turned inside-out. The skin you see on Le Loup-garou is the only one he owns. Nor has he been marked by the Devil, to which I have submitted sworn affidavits to the court. In fact, he doesn't bear any diagnostic marks of Satan's acolytes. Sum the facts to this point and it can be stated with certainty that Monsieur Loup-garou is surely not a voluntary werewolf, nor is he a fit for either of the other two species. He has never donned a magic girdle or used any of the sorcerer's charms, such as amulets and rings. He doesn't avert his eyes and tremble at the sight of the cross. He's unaware of any werewolfism in his lineage and doubts it exists. Neither the prosecutor nor I has information to the contrary. The thought of disrobing in public horrifies him, knowing it would embarrass nearby women and children, not to mention himself.

"During these episodes of strange behavior Le Loup-garou is never febrile, nor has he been wounded except by stray dogs. He has never applied unguents, salves, or similar magic ointments to his body, nor has anyone ever intervened to apply them on his behalf. He is a simple man, not a sorcerer or alchemist capable of concocting them. The thought of feeding on corpses and sucking the marrow from their rotting bones repels him, but not less so than the notion of devouring the tender flesh of freshly-killed children, prepubescent virgins in particular. To his knowledge a spell has never been cast on him. And I add one final comment, this in reference to

Institoris' famous *Malleus*. Werewolfism scarcely appears on its pages, the only mention being the case of William of Paris, who according to my classification wasn't a werewolf at all but a lycanthrope and insane. The *Malleus* considers a werewolf to fall squarely within the Augustinian model; that is, an actual wolf controlled by a demon that commits its atrocious acts while the human it represents lies elsewhere, his consciousness and animation suspended."

For a long moment I stood at the table with my documents before me and took a deep, ostentatious breath, as if weighty matters were about to be placed not just before the court but the whole of mankind. "I conclude these remarks with a plea for mercy in the event Monsieur Loup-garou is convicted of werewolfery and condemned to execution as a heretic. Such a decision would be a travesty of justice, although one for which my client and I have prepared. If it should become necessary I ask that he be strangled prior to being burned to spare him the unimaginable agony of the flames. This is the customary procedure in France, provided he fully confesses to the crimes of which he's accused. Meanwhile, I offer this alternative to execution if that should be the sentence.

"We must ask ourselves as Christians whether putting to death a man accused of shape-shifting is condign punishment and not simply murder. Suppose no one is capable of actual shape-shifting, in which case a werewolf is a *phantasticum* as Saint Augustine postulated more than a millennium ago. The possibility can't be ignored. Then the delusion will have been our own, and sentencing an innocent person to death makes us his murderers.

"Whether Le Loup-garou is a werewolf or lycanthrope is easily tested by incarcerating him for a full year. In the interest of justice he deserves such a reprieve and opportunity to prove his innocence. Sadly, the courts and the fates acting in concert have scuttled what few chances life offered. If within the span of one year the metamorphosis comes on him his geôliers will bear witness; if not, it can be reasonably concluded that my client is a harmless lunatic under the delusion of werewolfery and ought to be released back into society with a stern warning not to frequent graveyards and scare innocent citizens.

"My suggestion is buoyed by adequate precedent. The duke of Muscovy once held a deranged man for a year after attacking his cattle. When captured he was unkempt and dirty, his hair and nails like those of a wild animal. Metamorphosis did not occur during imprisonment, at which point it became clear that the poor soul suffered from lycanthropy, not werewolfism. A report of this event can be found in the writings of Simone Maiolo, bishop of Volterra, archived at Cathédrale Saint-Lazare d'Autun.

"Now I come to my major point: Monsieur Loup-garou, by rights and all evidence, should be declared legally insane and sentenced to live out his days in a monastery where God can whisper holy words in his ear. Being imprisoned in the bowels of the king's galleys where he was starved and beaten viciously year after year would drive even the strongest man insane. Imagine his life for a moment: a man who suffered years of being chained to an oar now finds himself chained to the walls of a cell; that is, when not chained to a post on public display. How would you fare?" I pointed to a spectator whose attention I had, then to another and two more.

"Your Grace, I now raise the case of Jean Grenier as precedent for declaring my client mad and as evidence that not all lycanthropes are intelligent and cunning and capable of carrying out evil with conscious intent. Numerous other such cases are on record. Take, for example, a man in Naples who in a frenzy of lycanthropy dug up a corpse and was arrested while wandering through the streets spewing nonsense at passersby, a rotting leg draped over his shoulder.

"Grenier's case of lycanthropy is noteworthy because the judge, a man ahead of his time, determined that Monsieur Grenier was not mentally competent and could not be held morally responsible for his actions. The examining doctors declared him to be malnourished and mentally defective, conditions that impaired his judgment. Instead of being executed he was incarcerated in a Franciscan monastery at Bordeaux where the monks could set him on a righteous path. It's interesting that during his testimony Grenier admitted matter-of-factly to the horrid crimes of attacking children, young girls in particular, and eating them. He claimed to have been transformed into a wolf when the Man of the Forest gave him a salve to rub on himself and then ordered him to don a wolf skin. Only eyewitness accounts of the trial survive. The details were so vile that all records of the proceeding were ordered burned.

"Grenier, an adolescent at the time of his sentencing, made no effort to defend himself, but instead confessed to these monstrous acts despite not being prompted or tortured, and without remorse. Remarkably, after observing the boy and listening to his openly self-incriminating statements and other evidence of astonishing and disruptive behavior recounted by his lawyer the judge rightly decided that Grenier lacked the capacity for rational thought. Here I must emphasize a critical point of law: *crimes committed by the insane aren't punishable in France, and like minors such persons are shielded from prosecution.*" For emphasis I curled my right hand into a tiny fist and pounded the table twice, satisfied by the surprised looks on the faces of the court's members and not a few of the spectators. Révigny's eyes turned orange, and he grinned greenly. I then turned to His Grace and said, "This concludes my closing statement." I had managed to finish it in a single oration.

"Well, that was a performance fit for the stage, Monsieur Chassenée," said His Grace. From its neutral tone the remark could be interpreted equally as a compliment or admonishment. "It's surely sufficient to end the day," and he dropped the gavel. "Monsieur Clerk? A few words, please."

The clerk stood. "Yes, Your Grace. Court will reconvene tomorrow, Thursday the 27th of September."

The days were shortening, and by vespers the last of the daylight was gone. Révigny and I had taken our customary seats in the tavern and were awaiting service while the innkeeper and his wife went table to table lighting candles. The air was chilly, and I looked forward to a bowl of hot soup. Suddenly, there were heavy footfalls. The floor under us shook as an enormous being stepped through the door. In the dim light I could only see the lower half of a man's body, and just this visible part portended a giant. He strode directly to our table, picked up an empty chair by the crook of his finger, and sat. When I finally dared to look at his face I saw a single black eye staring back. It seemed dark as the night. The other was white and obviously blind. His hair and beard were wild and unkempt, like those of a nomad or a hermit. The odor wafting from him contained all humanity squeezed into a very small place. He put a hand the size of a bear's paw on the table and said, "May I sit with you a while? I have a story to tell."

I was quaking with fear and unable to speak, but Révigny said, "Of course, my friend. Please reveal your name and estate."

"My name isn't important, but they call me Le Géant. My estate is a mercenary soldier, most lately in service to our newly late King Louis XII. I fought the Venetians at the battle of Agnadello on the 14th day of this past May where we routed the enemy, destroying his army but still failing to take Padua. On that afternoon I lost my eye. However, none of this matters in the moment. I've been watching the trial and must tell you that the man chained to the post is innocent, to which I can personally attest. He once was a werewolf but today not moreso than either of you. He simply retains no memory of the experience. I agree that he's insane."

The innkeeper brought two cups and a flagon of wine and set them down warily. "We shall need another flagon and cup," Révigny said, "and our companion will be joining us for supper . . ."

The giant interrupted and said, "Only the wine for me." When it arrived he pushed aside the cup and tipped the flagon to his lips, a rational gesture in this circumstance: the cup had looked ridiculously small, comparable to a thimble beside a hand of ordinary size.

When the buzz in the room attenuated and most of the patrons finished staring, Révigny said, "Please tell us your tale Monsieur Géant and how it affects our duties as lawyers for the prosecution and defense."

"Very well," he said. "As a mercenary I work for whichever army pays the most. I have no interest in politics or in the philosophies used to justify subduing other people. Kings strive to be kinglier, nobles to gain more nobility, the rich to accumulate greater wealth, all tiresome endeavors. In the end everyone is worm food. Perhaps they should strive instead to be the worms, eh? Meanwhile, what do I care? Their little games pay well. My only loyalty is to myself and my purse. I fight when I need money, and afterward when my purse is bulging I live the life of a nomad, traveling where the roads lead, stopping in towns where food, drink, and whores are plentiful. When my funds are exhausted I hire myself out to whichever army makes the best offer. There's always a war somewhere. Life is simple. I'm good at what I do, and I have no attachments to people or places. My only goal is to see what's over the horizon.

"Anyhow, I was walking along a deserted road on a night of no moon not that long ago. I had never traveled it before and was unfamiliar with its twists and turns, knowing only that it would lead to a city, as roads eventually do. As it happened the city was this one and not another. I could tell the countryside was haunted from the phosphorescent eyes darting here and there. I've been in many haunted places and never feared the resident demons. Most are forest hobgoblins, harmless but a nuisance. I started to feel them tap me playfully on my shoulders and calves, and for sport withdrew my sword and made occasional swipes at the darkness, knowing I was slicing some of them in half, but realizing that because hobgoblins consist entirely of air they were instantly reassembling themselves, probably delighted with my company. Everything is a game with hobgoblins, and I never take them seriously.

"I had passed a hermit's hut just as darkness fell, its single window illuminated by a tiny candle. As I rounded the next bend its glow vanished, pinched out between the thumb and forefinger of the night. I trudged on as the professional soldier I am, mindless of the steps, one foot ahead and the other behind preparing to take the place of the first. Few civilians realize that walking is alternately balancing on one foot and then the other. Only when standing are both feet solidly on the ground.

"The night was so black I couldn't see where to place my feet and relied on probing ahead with my walking stick to stay within the road's boundaries. Then coming toward me I saw a pair of fiery red eyes and knew instantly that this was no harmless demon. It came on, shuffling and emitting low growls and groans, as if in terrible pain or distress, and when we were nearly face to face the glow of its eyes highlighted enough detail to outline the countenance of a wolf walking on its hind legs, a wolf of huge proportions. I knew immediately I was confronted by a werewolf, that there was no escape or turning back, no negotiation. 'Drop your skin!' I shouted, at which point the monster turned its head and seemed to cower. If the beast was under a bewitchment it had no choice but to drop the skin, regain its human form, and do battle with me. The loser must then put on the skin and metamorphose into a werewolf. The winner could continue on his way in human form, free of the curse. These are the rules. Soon enough I heard the skin drop to the road and was overcome by a foul stench. The skin was rotting, and the man underneath who had acquired it smelled no fresher.

"Weapons are forbidden in these instances, and we locked in hand-to-hand combat. I'm large and powerful, as you can see. From what I could discern of my adversary he was a man of ordinary size, although of extraordinary strength and quickness. Before I could grab him he slipped behind me, jumped on my back, and was throttling me in a chokehold of such force as to nearly stop my breath. I reached over my shoulder trying to grab his head, but he cleverly pressed it between my shoulder blades where I was unable to reach it. Finally, I jumped into the air and landed backward. The impact knocked the air out of him, and he released his hold. I rolled over intending to grab him by the throat, but he stuck his finger in my good eye. Fearing total blindness I rolled away and immediately felt two blows to my kidneys and one full in the face. They had the impact of hammers, and for days afterward I pissed blood and my nose dripped it.

"I now realized that this man was the most dangerous opponent I had ever faced. Unless I wanted to be a werewolf I must defeat him, and the quicker the better. It's bad technique to lose your wits in close combat, but considering I had only one good eye and hoped to keep it I started flailing wildly with my fists. One found its mark, and I heard the man crumple and collapse. I dropped to my knees and felt around until grabbing his shoulder, then struck again where the head must be. He relaxed immediately.

"Ha! With him beside me the two of us could have slain half the Venetian army, a gang of underpaid and poorly trained mercenaries hired by greedy merchants." He turned his head and spat on the floor in disdain. "What a warrior! No combatant had ever touched my face with his hand until that night, when he cleverly got me onto the ground where all men are the same height and with a fist like iron broke my nose after pummeling my kidneys." He touched his nose gingerly. "It's crooked and still pains me. I felt the blood poured forth like a millstream, and with every twinge I think of him with awe and respect. The closest anyone ever came to my face was with a pike, which put out my eye, and an axe, which once grazed my forehead. Until him I believed I was invincible.

"I sat beside him breathing heavily and took a drink of water from my flagon, still attached to my waist, then shook him awake and offered him a swallow, which he accepted silently. Then he began to sob, a sound like choking and sucking air, saying he couldn't go on, that the wolf skin was that of his best friend. He asked me to kill him and end his anguish, but his story touched my heart, and I refused. Instead, I suggested we build a fire in the road and eat. We were both exhausted from our fray. I carried sausage, bread, and cheese in my knapsack, which I now sought to find, having dropped it when our tussle began. Meanwhile, he went in the other direction to gather firewood. I produced my flint and steel, and soon we had a cheery fire going. Then the werewolf told me his story.

"He said he had been sentenced to life pulling oars in the king's galleys after having been charged, essentially, with nothing at all. Compurgators had sworn to the truthfulness of his oath of innocence, and the mystery of why his wife and daughter had died was never solved. Nonetheless, the accusation of witchcraft stuck, but because of the mitigating circumstances the inquisitorial judge had reluctantly spared his life. After years of hardship and terror the galley in which he was chained sank in a ferocious storm and only by the grace of God he survived to crawl ashore at Normandy. From there he took up the life of a wandering beggar.

"One day as he walked along a large wolf burst from a marsh and accosted him. Strangely, the animal intended no malice and soon they became companions of the road. The beast was so tall that when it stood on its hind legs and put its forelegs on his shoulders it towered above him. It protected him, and each cherished the other's companionship. Then the wolf fought with a large dog, receiving wounds that never healed. He became weak and agitated, biting the man and slinking off to die in the woods. Greatly saddened, he continued on the road alone, unaware that a sorcerer in need of a wolf skin had been following them knowing the wolf was ill and waiting for it to die. A nobleman was willing to pay the sorcerer a considerable sum to transform his hated brother-in-law into a demon of some sort and get him out of the way. The sorcerer tracked the wolf to the place where it died, skinned it, then with the fresh skin in hand charmed the brother-in-law into putting it on and becoming a werewolf, thereby completing the contract and pocketing his fee. Our man, the one you call Le Loup-garou, became one of this werewolf's victims. He's a fierce warrior, to which I can attest, and so I was amazed when told how he came to wear the skin and become a werewolf himself.

"When the werewolf confronted him he spoke as I did, ordering the beast to take off the skin and do battle, never doubting he would win. It was a night of full moon, and he immediately recognized the skin as that of his friend. The sight of it rendered him so distraught that when his opponent stood before him in human form he refused to fight, thus accepting werewolfery as a sort of penance, although for what I couldn't say. He had no cause to feel guilt. Perhaps he did it out of melancholy."

"He never revealed this part of his story to us," Révigny said. "So he once was a werewolf of the involuntary kind?"

"I suppose so," said the giant. "If you mean by involuntary that he was tied magically to the wolf's hide, although voluntary if you consider he acquired it by refusing the brawl to avoid it." He drained the rest of the flagon, and Révigny ordered two more, one for the two of us to share.

The giant wiped his hand across his lips. "Your Monsieur Loup-garou continued talking until dawn peeked over the horizon, when I could see that his ears had been cut off and his eyes were empty and crazed. He still stank of a dead animal. Without a word he reached for the skin intending to put it on, but I stayed his hand. 'Let's burn it,' I said. 'That way no one will bear the curse again.' And so we did, although unknown to either of us in that moment the lingering effects of the curse would continue to haunt him. Afterward, we locked arms and vowed to be comrades wherever we met again, and like brothers come to the other's aid in time of crisis. Having made that promise we parted and continued down the road in opposite directions, never to be at the same place again until now, although surprisingly little time has passed." He drained the flagon in a few swallows and stood, kicking the chair out behind him.

Révigny started to protest, "But monsieur . . ."

The giant held up his hand, palm facing us. "No more words. I shall say only this: We three know that Le Loup-garou is sick with le rage. I've seen its effects several times in my travels. He infected me during our skirmish, and I'm starting to feel the disease consume my body. It will kill us both unless something else does first. And finally, I'm true to my vows, true all the way to the grave. If my comrade isn't exonerated by the court in quick order, for we both have little time, I shall free him myself and God help whoever stands in my way. Goodnight, sirs, and thank you for the wine." With that he turned and clomped out the door.

The wine, a haphazard blend of green Spanish swill and a moderately aged local product, was making me stupid, especially on an empty stomach. According to the innkeeper the stock of regional wine was in high demand. We had been paying extra for what he could supply, but his own stores were nearly exhausted. The blend had become our only choice, and I was destined for a fierce hangover if I kept imbibing. Being dead and ethereal, Révigny was spared such agony, and I silently resented him for that.

Moths fluttered aimlessly about the candle on our table. Révigny had been quiet and apparently feeling philosophical. He suddenly said, "Interesting objects, candles. Some components of candle wax are volatile, wafted into the air by the heat of the flame. We can smell many of them. The remainder change phase from solid to liquid and drip down the shaft to again become solid. Icarus flew too close to the sun, and his wings made of wax melted. He fell to Earth and died. These moths, notice the ones with phosphorescent eyes. They're repentant demons seeking redemption in death, letting the vaporous wax congeal on their wings, the added weight forcing them to the ground. There could be no redemption for Icarus. As a pagan, what could he repent?

"We—rather, you—humans aren't superior, dazzled though you are by the false illumination of manmade laws. Instead of salvation they bring sadness and death and in doing so destroy a natural completeness that already exists but which you try vainly to push out of sight. A moth that self-immolates trades the order of itself for its disordered constituents. Can such reductionism qualify as advancement?"

The moths seemed out of focus, but some did have phosphorescent eyes, or so they seemed. At this stage I would have accepted nearly any illusion. I knew I had to stop drinking and believing I was celebrating a victory when all I'd achieved had been completing my summation, in itself an empty exercise. I needed a clear head to assess Révigny's summation the next day.

We stood to leave. "Le Géant's pledge is ominous," Révigny said, "but the consequences ought to be enormously exciting." He grinned and stuck out his bifurcated tongue.

THURSDAY SEPTEMBER 27TH—RÉVIGNY PRESENTS HIS SUMMATION FOR THE PROSECUTION

WHEN COURT RECONVENED HIS GRACE IMMEDIATELY gave Révigny the floor. He rose slowly, deliberately, and spread his papers before him on the table. After looking at the mostly oblivious spectators a moment as if contemplating something, he began. "Some claim the eyes of a werewolf remain human even when under the spell, suggesting that the person is the same and has merely pulled a wolf skin over himself so as not to be recognized. Never are they the savage eyes of a wolf. Others claim different things." He pointed to the defendant and said, "Has this unfortunate pilgrim's voyage on the mystical sea of werewolfism been real or just a fever dream? We can argue the logic and evidence several ways, but as Monsieur Chassenée and I have insisted, only the facts matter. If ravishment and even murder have been inflicted on other human bodies and souls, whether the guilty party is a conventional or unconventional being is irrelevant. The crime and the criminal are inseparable. Sentencing must be the same in either situation.

"Someone accused of werewolfery is guilty if the facts point directly to him. Consider that if the culprit is an actual wolf then it needs to be put down both as punishment and to prevent further crimes, no different from cases in which a pig eats an untended infant or a horse kicks its owner in the head, killing him. And the same applies if he's a man whose morals have fallen precipitously into wolfish ways. Furthermore, it makes no difference if he's a victim of bewitchment or chooses to go on his rampages because of an evil nature." Révigny's voice now rose in intensity. "*He nonetheless must be judged on the results of his actions, not the source!*" His voice returning to its normal volume, he said, "Monsieur Chassenée has done a marvelous job of explaining the nature of werewolves, but philosophers and theologians will need to continue the ontological debate without us. The courts deal exclusively with crimes and their consequences, nothing else."

Révigny turned and waggled his forefinger at me. "Monsieur Chassenée advocates incarcerating Le Loup-garou a full year as a test of his ability to metamorphose, but this test might not be so valid as he thinks. Simon Goulart, writing in his *Thresor d'histoires admirables de memorables de nostre temps* (*Admirable and Memorable Histories of the Wonders of Our Times*) recounts cases of men languishing in dungeons shackled in irons whose corporeal forms never stirred, yet they flew far away over vast stretches of land and above wide rivers as phantoms of themselves. Upon arriving at their destinations they entered the bodies of wolves and inflicted great ravishment and pain on humans and livestock, returning eventually to occupy the bodies of the original imprisoned men. I acknowledge that these examples only reprise Augustine's theory of metamorphosis and the *phantasticum*, neither proven nor disproven.

"We know, as Monsieur Chassenée has reminded us, that werewolves can take different forms. He has given us three. I agree with his general classification but prefer to adduce their identifying qualities in my own words. In the first form a man becomes a wolf. This is the simplest transformation. In the second a demon occupies an actual wolf while the human body lies inert elsewhere with its soul intact. Saint Augustine teaches that body and soul are fused, separating only at the instant of death. Pardon the jocularity, but an appropriate mnemonic aid might be, 'when the body dies, the soul flies.'" He cackled hoarsely and seemed to shiver. The spectators looked at him curiously, but no one laughed. The judicial vicar and the clerk pretended not to notice. There was a moment's lapse while Révigny coughed violently several times and muttered under his breath something damning about brimstone. Gathering himself, he moved on. "In the third and most puzzling form the individual doesn't change at all; rather, the vision of those who see him becomes enchanted, and they *perceive* a wolf." Révigny now looked at my client. "It appears, Monsieur Loup-garou, that your method of metamorphosis involves none of these, and I'm inclined to agree with the diagnosis of Monsieur Chassenée that you suffer from the mental disease of lycanthropy.

"According to Monsieur Chassenée this condition is sufficient to exonerate and spare his client the flames, but is it? Not in my opinion. The defendant's ontological status and its tie to heresy might be the core issue of this case, although it isn't the only one. There's another, and while not directly relevant to the charges against him it has undeniable bearing on the sentence he receives.

"Le Loup-garou suffers from terminal effects of a terrible disease known as le rage, for which there is no cure. Le rage is a contagion ordinarily transmitted from the bite of an infected dog or wolf, although other animals can be infected too. Monsieur Loup-garou was bitten by his pet wolf, which later died of the affliction, and since then by many dogs that attacked him in the graveyard. Perhaps one or more of them was rabid too or became rabid from scuffling with Le Loup-garou. The specific offender is irrelevant; the important point is that Monsieur Loup-garou will soon die as a result, doubtless within days, a few weeks at most. I readily concede that le rage has driven him mad. It explains his hydrophobia, foaming of the mouth, and several other symptoms. For example . . ."

At that moment my client exploded in anger or perhaps mortal terror; under some conditions the two are indistinguishable. He roared and pulled at his chain with such violence that the audience gasped. Those standing nearest turned and ran, fearing he might break it off and flail them with it. He finally quit struggling and assumed a strange, rigid pose with his unchained arm behind his back, legs in a crouch as if ready to leap. His eyes were glassy, and he appeared confused as to his whereabouts. Apparently, the crowd noise had become painful or irritating to his hearing because he clamped his hands over what once had been his ears and unleashed a terrible shriek of anguish, falling to his knees and from there lunging prostrate onto the ground, then trying desperately to crawl away. Révigny, unflinching, observed these antics with stony detachment. He turned and looked at me. "Monsieur Chassenée, it seems Le Loup-garou is experiencing a fragile moment." He pointed to the base of the post where a puddle of muddy water had formed. Le Loup-garou had simply been trying to avoid stepping in it.

His Grace seemed shaken. "This is a serious matter, Monsieur Révigny, and the court thanks you for drawing attention to it. We must alert the king's guard to start killing the stray dogs of Magny-Cours immediately. I shall notify appropriate civil authorities to require that citizens confine pet dogs indoors and report dog bites and any symptoms of this terrible illness. We must isolate the carriers and stop its spread at all cost. Court is adjourned for today and canceled for tomorrow. Time is needed to implement these measures." He struck the sounding block with his gavel. "Monsieur Clerk?"

The clerk quickly composed himself and stood. "Court will reconvene at terce on Monday the 1st of October."

The day was barely past sext, and we were finished. Nothing would happen for the next three days. I had no intention of being alone with my client in his cell, especially now that all hope of a reprieve had disappeared. He was becoming more agitated and unstable with each passing day. Not only that, he would surely be sentenced to execution unless the disease killed him first.

At least I had negotiated a humane end, strangulation followed by burning of his remains. To avoid being burned alive required only his public confession of guilt to the charge of heresy by werewolfery, followed by an expression of remorse for his behavior. While allocution wasn't necessarily a requirement His Grace made clear that the civil judge who would carry out the sentence believed otherwise and might not accept the negotiated compromise. Furthermore, strangulation offered a nice ending, allowing Le Loup-garou to depart life with a priest's forgiveness, perhaps a modicum of sympathy from a minority of citizens, and a little dignity for himself. On the civil judge's command he would then be strangled at the same post to which he had been chained throughout the trial, except the bailiff's men would now bind him to it firmly. Any interested citizens were free to watch his face redden, his eyes bulge, and hear the pitiful gags as the rope tightened around his throat. The body would be taken to a place outside the city walls, tied to a stake, and ignited. This is how I anticipated the next week playing out. I had done everything possible, discharging my duties with honor and diligence. My client's fate and the ultimate disposition of his soul were now in God's hands. After checking in with Jamet to see if all was well I retired to my rented bed and napped away the remainder of the afternoon. Oddly, I was clear-headed despite the previous night's foul wine.

MONDAY OCTOBER 1ST—LE LOUP-GAROU SURPRISES BY
REFUSING TO CONFESS; HE DAMNS THE COURT AND CURSES THE
EXECUTIONER BY SUMMONING HIM TO THE VALLEY OF JOSEPHAT;
THE CIVIL JUDGE REQUIRES GUIDANCE FROM A HIGHER
AUTHORITY ON HOW TO PROCEED; THE EXECUTION IS POSTPONED
AND LE LOUP-GAROU RETURNED TO HIS CELL; LE GÉANT FREES
LE LOUP-GAROU; THE TWO KILL MANY KING'S GUARDSMEN AND
CIVILIANS AND ESCAPE; CHASSENÉE AND RÉVIGNY ARE SUMMONED
TO AN EMERGENCY MEETING OF THE COURT

AFTER THE CLERK OPENED COURT THE judge rose and ordered the bailiff to bring the prisoner and tie him to the post. A large crowd had gathered to watch, and entertainers of all sorts were present to enhance everyone's enjoyment. The morning was crisp, the sky a cloudless blue vault above which floated a flawless sun. Everything considered, a perfect day for an execution.

A civil judge charged with carrying out the sentence now occupied the center chair at the main table. He was standing and preparing to speak when a loud disturbance distracted him, and he turned his head to locate the source. I turned mine too in time to see several bodies go flying followed by shrieks of pain and surprise. Le Géant was striding through the crowd from the perimeter, kicking and hurling those in front out of his way. In seconds he stood alone before Le Loup-garou. The two men looked at each other silently and without expression. The bailiff's men approached Le Géant, who extended his arm and ordered them to stop or lose their lives. All doubts about his warning dissipated when he looked askance, piercing them with his savage eye, and slowly drew his massive sword.

The judge watched Le Géant nervously, momentarily confused, then pulled himself together and said, "The prisoner may now confess to his crime of heresy by means of werewolfery and give allocution."

Le Loup-garou, his face contorted in an awful grimace, the veins in his neck about to burst, spat foam and shouted back, "*I confess to nothing, and I do not accept this conviction! I have never been a heretic!*" Then turning his head sideways in a futile effort to face the executioner standing directly behind him: "*I summon you to the Valley of Josaphat!*" This was a curse no executioner can ignore because it denies him forgiveness by the prisoner he is about to kill. He then becomes a murderer if carrying through with his duty, and murder is a mortal sin.

Despite the chilly air the executioner began to sweat. Everyone knew about the agreement between the defense and prosecution and approved by the original presiding judge: the accused would be strangled and then burned, saving him the torment of the flames. This was why a gibbet with its dangling noose had not been erected in the square. Death would be by a short length of thick hemp passed underneath Le Loup-garou's chin, the ends wrapped in the fists of the executioner at his back.

The executioner was a fearful and superstitious man, sometimes driven to despair and bouts of melancholy by the ghosts of those he had killed. He looked at his hands, each wrapped in a single turn of the rope to avoid slippage. On the back of one hand was a fly of the sort attracted to the odor of human bodies, in particular human sweat. Unable to release his grip to swat it, he blew on it instead, but the insect didn't move. Its eyes seemed to glow with a green iridescence as the sunlight refracted through them. The executioner blew once more on the fly, again failing to dislodge it. Could it be a demon? He started to perspire more intensely, the sweat running from his forehead into his eyes, making them sting. The fly began to move slowly over the surface of his hand, probing between the hairs with its proboscis, searching methodically for . . . what? Could this be a sign?

He had forgotten to wear his lucky charm, an elliptical bezoar from the stomach of a stag, drilled to take a leather string and shiny from years of wear. He had worn it around his neck tucked beneath his tunic for every execution, beginning with his first years ago. It had belonged to his father before him and his grandfather before that, both executioners too. It protected them into old age against malevolent enchantments. He always hoped it would serve him the same way, but there wasn't time to retrieve it from his belongings, and crossing himself was impossible with his hands held at the ready awaiting the judge's word.

"Executioner, for the second time, stay your rope! Are you deaf?" Startled, he looked from his hand to the judge, oddly angelic in his white robe. The man seemed frantic, shouting and pointing at him. He relaxed his grip, allowing the rope to become limp. The crowd stirred and murmured, as yet too confused to protest. He looked again at his hand. The fly had departed. What had just happened?

The judge admonished the prisoner. "You understand full well, Monsieur Loup-garou, that terms of the sentence can't be fulfilled without your confession. You leave me few choices. I advise you to confess immediately to your crimes and then forgive the executioner for his pending act against your life. Allow him to strangle you before your earthly remains are burned for heresy. Save yourself the pain. I promise to honor my agreement with your lawyer and the prosecutor despite this needless interruption. Just say the words. Alternatively, I can have you tortured until you say them, and in the end we shall burn you alive and expel the evil demon from your shrieking body. Which do you choose?"

"I choose neither! I have never been a heretic! *I curse you and the entire court and condemn all your souls to burn with mine in Hell!*"

The crowd, having come together in a festive mood, gasped in shock and stepped back. The comforting structure of institutionalized death had just crumpled, exposing the ugly nakedness of mankind's unjust laws. The general aura at once turned uncertain and unnerved as though a satanic spell might break through at any moment and rip out the souls of the onlookers. Some glanced around furtively, terrorized by the unknown. Others stood poised to run. Food and drink vendors set down their burdens, unsure what to do next.

Children cried, confused and frightened by the abrupt change precipitated by Le Loup-garou's words inveighing against the only social order they knew, and by the frightening tone and certitude in their delivery. The naïve smiles anticipating a man's death dissolved from their faces, the tiny hands poised to clap with his final gasp fell to their sides. What had become of the harmless fun organized murder offered, little different from the routines of the mimes and acrobats? Earlier, the adults' happy demeanor had assured them that the residue of an execution stayed forever apart from their daily lives, never approaching close enough to tap them on the shoulder. It was God's will that prisoners die in these lethal plays staged for everyone's enjoyment. The accused was just another actor when his moment came, never mind the advent of dying on cue.

A balladeer carrying a small harp was thinking how he might expatiate in song about the event. He was a veteran observer of executions, you might even say a connoisseur, and already planning embellishments of the ballad he would compose about this one, eager to bring the soon-to-be-dead werewolf fearsomely to life. Recounting the details of such a well-known and popular execution could feed him for months as he moved from town to town, stopping in public squares to elaborate, adding layer upon layer of fiction and suspense. He held in memory a vast repertoire of these events and was a master of prosody, of building slowly to the dénouement when the executioner's axe sweeps downward, the first flames lick the living flesh like eager but tentative tongues, the hangman's noose intervenes to jerk the hurtling body to a midair stop. This event offered elements new even to a worldly balladeer. The accused had disrupted the trial's ineluctable progression by cursing not just his executioner but also the court. Such exciting possibilities!

The clerk, Révigny, and I clustered around the judge for a whispered conference. "I can't allow the execution to proceed without a confession and now a curse hanging over us all," said the judge. "The law states that a trial may not terminate without a confession. The allocution is optional, although I always insist on it just to gain a measure of completeness. At the very least a sentence can't be forced without the accused's public divulgence of guilt. As presiding secular judge I am prohibited from granting the executioner permission to perform supplicium if the accused refuses to forgive him. He is then within his rights to dismiss my order." To me he said, "Try persuading your client to recant and follow the rules, Monsieur Chassenée." And to the three of us, "I require guidance from a higher authority and will send a message this evening to the archbishopric at Bourges asking advice and stressing the urgency of a prompt reply. The archbishop, assuming he's presently in residence, no doubt will delegate the matter, but we should still hear from someone in authority within a week, God willing. Meanwhile, court is adjourned until I receive official instructions and have conferred with you. Monsieur Clerk, please make the announcement."

The volume of the crowd's low murmur was swelling. An occasional voice could be distinguished here and there advocating a range of solutions: burning the victim at once, hanging him, throttling him as planned, even releasing and banishing him from the city. The clerk stood at the edge of the platform with arms raised shouting for silence. When the noise abated he said in a loud, confident voice, "Because of the curses hurled at the executioner and the court by the accused, his execution is postponed until higher authorities have considered their consequences. When the answer has been received and assessed a crier will announce the court's decision in the town square at terce and again at vespers for two days prior to the civil court's reconvening and carrying out the sentence. Written notices containing the same information will be posted on churches and public buildings. That is all. Return to your homes or duties." The judge's gavel struck the sounding block, and the crowd started to disperse. "Monsieur Bailiff," said the judge, "please escort the prisoner to his cell."

The time was well past nones with evening just around the corner. Révigny and I retired to the tavern. I intended to calm my nerves with wine and wait until the restless crowd dispersed before venturing to the jail and reasoning with Le Loup-garou, who obviously was not in a rational state.

The world outside had turned dark. Révigny and I, having just finished supper, were enjoying a relaxing cup. I was lamenting how my impending meeting with Le Loup-garou would not come to anything. Nonetheless, I recognized my duty to try, as ordered by the civil judge, and was about to expound an opinion that only true believers in some cause or other are actually willing to face the flames rather than recant their beliefs, usually saints, martyrs, and other fanatics, and that my client's cause was merely his wasted life. I was puffing myself up in this way when a patron burst through the door with news that a giant seen lurking near the dungeon minutes earlier had killed two king's guardsmen attempting to interrogate him about his business there.

Révigny and I hurried out the back door. I grabbed a glowing lantern hanging at the barn's entrance, and we stumbled inside to rouse Jamet. I recognized the snoring of my footmen when their snouts have been rendered musical by too much wine. I swung the lantern into the first stall seeing only François and Alvin sleeping in each other's arms. Where was Jamet? I found him in the adjacent stall with a whore, both moaning softly and fully en flagrant délit. They were buried so deep in the hay I almost overlooked them. I raised the lantern above my head and said to Jamet, "Disengage and follow me at once! Le Loup-garou is about to escape from jail, and you must help part the crowd so Monsieur Révigny and I can reach him and prevent this disaster!"

"Yes, Master," he said, clamoring to his feet while desperately brushing aside the hay. "And François and Alvin?"

"They will only be in the way."

We arrived at the door to the dungeon to find two dead guardsmen and Le Géant negotiating his way down the stairs backward on hands and knees. He was too tall even to stoop underneath the arch stone. Gawkers had started to gather, but Le Géant scattered them with a shouted warning to leave immediately or be killed where they stood. To us he said, "Go back!"

"We can't," I said. "Le Loup-garou is my client and my responsibility, and he's also Monsieur Révigny's responsibility as prosecutor in the proceeding. What will you do with him?"

Le Géant raised his head and seemed to fix me with his terrible white eye. "Release him," he said simply. He reached the dungeon, and we heard his heavy footfalls on the stone floor.

We crept to the bottom of the stairs and watched in horror as Le Géant grabbed a geôlier by the throat and snapped his neck as easily as a farmer's wife breaks the neck of a fowl. The other geôlier bolted for the stairs, but Le Géant caught him by the tunic, yanked him back, and broke his neck too. He casually took the ring of keys from a hook on the wall, opened the door to Le Loup-garou's cell, and unlocked his shackles. Through all this neither said a word.

Halfway along the stairway to one side was a shallow niche. We squeezed into it. The men brushed against us one at a time as they departed, Le Géant again on hands and knees. They passed without a glance, as if we were invisible.

After a moment we followed and saw them walking toward the market, and at once Jamet began clearing a path for us, jabbing anyone in our way with his elbows or kicking them in the shins. News of the jail break traveled fast. The market denizens soon recognized Le Loup-garou from having seen him chained to the post. Many began pointing, shouting his name, and sounding a general alert: *"Look, the werewolf is loose! Run!"* Although Le Géant lacked

comparable celebrity, as Le Loup-garou's companion he was difficult to miss. Did the pair have a plan of action or was the intention
simply to cross the square and run for the countryside? If so, taking
to the streets instead of entering the crowded square would have
attracted less attention. They apparently had another motive.
Minutes passed while Le Loup-garou, appearing disoriented,
momentarily grappled with a beggar over a crust of bread and took
it from him. Le Géant gazed around absently. A bugle sounded, and
a squadron of the king's guard from the permanent garrison
arrived in the square, marching in formation to a drummer. This
had been the ploy: to discharge their pent-up anger and resentment
by taking on the established order.

The officer in charge was quickly pointed in the direction of the
fugitives and ordered two of his men to arrest them. The first to
approach was killed instantly, run through by Le Géant's heavy sword.
Le Loup-garou picked up the fallen guardsman's sword and beheaded
the second soldier as he stood transfixed in apparent shock. The head
rolled to a stop in front of Le Géant, who kicked it aside.

Instead of retreating the two men waded directly into the stunned
squadron, initially fifty soldiers and a commanding officer, swinging
their swords with the monotonous efficiency of farmers scything a
field of grain, killing or maiming all in their path and sending
screaming citizens to the safety of adjacent streets. They tipped over
the fragile stands and carts in their way, the wreckage igniting spontaneously as toppled candles delighted in these new sources of fuel.
Beggars scuttled in their wake like crabs, chasing the loaves, cheeses,
and fruits spilling onto the cobbles. Bystanders trapped in the confusion clasped their hands and wailed prayers, watching in disbelief as
the two men moved forward, their rippling black silhouettes misshapen and terrifying against the background of writhing flames.
Could this moment mark the coming of the apocalypse?

The nervous guardsmen retreated several steps before breaking
ranks and running, ignoring the shouts of their commanding

officer to maintain formation. Dropping sword and shield they became part of the irrational crowd, fleeing for their lives like everyone else. Révigny, Jamet, and I purposely fell behind. Soon only we three and the scavenging beggars remained to survey the carnage. It seemed incredible that two men could have devastated a city square and routed a full squadron of the king's garrison. Around us lay the evidence: the cobblestones slick with congealing blood, the burning rubble, the dozens of dead soldiers along with civilians slaughtered because they got in the way. Here and there a prone shape lay groaning or screaming in the flickering light of the fires, but there was nothing anyone could do. With few exceptions they would die before morning. Le Géant and Le Loup-garou had killed or maimed maybe sixty or seventy souls and vanished unscathed, silently, like angels of death.

The streets were in chaos, and when we returned to the tavern a court courier was waiting nervously, standing first on one foot then the other as if eager to run. "Thank God you're safe, monsieurs! I bring you this message from His Lordship, the civil judge. Please sign after reading it." The message summoned us to a meeting at the court's corner of the square the following morning at terce to discuss how to handle the prisoner's escape. The man dipped a quill in his portable bottle of ink, and Révigny and I scribbled our names at the bottom of the message. Then we sat and ordered wine. Jamet was still with us, and I asked the innkeeper to give him a flagon to take back to the barn, for which Jamet thanked me graciously. He had done well in the turmoil, keeping his head and making sure we were protected.

Révigny and I were just having a second cup. The tavern had filled with patrons talking excitedly about the evening's events. The innkeeper, his wife, and the serving girls were scurrying around attempting to profit as much as possible from the overflow crowd.

Tuesday October 2nd—Chassenée and Révigny Attend an Emergency Meeting of the Court; Chassenée Experiences One of His Dreams

THE MORNING ARRIVED OVERCAST WITH RAGGED gusts from the northwest. Dead leaves and debris blew across the square, interrupted here and there in their flight by piles of smoldering debris. Pedestrians with shawls and cloaks wrapped tightly around them poked with sticks among the remnants for salvageable items, although earlier arrivals probably had retrieved anything edible or otherwise of use. Révigny and I finished a warm breakfast of tea and spiced cake submerged in hot wine, then walked leisurely to the square. He, of course, didn't feel the cold or the food starting to warm his blood. What blood? Demons lack such essentials; they have no need to warm the fires that fuel movement and thought of the living.

We climbed the steps to the platform where His Lordship and the clerk of the court were trying unsuccessfully to arrange their documents. "Find some stones to weight them before we lose everything to the wind," His Lordship told the clerk, who descended the steps, nodding to us as he passed. The judge looked up on seeing us. "An unusual development, don't you think?"

"Indeed so," Révigny said. "Monsieur Chassenée and I discussed the situation over breakfast. We presume, first, that the king's guard has already departed for the countryside and is tracking the fugitives as we speak. Second, last night's event renders the case of heresy by werewolfery for naught, and when Le Loup-garou is captured the new charge of murder will override the other."

"Right on both counts, monsieur. With luck Le Géant will be captured too and returned to Magny-Cours where they will be tried together in my civil court and promptly hanged. What a disaster. The dead and soon-to-be dead are still being counted.

Apparently, some crawled away severely wounded and are under private care at various secret locations. We might never know the true extent of the slaughter."

"Despite their crimes they proved to be magnificent warriors," I said, then wished I hadn't.

His Lordship gave me a look of distaste, but withheld his tongue. He turned again to the documents, weighing them down with stones the clerk had retrieved. After a moment he stood and turned to the three of us. "Now, we must get to the details. Monsieur Clerk, please take a seat at the table and prepare to record your notes. The rest of us will stand in front. First, prior to arrival of the lawyers this morning I dictated a letter to the archbishop describing last night's events and their outcome. I explained how the situation now had changed completely, and we no longer need a recommendation on how to handle Le Loup-garou's curses directed at the executioner and the court. These are hardly relevant in the context of the recent murder of soldiers and civilians. I noted that the king's guard is presently in pursuit of the fugitives and will undoubtedly take them alive or dead within the next few days. If they are captured and returned to Magny-Cours I plan to charge them with murder, put them on trial, and see they receive the noose. Naturally, a prosecutor and defense attorney will be appointed and the procedure conducted according to legal protocol. These are the contents of my letter, which a clerk's assistant is now copying so you may examine them. I did not mention specifically who would prosecute and defend. However, for convenience and expediency will the two of you assume these tasks?"

"Of course, Your Lordship," Révigny and I said nearly in unison.

"Excellent! Thank you, gentlemen. A copy of my letter to the archbishop will be delivered to your inn this afternoon. You may begin preparing your cases. We now have only to wait until the perpetrators of this horrible crime return in chains to stand before us. Court is dismissed." He reached for the gavel and prepared to strike the sounding block.

For reasons unknown even to me I asked to speak for the record. The subject? I can't remember because the morning exploded suddenly in a light more intense than the first light of the world. All images vanished along with sounds, flushed like unnecessary clutter from the path of this splendid, omniscient energy. My mind devolved in a series of blinding flashes. I squeezed my eyelids shut, without effect. How could it be? Then I remembered that such moments occurred behind my eyes, not before them. They were predictable components of the excruciating headaches foreshadowing my dreams. There was nothing I could do, but this episode was more painful and frightening than any previous ones. I had entered a state where proprioception had slipped away, leaving the senses and awareness of my body unresponsive: I was here but simultaneously absent. My brain was swelling beyond the skull's volume to contain it, subjecting every nerve to scorching pain. I wanted to hold my head between my hands and dial down the pressure with extended shrieks. Instead, I continued speaking in a normal voice, unable to stop yet aware of the sentences disintegrating into gibberish as the words transposed themselves randomly. I heard them finally dissipate into echoes that ricocheted inside my skull, any original message vanishing like smoke up a chimney.

How much time had passed? Perhaps more sensibly, at what rate of speed was it passing? Stupid questions. Time had tiptoed away from this new order without past or future leaving only the now, a fleeting instant with an unremembered history, struggling to shift forward but frozen in transition.

The light began to dim. The scene of the square returned, first as jumping green-shifted silhouettes, then as distinct images with details painted in. Several spectators turned and looked at me, their movements languid as if held back by the viscosity of water. Next, segments of images whirled past, many tilted or upside-down: a kaleidoscope of caps, brows, eyes, noses, arms, a wheel of cheese, a mule's flaring nostrils, the curled lip of a hungry dog. Sound had returned too, but the noise of the market seemed far away as did I—from myself. Then I was floating, a nugatory entity in that familiar disembodied scene in which I gaze down at my physical body, watching it drift with limbs outspread, eyes empty and staring as if in death, hearing my voice not through unmoving lips but emanating from a discarnate mind somewhere on another plane.

The scene shifted abruptly, and I was standing as my reconstituted self now staring into the slowly roiling pot of stew beneath me. I felt detached, disinterested, yet unable to turn away. Bubbles burst softly as they wobbled up through the thick morass and broke the surface, their popping in rhythm with my heartbeat, reaching my ears as if enhanced by a mysterious auscultation. Familiar vegetables and cuts of meat rose into view, sank, and disappeared in the turbid brown fluid. Then a leg appeared, pale and stark against the background. Beside it a dusky elbow belonging to a different woman emerged followed by the hand and a finger on the hand that beckoned. Join us, it seemed to indicate. Everything is safe. Then a third image appeared, although at that instant I saw only a fish's tail, and as the surface grease slid away what looked like the lower body of a fish encased in reflective pearly scales. In previous dreams fishes had never been components of the stew.

The vision became mesmeric as the tail submerged and the creature's upper body floated toward the surface. Suddenly, the face of a beautiful girl broke through. Her hair was blonde and wafted like seaweed around her head, which was crowned with a sparkling diamond tiara. She looked up at me and smiled, teeth even and white. Her irises were blue, merging with the enlarged pupils to give her eyes the deep reflective appearance of translucent seawater. Despite her beauty there was no hint of personal warmth. Like all my dream women she was familiar yet a stranger, no one I had ever seen before. She was bare-breasted, her skin to the waist alabaster and entirely human, but from there down she was a fish. I wanted desperately to speak to her. I tried, but no words came.

She said, "What day is today?"

The question startled me. "What?"

"Try to focus. *To-day*. What day of the week is today?"

My mind seemed to be working at a crawl. "Uh, Tuesday. Wait . . . I think. Yes, today is Tuesday the 2nd of October in the year of grace 1515."

"I asked you just for the day of the week. I couldn't care less about the month and year, and I don't know anyone who does. No wonder I'm still half fish. I thought it was Saturday!" She laughed. It was an unexpectedly girlish laugh, musical and giggly. "How could I be so stupid?" She shook her head in comical disbelief, her swirling hair creating a minor disturbance in the stew. "Well," she said, "now you've seen me in my bath. By all rights I should transform into a dragon and flap away, but don't worry, it isn't your fault. For a minute I thought you'd broken your vow of letting me spend my Saturdays in secret. So, no harm done, nothing to forgive. Might as well jump in and join me."

"I can't swim," I said.

"It doesn't matter. You won't drown."

Here was an argument impossible to lose, the kind any lawyer relishes. "Of course I might drown! You're swimming around in a liquid, and it looks deep. Water, pot-au-feu, what's the difference? It seems plenty drownable from up here."

She cocked her head and gave me a puzzled look as if I might be a moron. "I repeat: you . . . can't . . . drown. Now, don't be truculent, just jump in. I'm losing patience."

I jumped. My mouth and eyes were instantly occluded with warm stew, and it occurred to me that I should have closed both and pinched off my nose, but too late now. Miraculously, I bobbed to the surface where my head stabilized at once, and I began breathing.

"See?" Again, that appealing laugh. "Excuse me while I undergo the metamorphosis and become myself again." She wriggled around. The turbidity of the stew combined with my shallow angle of sight from surface level precluded seeing what was happening below her waist. Abruptly, she was facing me, arms wrapped around my neck, legs locked around my hips. She pulled me against her.

"Are those your legs?" I said stupidly.

She laughed again. "Of course. Who else's?"

"Here," she said with a giggle, "have a stick of celery."

I looked at it and said, "Who are you?" In none of my previous dreams had I ever asked this question, but suddenly the urge to know was irresistible.

"I'm a woman in your dreams," she said.

"No, you're more than a dream figment. I can tell. I can feel it."

"For now my name is Mélusyne."

"The water sprite of legend?"

"Sure, why not?"

"Then am I Raymondyn, your husband?"

She bit off the end of the celery stick and looked at me with her depthless eyes, chewing slowly. "If you want to be him. Before we married I made you promise that I was to be free every Saturday. You weren't to ask where I went or why, but of course you couldn't resist knowing, so one Saturday you followed and found me in my bath, my legs turned into a fish's tail. Your gasp betrayed your presence, and on hearing it I changed into a dragon and flew away, never to return." She felt around in the grease. "This seems to be a carrot. Want it?"

After this exchange I must have blacked out, or at least spent a brief period trapped inside a black tunnel. The next I knew the bailiff was dabbing my forehead with a cool wet cloth and repeating, "Are you ill, Monsieur Chassenée?" Why, I wondered, is it always the bailiff who comes to my aid after one of these episodes happens in court? I opened my eyes and saw Révigny, the judge, and the clerk looking down at me, the latter two as if I were a strange species of insect. "What happened, monsieur?" said the judge.

"I must have fainted," I said. "Sometimes I have violent head-aches that come on me so quickly that . . ."

"Yes, but you were thrashing about as if having a fit while garbling incomprehensible sentences as if addressing the court. It was very strange. The words were distinct, but logically unconnected." His Lordship, I could tell, was attempting to decide if I had gone insane or simply experienced a moment of temporary disruption of my faculties.

"I've seen this before," Révigny said solemnly. "Monsieur Chassenée is plagued by a congenital condition that physicians have been unable to explain, although I assure the court that he's perfectly fit. All he requires is a calming cup or two at the tavern, a hot meal, and a night's sleep. I shall personally escort him back to the inn and guarantee his appearance when court next convenes."

"I see," said the judge, sounding unsure. "Very well, court is adjourned for today," and his gavel struck the sounding block. "I hope you're feeling better soon, monsieur. No doubt we shall all hear when the fugitives are captured. Then the clerk will notify you as to day and date for commencing the new trial. Public announcements will follow quickly. Good day, gentlemen."

I lay on the platform another few minutes while my head cleared, then nodded to the bailiff to help me to my feet. I toddled unsteadily down the steps to the square to be joined by Révigny, who gave me his frail arm for support. We went directly to the tavern and ordered wine.

WEDNESDAY OCTOBER 3RD—CHASSENÉE AWAKES
WITHOUT A HANGOVER AND SUGGESTS TO JAMET THAT
HIS ANIMALS RECEIVE SOME EXERCISE

I DON'T RECALL ANYTHING ELSE FROM that evening's conversation, or even making it to my bed, but the next morning I awoke without a hangover. From past experience I should have lain groaning until nearly sext, finally managing to stumble to the tavern for a midday meal alone. Why my fortune had changed in this respect was a mystery. Perhaps Révigny, who had not come to bed during the night in keeping with his alterity, could posit a theory. Where he traveled on his demoniacal errands in the black of night was anyone's guess.

After eating I went to the barn where the men were washing and grooming the animals, which looked in top condition. Jamet had taken a special interest in the palfrey, which stood blissfully in the crossties with his eyes closed. I suggested that the animals get some exercise, and that he should ride the palfrey.

"Do you mean it, Master?" He was obviously delighted by the prospect of riding this fine horse.

"Of course. François can ride the mule and Alvin the donkey. Go for a turn through the streets of Magny-Cours. All of you could do with a change of scenery. By the way, how are you feeling after the night before last?"

"If you mean from the drink I feel fine, Master. I returned to find François and Alvin awake and trembling after hearing the commotion. They could see the light from the flames above the rooftops and ran to hug me asking if we were going to die. I took only a few swallows from the flagon you graciously bought and gave them the rest to settle their nerves."

We could do nothing but wait for word from the king's garrison. A squadron of fifty was scouring the countryside looking for Le Loup-garou and Le Géant, hoping to take them alive for trial, but killing them if they resisted. There was no point in preparing for a prosecution and defense when the case might not happen. Révigny and I relaxed, taking in the fine autumn weather, chilly days of sunshine and colorful leaves and cold nights that now required two blankets. Our meals had improved since Révigny began paying the innkeeper to provide us with only the choicest fare he could manage. I naturally benefited more than my colleague with his peculiar digestive limitations, although he assured me his sense of taste remained fully functional.

FRIDAY OCTOBER 12TH—A COURIER FROM THE KING'S GUARD
SEARCHING FOR THE TWO FUGITIVES RETURNS WITH NEWS;
CHASSENÉE AND RÉVIGNY SUBMIT THEIR FINAL REPORTS
TO HIS LORDSHIP AND PREPARE TO LEAVE MAGNY-COURS

☙

WE WERE SITTING IN THE TAVERN having run out of subjects to discuss. Magny-Cours lacks many of Autun's amenities, and we had long since exhausted any interest in prowling the streets and alleys seeking pale amusements. We were bored and on the cusp of preparing our cases if only for some diversion. Then, just as the innkeeper was serving supper a courier from the king's garrison in pursuit of the fugitives walked through the door having just delivered his message to headquarters. He ordered a bowl of small beer, and the patrons clustered around him eagerly, peppering him with questions. He was a mere boy, but this was his shining moment and he took full advantage.

Révigny and I put down our spoons and turned our chairs toward the courier, who took a sip and gazed over the gathered heads, dramatically prolonging the moment. When the room had quieted, he said, "Le Loup-garou and Le Géant are dead."

The uproar was instantaneous. There were shouts demanding to know how they died, how many king's guardsmen they killed and wounded before succumbing to superior numbers, whether Le Loup-garou was a man or a werewolf during the battle and if the latter whether he regained human form at the moment of death. The courier looked around the room calmly, knowing he owned the moment and could justify the slight smirk on his lips. He took another sip of his small beer. There had not been a battle, he said. A wandering beggar had led the squadron into a field of grazing sheep and pointed to the unmolested bodies reposing peacefully in the grass, arms locked in the symbol of comradeship, beards thick with foam. Death had been recent because there was no odor or other signs of decay. The flies that follow death had just began to gather. Their buzzing and a slight breeze stirring the grass were the only sounds.

For a while the men had stood in awe. Their commander eventually ordered them to their knees, and the squadron's curé offered a prayer for the dead men's souls while the squadron to a man silently thanked God for not having to face them in combat, knowing they would never have let themselves be captured and that many guardsmen would have died in the attempt. This had been the universal fear during every hour of the march and every night of bivouacking in tenebrous fields, wondering and worrying aloud if that starry sky would be the last they see.

Then someone muttered that a wolf's tooth worn around the neck is an amulet against attacks by wild animals. This being so, imagine the protection gained from a werewolf's tooth. The scramble was on, and guardsman piled onto guardsman, the men on the bottom directly atop Le Loup-garou trying mightily to pull apart the jaws now locked in death. Knives were at the ready to pry teeth from bone or sever any competing fingers. Feeling euphoric and relieved at not facing Le Loup-garou in life they attacked his corpse as if extracting revenge, although the souvenir of a tooth was foremost in everyone's mind.

That the fugitives undoubtedly had died of le rage wasn't even considered. All soldiers on active duty bear at least minor cuts and nicks, if only from their training and in this case extended days on the march. Add to those older injuries newly acquired ones from scuffling and wallowing in Le Loup-garou's infected saliva over who gets the choice canines, who the lesser molars, who nothing but a wound for his failed effort. Perhaps all in the scrum were now infected with the distemper. In days or weeks at the outside most of the squadron would be foaming at the mouth and attacking one another like mad dogs. Eventually, the entire garrison could be afflicted.

The trial obviously would not happen, and a courier arrived the next morning from His Lordship requesting our final reports. We worked through the weekend, and the courier returned Monday the 15th to collect them. My men and I prepared to leave for home. The innkeeper told of several inns with taverns we would pass along the way and gave his recommendations. I suggested to Révigny that we make the journey together, but he claimed to have a few demon's errands awaiting his attention elsewhere, declining to elaborate.

Magny-Cours was alive with rumors, most started by the courier from the king's garrison. The squadron was en route, so he was the sole source of information. He spent considerable time in the taverns where patrons gladly paid for his food and drink while he recounted stories of how he and his comrades tracked their quarry, which mostly involved interviewing villagers and travelers they met along the main road west to Bourges, having received information that the pair had been seen walking in that direction.

The details were embellished with every telling and re-telling, and many a local man became a fleeting celebrity by claiming to have heard a story directly from the courier's mouth, which he could now repeat (never mind his own additions). When asked, many citizens along the route had reported seeing a giant accompanied by a lesser man, especially when prompted by an interlocutor dressed as a military officer. And yes, many often said, now that a little time had passed since the encounter the other wasn't an ordinary man at all, but undoubtedly a werewolf. Could there have been any doubt? Are you serious? Who could doubt his eyes when crossing paths with a giant and a werewolf! They aren't exactly common, you know. An old man at Saint-Parize-le-Châtel, bent double from a life of toiling in the fields, described Le Géant as taller than any tree he had ever seen. The old man himself probably measured slightly more than a meter from the bottoms of his bare feet to the top of his horizontal spine. A crone at Sermoise-sur-Loire, hump-backed and shuffling on two canes, managed to escape sexual ravishment by a werewolf (a very slow one, apparently) by taking to her heels and outrunning him.

MONDAY OCTOBER 15TH—CHASSENÉE AND RÉVIGNY SPEND
A FINAL EVENING IN THE TAVERN AT MAGNY-COURS;
A COURIER FROM THE ARCHIDIOCÈSE DE BOURGES ARRIVES

A COURIER FOR THE CIVIL COURT had picked up our reports earlier in the day, and we were settled in our chairs in the tavern and taking a second cup when I thanked my colleague for the several fine meals enjoyed at his expense toward the end of our stay.

"May I repay you in some way?" I said.

"Allow me a moment to consider." Révigny pulled himself upright, elbows on the table and forefinger pressed to his green lips behind which a green grin was spreading. The forefinger-to-lips was one of my staged mannerisms, and he was gently mocking me. The finger gradually lengthened and entered the right nostril. He jiggled his hand, making his nose move in peristaltic waves reminiscent of a caterpillar's crawl. The finger continued upward, pushing out the forehead incrementally before finally entering the skull where it jabbed enthusiastically at the underside of the bald pate, pushing it into points with each thrust as if probing for a soft place through which to poke a hole and escape. Révigny's head started jerking up and down in synchrony with the jabs. He bugged his eyes, flashing them through a fractured prism of hues and shades. The left eyeball popped out and hung limply by its twisted rope of muscles, blood vessels, and nerves before turning upward and staring at me eerily. "No," he said. "I can't think of anything."

We have little concept of how greatly the iris and opaque sclera contribute to our notion of humanity until confronted by a disembodied eye devoid of both, an unframed sphere that opens into emptiness. I looked away and refilled our glasses, and when I dared glance back everything had returned to the way it was before.

Révigny was obviously in a jocular mood, and so was I. And why not? Our legal endeavors were ending in unexpected and interesting ways. What future adventure did the fates have in store? Who—or what—would appear in the dock for me to defend and Révigny to prosecute, and in what legal playhouse would we perform? Révigny, reading these thoughts, grinned impishly. At that moment a man in a clearly agitated state burst through the door. He looked around as if seeking someone, then noticed the innkeeper sweeping the floor and approached him. The two spoke a moment, and the innkeeper pointed our way. The stranger pushed through the crowd and a moment later stood before us.

"Good evening, sirs, I bring a message from the archdiocese of Bourges. The bishop wishes to engage your services as prosecutor and defender of a young woman about to go before an inquisition on charges of witchcraft. The tribunal just ended in Magny-Cours has become famous throughout France and caught the bishop's attention. He wishes to engage your services. I rushed here with little sleep hoping to find you before you accepted another case elsewhere and departed."

We invited him to sit with us. Révigny raised his hand. "Innkeeper, another flagon and a cup for our visitor! And food! Now, please give us the details."

"Thank you, My Lord. I'm only the courier, and the contents of the message aren't mine to know. I can say that the defendant is a comely, disarming young woman accused of casting evil spells. It's said her skills are uncommonly powerful for one of so few years, and that she's open and fearless, brashly defending the practice of her craft instead of denying it."

He handed me a scroll stamped with the bishop's seal. In it was a brief description of the impending tribunal including charges against the defendant, opening date of the proceeding, and so forth. Notably, sitting in judgment would be Institoris, the most famous inquisitor of the age, known everywhere for his dedication to finding, persecuting, and burning witches. It could be said without exaggeration that he had sent hundreds to a fiery death. Any lawyer for the defense would be at an instant disadvantage, especially if his client had the courage to stand by her convictions and readily speak them.

I passed the document to Révigny, who scanned it quickly and looked at me, eyes pulsing orange. I felt his mounting excitement. The challenge was too good to refuse. The courier produced quill and ink, and Révigny and I signed our names. The men and I would not be going home after all. Instead, it was on to Bourges and my first inquisition.

— end —

About the Author

STEPHEN SPOTTE, A MARINE SCIENTIST BORN and raised in West Virginia, is the author of 23 books including seven works of fiction and two memoirs. Spotte has also published more than 80 papers on marine biology, ocean chemistry and engineering, and aquaculture. His field research has encompassed the Canadian Arctic, Bering Sea, West Indies, Indo-West Pacific, Central America, and the Amazon basin of Ecuador and Brazil. *Animal Wrongs* is his fifth novel. He lives in Longboat Key, Florida.

RECENT AND FORTHCOMING BOOKS FROM THREE ROOMS PRESS

FICTION

Lucy Jane Bledsoe
No Stopping Us Now

Rishab Borah
The Door to Inferna

Meagan Brothers
Weird Girl and What's His Name

Christopher Chambers
Scavenger

Ron Dakron
Hello Devilfish!

Robert Duncan
Loudmouth

Michael T. Fournier
Hidden Wheel
Swing State

Aaron Hamburger
Nirvana Is Here

William Least Heat-Moon
Celestial Mechanics

Aimee Herman
Everything Grows

Kelly Ann Jacobson
Tink and Wendy

Jethro K. Lieberman
Everything Is Jake

Eamon Loingsigh
Light of the Diddicoy
Exile on Bridge Street

John Marshall
The Greenfather

Aram Saroyan
Still Night in L.A.

Stephen Spotte
Animal Wrongs

Richard Vetere
The Writers Afterlife
Champagne and Cocaine

Julia Watts
Quiver
Needlework

Gina Yates
Narcissus Nobody

MEMOIR & BIOGRAPHY

Nassrine Azimi and Michel Wasserman
Last Boat to Yokohama: The Life and Legacy of Beate Sirota Gordon

William S. Burroughs & Allen Ginsberg
Don't Hide the Madness:
William S. Burroughs in Conversation with Allen Ginsberg
edited by Steven Taylor

James Carr
BAD: The Autobiography of James Carr

Judy Gumbo
Yippie Girl

Judith Malina
Full Moon Stages:
Personal Notes from 50 Years of The Living Theatre

Phil Marcade
Punk Avenue: Inside the New York City Underground, 1972–1982

Jillian Marshall
Japanthem: Music Connecting Cultures Across the Pacific

Alvin Orloff
Disasterama! Adventures in the Queer Underground 1977–1997

Nicca Ray
Ray by Ray: A Daughter's Take on the Legend of Nicholas Ray

Stephen Spotte
My Watery Self:
Memoirs of a Marine Scientist

PHOTOGRAPHY-MEMOIR

Mike Watt
On & Off Bass

SHORT STORY ANTHOLOGIES

SINGLE AUTHOR

The Alien Archives: Stories
by Robert Silverberg

First-Person Singularities: Stories
by Robert Silverberg
with an introduction by John Scalzi

Tales from the Eternal Café: Stories
by Janet Hamill, with an introduction
by Patti Smith

Time and Time Again:
Sixteen Trips in Time
by Robert Silverberg

Voyagers:
Twelve Journeys in Space and Time
by Robert Silverberg

MULTI-AUTHOR

Crime + Music: Twenty Stories of Music-Themed Noir
edited by Jim Fusilli

Dark City Lights: New York Stories
edited by Lawrence Block

The Faking of the President: Twenty Stories of White House Noir
edited by Peter Carlaftes

Florida Happens:
Bouchercon 2018 Anthology
edited by Greg Herren

Have a NYC I, II & III:
New York Short Stories;
edited by Peter Carlaftes
& Kat Georges

Songs of My Selfie:
An Anthology of Millennial Stories
edited by Constance Renfrow

The Obama Inheritance:
15 Stories of Conspiracy Noir
edited by Gary Phillips

This Way to the End Times:
Classic and New Stories of the Apocalypse
edited by Robert Silverberg

MIXED MEDIA

John S. Paul
Sign Language: A Painter's Notebook
(photography, poetry and prose)

DADA

Maintenant: A Journal of Contemporary Dada Writing & Art
(Annual, since 2008)

HUMOR

Peter Carlaftes
A Year on Facebook

FILM & PLAYS

Israel Horovitz
My Old Lady: Complete Stage Play and Screenplay with an Essay on Adaptation

Peter Carlaftes
Triumph For Rent (3 Plays)
Teatrophy (3 More Plays)

Kat Georges
Three Somebodies: Plays about Notorious Dissidents

TRANSLATIONS

Thomas Bernhard
On Earth and in Hell
(poems of Thomas Bernhard with English translations by Peter Waugh)

Patrizia Gattaceca
Isula d'Anima / Soul Island
(poems by the author in Corsican with English translations)

César Vallejo | Gerard Malanga
Malanga Chasing Vallejo
(selected poems of César Vallejo with English translations and additional notes by Gerard Malanga)

George Wallace
EOS: Abductor of Men
(selected poems in Greek & English)

ESSAYS

Richard Katrovas
Raising Girls in Bohemia:
Meditations of an American Father

Far Away From Close to Home
Vanessa Baden Kelly

Womentality: Thirteen Empowering Stories by Everyday Women Who Said Goodbye to the Workplace and Hello to Their Lives
edited by Erin Wildermuth

POETRY COLLECTIONS

Hala Alyan
Atrium

Peter Carlaftes
DrunkYard Dog
I Fold with the Hand I Was Dealt

Thomas Fucaloro
It Starts from the Belly and Blooms

Kat Georges
Our Lady of the Hunger

Robert Gibbons
Close to the Tree

Israel Horovitz
Heaven and Other Poems

David Lawton
Sharp Blue Stream

Jane LeCroy
Signature Play

Philip Meersman
This Is Belgian Chocolate

Jane Ormerod
Recreational Vehicles on Fire
Welcome to the Museum of Cattle

Lisa Panepinto
On This Borrowed Bike

George Wallace
Poppin' Johnny

Three Rooms Press | New York, NY | Current Catalog: www.threeroomspress.com
Three Rooms Press books are distributed by Publishers Group West: www.pgw.com

CPSIA information can be obtained
at www.ICGtesting.com
Printed in the USA
JSHW040950100921
18609JS00001B/1

9 781953 103093